ROLAND FISHMAN lives in Sydney with his partner, Kathleen Allen, who was integral to the writing of *No Man's Land*. After many years as a sports journalist with *The Sydney Morning Herald*, in 1992 Roland founded the Writers' Studio, a creative writing school that runs classes both live and online. Like Russell Carter, Roland has surfed since age ten and sees the sport as a metaphor for life.

ROLAND FISHMAN

NO MAN'S LAND

RISING
TIDE
BOOKS

Rising Tide Books
2/77 Hooper Street
Randwick NSW 2031
Australia
www.risingtidebooks.com.au

First published by Rising Tide Books in 2014

Cataloguing-in-Publication details are available from the National Library of Australia
www.trove.nla.gov.au

ISBN 978 0 99232 290 8

Front cover photograph © Eugene Tan, Aquabumps
Cover design, Luke Causby, Blue Cork

The poem quoted on page 311 comes from the work of Jalāl ad-Dīn Muhammad Rūmī,
translated by Coleman Barks and reproduced with his kind permission.

Set in 12/14.9 pt Adobe Garamond Pro by UnspacedEm

10 9 8 7 6 5 4 3 2 1

I dedicate this book to my partner, Kathleen Allen.
I couldn't have written it without her.

It is also dedicated to my mother, Joan Fishman, who could never do
enough for me, and father, Frank, who published three works of fiction
and set me on the writing path.

BOOK ONE

CHAPTER 1

Lennox Head, the far north coast of New South Wales, Australia,
5.30 a.m., Christmas Day

A breaking wave thumped into the sandbank two metres from where he stood and a fine cool mist of spray washed over him. He tightened his low-slung board shorts and shifted his six-footer from under his left arm to his right. The surf was pumping. It was shaping up as a solid day and he was itching to get amongst it.

But a man like Russell Carter knew when someone intended doing him serious bodily harm. Something about those three guys who'd pulled up next to him in the car park a few minutes earlier had triggered his internal alarm. It rarely let him down.

And it wouldn't shut up.

Full light was five to ten minutes away. The rising sun sat just below the ocean's horizon, hovering between the darkness and the light, the past and the future. He was standing alone on the jagged rocks, studying the break he'd been surfing since he was a kid, trying to get a read on it.

1

He took a deep breath and exhaled. The surf was his church, the one place where he found solace and the world made sense.

Since returning to his childhood home, more than a year ago now, he'd surfed this break every morning. Life was good. His past had stayed where it belonged.

He glanced over his shoulder. From where he stood, he couldn't see the car park. But nobody was coming down the dirt track towards him.

He was hung-over and hadn't had much sleep, and he'd been out of the game for over a year – perhaps there was nothing more to it than that. There was no reason to suspect trouble.

A huge wave boomed out to sea. He pushed his long black hair out of his eyes and watched the bubbling foam surge over the rocks below before retreating.

Then the ocean went quiet, as if holding its breath.

The lull between sets presented the window of calm he was waiting for.

He launched himself board first off the rocks and hit the water with a thud. He started stroking hard and deep, heading for the still-water channel that ran to the left of the break. The cool of the ocean and the feel of his board ploughing through the water helped to clear his head.

It took him five minutes to fight his way through the oncoming walls of surging foam and reach calm water. When he was halfway towards the take-off zone where the other surfers sat in a pack, he stopped paddling and looked towards the shore.

The three guys were already in the water, powering their boards through the first set of broken waves. They were heading towards him, negotiating the challenging surf like pros.

He lay back down and started stroking out to sea at a steady pace. He'd find out soon enough whether his instincts about them were on the mark or if it was just his hangover talking.

CHAPTER 2

Carter paddled into the line-up, where a dozen local surfers straddled their boards in the gathering light. The dawn patrol bobbed up and down with the incoming swell, staring out to sea like naked buddhas, giving nothing away.

He glided to a halt and sat upright, sinking the tail of his board into the water. His height and weight made him large for a surfer, even though he carried little body fat. At thirty-seven he was over a decade older than any of the other hardcore locals. They respected his ability but most of them gave him a wide berth.

In a few moments the feeling of calm surrounding the pack would evaporate and the dogfight for the first wave of the morning would begin. He ran his right hand unhurriedly along the smooth curved edges of his board, watching the three strangers approach the take-off zone.

As they came closer and the light improved, he pegged them as Indonesian. Before returning to Lennox, he'd spent the last twenty years living and working in South-East Asia.

They were in their early twenties, lean and compact with wispy goatees, and looked like typical surf rats from any of the legendary breaks in Indonesia, which possessed some of the best, most powerful and consistent waves on the planet.

Each wore a sleeveless wetsuit, which made them stand out; the locals wore only board shorts. The water was warm and, even at this early hour, the high level of humidity suggested a midsummer stinker of a day.

'Hey, Carter!'

He turned his board in a one hundred and eighty degree arc and saw a familiar figure paddling in his direction.

Knowlsie, a scrawny fourteen-year-old grommet with sun-bleached hair and a face full of freckles, was one of the few people in Lennox with whom Carter felt any real connection.

He was a young daredevil who'd take off on anything and thought he was bulletproof in the surf. Carter had been the same at his age.

Knowlsie pulled up beside him on a shiny cherry-coloured five-footer and grinned.

'Like your new board,' Carter said.

'Mum gave it to me last night for Chrissy. Can't wait to get me first wave.'

Carter gave him a half-smile. 'Merry Christmas, Knowlsie.'

'Yeah, you too,' the boy said. 'What did you get?'

'A few decent waves will do me.'

'I reckon Hughie's delivered on that.'

'He sure has.'

Hughie was the imaginary god of the ocean who surfers called upon to bring them good waves.

Knowlsie looked at the strangers and laughed. 'What about those dickheads all wearing the same wetties? You reckon they got 'em for Christmas?'

Carter didn't answer but nodded in the direction of the take-off zone. 'Go jag yourself a few. I'll join you in a sec. And if you hook into a big mother, charge.'

'Yeah, righto.'

Knowlsie lay down on his board and paddled away. Carter bobbed up and down, wondering whether he should warn Knowlsie to back off until he figured out what the three guys were up to.

He decided to stay put. After all, they wouldn't be after the kid.

To Carter's left, two seagulls squawked and dived beside a brown mat of seaweed that rose and fell as the first wave of the set passed underneath. It hit the sandbank and jacked up near vertical, creating a perfect clean wall of fast-moving water.

The pack sprung to life and converged on the critical take-off point, angling for pole position.

As Carter watched, one of the Indonesians paddled hard for the wave. So did two of the locals, who had the inside running. One of them, Knowlsie, got into the wave and leapt to his feet.

The stranger took off in front of him, gunning his board forwards and ignoring Knowlsie's right of way.

'*Oi, dickhead! My wave!*' Knowlsie screamed.

His board charged across the steep wave towards the Indonesian, who cut up and down the face.

The Indonesian shouted something back at him.

It was hard to hear from that distance, but it sounded to Carter like Javanese.

There was only room for one surfer on the hollow, breaking wave. The edge of the Indonesian's board caught the lip and stalled. Knowlsie kept charging like Carter had told him to and Carter swore under his breath.

The sharp crack of two boards colliding cut through the still air.

Both surfers were sent flying.

Knowlsie dropped straight down the face and ploughed into the foaming trough.

At the exact same moment the lip of the wave hit the stranger from behind, throwing him forwards.

The force of the water swept Knowlsie into no man's land, the one place a surfer didn't want to get caught.

In a war, 'no man's land' was the desolate and deadly zone that existed between enemy lines. In the surf, it was the wasteland between the rocks and where the waves broke, a washing machine of turbulent white water that drove you deeper and deeper towards the bottom.

If you kept your head and went with the flow of the ocean, you eventually rose to the surface and could paddle towards clear water. But inexperienced surfers often lost their centre, panicked and got into serious trouble.

Knowlsie could handle it under normal circumstances. But he'd been caught by surprise and might even have been knocked out by his board.

The Javanese guy had fared better. The angle of the hit had propelled him in the direction of the deepwater channel running alongside the break.

The second wave of the set, bigger and more powerful than the first, smashed hard into Knowlsie, pushing him closer to the rocky shoreline. Carter started paddling at full throttle straight for him.

The third wave, the biggest of the set, crashed onto the shallow bank. It created a two-metre wall of boiling foam, thrusting Knowlsie even deeper into the churn of violent water.

Carter just hoped the kid had managed to gulp down some air before getting chundered.

CHAPTER 3

Carter stroked hard across the strong rip sweeping towards the headland, focusing on the point where he expected Knowlsie to surface. The sharp nose of his board sliced through the chop.

Twenty metres in front of him, the ocean spat out three-quarters of a cherry board, minus the nose.

He slowed his paddle, just before Knowlsie's head popped up next to the busted board.

'Thank Christ,' Carter muttered under his breath.

Knowlsie shook his head and gasped for air.

Carter took four powerful strokes towards him and sat upright. 'You okay?'

Knowlsie, too out of breath to speak, nodded. He used his leg-rope to pull what was left of his broken board towards him and scrambled onto it.

Carter glanced back over his shoulder.

The Indonesian had surfaced much closer to the open water and was climbing back onto his undamaged board. His two mates paddled along the channel towards him.

'Shit, man!' Knowlsie said, still panting hard. 'Look at my stick!'

'Mate, it's only a board.'

'Mum's gonna kill me.'

'The point is you're okay. She'll get over it.'

'You don't know my mum.'

Carter smiled to himself and thought back to his own mother, who'd certainly ripped into him often enough over very little.

Knowlsie pointed at the three strangers sitting in a huddle forty metres away. 'What the hell is the story with those arseholes?'

'The world's full of them. Just worry about your own game.'

The comment didn't seem to register with Knowlsie. 'Bloody selfish drop-in artists,' he said. 'Disrespecting the local rules. They need to be taught a lesson.'

'That's how wars get started.'

Carter looked over at the Indonesians, who were discussing something. One of them pointed at him.

He needed to get Knowlsie out of there.

Besides the potential threat of violence, the rip was carrying the two of them at a steady rate back into the heart of no man's land. The next set was already building out to sea, rolling towards them.

'You need to head in,' Carter said.

Knowlsie scrunched up his freckled nose. 'Not before I tell those dickheads off.'

'Forget about 'em. They're not worth it.'

Knowlsie ignored him and started paddling across the rip towards the channel.

'Hey,' Carter said in a stronger tone.

Knowlsie stopped, turned his head and gave him a defiant stare.

Carter's gaze remained calm and steady.

After a few moments Knowlsie looked away, silently admitting defeat.

He turned his busted board towards the headland and started paddling towards it, managing to catch a small wave that carried him on his belly towards one of the few safe exit points on the rock-lined shore.

Knowlsie would be okay.

Carter turned out to sea. Another wave rushed towards him. He duck-dived through a wall of foam and popped out the other side.

When he'd negotiated the next two waves of the set, he slowed his paddle, looked up and scoped the three strangers. They sat astride their boards at twenty-metre intervals along the still waters of the channel, watching him.

He was starting to get a handle on what this was about.

At first he'd thought it unlikely anyone would choose to attack him in the surf. It would have been easier to take him out on dry land.

But now he understood. They were intending to attack him in no man's land and make his death look like an accident.

It wouldn't be hard on a day like this.

In theory, anyway.

One thing was for sure – they weren't there for a friendly chat.

If nothing else, the unexpected threat had shaken off the remnants of his hangover.

CHAPTER 4

Carter sat up on his board and savoured the fresh salty smell and tang of the ocean.

Waiting for them to take the initiative was out of the question. And if he struck first, he needed to go all out. Half-measures would get him killed.

He stretched his arms over his head and rotated his shoulders and neck, wondering what weapons might be concealed under their wetsuits.

Something to keep an eye on.

He slid off his board into the choppy water, detached the leg-rope from his right ankle and unhooked the other end from the tail of his board.

His movements galvanised the Indonesian closest to him into action, and he stroked furiously along the channel towards Carter.

Carter didn't waste a second.

He climbed back onto his board and lay prone, secured the leg-rope under his chest to keep it close and began paddling away from the approaching stranger at a forty-five-degree angle. He aimed his board for a position well inside the pack, where he figured a smaller but still solid wave would break. The other surfers kept their focus out to sea, watching for the next wave, oblivious to anything else.

Carter reached his targeted take-off point just before the incoming wave hit.

The lip curled and a wall of steep water reared up.

He whipped his board around, pointed the nose at a slanting angle towards the wave's face and powered his board forwards.

His board came to life. He grabbed the ends of the leg-rope in either hand and jumped to his feet, bending his knees to keep his centre of gravity low, and accelerated across the near-vertical face.

A quick backward glance told him he'd left the guy paddling towards him well behind, but one of his friends was now stroking at a frantic pace in an effort to cut Carter off.

He was just metres away when Carter shifted his weight on the sticky waxed deck of his board, lining its nose up with the man's forehead.

The startled Indonesian stopped paddling, sat up on his board and reached behind his back.

Too late.

Carter jammed down on his back foot, thrusting the speeding board forwards.

At the same instant he threw himself off the back of the wave into the arms of the ocean. The board flew through the air towards its target.

A second later Carter's head breached the surface.

Just in time to see the Indonesian collapsing forwards onto his board, blood streaming from a head wound.

The flying board had found its mark. He was out cold.

Carter switched his attention to the first guy, who was once again paddling straight for him.

Carter held his position in the water, still holding the leg-rope. There wasn't time to grab his board.

The Indonesian stopped and sat up four metres away. He reached into the back of his wetsuit.

Carter knew what was coming.

He took a deep breath, stuck the leg-rope between his teeth, dived underwater and swam under the assailant's board.

When he was half a body length behind the tail, he popped his head out of the water.

The Indonesian faced away from him, holding a fishing knife in his right hand and peering into the water from side to side, trying to figure out where Carter was.

Carter kicked hard to propel himself upwards out of the water and stretched his arms high in the air.

The guy started to turn his head.

Again, too late.

Carter looped the plastic-covered leash around his neck, yanked back and dragged him off his board, tightening the leg-rope like a hangman's noose.

The startled surfer tried to grab the rope with his left hand, while his right hand whipped the knife back and forth.

Carter pulled the rope even tighter with his left hand and smashed his right elbow against the base of the Indonesian's skull.

The strike was designed to pinch a nerve in his neck and paralyse the right side of his body. The knife dropped from his now limp hand and slid into the water.

Carter let go of his leg-rope, lifted the unconscious guy back onto his board and turned towards shore, leaving him floating there.

The final Indonesian was fifteen metres away and paddling towards him with an eight-inch dagger clenched between his teeth.

Carter recognised the distinctive pistol-grip hilt and wavy blade of a Javanese kris, an ancient weapon favoured by practitioners of pencak silat, the Indonesian martial art.

Carter swam towards his board, climbed onto it and faced his attacker.

The Indonesian stopped paddling two body lengths from him and straddled his board.

He took the dagger out of his mouth, pulled it back behind his ear and yelled, 'Allah akbar!' *God is great!*

CHAPTER 5

A split second before the kris left the Indonesian's hand, Carter slid off the tail of his board into the water. He grabbed the sides and held the fibreglass deck in front of him as a shield.

The dagger slammed into the board with a thud, slicing straight through its middle but holding firm at the hilt, the point of the blade stopping centimetres from Carter's face.

Carter rolled the board over and pulled the kris from the deck. The traditional blade was both weapon and holy object, believed to have a spiritual presence. Some blades bestowed good luck. Others bad. For its current owner, it was going to be all bad.

Carter flung the dagger at his assailant's right shoulder.

The kris penetrated the man's pectoral muscle, throwing him back on his board, screaming.

Carter swam up to him, grabbed his dreadlocked hair, pulled his head back and struck him behind the neck with a closed fist.

Knocking him out and shutting him up.

Religious fanatics, Carter thought. After living in the sleepy surf town of Lennox for a year, he thought he'd left this madness behind.

He laid the third surfer on his board and wrapped the man's leg-rope around him to secure his unconscious body. He did the same for the other two, glad they were still breathing.

Not because he thought the world would be better off with these three guys still in it. On the contrary. But dead bodies generated official investigations, creating a potential hassle he could do without.

Hopefully they'd come to and make it to shore. If not, too bad. He'd be long gone and would have to take his chances with the law. It wasn't like anyone would be filing an official complaint.

He paddled to shore and left the water by riding a surge onto the rocks. He stood with his board tucked under his arm and scanned the break. None of the surfers at the line-up were paying the slightest attention to anything beyond the next wave.

He shifted his focus to the grassy headland that rose out of the ocean like a lioness guarding her domain. A lone figure stood just on the edge of the car park, watching him, and he felt a pulse of adrenalin.

Though he hadn't seen her for over a year and had tried to make a relationship work with another woman, not a day went by that Erina wasn't in his thoughts.

She was a far tougher opponent than the three fanatics put together. And considering the morning's events, he knew she hadn't turned up to wish him a merry Christmas.

CHAPTER 6

Carter followed the dirt track up the gentle sloping hill towards her, carrying his badly dinged surfboard under his right arm. The coarse gravel pressed into the hardened soles of his bare feet. He noted a slight quickening of his heart rate.

Erina Wing leant against the bonnet of her black four-wheel drive, dressed in a white T-shirt, tight-fitting black jeans and sneakers. At thirty-two, she possessed the lithe body and grace of an Olympic gymnast.

A discreet black bag lay on the ground behind her. It looked like any normal sports bag, but instead of the usual make-up, deodorant and a towel, she'd be packing a handgun, poison darts and throwing knives.

He reached the edge of the car park and stopped. Behind him a powerful wave crashed against the rocks.

Erina touched the peak of her red San Francisco 49ers baseball cap and gave him an enigmatic smile.

The familiarity of her fine features stirred a host of memories. Part of him longed to hug her. Another wanted to turn and run.

He placed his board on the grass a metre and a half in front of her and said nothing. Any decisions he made now could have significant long-term implications and Erina wouldn't necessarily have his best interests at heart.

She removed her baseball cap and placed it on the bonnet, revealing jet-black hair tied in a loose ponytail. Fine wisps blew over her face in the gentle breeze. The rising sun created a luminous sheen across her head like a halo.

15

A dark angel.

She motioned her head towards the surf. 'Glad to see you didn't need me out there.'

'I get by okay on my own.'

He waited for her to make a move, trying to read from her body language what she wanted. Like him, Erina buried her true emotions deep, giving nothing away.

She took a couple of steps towards him. 'I know that attack probably took you by surprise, Carter, but as you can see, we've got a problem.'

'We?' he asked. 'What's it got to do with me?' His words came out harsher than he intended.

'It involves all of the order and then some. We need your help.'

Though her tone was light, he could tell she was serious.

'Erina, it's not the first time some fundamentalist wack job has tried to kill one of us.'

'This is different.'

'No, Erina. It's always the same.'

'This is the first time they've come to Australia. Why do you think that is?'

'I'll leave that for you guys to figure out.'

He looked down at his board as if expecting it to offer him some answers. The sooner he brought the conversation to an end and got out of there, the better. Now that everyone seemed to know where he lived, he needed to grab his stuff, make a swift exit and set up a new life somewhere else.

He knew how to disappear without leaving a trace.

The only thing keeping him at Lennox was the surf. All his friends from his early teens had long gone. Maybe Margaret River in Western Australia would be worth a shot. It was out of the way and he knew the surf ripped as good as Lennox.

He bent down to pick up his board.

'Thomas wants to fill you in on the details himself,' Erina said.

He stood up and left his board where it was. 'Thomas is here?'

She nodded. 'I'll take you to him.'

'Why didn't he come himself?'

'I offered to pick you up. I wanted to see you first.'

'I've got other plans for today.'

'What, another surf?'

'Maybe.'

She slipped her hands into the front pockets of her jeans and took a step towards him. 'Don't you care about anything beyond the next wave?'

He looked into her dark brown eyes. She didn't blink.

His heart quickened again.

Arguing with her was pointless, but he tried anyway. 'You know as well as I do that there are no winners in this kind of situation,' he said. 'Only losers. The harder we retaliate, the more they hate us. If we ignore them, they'll eventually go away.'

'You're not hearing me, Carter.'

All she cared about was getting him to do what she and Thomas wanted.

He looked over his shoulder.

The three guys were drifting out to sea, slumped over their boards.

Two of them were out for the long count, but the guy with the dreadlocks was starting to come to.

He needed to make a decision. Either go with Erina, meet with Thomas and be put through the emotional wringer once again, or just walk away.

Out the back of the break, an anonymous surfer took off on a screamer.

'Look at me, Carter.'

He turned his head and met her steely gaze.

'We're your family. You need to think about what kind of man you want to be.'

It was as much a threat as a plea, and deep down he recognised the truth of what she said. The order was the closest thing he had to a family, and he had to admit he'd struggled to live in the world without them.

Thomas would play on that.

But it wasn't going to happen. Not today.

He picked up his board. It felt light in his hands.

'So what's your answer?' she asked.

'I'm sorry, Erina,' he said, softening his tone. 'I'd like to help. But I can't.'

He kept his focus on her, pushing down the emotion welling in his chest. He needed to make her see he was serious so she would leave him alone.

After a few moments she raised her hands and smiled, revealing the single dimple in her left cheek.

'Okay,' she said. 'You do what you need to do. I'll respect your decision.'

Carter's shoulders relaxed. 'Thank you.'

'Thomas said if you wouldn't come back willingly, you'd be no use to us.'

'Thomas is a wise man.'

She extended her hand and he took it in his own. The familiar calluses from countless hours of martial-arts training, including up to a hundred chin-ups a day to maintain her upper-body strength, rubbed against his palm.

'We can do better than that,' she said.

She dropped his hand and held out her arms.

Without thinking, and still holding his board, he stepped into her embrace and felt her arms wrap around him.

He drank in the freshness of her hair and the warmth of her body. They fitted together like the last two pieces in a jigsaw puzzle.

Against his better judgement, he allowed his whole body to relax. He closed his eyes and for a fleeting moment felt like he'd come home.

Then a sharp shiver ran down his spine, breaking the potent spell.

A warning.

He started to pull back.

Too late.

He felt the sharp prick of a needle at the back of his neck.

Numbness spread down his shoulder and arm.

'Fuck you, Erina.'

He wanted to say more, but no words came out.

His muscles went slack. He heard the board drop onto the gravel.

There was a moment of great peace.

A sensation of falling.

She gently guided him to the ground, and his world faded to black.

CHAPTER 7

Carter drifted back into consciousness sitting in the front seat of Erina's four-wheel drive, speeding down a narrow tree-lined road.

The first thing he noticed was that his hands were cuffed and resting in his lap. He was still in his board shorts, and his naked back and legs sweated against the leather seats.

Every muscle ached. His stomach was queasy, his skin clammy and his bone-dry mouth tasted of zinc. She must have used scopolamine hydrobromide. In low doses it put the subject to sleep for under an hour and had no long-term effects.

He glanced out the tinted window and recognised the rolling hills behind the picturesque town of Mullumbimby, forty-odd kilometres north-west of Lennox. The aptly named Mount Warning, usually one of his favourite local landmarks, stood tall and remote in the hazy distance, its head lost in the clouds, removed from life below.

He moved his tongue, trying to work up some spit.

'You okay?' Erina asked.

He could barely form the word. 'Fantastic.'

'I'm really sorry about this,' she said gently. 'But avoiding Thomas wasn't an option today.'

'So it seems.'

'You never should've left without saying goodbye.'

Carter stayed silent and refrained from looking at her. He wasn't going there.

Erina was an elite member of the Order of the White Pole, a private black ops organisation based in South-East Asia. He'd been a member too, for over twenty years. The only way he'd managed to escape was to walk away without any explanation or argument and stay away.

'If you still refuse to join us after hearing him out,' she said, 'no one will try to stop you.'

He'd heard that one before.

'I promise,' she said, using her free left hand to lift a small plastic bottle with a straw to his lips.

He drank the warm milky antidote and flexed and relaxed his legs to get his blood flowing.

He wasn't thrilled with what she'd done, but blaming her was pointless. Thomas was not only her leader but also her father. And whatever feelings she might have once had for Carter were now long buried. For Erina, the ends always justified the means, and she wouldn't allow sentiment to cloud her actions.

On assignment her motto was *Get the job done or die trying*. That's what made her a dangerous opponent when you crossed her and a great ally when working on the same side – something he could no longer do.

He was mostly angry with himself. He should've been more alert. Getting close to Erina in any sense was way too dangerous.

'How's it going with that woman you left us for?' she asked. 'Jessica, wasn't it?'

'You know my leaving had nothing to do with her.'

She glanced at him sideways, as if she knew what had happened to him the night before, why he'd gone on such a bender.

'It's over,' he continued. 'She said she'd met laptop computers with more emotion.'

Erina giggled like a young girl, reminding him how sweet and lighthearted she could be. 'She obviously doesn't understand you.'

He looked out the window at the trees rushing by and said, 'I wouldn't have thought I was that complicated.'

She accelerated out of a tight corner. 'You need to find a woman who knows how to handle you.'

Carter looked across at her. 'What, like you do?'

An impish grin spread across her face. 'I never said that.'

He almost cracked a smile. 'No one would ever accuse you of letting your finer emotions get in the way.'

'I'll take that as a compliment.'

She held the bottle to his lips again and he took another long sip. The reason the relationship with Jessica had never worked was that his heart was never in it. He hated himself for hurting her. But he couldn't shake his feelings for Erina and wasn't about to tell either woman that.

He stretched his shoulders back and shook his head. The antidote was starting to kick in.

—

Erina turned right off the deserted bitumen road, slowed down and continued along a flat dirt track covered by overhanging foliage, which became thicker and denser the further they moved in.

The four-wheel drive bumped through the shadowy green tunnel for about a hundred and fifty metres until the thick vegetation opened up, revealing a lawn the size of a football field. The track led to a traditional country homestead, complete with sloping red-tile roof, brick chimney and wraparound verandah. Carter spotted several makeshift sensors and security cameras placed strategically around the grounds.

The wooden house stood in front of a hilly ridge that ran along the back of the property. A black four-wheel drive was parked to the left of the house under one of the half-dozen tall gum trees spread around the lawn area. The set-up guaranteed privacy, but Carter reckoned the place would be vulnerable to a well-organised attack. He wondered what had prompted the order to set up a temporary headquarters here.

Thomas would have his reasons.

The tyres crunched to a halt on the loose gravel.

Carter looked deep into the shade of the covered verandah. His pulse quickened as he recognised the familiar silhouette.

Thomas Wing stepped out of the shadows.

He walked down the stairs towards them and stopped. Standing just under six foot tall, Thomas wore a black cotton shirt, loose pants and sandals. The early-morning sunlight reflected off his bald head.

His features were distinctly Asian; he took after his Chinese mother, rather than his American father. He was sixty-eight, but could've easily passed for fifty.

Erina stepped out of the vehicle, walked round the front and opened Carter's door.

He breathed in the smell of moist grass. A kookaburra laughed as if amused by Carter's predicament.

Thomas moved towards him, calm and unhurried, stopping a metre from the open door.

His unlined face looked paler and gaunter than Carter remembered. Thomas's dark eyes examined him as though probing directly into his soul.

Carter wanted to look away but forced himself to maintain eye contact. Thomas and Erina were the only two people in the world who could throw him off balance with their eyes.

Thomas broke off his gaze, placed his hands in the prayer position and bowed his head.

'My heartfelt apologies,' he said. 'Desperation forced our hand.'

'You always said the ends never justify the means.'

'I did what I thought necessary given the circumstances.'

The hint of an ironic smile softened Thomas's face. He nodded at Erina, who unlocked Carter's handcuffs.

Carter stepped into the sunlight, kicked his legs out and shook his arms, wrists and shoulders.

Erina got back into her car, turned on the ignition and opened the window.

'Where are you going?' Carter asked.

'Unlike some people, I've got a job to do.'

'So the package has been delivered and you move on to the next assignment. Don't you ever clock off?'

'Life's too short. I'll be seeing you, Carter.'

'Don't count on it.'

She smiled at him and the tinted window slid up, hiding her from view.

The car rolled down the drive and gathered speed. He watched it disappear under the canopy of trees, feeling a curious mix of relief and disappointment.

Carter turned back to Thomas, who stood with his arms folded. A knowing smile broke the smooth lines of the older man's face.

'What?' Carter asked.

Thomas said nothing, just turned and walked towards the house.

Carter waited a moment and then followed.

CHAPTER 8

Thomas led Carter through the sparsely furnished house into an old-style kitchen at the rear. He gestured for him to sit on one of four wooden chairs placed around a rectangular table, bare except for a pile of documents and a slim MacBook Air sleeping at one end. A cool breeze drifted through the sun-filled room.

'I'll make some tea,' Thomas said.

Carter settled into his chair, stared out the window at the grey ghost gum standing alone against the pale blue sky and suppressed a sigh. *Accept what is, is*, he told himself. It was the first of the order's principles and one he had always struggled with. Another was *Expect the unexpected*. As he considered what had transpired that morning, Carter smiled wryly to himself. He'd clearly let that one slip over the past few months.

The order was based on the thousand-year-old White Pole school of martial arts. It'd been established in 1937 by a consortium of wealthy Shanghai families to protect Chinese citizens from being victimised by Japanese aggressors during the Second Sino-Japanese War. Its initial charter was to serve the weak and vulnerable, regardless of their ethnicity, financial status, political orientation or religious persuasion.

Over a number of decades the order's role had expanded and they began to operate throughout South-East Asia, guided always by spiritual and altruistic values. Carter's jobs had included smuggling refugees out of volatile border regions, rescuing women from slavery in the sex industry, cracking paedophile networks and intercepting drug and weapons shipments across unpatrolled seas.

The landscape had changed in the late nineties after the Asian financial crisis. Many voluntary supporters of the order could no longer donate regularly to keep it running. The society was forced to become fully self-supporting and obliged to work for business and government organisations to survive.

Further change had come after the first Bali bombing in 2002, when two hundred and two people, many of them young Australian tourists, were killed at the Sari Club in Kuta. The order had moved its primary base from Bangkok to Bali and started working with the Trident Bureau, an Australian government agency set up to run covert operations to fight terrorism in Indonesia, Malaysia and the Philippines. After the second Bali bombing in 2005, the order entered into an exclusive government contract with Trident, even though they did the occasional pro bono case on the side.

The lucrative agreement came with strict guidelines and reporting protocols. Political decisions were made in Sydney and Canberra with little or no regard for the needs of the operatives risking their lives in the field.

Carter glanced over at Thomas, who stood with his back to him, measuring precise quantities of tea into the pot.

After signing off on the Trident contract, Thomas's approach had changed. He'd always been the leader of the order, but now he became far less inclusive of the team when running operations, adopting a military style and imposing a clear chain of command to make sure that Trident policies were implemented.

Whenever Carter had voiced his concerns, Thomas patiently heard him out, but he never shifted his views or altered his leadership style. He claimed he always did what was best for the order to safeguard its survival. Carter understood where he was coming from but didn't agree.

And then there was the unwritten principle – no emotional attachments on the job. That one had done Erina's head in.

She and Carter had first become romantically involved when he was in his early thirties and she was twenty-six. She'd felt guilty about

26

betraying her father and his code. Thomas had been too smart to forbid them from seeing each other, but he never sanctioned the relationship either. He avoided teaming them up on assignment wherever possible and refused to discuss it with Carter, except to say that the order's principles, including the unwritten one, were there for a reason and it wasn't Carter's place to question them.

Ultimately, it was these changes to the order's modus operandi, Thomas's increasingly autocratic style and Carter's torturous relationship with Erina that caused him to walk away and stay away. They'd stopped being romantically involved nine months before he left. He'd felt much better being out of her orbit, even though he knew he'd left the order short handed. At the time of his departure there had been just fifteen active members, including two support staff and four trainees. Before the Asian financial crisis there'd been over two hundred members, many of whom had been volunteers.

Carter heard the back door open and close and a set of light footsteps tread across wooden floorboards towards the kitchen.

The kettle boiled. Thomas bowed his head over the pot.

CHAPTER 9

Wayan Gusti, Thomas's latest protégé, stood in the doorway holding his head high. When Carter had last seen him a year and a half ago, Wayan was a shy, slightly built sixteen-year-old Balinese boy. He'd developed into a fine-looking young man. He wore loose black trousers, a cutaway white cotton T-shirt and a black bandana wrapped around his forehead. His cheeks shone with a light sheen of sweat, suggesting he'd been working out. The muscle definition of his arms and chest was impressive. He'd developed strength and power to complement his natural agility and speed.

Wayan looked at Carter with a mixture of judgement and censure, suggesting he hadn't forgiven him for disappearing without saying goodbye.

Physically he looked ready to become a sanjuro, the name given to the order's elite field operatives. But Carter, who'd been the youngest member to graduate as a sanjuro in the order's history, wondered whether he yet possessed the emotional and spiritual maturity required. They were a warrior's most important qualities and were the hardest to master.

In his left hand Wayan carried a staff made from bamboo, a batang, the most versatile of the pencak silat weapons and a favourite of Carter's. Wayan held it like it was an extension of his body.

A good sign.

Carter stood up and was surprised at how tall Wayan had grown. He was nearly six foot, only a couple of inches shorter than himself.

Carter extended his hand. 'Good to see you.'

The young man shook it without enthusiasm. 'Thomas says you've become a full-time surfer. You like that?'

'It has its moments.'

'Why did you leave?'

'I needed some space.'

'You could've at least said goodbye.'

'I know. I'm sorry.'

They stood in an uncomfortable silence. Carter knew how much the younger man had looked up to him and understood his disappointment and hurt.

'Has Thomas sent you into the field yet?' Carter asked.

'He says I'm not ready. But I'm in the process of proving him wrong. Are you coming back?'

'That wasn't the plan when I woke up this morning.'

'So you're just going to keep drifting like a surf bum when there's important work to do?'

Carter didn't know what to say to that.

'We need you,' Wayan told him.

'Enough,' Thomas said, walking towards the table carrying a wooden tray with a Chinese teapot and three small cups on it. 'Fetch Carter a T-shirt. We need to get down to business.'

Wayan left the room. Thomas placed the tray on the table and turned his attention to Carter. 'As Erina has undoubtedly informed you, changing fortunes and the alignment of the stars mean your services are again required.'

Carter sat back down and rested his forearms on the table. 'Whether I like it or not?'

'I believe I have your best interests at heart.'

'Really?'

'Your trouble is you've lost your faith. You are no longer governed by your duty and the flow of the universe.'

Carter folded his arms and said nothing.

'Rather,' Thomas continued, 'you give every indication of following only the dictates of your ego. The order's principles apply to every aspect of your life, not just when you're on assignment.'

'The reason I left had nothing to do with me questioning the principles,' Carter said. 'It was the way you tried to impose your will on me and force me to do things I didn't believe in. You're still doing it, even now.'

'There is something much bigger going on here. The order needs you. This work is your calling, whether you realise it or not.'

'And you still won't listen to a word I say.'

'There has to be a chain of command. We each have to know our place within the chain. Life without faith, duty and discipline is meaningless.'

Thomas had been saying much the same thing since they first met at his Bangkok dojo when Carter was fourteen years old. The young Australian boy had been rebellious on the surface, but deep down, an insatiable hunger for guidance and order drove him. The dojo became his sanctuary, the only place in the chaotic city where he felt safe and at peace.

Up until then he'd been an outsider in Bangkok. The local kids had found out about his mother and called her a filthy junkie. Carter felt compelled to defend her honour, like he had at Lennox, and constantly fought against bigger and older local boys who saw him as a loner and a soft target with no one to back him up.

After a few months of intense training he began to combine what he learnt at the dojo with his natural talents and instincts on the streets to stunning effect. The boys soon stopped taunting him about his mother and his attackers left him alone. But he made no friends.

Thomas poured the steaming tea into each cup with silent reverence. The powerful aroma of fresh ginger and aniseed and the formality of Thomas's ceremony brought back a flood of memories.

Moving to Bangkok and meeting Thomas had changed his life forever. His mother had instigated the relocation from the country quiet of Lennox Head to the sleaze of the Patpong district – officially to teach English as a second language, unofficially for the smack, which was pure and cheap. More than once he'd come home to find her passed out on the couch with a needle sticking out of her arm. Two days before his fifteenth birthday she took an overdose and died.

As Carter had no living relatives in Australia, Thomas used his influential government contacts to become his guardian and introduced him to the order's strict training regimen and full range of mystical arts. It was a comprehensive and very different education to what he would've received in Australia.

On his eighteenth birthday, he became a fully fledged member of the order and was inducted as the youngest ever sanjuro.

Thomas placed a cup in front of Carter. 'Every disturbance has a spiritual cause. A man isn't an island. Tell me, how have you been faring on your own without a connection to a higher source?'

Wayan walked back into the kitchen and handed Carter a grey T-shirt.

He put it on, then took a sip of hot tea, savouring the sharp taste of his favourite blend, and said, 'Let's move on from my moral and spiritual shortcomings and get to what this is about, shall we?'

CHAPTER 10

Carter placed his cup back on the table and asked, 'Has someone issued a fatwa against the order?'

'Indeed they have,' Thomas said. 'The Sungkar clan have issued an edict saying the order is guilty of murder and we are enemies of God and Islam. A clan-controlled mufti has issued the fatwa, meaning a death sentence hangs over every one of us.'

In his last few years working for the order, Carter had plenty to do with the Sungkar clan. It was one of many powerful family organisations in Indonesia; such clans had controlled large sections of cities and entire villages for hundreds of years. It was impossible to sell a cup of tea in a clan's domain without paying a protection fee.

This wasn't a big deal in Indonesia, where petty extortion and corruption were an ingrained part of society. For the most part the clans were relatively harmless and fulfilled the useful role of maintaining law and order.

For twenty years Aamir Sungkar, a moderate Muslim, had led his clan and gathered significant wealth through traditional means – mainly protection and minor corruption. But when his oldest son, Arung, took over after his death, he had pushed the boundaries of tradition and law, expanding the Sungkar clan's interests to include drug trafficking, prostitution, gun running, piracy and people smuggling.

Arung was corrupt and ruthless, but he certainly wasn't a religious fanatic prone to issuing fatwas.

'Remember your last assignment with us?' Thomas said. 'You intercepted a shipment of the clan's guns being run across the Strait of Malacca from Indonesia to Malaysia?'

'Of course.'

Just thinking about it stirred a rush of anger in Carter's gut. As well as transporting weapons, he discovered, the targeted boat was also carrying five frightened young Hindu women from Bali, who he suspected had been kidnapped. He'd argued with Thomas, saying they should abort the operation, as the risk to the women was too great. Thomas had overruled his objections in no uncertain terms and ordered him to proceed.

Later he found out that Detachment 88, the brutal Indonesian anti-terrorist unit, had discovered the boat was also transporting C4 explosives to Malaysia. They, along with the cache of weapons, were being delivered to a known terrorist cell in Kuala Lumpur. When the Trident Bureau heard this, they insisted the operation be carried out and Thomas had complied.

'As you know,' Thomas said, 'one of their boats was blown up in the process, killing a number of crew and clan members.'

'Don't forget the five young women. You should've listened to me.'

'That's beside the point.'

'It actually is the point as far as I'm concerned—'

'What you don't know,' Thomas said, cutting him off, 'is that Arung Sungkar was killed in the explosion.'

'Can't say that upsets me. I've met sewer rats with more humanity.'

'That may be so, but every action creates a reaction. They now have a new leader.'

Thomas nodded at Wayan, who sat down at the table and clicked a key on the laptop's keyboard. An image of a slim Indonesian man in his mid-thirties appeared. He wore a white skullcap and flowing white robes. A wispy moustache and wiry goatee framed perfect white teeth and a smile full of mischief.

Carter remembered Arung's younger brother Samudra. His expression reminded him of one of the Bali bombers, Amrozi bin Nurhasyim, who, on hearing that he'd been sentenced to death, had welcomed the news with a huge smile and a thumbs up, saying, 'There will be a million more Amrozis to come.' He'd been executed in 2008, unrepentant to the end.

'Samudra Sungkar took over as leader eleven months ago,' Thomas said.

Carter knew the thirty-nine-year-old's history. He'd had a privileged upbringing and studied engineering and information technology at the University of New South Wales in Sydney. From what Carter had heard, Samudra, like Amrozi, had for many years strayed from the strict moral tenets of Islam. He drank, had sex with prostitutes and paid scant attention to the principles of his Muslim faith. Three years ago he had disappeared off the radar.

'He's a dangerous man,' Thomas said. 'He believes he knows God's will.'

'Not another one,' Carter said. 'I thought he was a party boy.'

'He was, but now he says he was corrupted by the decadence and moral depravation of life in Sydney. And that Australians are racist and treated him like a second-class citizen.'

'Something else must've turned him to the dark side, though?'

'Yes – it started when his younger brother was killed in Afghanistan in 2009 by Australian special forces in Helmand Province. It pushed him into the arms of the Islamic fundamentalists – his wealth and position meant they targeted him and gave him the full treatment.'

'I bet they did.'

'For two years he attended training camps in Malaysia, Pakistan and Afghanistan, where his instruction covered military tactics, propaganda, weapons and explosives, as well as extensive religious study. And now that Arung is dead, he's in charge.'

'Sounds like he's following in the footsteps of his grandfather.'

'So it seems,' Thomas said, topping up Carter's tea.

Samudra's grandfather, Fajar Sungkar, had been a member of the radical Indonesian fundamentalist sect Darul Islam, established in 1942 by Muslim militia. Its sole aim was to create an independent Islamic state where the only valid source of law was sharia, a legal code based on a strict interpretation of Islam.

They fought an armed rebellion against the Sukarno government in the 1950s and '60s. Later, a number of them travelled to camps in Pakistan and Afghanistan, where battle-hardened mujaheddin trained and inspired them to commit to a life of jihad.

The 'Afghans', as they called themselves, became the leaders, ideologues and commanders of Jemaah Islamiah, the violent extremist group responsible for the Bali bombings and other terrorist activities led by Abu Bakar Bashir.

One of their goals – introducing sharia law into Indonesian society – had met with partial success. The northern Indonesian province of Aceh was now legitimately ruled by sharia, its legal code based on their own interpretation of the Koran. He'd heard reports that people had been caned and even stoned for adultery.

Carter knew that the jihadi extremists were very much in the minority. The vast majority of Indonesia's Muslims were good, friendly people who contributed to society in a positive way – like the majority of people belonging to any other culture or religion. But Indonesia had the world's largest Muslim population – over two hundred million – which meant that even a small percentage of them represented a sizeable number.

'So what's God telling Samudra?' Carter asked.

'He's publicly declared that there is no nobler way to die than as a martyr. He's called on the members of the Sungkar clan and its international affiliates to pledge every cell of their being to wreaking God's vengeance on Australia and the order before the new year, less than a week away.'

'All because we killed Arung?'

'That was the tipping point that took him from being a radical fundamentalist to initiating a jihadist call to arms.'

'So you reckon Samudra sees himself as what? The next Osama bin Laden?'

'Correct.' Thomas took a delicate sip of tea and placed it on the table. 'And you are involved whether you like it or not.'

CHAPTER 11

Carter drained his teacup and looked out the open window, studying the shedding bark of a ghost gum. He wondered what Thomas wasn't telling him. Thomas only shared information on a need-to-know basis.

'How do you know it's not just the mad ranting of a fanatic preaching to the converted?' Carter asked. 'Why take it so seriously?'

'In case you've forgotten, three clan members did try to kill you this morning.'

'Could've just been a one-off act of revenge.'

'I can assure you it's not just about you. We have evidence that Samudra has set up a military-style training camp on Batak Island at the top end of Sumatra.'

'A bunch of radical Muslims running round in army fatigues on a remote tropical island and a revenge attempt on my life hardly constitute a threat to Australia's national security.'

'Perhaps not, but we've discovered a Sungkar clan cell four hours west of here, on a cattle property close to Boggabilla on the Queensland–New South Wales border.'

Carter put his hands behind his head and stretched back. There had been a couple of credible terrorist threats against Australia in the late nineties and in the aftermath of 9/11, both involving local branches of Jemaah Islamiah. One had involved the group Mantiqi IV, who had a base in the Blue Mountains, an hour and a half drive west of Sydney. Another group had set up a military-style training operation in Western

Australia – it had been run by the Ayub twins, who fled Australia after the 2002 Bali bombing. Despite the initial concern, neither had amounted to anything.

'What else?' Carter asked, knowing there must be more to it.

'Samudra's sister Kemala strongly maintains the Sungkar clan intends to wipe out the order and execute a jihad on Australian soil,' Thomas said. 'Most likely in Sydney.'

'Samudra's sister? Is she a reliable source?'

'Absolutely. Kemala has been actively watching Samudra's activities since he assumed leadership of the Sungkar clan shortly after you went walkabout.'

Carter detected a sly glance in his direction from Wayan, indicating that Thomas's interest in Kemala went beyond the purely professional. If that was the case, it was out of character. He filed the information away.

'Erina is in Boggabilla investigating the clan and has confirmed some disturbing activity,' Thomas continued. 'And there's one piece of information that will be of particular interest to you.'

Carter didn't respond. It felt like Thomas was playing him, drip-feeding information.

'Alex Botha has joined Samudra's clan.'

The mention of Alex's name caused Carter to sit up straighter in his chair.

In many ways Alex was his alter ego. He was South African by birth, a former member of the order and, like Carter and Erina, a sanjuro. He and Carter were the same age and shared the same birthday, 19 November. For a number of years they had been close friends. Alex and he shared a passion for the Japanese samurai tradition and both were master swordsmen. When Alex was training to be a sanjuro, they had often sparred for hours with wooden swords. But about five or six years before Carter left the order, Alex's arrogance and pride had begun to take over his personality.

They both collected replicas of famous swords, and when one of Carter's favourites disappeared – the 'Drying Pole', used by the famous samurai Kojiro – he confronted Alex, who claimed he'd never touched it. Their relationship had never been the same after that.

37

Alex had become increasingly competitive with Carter and started using his substantial talent for the martial arts and combat in a cruel and self-serving way. He'd stopped paying attention to the spiritual principles of the order and Carter suspected he was taking drugs, too.

When he shared his suspicions with Thomas, Thomas had tried to counsel Alex and bring him back into the fold. But it soon became clear that he was not only using drugs but also running them while on assignment with the order.

The problem had resolved itself two years ago when Alex was arrested at Jakarta Airport carrying half a kilo of heroin. Alex had sent messages to Thomas and Carter from jail, asking for their help, but they'd decided to let him sit in prison for six months, hoping it'd give him time to reflect on the choices he had made, and find his way back to the true path. Unbeknown to Alex, Thomas had used his influence to make sure the case would never come to trial. If he'd been convicted, he would've faced a firing squad.

After only a few months Alex had escaped – and that was the last they had heard from him. He hadn't created any trouble for them, and Thomas had decided against pursuing him.

'So what happened?' Carter asked.

'It turns out that he converted to Islam, joined the Sungkar clan and is now going by the name Abdul-Aleem.'

The fact that the clan had got to Alex both surprised and didn't surprise Carter. Muslim fundamentalists had for years maintained a level of covert control across many Indonesian prisons.

Following the Bali bombings, the Indonesian security forces and the Australian Federal Police had tracked down and arrested many terrorists. While incarcerated, they'd set up shadow governments in prisons, recruited members, sent money from jail to jail and, at least once, coordinated an outside terrorist attack. They also ran businesses, used mobile phones to preach sermons to followers outside and dominated prison mosques. Alex had a weakness for power and influence, and would naturally have been drawn to them. His use to them would have been immediately obvious – a westerner with his training and connections, bearing a grudge against their common enemy.

'The clan used their influence to get him out of jail,' Thomas continued, 'and helped him establish a new identity.'

'That's about the only path that'd lead Alex to God.'

'I agree. His conversion was, I suspect, motivated by his desire to save his skin rather than his soul.'

Carter nodded.

'Alex's reappearance is a major concern,' Thomas said. 'With his knowledge and experience, he could cause us a great deal of trouble – but Erina is taking care of things in Boggabilla for now. What I want you to do is go to Sydney and check out Trident for me, as I believe the bureau's security has been compromised.'

He reached into the bag sitting on the floor next to him and slid three stapled A4 pages across the table.

Carter leant forwards. His curiosity had been piqued. But before he had a chance to finish the first paragraph, Wayan's computer started to beep.

'You expecting more guests?' Carter asked.

Thomas shook his head.

Wayan hit a few buttons on the computer keyboard.

A map of the property appeared on screen. A red light flashed one-third of the way along the entrance road.

CHAPTER 12

Carter and Thomas stood on either side of Wayan, staring at the blinking light on the screen. The freshening nor'-easter rustled the stacked papers on the table and Carter placed his teacup on them.

Wayan explained how the property's security system worked. The laptop was linked wirelessly to eight motion sensors placed around the property, designed to alert them to intrusions along the perimeter.

Once alerted, four cameras, one pointing in each direction of the compass, could be used to determine what had set off the alarm. As Carter had noted earlier, though, the dense foliage that led into the property made it difficult to identify who or what had triggered the sensors until the intruder moved onto the open lawn.

Wayan clicked through four camera icons, north, south, east and west. The images that came up on his screen revealed nothing out of the ordinary.

He tapped another key and a map of the property appeared. A red light flashed along the track leading into the property about twenty metres from the point where the foliage and bush turned into lawn.

'Maybe it's Erina?' Carter asked.

'No. She would've called first.'

Wayan stood and picked up a daypack that was resting against the wall. 'I'm going to the ridge at the back of the house to see what I can from there.'

'No,' Carter said without hesitation. 'You stay on the computer. I'll go.'

Wayan looked at Thomas. 'But I know the layout of the property.'

Thomas gave his head a slight shake. 'You'll get your chance soon enough.'

Carter understood how Thomas operated. He knew the value of dealing in hope. All warriors in training craved recognition and the opportunity to prove themselves.

Wayan nodded and handed Carter the daypack. Carter placed it on the table, slid the zip open, reached inside and pulled out a Gore-Tex holster holding a Glock 18, his favoured handgun.

The beautifully balanced weapon had a sighting range of fifty metres, but it was only accurate up to twenty. It had a seventeen-shot magazine, which allowed the shooter to fire the first round without any preparation. Carter slid the weapon out of its holster and ran his hands over the cool steel of its lightly oiled barrel.

After checking the magazine, he hung a set of black Vivitar binoculars around his neck and returned the handgun and holster to the daypack, which he slung over his shoulders.

Thomas handed him a bluetooth earpiece and a satellite phone. Both looked like they had just come out of their packaging.

'Since when did satphones come with bluetooth?'

'It's the latest technology.'

'That's one benefit of working with the government,' Carter said, unable to hold back the barb.

'It's brand-new for you.'

'You're that confident I'll come on board?'

'You need to get moving,' Thomas said, ignoring the question. 'I've preset it with my number. As soon as you're in position, press 1 and report. Keep the line open.'

Carter nodded and headed towards the back door.

It took him a couple of minutes to climb the rocky ridge that ran along the top of the summit, using the trees and bushes for cover.

A wild rabbit ran across his path and disappeared. He followed it into the bushes and went as far along the ridge as he could without being exposed from below. He crawled into a small clearing surrounded by thick low scrub, lay on his belly, placed the bluetooth in his ear and the satphone in front of him.

He was about eighty metres from the back of the house, giving him a clear view of the property all the way to the main road he and Erina had driven along, about four hundred metres away. In the distance beyond the rich green of the long valley, he glimpsed the blue of the ocean. Thomas's four-wheel drive, parked in the shade of the gum tree, sat ten metres to the right of the house.

The only problem with his position was that he couldn't see the front or the left-hand side of the building. But that shouldn't be an issue. All he needed to do was identify what had triggered the alarm and warn Thomas.

He took the Glock and its stock out of the daypack and laid them next to the satphone, then focused the binoculars in the direction of where the sensor had been triggered. He scanned further along to the right, following the track to the main road, trying to locate anything through the foliage.

Nothing.

He pulled out the antenna on the side of the satphone, turned on the bluetooth and pressed 1. Thomas answered straightaway.

'What can you see?' he asked.

'All clear for now. Has the intruder changed position?'

'No change,' Thomas replied. 'Keep me posted.'

'Will do.'

All he could do was watch and wait.

CHAPTER 13

Carter lay motionless under the scrub, watching the property below through the binoculars and trying to get his head around everything Thomas had told him.

Most Australians believed a major terrorist attack on Sydney would never happen, but logistically it wouldn't be difficult. Security around Sydney, especially the harbour, the bridge and its foreshores, was lax. Which, if the clan was planning a significant strike around New Year's Eve, could create a serious problem.

He knew of plain-clothes police who'd entered the naval base at Garden Island on the harbour using library cards as ID. And, not so long ago, two state police agencies had discovered that a company subcontracted to guard HMAS *Penguin* and the Garden Island naval base was closely linked to the well-known organised crime figure Hassan Bakir, a member of the Iron Dogs outlaw motorcycle gang.

Also of concern was another hardcore bikie group, the Soldiers of Allah. Even before Carter had left the order, they'd been on a Trident watch list. Members of the group were known to have jobs in harbour security and were suspected of engaging in weapons smuggling and drug trafficking on a significant scale. If the clan had infiltrated one of these groups, they could use them to orchestrate an act of terrorism on Sydney Harbour, making the threat very real.

Carter ran his binoculars over the track that ran from the lawn to the main road, looking for any movement under the foliage. There was none. He switched his attention to the road leading to the ocean.

Did he want to get embroiled in a fight that'd been going on for centuries and where there were no winners?

The issues were far from simple. During his training with the order, Carter had studied Islamic history in an effort to understand the deeper dynamics of the fundamentalist Muslims' conflict with the West and what motivated modern-day terrorists.

It'd surprised him to learn that the period of Islamic supremacy, beginning in the eighth century and continuing into the twelfth, had been a time of relative peace, prosperity and cultural and technological advancement. Different religions, including Judaism and Christianity, had been tolerated under Islamic rule. This was known as the Golden Age of Islam.

The fuelling of the jihadists' religious fervour began in the eleventh century with the first of the Christian crusades, initiated by Pope Urban II; the aim had been to restore Christian access to the holy places in and near Jerusalem. The city was a sacred site for all three major Abrahamic faiths: Judaism, Christianity and Islam.

Throughout the next two centuries, the Muslims maintained the strength of their powerful empire, which stretched across Middle and Eastern Europe and into Asia, managing to repel the crusaders, who came from all over Western Europe. In later centuries, though, the western invaders had more success, and many Muslims came to see westerners as the enemy, intent on humiliating and subjugating all devout followers of Islam.

In Europe the period from the fourteenth to the seventeenth centuries was a time of great scientific, artistic, philosophical and – most importantly – industrial expansion, propelling the western world out of the Middle Ages and into the modern era.

As Islamic power waned and the western powers seized control of large parts of the globe, Muslim clerics claimed that the followers of Islam were suffering because they'd strayed from the path laid out in the Koran and were being punished for their sins. The solution, they preached (according to historians), was to return to the practice of Islam as it'd been in the time of Mohammed, more than a thousand years earlier. They rejected industrialisation and modernisation, and instead sought to enforce the strictest possible interpretation of the Koran.

While the twentieth century witnessed the independence of numerous Muslim countries from colonial rule, many of their leaders regarded the establishment of Israel as an extension of a historic campaign against Islamic lands. The West, particularly the United States, was held responsible for supporting the original intrusion and for subsequently sustaining the Jewish state in the Middle East.

Ironically, in the 1980s, the United States worked with the Afghan Muslims in their fight against the Soviets. The CIA gave over nine hundred surface-to-air Stinger missiles to the mujaheddin, handing them out like they were lollipops.

All that changed in the early nineties, when George Bush snr sent armed forces into Saudi Arabia. Osama bin Laden described the huge influx of US troops into what he regarded as the holiest land of Islam as the greatest disaster since the death of Mohammed. He saw it as the final insult after centuries of western victimisation of the Muslim world.

According to bin Laden, that was the action that drove him to strike back at 'the American soldiers of Satan and their allies of the devil'.

In the current international climate, post 9/11, there was a tendency to view the historical relations between Islam and the West in simplistic terms. The current conflict was often portrayed in the western media as the struggle of freedom versus oppression, tolerance versus fanaticism, civilisation versus barbarism. When put into religious terms, it became Christianity versus Islam, and finally it was reduced to the ultimate moral battle of good versus evil.

A flock of squawking white cockatoos flew across the sky above Carter, interrupting his thoughts. He watched them swoop down as if dive-bombing the ground before flying away.

Again he scanned the property and the bushland surrounding the perimeter. Still no sign of activity.

Like most people, he had no time for fundamentalism of any sort – and that included Christian fundamentalism. He believed every individual ought to be free to worship any god and follow their own path to him or her. Many roads led to the top of the mountain.

The struggle between religions brought out the worst in both sides. He'd seen it firsthand, and it was ugly. The fact that Alex had joined the Sungkar clan disturbed him. Alex was highly trained, dangerous and almost certainly driven to seek revenge against the order.

But that didn't mean Carter had to be the one to stop him. If Thomas had listened to him earlier, none of this would have happened.

He made a decision.

As soon as this present trouble with the Sungkar clan was resolved and Thomas, Erina and Wayan were free to go about their business, he'd head back to Lennox, grab his stuff and disappear.

Margaret River with its cranking waves and remote location was looking as good as anywhere.

A movement to his right on the main road that ran alongside the property caught his attention. He pointed his binoculars towards it. A large white freight truck, with the words *Rapid Transfer* painted on the side in red, slowed. It passed the entrance, stopped and then started reversing into the dirt track leading to the property.

'Thomas,' Carter said.

There was no answer. The line had dropped out. He pressed 1 on the keypad.

CHAPTER 14

Thomas answered on the first ring and said, 'What can you see?'

'There's a freight truck backing into the property. It could be just turning around, but I doubt it.'

'Maintain your position and monitor the situation for one minute. Then report.'

'Will do.'

Carter scanned the track again all the way back to the homestead.

Nothing.

He looked back at the truck. It'd reversed most of the way in and stopped. The front half of the cabin jutted out onto the main road. A man stepped out of the cabin's passenger seat, followed closely by the driver, who walked around the front of the cabin and joined him.

Carter focused on them. They were Caucasian and both wore T-shirts, dark blue jeans, baseball caps and wraparound sunglasses. Nothing out of the ordinary, except for the intricate tattoos leaking from under their sleeves and the handguns they shoved down the back of their pants.

The driver put a phone to his ear and began talking.

Carter was about to give Thomas an update when he heard a loud clap followed by a whooshing sound coming from the bush near the homestead.

Half a second later the unmistakable crash of breaking glass from the house caused his gut to tighten.

The sound almost certainly came from a high-tech grenade launcher firing a gas canister through a window. If he was right, the gas would knock them out within seconds.

'Thomas, Wayan. If you can hear me, get the fuck out of there.'

There was no answer over the phone.

'Thomas, can you hear me?'

No reply came. Instead, he heard the faint whir of an engine starting and switched his attention back to where the track met the lawn.

A glint of metal flashed through the overhanging trees and a khaki-coloured Humvee with a bull bar at the front glided out of the bushes.

The three-tonne metal monster headed straight for the homestead at around ten kilometres an hour, barely making a sound as it moved across the grass. The vehicle had bulletproof tyres, was powered by an electric engine and didn't appear to be in a hurry.

He put the binoculars down and, in a reflex action, fitted the Glock to its stock and jammed it against his right shoulder, lining up the Humvee in his sights and brushing the trigger with his finger.

A slow breath helped calm his mind. The last thing he needed was to act impulsively and make a bad situation worse.

He eased his finger off the trigger, laid the weapon on the ground and stared through the binoculars.

The Humvee disappeared from Carter's line of sight, presumably pulling up close to the front of the house.

The sound of the vehicle's doors opening and closing cut through the quiet of the bush. After a brief silence the front door of the house slammed shut.

Carter was about to move further down the ridge when a solidly built Indonesian dressed in dark brown overalls, probably a clan member, ran around the corner of the house, carrying an automatic assault weapon in two hands. He looked through the windows of Thomas's four-wheel drive and then underneath it before heading to the back of the house, swinging his gun in an arc, scanning the ridge where Carter lay hidden as if expecting to find someone, probably him.

Carter didn't move a muscle. An eerie silence descended over the property. Every cell in his body wanted to charge down the hill and attack the intruders. He reminded himself that any rash action on his part would only put Thomas and Wayan's lives in even greater danger.

An excruciating thirty seconds ticked by. Even the birds had gone quiet, as if sensing trouble brewing.

He heard the front door opening, followed by three Humvee doors opening and closing, one after the other. He saw the vehicle appear again as it slowly backed away from the house, veering to the right before coming to a stop.

The guard at the back abandoned his post and ran towards the front of the house. The vehicle's passenger window slid down and a man shouted, 'Kamu melihatnja?' *You see him?*

The guard shook his head.

The man in the Humvee said something Carter couldn't quite hear and the guard turned and walked back towards Thomas's four-wheel drive.

Carter raised the Glock's stock to his shoulder and tried to line up the guy's head in the gun sight. But he knew a hundred metres was way too far to even consider taking a shot. To do so would've been pointless.

He put the gun down.

The guard moved around the four-wheel drive and shot out each tyre. The vehicle sunk to the rims. He then ran to the Humvee, opened the back door and climbed in. The vehicle turned and headed across the open lawn at a steady pace before disappearing under the canopy of trees.

Carter grabbed the binoculars and trained them on the stationary truck out on the main road. The back door was now open and a ramp led up to it.

The Humvee emerged from the cover of foliage and drove up into the truck's bowels. The two Caucasians loaded the ramp and shut the back door before climbing into the cabin. Carter heard the engine growl to life and watched smoke billow from the exhaust. The truck turned right and accelerated down the main road away from the coast.

Carter watched it swing around a bend and disappear from sight. Several seconds later he was unable to hear the engine. It would be just another anonymous truck rumbling down the road.

The well-executed attack had taken exactly three minutes from start to finish.

CHAPTER 15

Carter waited and watched for eight minutes without moving, even though it felt like his whole world had been turned upside down.

He crawled down the hill and crouched behind a burnt eucalypt stump, thirty metres from the back door of the homestead, and waited some more, looking for any movement or sign of activity inside.

Thomas and Wayan were either dead or at best unconscious and miles away in the back of the speeding truck.

He had to make sure, one way or the other, before making any decisions. Plus, if possible, he needed to get his hands on the laptop and the documents Thomas had wanted to give him.

He resisted the urge to rush in.

It seemed likely the clan members knew he was in the area and were looking for him. There was a good chance one of them had remained behind, armed and waiting inside the house.

He needed to exercise patience and give events time to unfold. On several occasions waiting that extra five minutes had saved his life.

The seconds crawled by without incident. The house was still and silent.

He rechecked the Glock, counted to three and then sprinted at full pace towards the house, keeping his body at a forty-five-degree angle to the ground.

It took six seconds to reach the back wall near the kitchen and press his back flush against it.

He listened.

Nothing.

He crept along the side of the house, pausing every five metres.

Again, nothing out of the ordinary grabbed his attention.

He reached the front verandah and scanned the grounds and nearby bushes, checking for any sign of life. The only movement came from the leaves quivering in the light nor'-easter.

It was time to move.

He climbed the verandah stairs without making a sound, crouched low beside the front door and put his ear against it.

Not a sound.

He noticed a strong smell, though – the pungent odour of a noxious gas.

When it was first released into the air, it would have taken only a tiny amount to knock a person out, but by now the gas would've dispersed and lost much of its toxicity.

He turned his head and breathed in a lungful of fresh air. Then he dropped his shoulder into the wooden door, pushed it open and plunged inside, holding the Glock two-handed in front of him.

He made his way carefully through the deserted living room, along the hallway and into the kitchen.

There was no sign of Thomas or Wayan. The laptop and the pile of documents were gone.

He checked all six rooms, looking for any useful source of information, like a backup hard drive, a memory stick or notebooks. All he found was the satphone charger alongside its packaging in one of the spare bedrooms. Apart from that, nothing.

They'd done a clean, professional job. Any further search was a waste of time.

His lungs were crying out for oxygen. Carter grabbed the charger and ran back through the house. Out on the verandah he sucked in three huge breaths of fresh air. He shoved the Glock into the daypack and ran along the track away from the homestead, heading for Lennox Head.

BOOK TWO

CHAPTER 1

Four and a half hours later Carter was gunning his white Ford Falcon ute down the straight black line of the two-lane highway heading for Boggabilla, population six hundred and fifty-seven.

He'd managed to hitch a ride back to his place at Lennox, where he grabbed the daypack he kept hidden at the back of his bedroom cupboard and combined its contents with the one Wayan had given him. It now sat on the seat beside him, containing a Glock 18, binoculars, a noise suppressor, a blowpipe, poison darts, throwing knives, a balaclava, lock picks, three gas canisters, twelve hundred dollars, an iPad and his passport. He'd brought his mobile phone, too, even though the battery was low. If he was lucky, there'd be a chance to charge it soon. You couldn't always rely on a satphone.

The blazing sun beat down overhead and the hot, dry breath of the outback blew through the open cabin windows. Outside, the temperature must've been pushing forty degrees Celsius.

He'd been driving nonstop for over three hours, well above the hundred-and-ten-kilometre speed limit. He was working on the presumption that the clan had taken Thomas and Wayan to the cattle property near Boggabilla.

The first thirty-six hours following any abduction were critical. After that the odds of rescue diminished dramatically.

His plan was to track Erina down and go from there, but her old mobile number was no longer working, which came as no surprise. Members of the order often switched their numbers and used prepaids when out in the field.

To get Erina's current number, he'd been trying to reach the order's operations and logistics man in Bali, Jacko MacDonald, but his phone kept going straight to voicemail.

Jacko was the closest thing Carter had to a true friend and brother. They'd covered each other's backs on dozens of assignments throughout South-East Asia. No job was too big, too small or too hard for Jacko. He always came through.

Carter reached for the bottle nestled between his thighs, took a long pull of tepid water and reminded himself he needed to stay in the moment. *Take it one step at a time.*

The wilder and more out of control the world was around you, the calmer and stiller you needed to become inside.

He looked out at the monotonous flat brown plains stretching out to the horizon on either side of the road.

Boggabilla was a local Aboriginal word meaning 'full of creeks' – he was sure he'd read that somewhere. Ironic, because the district was famous for getting either not enough rain or too much. Drought and the occasional flood were a way of life for the locals – a harsh reality that hung over everything they did, making them as parched and stubborn as the arid land they worked.

He tried Jacko again without success and checked the phone's battery. It was getting close to red.

Jacko had grown up in surroundings as flat and unyielding as the country rushing by Carter's windows now. He had sometimes talked about his home in Central Queensland, and his love for the place was clear, though it sounded tough, and its climate unrelenting.

The MacDonalds had worked their cattle property for three generations until crippling debt forced them off it for good, compelling Jacko to join the army when he was twenty. He'd eventually become a warrant officer in the SAS before entering the order.

A huge semitrailer loomed ahead on the other side of the road. The driver tooted, gave a friendly wave and sped past. The wind generated by its slipstream buffeted Carter's ute, causing him to tighten his hold on the wheel.

He stretched his jaw, relaxed his grip on the wheel and pressed Jacko's number on redial for the sixteenth time.

CHAPTER 2

The phone answered on the fourth ring.

'Jacko. It's Carter.'

'Carter, you old bastard.' There was a pause. 'I'll call you right back on a secure line.'

Thirty seconds later the mobile started vibrating in Carter's lap. He switched on the speaker and answered after the second ring.

'Mate, great to hear from you,' Jacko said. He sounded exhausted.

'What's up?'

'We've got a serious shit storm going down.'

His blokey tone, usually full of laconic Aussie humour, had a brittle edge to it.

'What's up?' Carter asked again.

'Some fuckin' wack job drove a car bomb into our rural joint near Ubud at five-thirty this morning. It has to be the Sungkar clan.'

Carter did the time-difference calculation in his head. It was almost the exact same time as when Thomas's property had been hit, which explained why Carter hadn't been able to contact him.

'Shit,' Carter said. 'Everyone whole?'

'Six people are in the local hospital.'

'Are they going to be okay?'

'Mate, it's pretty ugly. Multiple fractures, third-degree burns, that sort of thing. Josh is the biggest worry. There's some internal bleeding on the brain. But he's one tough bugger.'

Silence hung over the line.

'Where are the others?' Carter finally asked.

'Jean, Teck and Hiroshi are doing a job along the Thai–Burmese border. Patah and Lui are in East Timor. Can't get hold of anyone else. Thomas and Erina are on the north coast of New South Wales with Wayan, but I can't raise any of them. Thomas's satellite phone's not answering and the other two are reporting directly to him, so I don't have numbers for them. I wish to fuck they'd remember to tell me when they get new prepaids – it would make my job a hell of a lot easier. Right now I'm the only one manning the fort, bung leg and all.'

Jacko had been shot in the left knee two years ago and the injury made it impossible for him to work in the field. That meant Carter and Erina were now the only active operatives on deck.

'I'm afraid I've got more bad news,' Carter said.

'Shit … Hit me with it.'

Carter filled him in on what had happened to Thomas and Wayan, including a brief summary of the events leading up to the abduction.

'Bloody hell,' Jacko said. 'You reckon they're still alive?'

'Hard to say, but I suspect if they'd killed them, they'd have left their bodies behind.'

'That sounds right. Where do you reckon they're taking them?'

'My best guess is the cattle property in Boggabilla.'

'Makes sense. Did Thomas tell you they're shooting a movie there or some such bullshit?'

'A movie?'

'Yeah, some Indonesian martial-arts feature film. Apparently half-a-dozen Sungkar clan members are working on the shoot. And that dysfunctional dipshit Alex Botha has been spotted a couple of times in the area. Did Thomas tell you about him?'

'Yeah.'

'Having him running around on the loose with those fanatics is a real worry. He's a bloody good operator and he knows our systems inside out.'

Out of nowhere two kangaroos hopped across the road in tandem. Carter hit the brakes and the car slowed, letting them pass.

Alex's involvement with the clan took the threat they posed to another level and explained how they'd managed to break through the order's defences so easily, both at the country property near Lennox and in Ubud. Carter would have to deal with Alex at some point. But for now he needed to get as much information as possible from Jacko before his phone cut out.

He accelerated and asked, 'So what's the story with Trident? Any idea who might've turned?'

'Earl Callaghan, the CEO, strikes me as being one dodgy unit. Been divorced a couple of times and his finances are in a right mess. Plus there's been talk his only kid has gone AWOL in Bali. She's seventeen and a bit of a wildcat. Last seen outside a nightclub in Kuta.'

'Blackmail?'

'Could be.'

Kidnapping was one of the clan's specialties.

'Tell me what you know about Samudra's sister,' Carter said.

There was a brief pause, then he heard the click of a cigarette lighter.

'Kemala Sungkar has an MBA from Stanford – she's one smart cookie. Over the last year she's become pretty tight with Thomas. First woman I've seen get under his skin.'

'Under different circumstances that'd be big news.'

'Huge. She's worried about where her lunatic brother is taking the clan. Thomas was going to hook up with her in Jakarta tomorrow, but he's been unable to make contact.'

'Maybe her brother nabbed her as well.'

'Quite possible. She's got a local working for her undercover on Batak Island where Samudra's set up his training compound. I'll try and contact the guy directly.'

'Who's he?'

'Name's Djoran. He grew up on the island and knows it like the back of his hand. You'd like him. He's smart as a whippet with a ton of guts. He's a Sufi, too, which is how he met Kemala, at some conference in Jakarta six years ago.'

Carter was familiar with Sufism. It was a mystical branch of Islam whose adherents strived to be close to God in every moment and every movement. A Sufi acquaintance in Jakarta had once said to him, 'I possess nothing in the material world and nothing possesses me. Sufism is not the wearing of wool and shabby clothes, rather the excellence of conduct and moral character.' But why would a Sufi get involved in something like this?

He looked at his phone. The battery was now showing red.

'I'm about to cut out. So where exactly will I find Erina?'

'She's operating out of the film's production office, pretending to work for Screen Australia. Using the name Nicole Davey.'

'So where is it?'

'Sorry, mate. All I know is that it's somewhere between Boggabilla and Moree.'

'Okay, I'll hit the first pub I see in Boggabilla and gather some local intel.'

'Don't get caught in a bloody shout with a bunch of bushies. Once they buy you one beer, they'll expect you to be there until closing time.'

Carter almost smiled. 'Thanks for the tip.'

'Good luck.'

'You too. Give my best to the guys in hospital. I'll be in touch.'

The phone went dead. Carter dropped it on the passenger seat and took a sip of lukewarm water. Knowing Jacko was on the case in Indonesia allowed him to focus exclusively on Boggabilla.

He glanced at his daypack and patted it like an old faithful dog, then concentrated on the black line of road shimmering into the distance.

CHAPTER 3

At a little after 2 p.m. a sign flashed by. *Boggabilla 10 kilometres.*

A few minutes later the ute crunched to a halt on the gravel opposite a faded yellow cement-rendered building. A name was painted above its door: *The Wobbly Boot.*

Carter ran his eye over the old-fashioned pub, noting the peeling artwork – a brown laced-up workboot overflowing with frosted frothy beer.

A dozen cars were parked outside, mostly dusty utes with large roo bars and black tarps stretched over the back trays. There were also a couple of road bikes – a Harley-Davidson and a souped-up Yamaha 750.

He stepped out into the dry, burning heat and looked around. The air was still and he saw no sign of a living creature. He leant back into the cabin and grabbed the daypack from the passenger seat. When working for the order, he made it a habit to carry it with him wherever he went.

After locking his car, he slung the pack over his shoulders, walked across the street and pushed through the pub's door.

The chill of air conditioning welcomed him, along with the loud buzz of indecipherable chatter and the country twang of Hank Williams singing 'Honky Tonkin''.

He crossed a green sea of sticky shag-pile carpet and walked towards the counter. Twenty or so white males were gathered around the bar, dressed in shirts, jeans, moleskins and bush hats, all drinking schooners of frothy beer.

In the far corner three middle-aged Aboriginal men sat under a well-used dartboard, drinking longnecks. Two bikies sat at a table near the jukebox. They didn't look at him directly, but he sensed they were checking him out.

He manoeuvred his way to the bar and read the blackboard menu. *Wobbly Boot Sportsman's Special, Pie and Chips with Gravy.*

A rake-thin woman in her late forties stood behind the bar, looking his way. She had fine mousy hair and the deeply lined, sallow skin of a pack-a-day-plus smoker.

'What'll it be, love?' she asked, without a drop of warmth in her voice. 'We've got cans of Fourex and Fourex on tap.'

'Any chance of getting a feed?'

'Kitchen closed at two.' She let out a hacking cough and pointed at the vending machine across the bar. 'We got chips, nuts, Twisties and Kit Kats. Help yourself.'

'Just give me a large bottle of water then.'

She reached into the fridge behind her and placed a bottle on the counter.

From the other end of the bar, a voice boomed, 'Mate, this is a pub. Not a flaming milk bar!'

Suppressed laughter and a faint cheer rippled through the room.

Carter thanked the woman, grabbed the bottle, undid the cap and took a long, cool swig. Then he turned towards the voice.

A barrel-chested bushie with a curly mop of rust-coloured hair stared at him.

'Really?' Carter said. 'I suppose a chocolate malted milkshake is out of the question then?'

A couple of people groaned at the attempted joke.

Must have been his timing.

The guy started walking towards him and the crowd parted in silence.

The breadth of his shoulders, his bulging biceps and powerful chest suggested he'd been tossing steers in his backyard since he was five.

He pulled his six-foot-six frame to its full height, stood unnecessarily close to Carter and eyeballed him. Judging by his swaying swagger and the glazed look in his eyes, he'd already put a good few beers away.

'Mate, I thought that was pretty funny,' he said. 'But I wouldn't quit your day job.'

Carter smiled.

'You here for that kung-fu movie?' The bushie waved his arms in circles in the air in a mock martial-arts move. 'You pretty good at kung-fu?'

'Just passing through.'

A big smirk appeared across the guy's sun-lined face.

'Fair enough.'

He put out his big meaty right hand.

Carter took it. The big bushie clamped down hard, as if trying to break the bones in his fingers.

'Don't hurt him, Bluey!' someone yelled, then laughed. 'We don't want a bloody ambulance and a bunch of medics interfering with our drinking.'

Carter adjusted his grip and drilled his thumb into the pressure point between Bluey's thumb and forefinger.

Seven long, silent seconds passed.

Bluey grimaced, turned away and said, through gritted teeth, 'Fuck me …'

But he didn't let go.

Carter glanced around the room. All eyes were on them. If this turned into a fight, it'd be on for young and old and he'd find out nothing.

He eased the pressure. Bluey let go.

Carter took half a step back.

Bluey flicked his hand in the air and glared at Carter.

'Let me buy you a beer,' Carter said, 'and we'll call it quits.'

Bluey said nothing. Carter watched the cogs turning slowly in his beer-addled brain.

'No,' the man said. 'It's my shout.' His face broke into a broad grin. 'You sure you're not in that kung-fu movie?'

Carter smiled and shook his head.

Bluey beckoned to the woman behind the bar. 'Cheryl, pull us a couple of schooners would you, love?'

'Mate, gotta fair way to drive,' Carter said. 'Let me buy you one. I'll stick with the water.'

While on assignment, Carter rarely drank. Alcohol muddied his perception, slowed him down and cut him off from his higher instincts. After his binge the night before, the last thing he needed was more alcohol.

'Round here we find it hard to trust a bloke who won't sink a schooner or ten with you,' Bluey said.

Carter needed information and Bluey seemed as good a source as any to gather it from. He nodded at Cheryl. Fourex was the glue that bound men in these parts.

'A schooner of Gold,' he said.

Bluey patted Carter on the back.

Cheryl pulled two foaming beers and placed them on the counter.

Bluey grabbed one of the frosted glasses and downed a third in one gulp. He leant on the bar. 'So what brings you to this neck of the woods?'

'I'm looking for someone on that film shoot.'

'Won't find them here, mate. Mostly Indos on that gig. They never venture far off the reservation. Mostly stick together and say their prayers.' Bluey lifted his schooner level with his eyes. 'This is my god.'

'You know where the production office is?'

'Maybe I do. But someone who doesn't appreciate the beauty of the sacred amber fluid is no friend of mine. Not someone I can share my truth with, if you get my drift.'

Carter took the hint, realising this was one argument he'd never win. Drinking great quantities of cold beer was the religion of the bush and the passport to the pub brotherhood.

He raised his schooner towards Bluey in a salute, put the ice-cold beer to his lips and drank down the lot.

Bluey's face lit up like he'd found a soulmate.

Carter placed the glass on the table and said, 'You were about to tell me how to find the film's production office?'

Bluey nodded at Cheryl. 'Another round, love.'

Cheryl placed two more schooners on the bar.

'It's at Jambaroo Springs, a cross between a motel and a resort built on a natural hot spring.' Bluey picked up his fresh schooner and again downed a third in one go. 'Buggered if I know why anyone would pay good money to sit in a tub of hot salty water.'

Carter picked up his beer and drank half of it. 'Where is it exactly?'

'You head down the Boomi Road for about thirty-five clicks and hang a left at the sign. Can't miss it. When you plan on going?'

'Right now.'

'You got an invitation?'

Carter shook his head.

'Security's pretty bloody tight and they don't welcome strangers. They've got a three-metre fence around the joint. Are you looking for someone in particular or you after a part in the flick? You look scruffy enough to be an actor.'

'I'm looking for a woman.'

Bluey winked and gave him a playful shove. 'Aren't we all? Tell you what, mate, I can give you a leg in. A good buddy of mine, Dazza, is manning the gate. I'll give him a bell.'

'Thanks, mate,' Carter said. 'Appreciate it.'

Carter didn't need to see Jambaroo Springs to know whatever security they might have was unlikely to present a problem. Breaking into places like that without a fuss was what he did. But it was always better to take the easy route and enter through the front door.

Bluey drained his schooner, let out a satisfied sigh and thumped the glass on the counter. 'That hit the spot.'

Out of the corner of his eye, Carter noticed the two bikies heading towards the front door.

'You know those two?' Carter asked.

'Never seen 'em before in my life.'

Carter wondered if they could be somehow mixed up with the Sungkar clan.

Bluey pointed at Carter's half-empty glass. 'Come on, mate. Get that beer into ya. A man could die of thirst waiting for your shout.'

CHAPTER 4

Two schooners and one hour later, Carter drove along the highway towards a sign that read: *Jambaroo Natural Spa and Hot Springs, 200 metres.*

He turned left off the highway following Bluey's directions. If all went according to plan, he'd enter the resort, locate Erina and then leave with her, without attracting undue attention.

The ute rolled down the drive. Harsh sunlight shimmered off the white walls of a large, drab two-storey building with a three-metre wire fence running around the perimeter.

He pulled up in front of a red boom gate next to a white gatehouse. A lanky guard dressed in a short-sleeved khaki shirt, long grey pants and a broad-brimmed hat strolled towards him. It could only be Dazza.

Carter grinned at him. 'G'day, mate. How're you doin'?'

The guard stood a metre from the car, swatting flies. 'Fair to middling. Has to be forty degrees in the flaming waterbag. And you must be Bluey's new drinkin' mate? He warned me not to shake your hand.'

Dazza's infectious good humour made Carter smile. 'I wish someone had warned me not to get into a shout with Bluey.'

Dazza chuckled. 'He loves a beer or twenty. Who is it you wanna see?'

'You know Nicole Davey?'

Dazza nodded. 'Good-looking sort. You want me to try and get her on the blower?'

'Yeah, give it a shot.'

Dazza ducked back into the guardhouse, leaving Carter in the stifling heat.

Less than a minute later he stepped back out and said, 'The receptionist reckons she can't track her down. She wants to know your name. What'll I say?'

'Tell her I had to shoot through. I'll be back later.'

Dazza disappeared into the guardhouse again. When he emerged thirty seconds later, Carter asked, 'Nicole is actually somewhere around, I presume?'

'Came in two or three hours ago and hasn't left. Maybe she's avoiding you?'

'Maybe she is. You know women. You can never tell what they're thinking.'

'You're not wrong there.'

'Any chance of letting me in so I can surprise her?'

'Gettin' you through the gate ain't a big drama. But I gotta warn you, unless you've got an appointment, getting past the receptionist to see someone unannounced is like being granted an audience with the Pope.'

'I'll take my chances.'

Dazza pressed a button on a handheld remote and the boom gate lifted.

'Cheers, mate,' Carter said. He gave Dazza a two-finger salute and drove into the grounds.

—

Carter picked out a deserted corner of the parking lot and pulled in under the shadow of one wing of the resort.

He locked the car, slung his daypack over his left shoulder and walked through the dry, harsh heat.

A glass door slid open. Once again, the welcoming breath of air-conditioned cool came as a pleasant relief.

He headed straight for reception, where a woman sat behind a shiny white counter.

She looked Indonesian, around thirty years of age, and wore a dark blue blazer and white shirt. Her hair was tied back in a tight bun.

She lifted her attention from the computer screen and gave him a questioning stare.

'Good afternoon, sir. Do you have an appointment?'

'I'm here to see Nicole Davey.'

'Your name?'

'Sinclair. Brett Sinclair. From the Commonwealth Bank.'

She typed something into the computer, then looked up and shook her head. 'I'm sorry, sir, but you have no appointment. You can't see anyone here without an appointment. That is company policy.'

Her mouth smiled at him, yet her dark eyes were ice-cold. He had no idea if she knew who he was, but he understood her culture and could read her manner. She wasn't going to let him in and intended to report his appearance to her immediate superior as soon as he left.

Whatever he said would fail to budge her one millimetre. But nothing was impossible if you knew the correct approach and used the appropriate language. He suspected she wouldn't say no to some quick cash on the side.

He reached into his pocket, pulled out his wallet, extracted a crisp fifty-dollar bill and placed it on the table.

She looked at the money and then at him, unmoved.

He placed another fifty on top of the first.

She glanced around the room, checking to see if anyone was watching.

In any act of bargaining the trick was to know a person's limit. If you offered too much or too little, you lost respect.

More slowly this time, he lay down a third.

She raised an eyebrow and glanced at the money, then at the black book on the table next to her iMac.

Her hand reached out for the money like a hungry snake stalking a mouse.

He snapped his hand back over the notes before she got even close.

'Where will I find Miss Davey?'

—

Carter raced two steps at a time up the stairwell that led to the second floor and Erina's office.

He spotted the minute eye of a camera attached to the concrete ceiling and wondered if Erina had hooked it up to her computer, enabling her to track anyone's movements as they came up the stairs.

As well as being an expert in the martial arts, she was an IT whiz, and with Alex in the vicinity she couldn't afford to be caught unaware.

She stood waiting for him as he entered the open door of the bare rectangular room. The window gave her an uninterrupted view of the grey concrete wall of the other wing of the building.

She was leaning on the edge of the black desk, facing the door with her arms folded, glaring at him.

He took a step back and studied her disguise.

She wore a shoulder-length black wig with a fringe, red-rimmed glasses, a white blouse, black jacket and a matching pencil skirt that just covered her knees. Her shiny black shoes had three-inch heels; red lacquered toenails peeked from the open toe. An unfamiliar small tattoo of two hearts entwined sat just above the inside of her right ankle and her daypack lay behind her feet within easy reach.

Her outfit created the impression of a woman making her way up the corporate ladder. The major difference being that Erina would have at least two lethal weapons concealed on her body.

She pushed off the desk and stood upright. 'What the fuck are you doing here?'

'Great to see you again too,' he said.

'You're supposed to be on your way to Sydney.'

'Change of plan.'

He walked behind the desk, free of clutter except for an open bottle of still mineral water, a set of keys and an eleven-inch MacBook Air hooked up to a screen and keyboard.

She followed his every move.

He took a long sip of cool water from the bottle, screwed on the lid and placed it back on the table. He then unplugged her laptop.

'What do you think you're doing?' she asked.

Paying off the receptionist had bought him a little information and some time, but not a whole lot more, certainly not her loyalty.

He picked up her keys and laptop and held them out. 'Your film-industry days are over. We need to get out of here.'

Erina understood him well enough to recognise when it was best to take notice of what he said and follow his lead.

She took her things from him and said, 'I trust you know what you're doing.'

CHAPTER 5

Five minutes later Carter was driving along the two-lane highway at a hundred and twenty kilometres an hour, several car lengths behind Erina's black four-wheel drive. They were heading towards a local restaurant, which she said served breakfast and lunch all day. He was in need of food. He hadn't eaten anything except for a banana he'd grabbed when he went home that morning to pick up his daypack and ute.

He glanced in the rear-view mirror for the third time. An iron-grey van maintained an even distance of a hundred and fifty metres behind him. It suggested his visit to the resort hadn't passed unnoticed.

Erina would've spotted the tail as well.

Up ahead he saw a sign for the Billabong Restaurant and Guesthouse.

Erina's four-wheel drive turned right and headed towards a weatherboard cottage with a bullnose verandah sitting seventy-five metres in from the highway. A parking area in front of the verandah was marked *Restaurant Visitors*. A single-storey red-brick motel wing had been built to the left of the restaurant, looking like it'd been tacked on as an afterthought without any effort to match the original homestead-style architecture. It had a flat roof with a large white satellite dish placed on top of it at the far end of the building. There were car spaces in front of each of the six rooms, none of which was occupied.

Further to the left of the motel there was an additional parking area marked *Coaches and Truck Stop*, which backed onto thick scrubland. That was empty.

He pulled into a car space in front of the restaurant between Erina's car and a white Winnebago motorhome covered with fine red dust, the only other vehicle.

After switching off the ignition, he looked in the rear-view mirror. The van slowed while it passed the restaurant, then accelerated away.

Carter pulled the binoculars from the bottom of his daypack, stepped out of his ute and watched the van speed off towards the horizon.

Erina climbed out of her vehicle and stood next to him. 'Great work, Carter. First you blow my cover and now you pick up a tail. I hope you've got a good explanation.'

'Let's grab a table and I'll fill you in.'

Carter followed Erina up three wooden stairs to the verandah, which led into a surprisingly modern sun-drenched interior. He paused inside the front door and noted three potential exit points: the entrance, kitchen and bathroom. The kitchen and bathroom were both situated at the rear left of the square room.

An elderly couple, the only other guests, sat eating their meal in the middle of the restaurant, facing a floor-to-ceiling window at the back. It framed a natural billabong, a small pond created after a river changes its course. It was surrounded by tall spindly gums and low-lying bush. Soft jazz played in the background.

Carter and Erina exchanged a look and chose a table at the front of the restaurant near the right side wall. Erina's high heels clipped over the polished wooden floorboards. They both sat facing the entrance, their backs to the billabong, giving them a clear line of sight out to the highway.

'Okay, we're sitting down,' Erina said. 'Start talking.'

She sounded angry, but Carter didn't respond. He was waiting for the van that had been following them to return.

'Don't even think about messing with me,' she said.

'What are you going to do? Knock me out again? Trust me, I'm not here because I want to be.'

'Just tell me what's happened.'

'Erina, you need to chill out.'

'Don't tell me what to do.'

71

He'd forgotten how fired up she became if she felt he'd slighted her.

A young waitress approached and handed them a menu. With a warm smile, she asked, 'Can I get you something to drink?'

Outside, above the hum of the air conditioning and the light clatter from the kitchen, Carter identified the sound he'd been expecting: the purr of an engine and tyres crunching on gravel.

They both looked out the window at the same time. Erina had clearly heard it too. It was the grey van.

'We'll order in a minute,' Erina said to the waitress, who nodded and walked away.

Twenty metres from the restaurant the van veered along the path that led to the truck and coaches parking area, out of sight from where they sat. The vehicle's windows were heavily tinted, making it impossible to see who was inside.

Erina stood, took off her glasses and placed them on the table.

'What are you doing?' he asked.

'I'm going to check it out.'

He stood up. 'Let me do it.'

'Why?'

'I'd hate to see you ruin your outfit. Especially the heels.' He looked her directly in the eye. 'You look good.'

She stared back at him without acknowledging the compliment.

After a few seconds' thought, she sat back down and with the hint of a smile said, 'Okay, it's about time you did some work.'

She pulled her phone out of her shoulder bag. 'I'll call Thomas and find out why the change of plan.'

'You do that.'

He slung the daypack over his left shoulder and perused the menu while he stood. 'And while you're at it, order me two turkey sandwiches on rye and a double-shot, extra-hot long black.'

Without waiting for a response, he headed for the rest room at the back of the restaurant.

CHAPTER 6

Carter pushed through the door of the men's room and locked it behind him. There was an opaque glass window a metre above the single toilet's cistern. He grabbed the handtowel from next to the sink and shoved it into his daypack.

He closed the toilet seat cover, stood on it and examined the window. It was open a few centimetres at the base, as far as it would go without breaking. Carter lined up the heel of his hand with the window base and struck hard. The cheap lock and hinge exploded, dropping to the ground, and the window snapped wide open.

He stepped onto the cistern, squeezed his head and shoulders through the opening and studied the terrain. A dirt path ran behind the restaurant, in front of the billabong, and continued behind the back of the motel. It led to the coach and truck-parking stop, which he couldn't see from the window. A thick cover of scrub surrounded the back of the property on the other side of the dirt track. It'd provide good cover.

He tossed his daypack out the window, then stuck his head and shoulders through again and inched his torso forwards, to a point where he was half in and half out. The top of his thighs balanced on the window ledge. He looked down at the three-metre drop to the ground, hanging in limbo for two breaths, then pushed himself further forwards until gravity kicked in.

His body began sliding towards the ground. He raised his legs, arched his back and pressed his hands against the outside wall.

73

His slide gathered momentum.

At the critical moment, just before he started to freefall, he shoved hard against the wall with both hands and, tucking his head onto his chest, used his stomach muscles to force his legs over his head into a pike, doing a backflip in midair. He landed on the balls of his feet and stumbled a few steps forwards to regain his balance.

It'd been a long time since he'd done something like that. He looked up at the open window and gave himself a 7.6 out of 10 for the effort.

Then he switched his attention to the roof of the motel. He needed to climb up and see what he was up against. Once he knew the strength, size and nature of the threat, his next move would become obvious.

A rusty drainpipe ran up the middle of the five-metre-high brick wall of the motel. He tested the pipe's strength with both hands. The metal was hot enough to brand a cow, but it'd hold his weight and get him to the roof.

He took the handtowel from his pack, ripped it in two and wound the two halves around his hands. Then he climbed the wall, using the drainpipe for purchase.

When his head came level with the guttering that ran around the roof, he checked the ground below him.

Right then left. All clear.

He pulled himself onto the flat tiled roof, padded across it and squatted behind the satellite dish that sat above the last guestroom, closest to the truck stop, glad the fierce sun was at his back.

He removed a small leather pouch from his pack, hung it around his neck and peered around the satellite dish. About thirty metres away he spotted two men leaning on the bonnet of the grey van. He recognised them as the two bikers from the Wobbly Boot.

Just two things were different. They'd traded their bikes for a van and had handguns shoved down the front of their belts. The taller of the two handed a packet of tobacco to the other, who started rolling a cigarette.

A third guy was walking away from them and heading towards the back of the motel. He was short and stocky and wore a battered akubra hat, blue jeans that sat below his potbelly and scuffed riding boots. He held a lit cigarette in his left hand and a pump-action shotgun in his right.

If there was one weapon Carter hated coming up against, it was a shotgun – a lazy weapon that required no skill or finesse. All the person holding the weapon had to do was point the thing in the general direction of their target and pull the trigger. Even an incompetent amateur could neutralise the most highly skilled adversary. Carter rarely used one because of the danger of injuring others nearby.

The shotgun glinted in the sunlight. The man reached the back wall of the motel directly below where Carter crouched.

Carter blinked the sweat out of his eyes and held himself perfectly still, breathing softly. He ignored the flies crawling over his face. He needed to take the guy out before he knew what hit him. But first the guy had to move forwards another few paces so he was hidden from his two mates.

Carter shifted his weight to the balls of his feet and adjusted his position as he watched the guy walk past him slowly.

The man tossed his cigarette on the ground and held his weapon with both hands, like he was expecting trouble.

Then he turned and looked up at the roof.

Carter realised his body must have thrown a slight shadow across the ground. Something he should've anticipated. He was out of practice.

The man squinted and started to raise the shotgun to his shoulder.

CHAPTER 7

Carter's body responded without conscious thought. He leapt off the roof, flying feet first through the air.

The guy wasn't so well trained. His eyes widened and his body froze.

The heel of Carter's shoe smashed into the guy's temple, hitting the vulnerable point level with the top of his right ear.

Carter hit the ground hard, landing on his back.

The shotgun dropped onto the track and the man's body collapsed backwards like a sack of potatoes, making little sound.

Carter moved behind the guy and grabbed his head and shoulders, clamping his left forearm under the guy's chin and around his neck, ready to pull back if he met any resistance, but there was none. He was out cold.

Carter released his hold, reached into the leather pouch around his neck and extracted a drug-tipped dart. He removed the plastic tip with his teeth and jabbed the sharp point into the guy's neck. That'd keep him out of action for at least a couple of hours.

He rolled the unconscious man over, emptied the pockets of his moleskins and found a set of keys, a mobile phone and a leather wallet. All of which went into his daypack.

He dragged the guy into the shadowy space underneath the restaurant's rest room and hid the shotgun in the bushes. Then he moved down the path to the end of the motel and checked that the guy's two mates were still at the van. They hadn't moved.

He veered to his right into the thick undergrowth and circled around the coach and truck stop until he reached a position on the far side. The van was about twenty metres away now, and his two targets just in front of it. The smell of cigarette smoke drifted across the hot air.

The two men stood staring in the direction of the restaurant, looking away from where Carter was.

He opened his daypack, took out two thin black cylinders and screwed them together, creating one of his favourite weapons, a twelve-inch blowpipe.

Next he extracted two darts from the leather pouch, removed the plastic tips with his teeth and started counting down his breaths. *Ten, nine, eight …*

When he got to three, he started walking out of the bushes towards the van, treading lightly to make as little noise as possible on the gravel. He stopped at the back of the van, only metres from them, and stood motionless.

'What I wouldn't do for a few cold beers,' one of the men said.

'How about after we grab these fuckers, we head into town, go to the whorehouse, get drunk and fuck ourselves silly?'

'Have to twist me arm.'

They laughed, like this was a great joke.

Carter slipped one of the darts into his mouth, lifted the blowpipe to his lips and sucked in a lungful of air.

He stepped out from behind the van. The men were still watching the restaurant while they smoked.

The bigger of the two started to turn in Carter's direction.

Carter blew hard.

The guy grabbed his cheek. 'What the …'

His body slumped forwards.

The other guy turned, opened his mouth and reached for his gun.

Too late.

The second dart caught him in the throat.

He collapsed onto the ground on top of his mate.

Carter dragged the two men behind the van and into the scrub.

Like their mate, they'd be out of action for at least two hours. He'd give them a wake-up dose if he needed to interrogate them.

He searched their clothing and came up with two handguns, both high-calibre Smith & Wessons, two mobile phones, two wallets, two sets of keys and two packs of gum, one spearmint and the other extra-white, for a brighter smile.

He stuffed the phones, the wallet and the guns into his daypack and the gum into his trouser pocket. Then he stood up.

The three guys would keep until after he'd eaten.

CHAPTER 8

Carter walked back towards the restaurant, pushing his hair back into place and brushing the red dust and grime off his T-shirt and trousers. He was wondering how Erina would take the news when he told her about Thomas and Wayan.

Erina was ice-cool in the execution of her duties – even clinical – but this wasn't an ordinary job. Thomas was her father.

Carter had only seen Erina really lose it once, but it had genuinely frightened him. One time, before their brief affair, they'd busted a paedophile gang in Bangkok. A ringleader led them to a secret underground chamber where he kept a select number of underage workers for his own pleasure, some as young as six, lying naked and mute in steel cages. Erina exploded, blowing their cover and jeopardising the operation. She would've killed him but for Carter's intervention.

Erina's past was even more challenging than his own. When she was fifteen and Carter twenty, she'd been kidnapped by an organised crime gang off the streets of Bangkok. They had used her as a bargaining chip in an effort to force the order to drop an investigation into one of their leaders. It had taken Carter and Thomas two weeks to track her down and rescue her from a property near Chiang Mai, from where she was taken to hospital and examined. No serious injuries or evidence of sexual abuse were found, but she'd refused to this day to speak about what had happened.

A month after Erina's return, her American mother had announced that she was leaving Thomas and returning to Boston, taking their only child with her. It proved to be a defining moment in Erina's life. She refused to go. She'd always been Thomas's daughter, a fighter who had more courage in her than most adults.

She'd begun training from the age of five and was already highly skilled in the martial arts at the time of her abduction. The experience motivated her to work even harder to become a sanjuro and fight for those unable to protect themselves. It'd also made her wary of physical and emotional intimacy with anyone she didn't trust completely.

Carter entered the cool of the restaurant and exchanged a nod with the grey-haired couple paying their bill, then headed towards the table where Erina sat holding a fork in one hand, hovering over a green salad, while staring at her mobile as if willing it to ring.

She looked up and ran her eyes over him. 'You've certainly made a mess of yourself.'

'Better me than you,' he said, brushing at the stains on his shirt.

He settled in the seat opposite her, drank down the glass of water the waitress had left and took a bite of his turkey sandwich without really tasting it.

She placed her phone on the table. 'What happened?'

He opened his daypack, checking that the two guns and mobile phones were there on top, then slid the bag along the floor towards her.

She peered inside. 'So they weren't making a social call?'

He took a sip of lukewarm coffee. 'You could say that.'

'Where are they now?'

He jerked his head towards the bushes outside. 'Sound asleep.'

'Caucasians or Indonesians?'

'Caucasian.'

'I'm sure I know who they work for.'

He took another bite of sandwich, waiting for her to say more. She looked at him sideways.

'Something's happened to Thomas, hasn't it?'

He pushed his plate to one side and gave her his full attention. 'Yes.'

She mouthed the word *fuck* and said, 'Tell me everything.'

He gave her a detailed run-down of what had unfolded since she'd driven off from the property outside of Lennox that morning, including the attack on the order at Ubud. He knew better than to try to keep anything from her.

She sat in silence while he spoke and never took her focus off him.

When he finished, he leant back in his chair and let what he'd said sink in.

She kept her voice low and controlled. 'Those Sungkar bastards.' Then she put her glasses and phone in her shoulder bag and stood up.

Carter got to his feet. 'What are you doing?'

'I know where the clan will be holding them.'

He grabbed her keys from the table. 'Sit down. I saw how they operated at Lennox. They're far from amateurs. We need to think this through.'

They stood looking at each other without moving. Neither said a word.

The kitchen door swung open. The waitress walked across the dining room and said, 'Is everything all right?'

'Can I get a fresh coffee, please?' Carter asked. 'Erina, you want anything?'

She shook her head.

The waitress forced a smile and said, 'Be right back.'

She turned and walked back to the kitchen.

He placed his right hand on Erina's shoulder. 'We're going to get them back,' he said. 'I promise.'

Her head dropped and she took a deep breath.

'Whatever it takes,' he said. 'Now sit down and talk to me.' He guided her back into her chair. 'So, who do you reckon these guys work for?'

Erina put out her hand. 'Give me their phones.'

CHAPTER 9

Carter watched Erina work the phones and the computer, her expression cold and dispassionate now.

Like him, she'd witnessed firsthand the inhumanity and depravity of the human race. She'd seen many friends and enemies die. And even though she'd learnt to suppress her emotions to get the job done, there was no doubt it had affected her at a deep psychic level.

From the restaurant's kitchen he heard pots and pans clang and the hiss of an espresso machine. He sipped his fresh long black and ate his second turkey sandwich slowly.

Erina checked a final number and dropped the two mobiles into his daypack. She pushed it across the floor towards him and said, 'Just as I thought. The phones lead to Hamish T. Woodforde, owner of the property where the film is being shot. I'm sure Thomas and Wayan have been taken there.'

She reached into her daypack and handed him a manila folder. He pushed his cup and plate to one side and opened it.

A large photo of a heavily jowled man in his early fifties stared back at him. He had a ruddy complexion, thinning grey hair and a protruding beer belly. His most telling feature was a look of smug entitlement.

'Hamish Woodforde,' Erina said. 'The motherfucker has a finger in half-a-dozen crooked pies. Brothels, gambling, drugs and stolen goods. He even supplies alcohol covertly to the Aboriginal community.'

'Greed is an ugly religion.'

'He controls several businesses and spends a great deal of money in the district. When I questioned a handful of local shopkeepers, publicans and the local police, they clammed up at the mention of his name.'

'So we can assume the police are in Woodforde's pocket.'

'The best money can buy.'

Carter put the photo to one side and scanned the two-page dossier. He finished reading and asked, 'How does a fourth-generation farmer in the middle of the outback get into bed with the Sungkar clan?'

'Believe it or not, through playing polo. He met Arung Sungkar at the exclusive Nusantara Polo Club near Jakarta nine years ago. He ended up marrying Arung's cousin.'

'Arranged?' he asked.

'Yeah. Not exactly a match made in heaven.' She paused. 'For her, anyway.'

'But good for the family?'

'Very. It's allowed the Sungkar family and various clan members to move freely in and out of Australia for a number of years.'

He slid the folder back towards her. 'What's in it for Woodforde?'

She put the dossier back in her daypack and said, 'The clan saved his arse. He prefers the ageing playboy lifestyle to working his butt off on the family farm. He owes the Bank of Queensland four million dollars and couldn't keep up with his payments – he was on the verge of losing it all. Arung obliged and bailed him out, making him the managing director of a clan-controlled transport company, Rapid Transfer, now based on Woodforde's property.'

'The perfect cover.'

'We suspect the trucks distribute stolen and illegal goods throughout Australia.'

An image of the truck at Thomas's property flashed across his mind. The name *Rapid Transfer* had been painted on its side.

'What's his relationship with Samudra like?' he asked.

'Basically, he does whatever the clan ask him to do and they tolerate his gross behaviour.'

Carter shook his head. 'The God of the fanatic moves in mysterious ways.'

'When it suits them.'

He glanced out the window. A black ute flashed down the highway. Guys like Woodforde, motivated purely by greed, pissed him off even more than terrorists. At least most religious fanatics acted out of the misguided belief that they were doing God's will. Which made him think of Alex Botha.

'Talking of arseholes, what's the latest with Alex or Abdul-Aleem or whatever he goes by now?' he asked.

'All I know is that he's Samudra's right-hand man. Been in the production office a couple of times, but I've managed to avoid him. He left the property with three Indonesians this morning in a big truck. It could be an advance party for a possible terrorist attack.'

'We can't worry about that until we get Thomas and Wayan back.'

'Agreed.'

'What's the set-up at Woodforde's property like?'

'Considering it's in the middle of nowhere, the security is incredibly tight. Fenced-off compound and all. You'd think Woodforde was a Colombian drug lord.'

Carter finished his coffee. 'So rushing in now will only tip them off.'

'We need to go in late tonight.'

They sat in silence. Carter ran through everything in his mind.

'Do you reckon this film is legit?' he asked.

She shrugged. 'I don't know. They're well organised and the paper-work appears up to date. I've seen boom mikes and cameramen filming guys in military uniforms running around carrying automatic rifles. The film could be legit – maybe fundamentalist propaganda – or it could be a front for getting members of the Sungkar clan into the country and marshalling them for a terrorist attack. Whatever they're up to, the irony is the Australian and Indonesian governments are funding it.'

She finished her glass of water.

'Let's move,' she said. 'I can't sit here doing nothing.'

Carter stood up. 'Okay, let's grab the sleeping beauties outside and find out what they know.'

'I've got just the place for a quiet chat. Follow me.'

She slipped her computer into her daypack and stood up. 'By the way, where are you staying?' she asked.

'Haven't thought that far ahead.'

'You'll stay with me. I've got a suite in Moree.'

It wasn't a question.

She turned and walked towards the 'pay here' counter.

CHAPTER 10

Just after 8 p.m., Carter sank into the soft embroidered lounge in Erina's spacious motel suite just out of Moree on the Newell Highway. She said it was the only room she could find in the area that wasn't a gloomy soulless box with a low cement-rendered ceiling.

The sound of the kettle boiling and the smell of fresh ginger wafted into the living room from the kitchenette. Crockery rattled. The fridge door opened and closed. She'd insisted on making tea before outlining how she intended to break into Woodforde's property. He knew better than to rush her, but hoped the plan she came up with wouldn't be too elaborate. He preferred the simple direct approach.

He looked through the open sliding door towards the outback sky. The sun had melted into the horizon, creating a spectacular red, yellow and black sunset, the colours of the Aboriginal flag.

The relative cool and stillness of the end of the day evoked a sense of calm, giving him the opportunity to run through in his mind the information they'd gathered. He'd interrogated Woodforde's men while Erina had prepared the night's assault on the property.

The three guys were hired standover men who basically did whatever Woodforde told them to do without question. It didn't take a lot to get them talking. Just a bit of pain and the threat of far greater injury if they failed to cooperate.

They confirmed that a Rapid Transfer truck had arrived at Woodforde's property around lunchtime, but they hadn't been told who or what was inside. All they knew was that Alex had left that morning with three Indonesians and that Samudra and two of his men had flown in by light plane two days before.

They had also provided some key pieces of pertinent information.

Woodforde slept on the top floor of the main homestead, they had told him, in the master bedroom above the entrance, usually with a much younger woman. His wife was in Indonesia and no one else slept in the house.

The property's employees lived in the shearers' quarters at the back of the compound. The visiting Indonesians bunked down in a barn on the northern boundary. Alex and members of the Sungkar clan occupied the visitors' cottage behind the main homestead when they stayed.

Four of the large barns spread around the property were used to grow marijuana hydroponically and to store stolen goods. The three men said this was why Woodforde had installed the state-of-the-art security system.

Footsteps padded across the carpet. Carter turned to see Erina walking towards him carrying two mugs of steaming tea. She'd ditched the wig, suit and shoes and changed into the more familiar loose black pants and white T-shirt. Her feet were bare and her hair was pulled back in a ponytail that hung over her right shoulder.

Carter thought she always looked good, regardless of what she wore.

She handed him a mug and sat down facing him, tucking her legs under her and draping her free arm on the back of the sofa.

'What've you come up with?' he asked, resting the mug on his thigh.

'You're not going to like it.'

'That's never bothered you before.'

She flicked her ponytail behind her shoulder. 'One of the security guys took a shine to me when I paid the property a visit a few days ago and was good enough to show me how their security system works.'

'You can charm the pants off any man when you want something.'

She brought the mug to her lips and drank a mouthful. 'But you've become immune?'

'I've managed to build up some resistance.' He lifted his mug and crossed his legs away from her. 'So what's your plan?'

'The guy told me he was on duty tonight at the gatehouse and asked me to pop in and say hi, if I was free.'

Carter took a sip of tea and said, 'Go on.'

'After a few polite niceties, I'll put him to sleep and shut down security. Then we wake up Woodforde for a chat. Make him tell us where Thomas and Wayan are.'

'Sounds good,' he said.

As far as plans went, he had no problem with it. But in a situation like this the plan was usually only the starting point. Something always went wrong, but there was no point worrying about it now. She knew that too.

'We leave at the usual time?' he asked.

She nodded.

They always made night-time incursions at 2.30 a.m. It was the time when people were at their most vulnerable.

He took another mouthful of tea and looked out through the sliding door. The sun was no longer visible. A reddish tinge was all that remained on the horizon. It was nearly half past eight.

'We should get some sleep,' he said. 'I suppose I'm bunking down on the couch?'

'You'll get into less trouble there.'

'Who says I'm afraid of trouble?'

'Carter, are you trying to flirt with me?'

'I said I've built up some resistance – I didn't say I was immune.'

She smiled, revealing her dimple.

He watched her stand and walk towards the bedroom.

She turned just before reaching the door. 'I'll get you a blanket.'

CHAPTER 11

Carter sat in the passenger seat in the air-conditioned cool of Erina's four-wheel drive. It was 2.06 a.m. He'd slept for four and a half hours on the couch and felt wide-awake and ready for whatever lay before them.

The headlights' high beam lit up the road ahead and the surrounding narrow band of stark, flat farmland. On their left a 'beware of kangaroos' sign flashed by.

He glanced at Erina, intent on the two-lane highway ahead, gunning the four-wheel drive through the inky blackness towards Woodforde's property. The speedo hovered just under a hundred and forty kilometres an hour. They'd travelled in a comfortable silence for fifteen minutes. Both liked to still their minds and clear their thinking before a job.

Before leaving, Carter had watched Erina put on the black wig for her encounter with the gate guard. She then slid a small Beretta into the Gore-Tex holster under her left armpit and finally placed a pack of drug-tipped darts, an Emerson throwing knife, a cigarette lighter and a packet of Marlboro into her leather shoulder bag. She didn't smoke, but cigarettes often came in handy when you needed information from an uncooperative source. His weapons were tucked into his daypack, lying at his feet.

A still, bright light loomed ahead of them to the right, a blazing beacon in an ocean of dark. Erina veered off the bitumen, hit the brakes and killed the headlights.

Carter felt a slight rush of adrenalin quicken his heart rate.

She pointed at the light, about seven hundred metres away at a diagonal angle from where they were parked. 'That's the gatehouse where my dream date awaits me.'

'Let's hope he doesn't turn into a nightmare.'

'Whatever, I'll handle him.'

Carter grabbed his daypack and stepped out of the vehicle. He climbed onto the four-wheel drive's crash bar, took out his night-vision binoculars and studied the small building. Two bright lights mounted on its roof threw out a fifteen-metre arc of light, illuminating a high barbed-wire fence, which presumably cordoned off Woodforde's inner compound.

Erina stood on the road beside the four-wheel drive. 'To get there,' she said, pointing down the highway, 'we turn right up ahead, travel three hundred metres along a dirt road and cross a cattle ramp.'

He scanned the grounds beyond the light and noted the dark shadows of two utes parked about fifteen metres from the gatehouse.

'I thought you were expecting just one guard,' he said.

'That's what he said.'

'Looks like there's two. Maybe your boyfriend was thinking along the lines of a threesome.'

Erina ignored him.

He turned his head and looked out into the darkness. To his left the moon shone behind a single majestic gum, creating a ghostlike silhouette. Already the plan was bending out of shape.

'Whatever you're thinking,' she said, 'there's no time for second-guessing. We have to go in. Now.'

He turned to face her. 'Agreed.'

—

It took Carter three minutes to organise himself in his hiding place underneath the chassis of the four-wheel drive.

He lay in a sling he'd created from a hessian bag, suspended twenty centimetres above the black bitumen with his feet pointing towards the front, parallel to the highway. His nose just cleared a hot metal pipe and rope dug into his back, thighs and calves.

The engine purred to life and the vehicle moved down the highway towards the turn-off to the gatehouse at around twenty kilometres an hour. He twisted his head in an effort to avoid the harsh fumes of engine oil. Not exactly first class, but it would get him through the front gate.

In his left hand he gripped one of the suspension ropes. In his right he held the Glock 18 close to his chest, fitted with a silencer. He hoped he wouldn't need the weapon but it was best to be prepared. The four-wheel drive's spare keys were tucked away in his pants pocket.

He felt the vehicle brake, then they turned right off the smooth highway and rumbled along a gravel road.

The four-wheel drive decelerated further, rattled over a cattle grid and then came to a halt.

He heard the front window slide down and an intercom buzz. 'I'm looking for Pete Stanley,' Erina said. 'He's expecting me.'

A hoarse, raspy voice crackled, 'State your name.'

'Nicole Davey from Screen Australia.'

'Are you alone?'

'Yes.'

'Come on in. Don't exceed ten kilometres an hour and stop at the gatehouse. Understood?'

'Absolutely.'

Carter heard the gate click open. The four-wheel drive rumbled slowly along the gravel and came to a gentle stop.

Light flooded underneath the vehicle.

Two sets of dark boots strode towards the four-wheel drive.

Carter heard the distinct sound of a pump-action cocking and a shell crunching into the chamber ready to fire.

Shotguns weren't part of the plan.

'This is all very melodramatic,' Erina said, her tone playful and light. 'I just came by to see Pete.'

A hoarse voice answered her. 'Pete's not here. Get out of the car and keep your hands where I can see 'em.'

Carter ran his forefinger over the well-oiled barrel of his Glock.

'Really, guys,' Erina said, 'I'm just coming back from Brisbane. Pete said he was on night shift this week and asked me to drop by.'

She hadn't missed a beat.

'Get out of the car,' the hoarse voice repeated.

The driver's door opened and Erina stepped out.

'Leave the bag on the seat.'

'Why are you making such a fuss?'

Carter imagined her staring down the barrel, calculating the odds, deciding whether she should attempt to take the guy out.

A set of boots moved towards her.

Carter hoped she'd play it low-key and bide her time. With a shotgun pointing at your head, the percentages were too low to make a move, but eventually an opening would present itself and they'd sort it out. He was counting on her having faith in him, even though they hadn't worked together for two years.

'Put the shotgun to her head, Smokey, and if she moves so much as a muscle pull the trigger and blow her pretty head off.'

'No worries, Mick.'

Carter watched a pair of boots move to Erina's left. The other boots stepped forwards.

Mick's husky voice said, 'What's this?'

Carter figured he was frisking her.

'She's got a gun under her armpit.'

Erina's Beretta landed on the ground and a boot kicked it away.

'A woman in the bush needs to protect herself,' Erina said. 'You have no right to—'

The sharp crack of an open hand hitting flesh made Carter hold his breath.

A moment of silence followed.

'Fucking arsehole,' she said.

Another sharp crack rang out. 'Shut the fuck up, you stupid bitch, or I'll spread that cute little nose across your face.'

Adrenalin coursed through Carter's veins and his pulse quickened, but his mind was crystal-clear. He needed to rescue Erina before either of the guards called the house and warned whoever was there.

A handcuff clicked open and then closed.

'Smokey, check the car.'

A set of boots strode towards the car. The door opened.

Smokey stepped inside – a big guy judging by the downward movement of the vehicle.

Carter slipped his finger around the trigger of the Glock.

Half a minute later the car bounced up and the door slammed shut.

'All clear, Mick,' Smokey said. 'The bitch is alone.'

'Sweet. I'm going to radio the house and find out what the boss wants us to do with her.'

'Don't start feeling her up without me.'

'No need to get your tits in a tangle, Smokey – I'm not greedy. I like to share.'

Their laughter had a strange, almost hysterical quality.

'You stay here,' Mick said. 'Keep your eyes open.'

'Yep.'

Carter saw Erina's running shoes move away, followed by a set of boots that presumably belonged to Mick.

'Hey, mate,' his friend called.

The boots stopped.

'You reckon we should have ourselves a bit of fun before handing her over?'

'Why not?' Mick said. 'You're only young once. Just stay alert and you can go seconds.'

'Roger that.'

'Remember the boss reckons there's a guy with her. Some dangerous motherfucker. Might be following her. You need to cover my skinny arse while I lighten my load.'

'It's not like I'm going to fall asleep. I've had enough goey to keep me awake for a week.'

Goey was slang for speed. That accounted for the mad edge to their voices and laughter. These guys were wired on amphetamines, making them unpredictable, but also prone to mistakes.

Carter saw a hand pick up the Beretta. A pair of boots and Erina's shoes crunched across the ground towards the gatehouse.

CHAPTER 12

Carter untied the knots in the rope supporting the sling and lowered himself inch by inch towards the ground.

His back touched down on the hard gravel surface. He rolled onto his belly, slid his legs around behind him without making a sound and stared into the brightly lit night towards the gatehouse.

Smokey's black boots stood two body lengths away from Carter, pointing towards the four-wheel drive.

They shuffled back and forth.

Carter peered towards the open door of the gatehouse, a further four body lengths away. All he could see was Mick's broad back filling the doorway, obscuring Erina.

'Get your fuckin' hands in the air,' Mick said.

Erina's clear voice carried through the still night. 'What are you doing? I think you've mistaken me for someone else.'

'Raise your fuckin' hands in the fuckin' air or I'll jam this butt into your fuckin' gut.' He chuckled. 'Hey, I'm a fucking poet and don't even know it. But that don't mean I'm soft. Now lift 'em.'

Carter saw her handcuffed hands extend above Mick's head.

'That's a good girl.'

Mick took a few steps back. Still aiming the shotgun at Erina, he grabbed a length of rope, looped it through her handcuffs and slung it over a pipe that ran parallel under the ceiling.

Carter breathed out slowly, glad Erina hadn't tried to take Mick

94

out. It was too risky. If either of the two armed guards fired a shot, the element of surprise would be lost and their plan would unravel.

Mick yanked down on the rope, pulling Erina to full stretch, and tied it off behind the open door. He moved to one side, giving Carter a clear view of Erina. Her head swivelled to the left and then to the right as if she was trying to figure out a way of striking back.

'You guys are in deep shit,' she said, her voice full of controlled defiance. 'But you can still save yourselves. Let me go right now and I'll forget this incident occurred.'

'Who the fuck do you think you are?' Mick asked. 'Waltzing in here as if you own the fuckin' joint.'

'I just popped in to say hi to Pete.'

'At two in the fuckin' morning? What did you want to see him for?'

'We struck up a bit of a friendship. I wasn't tired. Just wanted a bit of company and maybe a coffee.'

'Yeah, and I'm the next fucking king of England.'

Erina didn't reply.

Mick moved back in front of her. Carter had to strain to make out what he was saying.

'You figure we're a couple of rednecks with shit for brains,' Mick said. 'Well, don't worry, sweetheart, we'll give you more than fucking coffee. The party's about to begin.'

Mick turned to his left and started rummaging through a set of cupboard drawers.

Carter caught a glimpse of Erina's face and the look of steely determination etched across it.

He shifted his attention from Mick to Smokey's black boots. They still pointed towards him, shuffling back and forth.

'Don't even think about it,' Erina said. 'I won't warn you again.'

Carter shifted his focus back to the gatehouse.

Mick moved behind Erina, wrenched her head back and slapped a strip of metallic tape across her mouth.

He then put one arm around her throat, ripped the front of her shirt open and yanked her bra up, exposing her breasts.

Carter swallowed hard.

Mick grabbed her right breast and squeezed.

For a moment the night continued still and silent.

Then Erina went wild, thrashing about like a wounded tiger, hurling her body back and forth. When her rage exploded to the surface, she became far more dangerous and at the same time more vulnerable.

Even in a fight where you were at a severe disadvantage, you couldn't allow your opponent to dictate terms. By fighting back, she'd seized the initiative and potentially opened up a space for Carter to act. The danger was that her actions could provoke Mick into lashing out at her with his knife or even shooting her.

Her foot kicked out at him.

Once.

Twice.

Both times she hit nothing but air.

Mick let go of her and laughed.

Big mistake.

The third kick struck his shin.

He doubled over, clutching his leg.

Erina had picked her target well. The shin was a weak point.

Carter glanced at Smokey's boots, still pointing towards the four-wheel drive and jiggling up and down as though he was moving to a musical beat. Carter figured he must be listening to an iPod.

Carter grabbed a handful of small stones with his left hand and turned his attention back to the gatehouse.

Mick stood to one side of Erina. 'I'm going to make you pay for that, bitch.'

He looked like he was about to grab her.

Carter held his breath.

She reared her head back. Her forehead flew forwards, catching Mick square on the nose.

The sickening crunch of bone smashing on bone made Carter wince.

The forehead was the hardest bone in the human body, a lethal weapon. It would've been the last thing Mick expected from a handcuffed woman.

A high-pitched male scream cut through the night.

Erina was on the balls of her feet, facing him, her body coiled like a spring.

Carter was pleased to see she'd regained control of her anger and was ready for his next move. He couldn't see Mick but could imagine the look of bewilderment on his battered face. Headbutting a man while handcuffed was a calculated act of extreme courage.

It was what he loved about her.

'You stupid fucking bitch,' Mick yelled. 'You're going to be so fucking sorry you did that.'

Judging by the rage in his voice, the wired-up Mick was capable of anything.

Carter looked back at Smokey's boots.

They'd turned a hundred and eighty degrees towards the gatehouse, his heels facing Carter.

They'd stopped jiggling.

The window Carter was waiting for had just opened.

CHAPTER 13

Carter propelled himself from underneath the right-hand side of the four-wheel drive and sprung to his feet, knowing exactly what he needed to do.

The spotlight lit up Smokey, striding away from him towards the guardhouse. He was a big paunchy guy carrying a pump-action shotgun loosely in his right hand. He'd pulled his earphones out and they hung over his chest.

Carter needed to take him out before he had a chance to squeeze the trigger. He shifted his weight to the balls of his feet and lobbed the handful of stones ten metres to Smokey's left.

An old trick, but it worked.

Smokey spun around, lifted his shotgun and aimed it at the point where the sound had come from.

Carter moved towards him from the opposite direction, holding the Glock's barrel in his right hand and making barely a sound.

In four strides he closed the gap between them to a body length and started to lift his arm, preparing to strike.

But before he had a chance, he stepped on something hard.

A brittle stick gave a distinct crack.

Smokey stopped dead and turned, backlit by the gatehouse light behind him.

His jaw dropped. He started to bring his shotgun around when Carter smashed the butt of the Glock into his temple.

The shotgun went flying.

Carter lunged forwards and caught the weapon by the barrel with his left hand, midair, before it hit the ground.

Without dropping his own weapon, he simultaneously grabbed hold of the dazed Smokey, still standing but swaying. He twirled the shotgun around and smashed the butt into his other temple, delivering a knockout blow.

Smokey's body went limp. Carter lowered him to the earth like he was putting a sleeping baby to bed. Except this baby weighed over a hundred kilograms and dark blood oozed down his face from the wounds he'd just received.

Carter turned towards the illuminated gatehouse.

Mick had been busy. He'd tied rope around Erina's neck to form a noose, pulled it tight and fastened one end to the pipe near the ceiling. He'd also wrapped gaffer tape around her ankles, rendering her helpless.

He stood behind her, pushing his blue jeans down over his skinny backside.

Carter weighed up the odds and decided it was too risky to fire at him or try to take him out with his bare hands. He needed to manoeuvre him out of the gatehouse.

He sprinted ten metres to where one of the utes was parked and slid under the chassis feet first.

In one smooth movement he rolled onto his stomach, lay prone next to the driver's wheel and adjusted his position so he had a clear view inside the gatehouse.

Mick was yanking Erina's black cotton trousers down. She threw her hips back and forth, but there wasn't much she could do.

Carter reached into his cargo pants with his left hand, pulled out the four-wheel drive's keys, aimed the remote device at the vehicle and pressed the button.

The vehicle quacked twice.

Mick spun around and stared into the night. His jeans were bunched around his ankles and his pale blue shirt hung over his thighs.

If the stakes weren't so high, the image would've been comical.

Mick pulled up his jeans and held Erina's Beretta to her throat. He quickly cut the tape holding her ankles and the rope forming the noose, then yanked her pants up and pulled her in front of him as a shield.

'You try anything,' Carter heard him say to her, 'and I put a bullet through you.'

The guard pushed Erina through the gatehouse door and stopped just outside.

The bright spotlight lit up her exposed breasts. Her bra hung around her neck, her torn T-shirt fell off her arms and her trouser belt was undone. Blood dripped down from her shoulder, and tape covered her mouth.

Mick pressed the barrel of the Beretta against her chin. Her eyes flicked from right to left, seeking Carter out.

Lying on his stomach under the ute, Carter dropped the keys and lifted the Glock to eye level with both hands. His elbows rested on the rock-hard ground to form a solid base.

He took aim at Mick's head, but there was no clear shot. Erina was still in the line of fire.

The guard's darting eyes reflected his agitation. They looked as if they were about to pop out of their sockets.

'Smokey,' he said, 'where the fuck are you?'

In his addled state he'd obviously missed his unconscious colleague sprawled in the dirt.

He pushed Erina forwards and shuffled across the open ground behind her, making sure she continued to shield him.

When he was a metre from his partner's body lying spread-eagled on the ground, he stopped.

'What the …?' he muttered.

Carter's finger caressed the trigger.

A shot was still too dangerous. He needed to wait until Mick had moved away from Erina.

Unfortunately, Mick did exactly what Carter had hoped he wouldn't. He backed into the gatehouse with Erina and shut the door.

The only option was to hang tight and hope that Mick was too drug-addled to call the house for backup.

From inside the gatehouse Carter heard feet scuffle, followed by a brief silence.

The door swung open.

Mick again pushed Erina out of the gatehouse in front of him.

He was now holding the point of a knife at her throat with one hand and his shotgun in the other, the barrel poking out from under Erina's right armpit. Mick's chin was just above her shoulder. She kept her eyes fixed straight ahead, staring into the night.

Carter lined up a spot above Mick's right eye.

The angles looked good.

If he hit his target, the bullet would take out Mick, miss Erina and pass harmlessly into the night. Ideally Erina would somehow put a little more space between them before he opened fire to reduce the margin of error.

Mick swung the shotgun in an arc in front of him.

'If you don't want me to cut the bitch,' he snarled, 'you'll come out with your hands high in the air. I'm gonna count to three.'

Carter remained motionless.

'And I promise you. I will do it.'

CHAPTER 14

Carter relaxed his shoulders and focused on his target. He'd made tough shots like this many times.

The distance, the tight angle between him and the target and its size weren't the issue.

He was.

The last time he'd fired a handgun had been well over a year ago. It wasn't the physical challenge that concerned him. Rather the mental, emotional and spiritual readiness required to take a shot when someone's life was at stake. Especially when that person was Erina.

He needed to be still and clear.

His mind flashed back to a training camp he'd done on a tiny uninhabited island off the western coast of Sumatra when he was seventeen years old. Thomas had been instructing him in the finer points of shooting a crossbow. His task had been to lie prone on the ground and hit a coconut with a red cross painted on it dangling from a tree seventy metres away.

After he'd missed the target twenty times, Thomas knelt beside him, touched him on the shoulder and whispered, 'A true marksman shoots with his whole being. Not just his eye.'

The memory made Carter relax and take a deep breath.

'The count starts now,' Mick said. 'If you don't show your fucking face, I'll start by cutting the bitch's tit off.'

Mick dropped the knife from Erina's throat to below her left breast and used the flat of the blade to push it up.

Carter saw her body tense and willed her to remain still.

'One,' Mick said.

Carter inhaled into his *hara*, the point below the bellybutton, which was the centre of a man's chi, the subtle energy system the ancient Chinese described as a man's life force and the true source of his power.

He exhaled slowly and felt the air passing through the fine hair of his nostrils.

His shoulder muscles relaxed.

Everything around him slowed.

Mick's bushy eyebrows, his high forehead and the dark stubble on his chin came into sharp focus.

Carter caressed the trigger.

No conscious thought intruded. No emotion upset the calm and clarity of his mind.

There was just him, the gun and the target, united through his even breath.

'Two.'

A smile twisted Mick's face. He turned the knife over and jabbed the point into Erina's skin just below the nipple.

Her head and body jerked upwards, causing Mick to throw his head back.

Erina seized the moment. She threw her body forwards, breaking Mick's grip, then spun around on her left foot and kicked him in the throat with her right.

Thrown off guard, Mick reeled back.

Carter kept the sights on Mick's head, waiting for the right moment to shoot.

Erina kicked Mick's wrist and he dropped the knife, but he managed to raise the shotgun, aiming it at her stomach.

Erina dived forwards, giving Carter a clean line of sight.

He squeezed the trigger.

The silenced shot made a short *pssst* sound like air rushing out of a tyre. The lights lit up a mist of pink spray and Mick dropped to the ground.

Erina collapsed on the ground next to him.

A chill passed through Carter. He feared he'd taken out both of them with the one shot. He slid on his belly from under the vehicle, jumped to his feet and sprinted to her.

She lay facedown on the bare earth, perfectly still.

He crouched beside her and gently pulled off her wig. To his relief, she moved her head.

A set of keys lay on the ground behind her. He grabbed them and gently rolled her over.

Her eyes were open. Their gaze locked for a brief second. He gripped one end of the tape between his fingers and peeled it back far enough to get a firm grip. She winced as he ripped it off.

'You okay?' he asked.

Her face was red where she'd been slapped and there was a swelling the size of a golf ball on her forehead from headbutting Mick.

She moved her mouth back and forth. 'Yeah. Soon as I get some feeling back into my lips.'

He stayed put on his haunches, giving her some space to recover from the shock.

'You sure took your time,' she said.

'And that's the thanks I get?'

'You nearly shot me.'

He tried one of the keys in the handcuffs.

'But I didn't, did I?'

He tried another key in the handcuffs and then another.

'Maybe you got lucky,' she said.

The fourth opened the lock.

'Luck had nothing to do with it,' he said.

He took her hand and pulled her to her feet. She turned away from him, adjusted her pants and manoeuvred her bra back in place.

He slipped off his T-shirt and held it out for her.

'You keep it,' she said. 'I've got one in the car.'

She looked down at Mick's body.

Hollow-point bullets expanded outwards on impact, destroying surrounding tissue and shattering bone. Carter had hit Mick right in the centre of the forehead, blowing his head apart. A pool of blood and brain matter soaked into the earth beneath him.

'What a sick motherfucker,' she said.

Carter pulled his T-shirt back over his head. 'Not anymore.'

'What about the other guy?'

They walked over to where Smokey lay spread-eagled on the ground, barely breathing. Blood trickled down both sides of his face. His mouth hung open.

Carter wasn't a doctor but recognised a fatal injury when he saw one. He crouched beside Smokey, tried to find a pulse on his wrist and stood up.

'He's history too,' he said.

'Can't say I'm sorry,' she said, tying her hair back in a ponytail. 'Give me two minutes to disable the security system, and then we'll go make Woodforde talk.'

CHAPTER 15

Carter drove one of the black utes parked near the gatehouse down the gravel drive, using only the light from a three-quarter moon and the unlimited abundance of outback stars to guide him towards Woodforde's house. Erina sat beside him in the passenger seat.

If anyone on the property spotted them, the car would be recognised as belonging to one of their own and was unlikely to arouse suspicion.

The ute's cabin smelt like the aftermath of a one-man party, reeking of stale hamburgers, marijuana smoke and beer. Carter rolled the driver's seat window down and breathed in the warm night air.

Adrenalin raced through him after the encounter with the gate guards and he consciously slowed his breathing to bring his heart rate back to normal.

He turned towards Erina. 'You okay?'

'Apart from the fact I have a golf ball on my forehead and that killing those guys means at some point we may have a police investigation to deal with?'

'We'll worry about that if and when it happens.'

'Those arseholes deserved to be put down.'

She turned and looked through the passenger-seat window, signalling an end to the conversation.

Carter concentrated on the road ahead. He wasn't one to talk about his feelings. He'd learnt not to dwell on the fate of people like Mick and Smokey. They'd made their choices and paid the ultimate price.

In a fight where the stakes were life and death, you couldn't hold back and hope to get the job done – but every time you took a man's life, a part of you died with him. Something you never got back. A fact of life he'd learnt to live with.

—

The single light blazing on the porch of the large Queenslander brought his thoughts back to the present.

He parked near the eastern wall of the house, well away from any lights, and turned off the engine.

Erina checked her watch and broke the silence. 'Three twelve a.m. Only twenty minutes behind schedule.'

She took two cotton balaclavas from her daypack and handed him one. He pulled it over his head and shoved the Glock and a six-inch knife into a black pouch, then clipped it onto the front of his web belt. They exchanged a nod and stepped out of the car.

He crouched next to her beside a large tractor parked twenty metres from the side of the house and studied the layout.

The moonlight reflected off the wide master-bedroom window on the top floor. The blinds were drawn, making it impossible to tell whether anyone was awake.

There was no sign of movement outside the house. He doubted they'd have lookouts posted inside the grounds.

They walked without rushing to the front door. Erina used a lock-picking device from her daypack to jimmy it open in three seconds and led the way in.

Carter closed the door behind him. It was pitch-black inside. The only sound came from a ticking clock.

Erina switched on a pencil-thin flashlight, lighting up a short hallway and a coat rack. They followed the narrow beam into a large living room.

A colourful Indonesian carpet and a rug made from steer's hide lay beside each other on dark wooden floorboards. Christmas tinsel hung over a painting of a bush landscape. A metre-high fir tree sat in one corner, decorated with baubles and stars.

Erina pointed the flashlight towards a wooden stairway. She led him up the stairs, walking on the side of her feet to avoid making a sound. They padded side by side along a carpeted hallway and stopped outside Woodforde's bedroom.

The dull light from a muted television leaked out under the closed wooden door. Carter heard the quiet hum of air conditioning and someone snoring.

Erina stepped to one side.

Carter adjusted the balaclava so that his mouth was completely free of the rough cotton, opened the door and poked his head into the bedroom.

A large plasma television sat on a waist-high chrome stand at the end of the bed, lighting up the room. On screen, the talk-show host David Letterman sat at his desk, armed with his coffee cup, interviewing a smiling male in his late twenties.

Carter stepped inside and walked over the thick shag-pile carpet. Erina took up a position just inside the door. The smell of hash, cigarette smoke and stale sex hung in the air.

In the flickering light of the television, Carter made out two bodies, one much bigger than the other. Both asleep. A half-metre-wide valley of bed separated them. On the left side a large male snored. On the other a much smaller figure, a woman, lay on her back, also asleep.

The leftovers of a party lay on the floor and bedside table – an empty condom packet, male and female underwear, a half-full bottle of Bundaberg Rum, cigarettes, a block of hash and a pipe.

He placed a dart between his teeth and crossed the thick carpet, stopping beside the messed-up bed, next to the sleeping woman.

She was young and blonde, with headphones in her ears. She looked like she was in her late teens. Clearly not Woodforde's Indonesian wife.

Carter took the dart in one hand, reached out and pricked her neck, just below the ear.

He counted to three and pinched her cheek.

She was out cold.

He moved to the other side of the bed and pulled back the sheet and blanket, exposing Hamish Woodforde sprawled out on his back snoring, naked except for a black eye mask and a pink condom attached to his flaccid penis.

Woodforde was over six foot and would've weighed more than a hundred and ten kilograms. There was a fair bit of fat, but also plenty of muscle. Not a guy to be messed with lightly.

Carter slapped him hard across the face and Woodforde's whole body twitched. He struggled to pull himself up, reached for his eye mask and began to open his mouth.

Before a word came out, Carter lined up the pressure point five centimetres above the jaw and let go a rabbit-punch.

Woodforde's head snapped back and dropped to the pillow.

Carter walked to the television, lifted the set off its stand and placed it face up on the thick carpet, giving him light to work by. He slung Woodforde's limp body over his shoulder, carried him to the waist-high TV stand and laid him on top. Woodforde's arms and legs dangled over the sides.

Carter used an extension cord from the DVD player to strap him to the stand, trussing him up tight. He then went to the ensuite bathroom and came back with two full glasses of water, a bath towel and a couple of small handtowels.

He took a long drink from one glass, threw the contents of the other into Woodforde's face and slapped his cheek twice. He pulled the knife from his web belt and held it ten centimetres from the man's right eye.

Woodforde opened his eyes, looking like he'd just woken from a strong anaesthetic. His bloodshot eyes darted around the room before focusing on the point of the knife.

He glared at Carter and tried to move his arms and legs without success, appearing more angry than scared.

'What the fuck do you think you're doing?' he said.

His gruff tone indicated he was a man used to giving orders rather than taking them.

Carter jabbed the knife through the air, stopping a centimetre from the man's eye. Woodforde flinched.

'Keep the volume down,' Carter said.

'What do you want?' Woodforde asked in a loud whisper.

Carter leant forwards. 'Information.'

'You really think you can bully and intimidate a man like me?'

'That's the plan.'

CHAPTER 16

Carter looked down at Woodforde's hairy belly through the slits of the balaclava. The man lay completely naked and vulnerable, lit by the soft glow of the television. His limp penis hung to one side. The condom had fallen off in the bed. His breath came in short sharp wheezes.

Torturing another human being never sat well with Carter, but it was the only viable means of extracting information from an unwilling subject in a short amount of time.

There was little grey area in this case anyway: Woodforde's conduct in his business and personal life crossed the bounds of human decency. His actions threatened the lives of Thomas, Wayan and potentially countless other innocent people, meaning that Carter could assume the role of judge, jury and torturer with a clear conscience. Still, he hoped the threat of intense physical pain alone would convince Woodforde to supply the required information, without the need for much actual violence. It'd call for a high level of theatre.

Carter ran his fingers over the cool blade and placed the point of the knife against Woodforde's stomach, just below the bellybutton.

Woodforde glared at him. 'You know how much I'm worth?'

Carter slid the knife tip down his belly, tracing carefully around his genitals and bringing it to rest just below his scrotum.

Woodforde's eyes bulged.

Carter knew the man would be loath to betray the brutal and unforgiving Sungkar clan – but for most men, future dangers paled into insignificance in the face of imminent excruciating pain and permanent disfigurement. The hardest people to break were usually religious fanatics and patriots – people with a commitment to a higher ideal, to something bigger than themselves. Woodforde fitted neither category.

Carter pushed the point of the knife into the top of Woodforde's muscular thigh, near the pubic bone, drawing blood. Woodforde flinched again.

Carter wiped the bloody blade on the man's unshaven cheek and asked, 'How much do you reckon a functioning penis is worth?'

Despite the cool air conditioning, beads of sweat formed on Woodforde's brow and above his top lip. His eyes jumped from left to right and he swallowed hard. The sight and smell of a man's own blood tended to remind him of his humble place in the universe.

'We can do this the easy or the hard way,' Carter said. 'Tell me what I need to know and I won't hurt anything except your pride.'

Woodforde struggled against his bonds.

'Are you going to cooperate?'

Woodforde set his jaw. 'You touch me again, you're a dead man.'

Carter made the honking sound of a buzzer in a game show. 'Wrong answer.'

He rolled up the handtowel and leant in close enough to smell the rum and tobacco on his captive's breath.

'There's only one thing you need to know about me,' Carter said, stuffing one end of the handtowel into Woodforde's mouth and speaking slowly. 'If I say I'll do something, I'll do it. You want this to stop, blink twice. But make sure you're prepared to tell the truth and nothing but the truth.'

Woodforde's attention flicked to Erina, standing by the door, before returning to Carter.

'We've just killed two of your guards and I'd prefer to do this without maiming you.'

There was fear in Woodforde's eyes and sweat rolled down his face, but he didn't blink. The guy was far tougher and had more arrogant pride than Carter had given him credit for. Plus, he'd be well aware of the clan's harsh reprisal should he betray them.

To get him talking freely would require more than the mere threat of pain.

Carter glanced back at Erina. She gave him a short nod.

He put the knife down on the television stand next to Woodforde's head and stared at him.

In a blur of movement he clamped his hand over Woodforde's left wrist and turned the palm up.

His skin was hot and sticky.

Carter used the heel of his hand to push the little finger back, close to breaking point.

Woodforde threw his head from side to side and tried to pull away.

'Are you ready to talk?'

Woodforde stopped moving and turned his eyes towards him.

Carter pushed hard.

There was a snap, like a large twig breaking.

Woodforde thrashed back and forth. He screamed through the gag. The sound came out muffled and indistinct.

Carter gripped his wrist tighter and turned the hand over.

Shaking, Woodforde tried to clench his good fingers into a fist. Tears streamed down his cheeks.

Carter drilled his thumb into a pressure point at the top of the wrist. The hand snapped open.

Carter slid the heel of his hand up Woodforde's palm and pushed it against his index finger. 'Look at me,' he said.

Woodforde did so. The anger and arrogance had disappeared. The only emotion in his eyes now was sheer terror.

Carter pushed the finger almost to its breaking point, then paused.

Woodforde squirmed. His body tensed.

Carter shoved back hard.

Another snap.

There could be no letting up. The subject had to believe the pain would only cease when he cooperated.

'I'm going to take the gag out,' Carter told him. 'You scream, I'll break your nose, then your thumbs. Got it?'

Woodforde moved his head.

Carter removed the gag and kept his fist cocked ten centimetres from Woodforde's nose. 'We're looking for a man in his sixties and an eighteen-year-old boy. Are they on the property?'

Woodforde's response came as a hiss. 'I don't know what you're talking about.'

Carter stuffed the gag back into his mouth.

He looked over at Erina.

She walked across the carpet and stood over Woodforde's head.

'I was hoping to do this the easy way,' Carter said. 'But it looks like the easy way isn't working, and my associate's preference is that you pay for your sins.'

Erina placed a Marlboro through the slit in her mask and between her lips. As she lit it, the flame of the cigarette lighter illuminated her dark eyes.

'And by the way,' Carter said, 'she doesn't smoke.'

CHAPTER 17

Erina drew on her cigarette, held the glowing end five centimetres from Woodforde's face and blew the smoke into his eyes, causing him to squint.

She placed it on the television stand next to his head and grabbed the remaining handtowel. She wrapped it round her right hand, reached down, took hold of Woodforde's scrotum and squeezed hard.

He struggled against his cords like he had an electrified cattle prod shoved up his backside. Tears poured down his cheeks and he made a pathetic moaning sound through the gag. The cigarette fell from the stand.

Erina wasn't holding back.

Woodforde's pleading eyes jumped to Carter, who stood by the door with his arms folded. He seemed to hope another man might feel sympathy for him.

Without letting go of his scrotum, Erina knelt and picked up the cigarette from the carpet. She stood back up, inhaled until the cigarette glowed bright and then placed the burning end just centimetres from Woodforde's barrel chest.

The hair crackled and flared, releasing an acrid smell as it singed and burnt. His chest heaved and he threw his head sideways.

Erina leant in close and spoke slowly and softly. 'Are the two men my associate spoke about on the property?'

Woodforde stared at her, wheezing.

'I'm going to count to three,' she said. 'If you haven't answered by the time I do, I'm going to stub this cigarette out on the end of your limp dick, then turn your hairy balls into mashed potato. And if that fails to motivate you, I'll shove a six-inch needle into your left eye. Followed by your right. You get the picture.'

Woodforde's body went rigid.

'Are they on the property? Two blinks means yes. One no.'

Woodforde appeared to be holding his breath. His face was bright red.

He blinked once.

Erina stiffened.

'I'm going to pull the gag out,' she said. 'You yell out, or do anything to upset me, you'll wish you hadn't been born. Understood?'

He blinked twice.

She put the cigarette in her mouth, pulled the gag out and placed it on his chest. She continued to hold on to his testicles with her right hand.

Woodforde coughed and gulped mouthfuls of air.

She took the cigarette out and asked, 'Where are they?'

'You have no idea what Samudra will do to me if he finds out I've betrayed him.'

'You think I give a shit?'

She squeezed his testicles just enough to get his attention, but not enough to make him thrash about.

'Where are they? Last chance.'

Woodforde swallowed hard and took a deep breath.

She moved the cigarette to his eyeball. He closed his eyes, but Carter knew he'd feel the heat from the lit end.

'Open your eyes,' she ordered.

He obeyed.

She pulled the cigarette slightly back. 'I asked you a question.'

Woodforde looked at her. Carter could see that his resistance was broken.

'Two people were flown out at ten o'clock.'

'Where to?'

'Batak Island.'

She glanced at Carter, who walked to the other side of Woodforde.

Carter asked, 'With Samudra?'

'Yes.'

'You know what he's planning?'

Woodforde swallowed. 'Samudra tells me nothing.'

Erina squeezed his testicles again, causing his body to arch. 'Don't even think about lying to us!'

He gritted his teeth. 'I'm telling the truth. I swear. Samudra is crazy. Thinks he's going to be the next Osama bin Laden.'

Carter put his hand under Woodforde's bristly, sweaty chin and turned his head towards him. 'Where's the South African headed?'

'Sydney.'

'What's in the truck?' Carter asked.

'I saw them loading explosives and automatic weapons. Plus some other stuff.'

Erina leant over Woodforde. 'What's the target?'

He shook his head, tears flowing down his cheeks. 'I swear on my mother's grave I don't know. The only thing I heard was something about a great victory for the new year.'

'Anything else?'

'That's all. I swear. You've got to believe me.'

Erina released her grip on Woodforde's scrotum, shoved the gag back into his mouth and held the lit cigarette in the air for a moment.

Then she dropped it onto the carpet and ground it out.

BOOK THREE

CHAPTER 1

Eight hours later, Carter and Erina sat next to each other in the packed economy section of the Virgin Australia flight from Brisbane to Bali. They were due to land at Denpasar Airport at 3.10 p.m. Bali time. Over thirty hours had passed since Erina had kidnapped him from the headland at Lennox.

There were just five days left until the end of the year. According to Woodforde, that was the time frame during which the clan were expecting a 'great victory', which fitted in with Thomas's intel. Alex and his men were headed to Sydney with weapons and explosives, which meant this was a threat that had to be taken seriously.

Carter and Erina had figured that the most likely date of a planned clan attack was New Year's Eve. It was an educated guess based on the available facts and their gut instinct. In a situation like this it was the only way you could operate.

119

On the surface they'd faced an impossible moral choice – either fly to Indonesia to rescue Thomas and Wayan or go to Sydney first to track down Alex and the other clansmen. But there was no option. Neither of them even contemplated abandoning Thomas and Wayan. Every decision flowed from that. There would be time enough afterwards to fly back to Sydney and figure out how to stop Alex's team.

Carter needed to get Jacko on the case ASAP and had tried to phone him at least a dozen times before they'd boarded the plane, but his calls had gone straight to voicemail and it had him worried. They needed Jacko to take care of the logistics, arranging for them to travel to Samudra's island camp and setting in train an investigation into what was happening with Alex and his men – and it all had to happen without Trident's knowledge. At some point they might be forced to hand the matter over to the Federal Police, but Carter didn't want to do that unless he had to, as he knew he and Erina were best equipped to find and stop Alex.

He glanced to his right at Erina. Her head rested on a pillow against the window. Ever since they'd discovered that Thomas and Wayan had been taken out of the country, she'd retreated into herself and avoided all unnecessary conversation.

Carter figured she was either consciously or unconsciously blaming him for putting the order at risk by walking out. The unspoken rift between them threw him off centre. To have any chance of succeeding they needed to be working as one mind, but shutting down was her way of dealing with uncomfortable emotions, particularly where he was concerned.

She'd drifted off to sleep soon after take-off, skipped breakfast and had barely stirred since. Like him, she'd learnt to grab sleep whenever she could, no matter how she was feeling, realising you never knew when the next opportunity might come. But he wasn't prepared to switch off until he spoke to Jacko.

He'd give the flight stewards another five minutes to complete the breakfast shift before making the call. He swigged the last dregs of lukewarm water from the small plastic bottle provided by the airline and closed his eyes.

Sitting so close to Erina stirred memories of the good times as well as the bad. He recalled images of the two of them lying together on a carved wooden bed in a resort off Malaysia two and a half years ago – entwined, naked, her head resting on his shoulder and her breathing soft. The memory reminded him of just how close they could be.

For a long time, until Erina was in her mid-twenties and shortly after Carter turned thirty, they never crossed the line between friendship and romance, due partly to Thomas's close oversight of his daughter, but also because of their loyalty to the order and obedience to its principles.

That all changed during a layover after a particularly tough assignment at the idyllic Malay resort. A mutual friend had been killed. They'd drowned their grief with shots of tequila. They'd wound up in bed and stayed there for five days. After that, Carter knew he could never be happy with another woman.

But as soon as they'd reported back for duty and it became obvious that Thomas was displeased, their relationship began to unravel. Carter started to wonder if he and Erina could ever find any kind of peace together. His bond with Thomas deteriorated, and the man he'd thought of as a father became cold and distant.

The woman to his left in the aisle seat unbuckled her seatbelt. His eyes flickered open and he watched the skirt of her floral dress sway as she headed towards the back of the plane.

He would let Erina sleep while he went and made the call. But first he needed to retrieve the satphone from her daypack, lying at her feet. She'd taken charge of it without offering any explanation, which was fine with him. He reached down slowly across his body towards it, trying not to disturb her.

His fingers touched the zip a fraction of a second before her left hand clamped over his forearm. She was wide-awake in an instant.

'What are you doing?' she asked.

'I'm going to call Jacko.'

'Without me?'

'It makes no sense for the two of us to go.'

She reached into her daypack, pulled out the phone, unbuckled her seatbelt and stood up.

He did the same. They stood in front of their seats, neither budging an inch.

'Erina, wait here.'

'No.'

'There's no need to draw attention to ourselves and cause a fuss.'

'What are the cabin crew going to do, throw us off the plane?'

'I'll fill you in on every detail.'

'How about I call Jacko and you stay here?'

Carter sighed. Fighting her when she'd already made up her mind was a waste of time.

The woman in the floral dress returned from the rest room and stood by her seat in the aisle, waiting for them to make a move. He nodded at her and she stepped back, allowing them to move into the aisle.

'Some things never change,' he muttered.

Erina, who was right behind him, asked, 'What's that supposed to mean?'

'You won't be told.'

'And don't you forget it.'

—

Carter sat on the closed plastic toilet seat in the rest room at the back of the plane, breathing in the smell of human waste and cheap soap.

Erina locked the metal door and an exhaust fan whirred overhead. She handed Carter the satphone and leant against the sink with her arms folded, their knees touching.

He dialled Jacko's number.

On the sixth ring the line clicked. 'That you, Carter?'

Jacko's voice was music to his ears.

'Yep.'

He put the phone on speaker and held it so Erina could also hear.

'Thank bloody Christ,' Jacko said. 'I knew you might be trying to contact me. But I've been running round all night like a blue-arsed fly. The officious pricks at the hospital make everyone hand in their cell phones at the front desk and somehow they managed to lose mine. I only just got it back.'

'So how's everyone?'

'Hanging in there.'

'What about Josh?'

'He's stabilised. Won't know for sure whether he'll pull through until later this arvo. Did you track down Thomas and Wayan?'

'Afraid not.' Carter looked at Erina. 'Apparently they're en route to Batak Island.'

There was a heavy silence.

After a few seconds Jacko came back on the line. 'Where the hell are you?'

'The rest room of a plane heading your way. I'm with Erina.'

'Yeah? You aiming to join the mile-high club or have you two done the deed already?'

Erina rolled her eyes. 'Good morning, Jacko.'

A cigarette lighter clicked on the other end of the line. Carter heard Jacko inhale.

'Hello, love, just wanted to hear your voice,' Jacko said. 'Fill us in on what's happening at your end.'

They told him everything that had gone down, finishing with Alex heading to Sydney with the truckload of explosives.

'I'll line everything up so we can get you two guys to Batak Island first thing in the morning,' Jacko said.

Erina leant over the phone. 'We also need you to suss out everything you can about the Sungkar clan's connections in Sydney and find out if the threat is real without alerting Trident to what's going on.'

'Gotcha.'

There was a loud knock on the door.

'What was that?' Jacko asked.

'Someone wants to use the john,' Carter said.

There was another knock, louder still.

'Open up,' a high-pitched male voice said. 'I'm in charge of the cabin crew.'

Erina turned to face the door and said, 'And I'm a full-paying passenger. What's your problem?'

'Are you alone in there?'

123

'None of your business. What's your name?'

There was silence on the other side of the door.

'Just hurry up,' the steward said. 'There are people waiting.'

Carter shifted the phone away from the door.

'Anything else you need to know?' Jacko asked.

Carter looked at Erina, who shook her head.

'Nothing that can't wait until we land,' he said.

'Okay, call me when you touch down and we'll meet at the Green Monkey Cafe,' Jacko said.

The line went dead.

—

Carter followed Erina down the aisle, ignoring the looks of several passengers standing at the rear of the plane. They edged their way past the woman in the aisle seat reading her Kindle and Erina sat down. He remained standing, waiting for Erina to put the phone back into her daypack and make herself comfortable.

She turned her body from him and stared out the window, a clear message that she didn't want to talk.

He dropped into his seat. A wave of tiredness washed over him.

This wasn't the time to push her. They'd done all they could for now. He pressed the button on the armrest, leant back and stretched his legs under the row in front as best he could.

He closed his eyes, focused on the drone of the plane and felt himself drifting off.

CHAPTER 2

Carter lay back with his head against the seat in a state of deep relaxation, somewhere between light sleep and meditation. It enabled him to refresh his mind, body and spirit while at the same time remaining attuned to any changes in the world around him.

The plane slowed and the angle of the nose dipped. They were starting their descent into Denpasar, the tourist gateway into Bali.

He turned his wrist and checked the time. It was 2.45 p.m., Bali time. He glanced at Erina.

Her eyes were closed, but that didn't mean she was sleeping.

He took a long sip of cool water from a new bottle that a flight attendant placed in front of him. The Sungkar clan would, he felt sure, have people watching for them at the airport when they touched down in less than thirty minutes.

For most Australians, Indonesia conjured images of pristine ocean beaches, perfect barrelling waves, majestic cloud-capped mountains and lush tropical rainforests – a holiday paradise. For Carter, it meant something more. The sprawl of islands had been his home for many years, and for him the landscape possessed an ethereal natural beauty touched by the hand of God. He felt a spiritual connection to the place, and it tugged at him no matter how far away he travelled or how long he stayed away.

He wasn't blind to its flaws, though. Like many developing countries where a huge gap existed between rich and poor, Indonesia was riddled with corruption and vice. If you strayed too far off the beaten track, you entered a shadowy realm full of dangers. This was a parallel universe to the land he loved and worlds away from the picture-postcard images presented to pleasure-seeking tourists.

He'd read the figures. On average around forty Australians died in Bali every year and a hundred sought help from the consulate after being taken to hospital. Countless victims of assault and robbery failed to report such incidents to the local police because they believed them to be corrupt.

This violence and crime was not limited to tourist zones. With a population exceeding two hundred and forty-five million spread over seventeen and a half thousand islands, parts of Indonesia were out of control. In some remote or isolated areas Indonesian law enforcement had little effect, and traditional cultural or religious codes prevailed. In many villages chaos reigned.

Instinctively he knew that Thomas and Wayan were still alive and being held in just such a place.

—

They touched down at Denpasar Airport with a heavy thud. Erina opened her eyes but said nothing. Carter looked across her and out through the porthole. Tiny droplets of water from a light shower of rain raced across the window. The plane taxied along the runway, passing the familiar dark stone gate on which Hindu carvings and images welcomed visitors to the island.

While Indonesia had the world's largest Muslim population, more Hindus lived in Bali than any other country outside of India. Unlike Islam, Hinduism didn't have a single founder or prophet. And even though Hindus believed in only one god, their notion of god manifested in many forms and was both male and female. The Balinese strand of Hinduism was particularly flexible, offering its followers far more freedom than the Indian. They weren't obliged to study sacred texts or follow any strict doctrine or scripture. There were no prescribed prayers or fixed moments of devotion, and they had no caste system.

Hindu spirituality in Bali embraced oneness and tolerance. Balinese Hindus were the polar opposite of monotheistic Muslim and Christian fundamentalists who maintained that anyone who failed to worship their god deserved to go to hell.

The plane slowed to a halt and the *fasten seatbelt* signs switched off.

—

Once Carter and Erina had cleared immigration and customs and retrieved their minimal luggage, they used one of the airport's cash machines to withdraw five million rupiah each, equivalent to a little over four hundred and fifty Australian dollars. Then they navigated their way through the stream of travellers towards the exit.

As they stepped out of the relative calm of the airport, the over-whelming heat and humidity of Indonesia greeted them, along with a swarm of taxi touts, all pushing, jostling and calling out to get their attention.

Carter and Erina walked through the crowd and climbed into the back seat of a beat-up taxi, the first in a long line of waiting cabs whose drivers sat patiently at the wheel. The vehicle reeked of stale body odour and clove cigarettes. They both immediately wound down the finger-smudged windows. The engine growled to life and the taxi moved into the traffic. Jacko was less than half an hour away at the Green Monkey Cafe.

The taxi accelerated through an orange light, turned left and came to a screeching halt behind a line of banked-up traffic.

Petrol fumes and the familiar aroma of earthy spices cooking in hot oil hung in the stifling air. Carter checked out the sea of vehicles surrounding them. A dozen Honda motor scooters buzzed around them, dancing through the lines of cars.

Any number of them could've been Sungkar clan tails. Alex would've anticipated that they'd come to Bali and hook up with Jacko. Even though Carter had failed to identify anyone following them, someone would've been watching for them at the airport and was almost certainly tailing them now.

The taxidriver pulled into the left lane and turned off the main road into a side street. The cab dodged a group of bare-chested western men in their early twenties staggering across the road, swilling beer from giant cans of Foster's. They turned to face the taxi, raised their cans above their heads and cheered.

The driver glanced over his shoulder. 'You want hashish? Ecstasy?'

The phone began to ring in Erina's bag.

'Just drive,' Carter said.

She pulled her mobile out and put it on speaker.

'Jacko,' she said. 'I was just about to call.'

'Listen,' he said, 'I received an email from Samudra half an hour ago.'

Carter looked at Erina. 'What's it say?' she asked.

The taxi swerved to the right, just missing a bemo, a mini-van used to transport tourists. A series of horns blared. Someone outside yelled, 'Ngentot lu!' *Fuck you!*

Carter missed Jacko's reply. He wound the window up.

'Come again?' Erina asked.

'Thomas and Wayan are alive,' Jacko said.

Carter watched Erina exhale, close her eyes and sink into the seat.

A wave of relief washed through him. Even though neither of them had talked about it, both knew Thomas and Wayan's fate hung by the thinnest thread and there'd been every chance they were already dead.

'There was a photo attached,' Jacko said. 'He's definitely holding them prisoner on Batak Island.'

The taxi screeched to a halt at a set of lights, throwing Carter and Erina forwards. The driver leant on his horn.

'Mate, give it a rest,' Carter said. His meaning was clear, even though he spoke in English.

The driver stopped honking.

'What was that, Jacko?' Erina asked.

'He says if we contact the authorities, he'll execute them immediately. If we do nothing, he'll release them on the first of January.'

'In other words,' she said, 'he's sent us a written invitation to pay him a visit on Batak Island and will be expecting us.'

'You could say that. Listen, I've got another call coming in. I think it's the helicopter pilot. See you at four.'

CHAPTER 3

Four kilometres away in a cheap hotel on the main street of Kuta, eighteen-year-old Awan Darang had just vomited for the third time in an hour.

He'd been so proud when Samudra had chosen him for this mission. This was supposed to be the greatest day of his life. He'd been training for months for this opportunity to go all the way for God. But now the time was so near, fear wracked his body.

He rocked back and forth on a wooden chair, rubbing his sweaty palms over his thighs and inhaling deeply in an effort to stop the burning bile rising from his stomach into his throat.

His most esteemed leader, Samudra Sungkar, had departed an hour ago and was due to return any minute. Awan had been left alone in this sparse room on the first floor of the Hotel Maria, just a few blocks from Kuta Beach and overlooking a street choked with traffic. He wore a pair of black pants, a crisp, freshly ironed short-sleeved shirt and his best leather shoes, which he'd polished shiny for the occasion.

His attention darted around the room. The four white walls were bare except for a single photograph of two pink lotus flowers lying in a pond of green and orange leaves.

The flowers' simple beauty reminded him of his home in Nalang, the tiny inland village in northern Java where he'd grown up in a strict Muslim family. He'd spent the first seventeen and a half years of his life sharing a four-room hut with his mother, father and two younger sisters. He'd attended the local school and been a good student.

Eight months ago he and a dozen other young men from his village had gone to a meeting at the local mosque to hear Samudra Sungkar speak. Up until that point, even though he'd received a good education, his life had lacked meaning and direction. Samudra's sermon, concerning service to God, and its relationship to Islam and jihad, ignited a passion in his heart and imagination. For the first time in his short life a holy purpose inspired him and he knew happiness. He wanted to do something great for God.

He and four friends from his village had formed a young people's mujaheddin group. They met every night to discuss the true meaning of the Koran and what it meant to be a good Muslim. After three months Samudra had invited them to his compound at Batak Island and their training had begun. It was the most exciting time of his life.

Samudra had explained many times how dedicating one's life to jihad represented the truest path to God. It all seemed so clear and made perfect sense when Samudra spoke. But sitting alone in the unfamiliar hotel room thinking of his home and family made Awan question whether he was truly ready to give his life for God.

He turned towards the warm afternoon sunlight streaming through a half-open window, bowed his head and prayed. 'In the name of Allah, the most beneficent, the most merciful. You alone do I worship. You alone do I seek for guidance.'

Outside in the hall, as if answering his prayer, footsteps approached.

His heart started to race. He stared at the door, feeling like he wanted to be sick again.

A key clicked into the lock and the doorknob turned.

A jolt of adrenalin shot through his body and he feared his bowels might open right where he sat. His legs went to jelly and he found it difficult to rise from the chair.

Samudra Sungkar stepped through the door wearing a short-sleeved batik shirt, slim black pants and leather sandals. He dragged a small businessman's suitcase on wheels behind him. A leather satchel hung over his shoulder. Even though he was not tall, he had a very great presence. He was the most wonderful man Awan had ever known.

'Allah akbar,' Samudra said.

Awan repeated the greeting and dropped his head. Looking down at the table, he felt Samudra's brown eyes fixed upon him, but he was unable to meet his master's gaze.

'My young brother,' Samudra said in a soft, gentle tone. 'We are all afraid. It is nothing to be ashamed of.'

Awan lifted his eyes. 'Even you?'

'Yes, of course. Fear has a holy purpose. It reminds us of God's presence and greatness. If you continue to pray and strive to do his will, he will always be with you, and when this great task is over, he will welcome you into paradise with open arms. You will be warmed by his embrace. As the great Osama once said, "To kill the Americans and their allies – civilians and military – is an individual duty for every Muslim who can do it in any country in which it is possible to do it. In our religion, there is a special place in the hereafter for those who participate in jihad."'

Awan nodded.

'And of course,' Samudra said, 'you will bring great prosperity and honour to your family. You want them to be proud of you, don't you?'

Awan nodded again.

Samudra placed his hand on Awan's shoulder. 'But you must do this for the right reasons. Not to be a hero or to be seen to be courageous or to gain my respect or for any other bad reason. You must do this only for the glory of Allah.'

Awan's spine straightened. 'I understand.'

Samudra's familiar smile lit up his face. 'Very good.'

He produced a pad and pen from his satchel and placed them in front of Awan on the table. 'Now, please write to your family and tell them of your great legacy.'

As always, Awan did what he was told. He sat down at the desk, closed his eyes and asked Allah for guidance, that he might find the right words. After a few moments he picked up the pen and started to write, shakily at first, then faster as the ideas started to flow – ideas Samudra had introduced him to.

I am so blessed and grateful to do God's work. Holy Jihad. I thank Allah for this opportunity. I ask you, my beloved family, for your prayers and support in carrying out the great cause. There is much work that must be done for the sake of the struggle against the infidels.

America and Australia and all their allies must be destroyed. Even if it takes a hundred years, we must keep fighting until we win.

We must all sacrifice ourselves and spill blood that we may return Islam and our brothers to glory. I pray that my martyrdom may inspire others to do great deeds that will trigger the growth of the fellowship of mujaheddin.

What good is a life that does not involve love and sacrifice? We must not live a life that will shame us before Allah. Jihad is my divine purpose. My destiny.

So, please, shed only tears of joy for me.

I love you.

Allah akbar.

He signed his name, placed the letter in an envelope, sealed it and handed it to Samudra, who slipped it into his bag.

'Thank you,' Samudra said. 'Now please stand.'

Awan did as instructed. Samudra opened his suitcase and extracted a vest packed with four fifteen-centimetre sticks of dynamite in the front pockets and two in the back.

The boy stood still as Samudra slipped the lethal garment over his shoulders and secured the plastic buttons at the front for him.

A shiver ran through his body from head to foot. He was a mujaheddin, a holy warrior for God. This was his destiny.

Soon he would know glory and enter paradise.

God was great.

Samudra reached into his suitcase, held up a casual black cotton jacket, presented it to him and smiled.

Awan slipped his arms through the sleeves.

The great man's tenderness gave him strength.

He hoped Samudra would not notice the sweat trickling down the side of his face.

Samudra zipped up the jacket's front and adjusted the collar, reminding Awan of how his father had dressed him for school as a young boy.

Samudra held a mobile phone in his right hand. 'All you have to do, my brother, is walk into the cafe. I shall do the rest.'

CHAPTER 4

Carter paid the taxidriver and they negotiated their way along one of the cluttered streets that led to Kuta Beach and the Green Monkey, where they were due to meet Jacko in less than twenty minutes.

They turned into Legian Street, the main drag of Bali's central tourist district, and walked towards the site of Paddy's Pub, one of the two targets in the 2002 terrorist bombings, the other being the Sari Club. They stopped in front of an intricately carved stone monument, created to honour the victims of the bombings.

He scanned the pedestrian traffic but couldn't see anyone watching them.

Across the street a neon sign read: *Pirates, Dance Party, Bounty Discothèque*. Despite the brutal tragedy, the party continued unabated in Kuta. The nightclubs still attracted plenty of hedonistic young western backpackers and high-school graduates. Another bar, Paddy's Reloaded, had opened down the street.

Jacko claimed he loved the life and energy of Kuta, saying it made him feel young at heart. Carter found the pollution, congestion, constant noise and swarms of tourists intolerable.

For their current purposes, though, Carter had to admit that Kuta had a few things going for it. It allowed them to blend into the background without attracting too much attention, and police officers patrolled the streets regularly, meaning an attack in the open was unlikely.

Erina bought a small bunch of white flowers from a street vendor and placed them on the monument. They then resumed their walk down Legian Street, heading in the direction of the Green Monkey.

They didn't speak, each too busy scanning the streets as they walked. They moved at a leisurely pace like a couple of tourists, passing shops selling low-priced T-shirts, pirated CDs and DVDs, and tiny restaurants serving cheap food and booze.

Traditional gamelan music competed with hip-hop and classic rock. That, combined with the constant tooting of car horns and revving of motorbike engines, made it too noisy to think let alone talk.

They'd just passed a dress shop when Carter noticed two young men loitering in front of a music stand set up on the pavement on the other side of the street. The Doors' 'Light My Fire' blared from a set of cheap speakers.

Erina turned towards him. She'd spotted them too.

He gestured towards a Starbucks fifty metres down from them, across the street, and said, 'Let's grab a coffee.'

They navigated their way across the sea of idling traffic and belching petrol fumes.

A stone statue of Kali, the Hindu goddess of time and change, stood outside the cafe. Flowers and burning incense lay at her feet. Similar offerings could be seen outside practically every Balinese-owned shopfront, demonstrating the reverence most Balinese practised in their daily life. The simple everyday spirituality was something Carter loved about the place.

He followed Erina into the cafe's air-conditioned cool. Except for the Balinese serving staff dressed in black, they could've been in a Starbucks anywhere in the world. If they weren't being followed, he'd take the opportunity to try to get Erina to talk about what was bothering her.

A quick study revealed nothing out of the ordinary. The cafe was full of westerners, except for two young Indonesian women sitting with a group of western backpackers.

Carter said to Erina, 'Get me an espresso and I'll check the back exit.'

She looked at him for a moment as if tossing up whether to do what he asked and then walked to the counter.

He made his way to the back of the cafe, past the bathrooms, and headed down a narrow hallway, stopping in front of a door that stood ajar with a key in the lock. He checked behind him to make sure no one was watching and opened it a little wider. It was a walk-in cupboard half-stocked with cleaning products. He left the door ajar as he'd found it and continued on to the back exit.

He pushed the rusty iron door open and looked outside. A shaded alley ran down the side of the restaurant and intersected with a main road about a hundred metres away.

Satisfied there was no immediate danger and having established a clear exit route, he headed back inside.

Erina stood at the counter, placing an order. He chose a table set against the back wall and waited. They'd have their coffee and, if no one suspicious turned up, leave through the back lane.

The front door swung open.

Two elderly female tourists with pale skin and bright red, sweaty faces entered. They wore matching blue and white Hawaiian shirts and their bodies visibly relaxed in the air-conditioned cool after the heat and humidity outside.

They headed for the counter, passing Erina, who was making for Carter's table carrying a tray with two takeaway coffee cups and a white paper bag.

Behind her, two teenage girls with long blonde hair pushed through the entrance wearing sarongs and bikini tops, listening to their iPods.

Erina placed his coffee in front of him, sat down and tore the bag open. Inside was a coconut and palm sugar slice, her favourite.

The front door of the cafe swung open again and the two young Indonesian men they'd spotted on the street came in. They stood at the entrance, scanning the room. One of them looked over at Carter, leant close to his mate and whispered something.

Carter and Erina stood up at once and walked towards a sign that read *Rest Rooms*. Five metres past it, they turned down the hallway and broke into a jog.

When they came to the cleaning cupboard, Carter grabbed Erina's arm and then glanced behind him, checking that the two men weren't yet following them.

No one was watching. He opened the door wide for Erina. She stepped inside. He took out the key, squeezed in beside her and closed the door, locking it.

A dim light leaked under the bottom.

He grabbed the smooth handle of a mop in his left hand and listened. The distant hum of the cafe echoed through the thin walls.

For twenty seconds they stood absolutely still, breathing in the sharp smell of bleach. At first Carter heard nothing out of the ordinary, but then the sound of two sets of footsteps walking on concrete came towards them.

The footsteps stopped outside the cupboard.

A shadow blocked the light coming under the door.

Carter clenched his right hand into a fist and shifted his weight onto the balls of his feet. He felt Erina tensing beside him, controlling her soft breath, preparing herself to strike.

Someone turned the doorhandle back and forth twice and pushed against the door.

Time crawled by. Then the footsteps started up again, moving down the hallway away from them, gathering speed as they neared the back exit.

A door opened and then slammed shut.

Carter waited a few seconds. He then unlocked the door, pushed it open and looked up and down the deserted hallway. The two Sungkar clan spies had obviously headed straight for the back alley, thinking he and Erina had exited that way.

They stepped out of the cupboard and walked at a brisk pace back into the cafe. Before heading out the door, they grabbed their takeaway coffees and the coconut slice, which were still sitting at the table.

Outside in the street Carter turned towards the shrill ring of a bell. A bright red three-wheeled motorised taxi was heading towards them.

He hailed it and they slid onto the seat, under the shade of a cloth canopy. It wasn't a perfect hide-out, but it'd do for now and get them away from Starbucks.

Erina leant forwards and said to the driver, 'Terus sitir.' *Just drive.*

CHAPTER 5

Carter and Erina stepped out of the vehicle and headed towards the Green Monkey Cafe, one of a string of thatch-roofed coffee shops and restaurants that lined Kuta Beach and attracted a young backpacker crowd.

They entered via an alley that ran along the back to reduce the likelihood of being seen. Once inside, Carter saw no sign of Jacko, even though he and Erina were ten minutes late for their 4 p.m. meeting.

He looked through the front opening and onto the beach, where a dozen men and women in their late teens and early twenties sat in a circle on white plastic chairs under raffia beach umbrellas, playing a drinking game. The Eagles' 'Take It Easy' rang out from a set of speakers outside.

The song transported him back to the fibro shack he'd lived in with his mother in Lennox, back when he was a kid. She'd loved seventies music. He remembered her sitting on the back porch of their house when he was around six years old, singing along with the Eagles on the radio while smoking what he now knew was a marijuana joint.

'You want me to call Jacko?' Erina asked.

'Let's give him a few more minutes.'

One of the backpackers, a young blonde guy with a goatee and frizzy hair, lifted a coconut to his mouth, threw his head back and drank to the chant of 'drink it down, down, down'.

He was most likely drinking an 'Arak Attack', a potent mixture of the local liquor, which was fifty per cent alcohol, with orange and coconut juice. He drained the coconut, banged it down on the table and burped.

The other players laughed and clapped.

A young Balinese waitress in a pink and yellow dress carried a tray of empty bottles and dirty glasses through the entrance.

Erina called out to her, 'You seen Jacko?'

'No,' she replied. 'You like cold drink?'

Erina looked at Carter, who shook his head. 'We'll wait, thanks,' she said.

The backpackers outside erupted in another round of wild cheering, drowning out the iconic opening bars of Elton John's 'Benny and the Jets'.

Carter looked around the indoor section of the cafe. Jacko called this place his second office. It was fairly basic: a dozen tables covered by red and white plastic tablecloths and bare wooden walls.

Carter was about to sit down at one of the tables when he heard a familiar voice from the rear of the cafe and glanced behind him.

A big bear of a man with shoulder-length sun-bleached hair filled the back door. He wore a short-sleeved batik cotton shirt, black board shorts and green thongs. At first glance he looked like a typical Australian tourist, interested primarily in drinking beer and having a good time, but he had a laptop bag slung over one shoulder, and to Carter he looked tired and drawn, and older than his forty-five years. Clearly the events of the last twenty-four hours had affected him. Still, when he saw Carter and Erina, his face lit up with a broad, welcoming grin.

Carter walked towards him and put out his hand.

'Don't give me this "shake your hand" bullshit,' Jacko said. 'Give us a hug, you old bastard.'

He dropped his bag beside the table, wrapped his arms around Carter and squeezed tight.

Carter breathed in the familiar combination of aftershave, deodorant and clove cigarettes, relieved to see his friend.

Jacko released his grip, turned towards Erina and put out his arms. 'I'm so sorry, love, I really am. We'll get 'em back. Promise.'

He threw his arms around her. Jacko was one of the few people Erina let hug her. They held each other tight.

After a moment or two she patted him on the shoulder, gently pulled away from him and asked, 'So what's the latest at the hospital?'

'It looks like everyone's going to pull through, thank Christ. But I'm buggered if I know where this'll leave us. The order's been well and truly fucked over.'

Carter looked at Erina, who dropped her gaze. They both sat down.

Jacko settled in a seat opposite them. 'Sorry I'm late, but I just got off the blower with Djoran. He's expecting you.'

'I'll bet he is,' Erina said.

'What do you mean by that?' Jacko asked.

'How well do you know this guy?'

'Well enough,' Jacko said. 'He's very tight with Kemala.'

'That's not what I asked.'

'Djoran's a top bloke. He's been undercover, training as one of Samudra's mujaheddin for the last five months. In my book, that takes a huge ticker.'

'What's a Sufi doing getting involved in a fight against terrorism? They're supposed to spend their time transcending the physical world and getting high on God.'

'I'm buggered if I know what motivates him. But Kemala vouches for him one hundred per cent.'

'That's my point.'

'What?'

'I've been concerned about her relationship with Thomas ever since they became close,' Erina continued. 'I'm starting to wonder whether Kemala is the saint everyone thinks she is.'

'Have you ever brought it up with him?' Carter asked, knowing Thomas rarely discussed his personal affairs with anyone, including his daughter.

'I tried a few times,' she said, 'but he wouldn't go there. Look, I doubt they're having a full-on sexual relationship, because of her beliefs, but he's besotted with her. It's ridiculous – he's like a teenager. Though he'd never admit it.'

'And?' Carter asked, though he suspected he knew where this was going.

'She's Samudra's sister. The whole family is corrupt in one way or another and they hate the order for killing Arung. Just because she's a woman doesn't mean she's above scrutiny.'

'And just because she's a Muslim and belongs to the Sungkar family doesn't make her a terrorist,' Carter said.

'Don't forget,' Jacko said, 'she's the one who alerted Thomas to Samudra's intentions.'

'That could've all been part of a plan to infiltrate the order.'

'That's a real stretch,' Jacko said.

Erina shrugged. 'Think about it. Kemala disappeared four days before the attacks on the order began.'

'You're being paranoid,' Jacko said. 'Your father trusts her completely.'

'And maybe his blind trust helped get us into the position we're in,' Erina said. 'They've been one step ahead of us with each of these attacks. We can't assume anything.'

She leant back in her chair.

Carter glanced at Jacko. 'What do you reckon?' he asked.

'I reckon she's the best thing that's happened to Thomas for a long while. She just has to walk into a room to bring a smile to his face. And they've known each other on and off for ten years.'

'But they've only been close for less than a year,' Erina said, 'since Samudra took over the clan. Samudra and Kemala could've hatched something together.'

'You sure you're not being overprotective or even a tad jealous?' Jacko asked.

She tied her hair up into a loose bun. 'Some women will do anything to protect their family.'

'Maybe,' Carter said. 'But Thomas does nothing without thinking it through. I reckon Jacko's right. If Thomas trusts her, so can we.'

'What you're both overlooking is that most men, including my father, are hopeless when it comes to relationships.'

Carter shifted in his seat. 'And you're good at them?'

'At least I don't get taken advantage of.'

'You never hang around long enough to let that happen.'

She gave him a withering look. 'We both know you don't stay alive in this game for very long if you expect the best of everyone.'

'Nor if you always expect the worst.'

She sat up straighter. 'These attacks on the order are game-changers.

We can't overlook any possibilities. It's no time to be oversensitive.'

'And it's no time to shut down.'

'What—'

'Hang on, you two,' Jacko interrupted. 'We're getting off track. The situation is what it is. We have to deal with what's in front of us.'

He stood up. 'And if you'd let me get a word in, I was about say Djoran told me where Thomas and Wayan are being held on the island.'

He started walking to the kitchen.

'What are you doing?' Erina asked.

'I've been running around like a headless chook all day and I'm starved. I'm going to organise something to eat and drink before we get down to business. Then I'll show you what I've got.'

He walked a few more steps and turned back to Erina.

'He also informed me that Kemala is on the island. And here's the kicker. She's being held prisoner under armed guard on order from Samudra.'

Carter looked at Erina, whose expression revealed nothing. He knew this would have taken her by surprise, even if she didn't buy it or wasn't prepared to admit it.

CHAPTER 6

Carter watched Jacko take a long pull of beer from his bottle of Victoria Bitter, push it to one side and reach for his bag. Jacko set up his laptop on the table so Carter and Erina could both see and fired it up. A topographical map of Batak Island appeared on screen.

Despite his casual manner, Jacko had an uncanny ability to organise an operation to the last detail with a minimum of drama.

'We've been checking out the island and the clan's activity for the last month,' Jacko said. 'Since Samudra took over, he's turned it into an unofficial Islamic state governed by sharia law. I saw a video on his website of a young woman being stoned for adultery.'

Erina poured sparkling mineral water into a glass and said, 'I've seen the site too – there's some spooky shit going down on that island.'

Outside, the backpackers let out yet another round of cheers.

Jacko's forefinger ran down the middle of the map.

'The island is divided in two by this mountain range. On the southern side is a village of peasant farmers and fishermen. The Sungkar clan control the mosques and clerics, which gives them huge influence over the people on the island, all strict Muslims. Though there are pockets of dissent.'

He tapped another key. An aerial photograph appeared, showing what looked like a military training complex with a large white mosque in the centre.

'This is Samudra's compound on the northern side,' Jacko said. 'It's a full-blown training camp for his mujaheddin.'

His forefinger circled a group of buildings and bungalows. 'That's the accommodation and admin block, where a high-tech command centre has been set up. And that's the airstrip. They own a light plane and a helicopter, which means they can fly in and out without bothering too much about airport security.'

He pointed to a fenced-off enclosure housing two cell-like buildings. 'This is where Djoran reckons Thomas and Wayan are being held.'

'Can we land on the island?' Carter asked.

'No way, Jose. Security's tighter than a fish's arsehole. The pilot I've lined up will drop you at an atoll five clicks away. Then you'll take a jet ski to the island. Budget fifty minutes for the one-way ocean trip. If you travel at low throttle and keep engine noise to a minimum, you'll sound like a regular fishing boat and won't set off any alarms.'

Jacko took a sip of beer and tapped another key. The map of Batak Island reappeared. He indicated a rocky cove on the village side of the island. 'You land here. Then I suggest you make your way to this point.'

He touched a clearing at the edge of the mountains that cut the island in two. 'There's a steep cliff you'll need to climb to reach the compound's perimeter. It'll shield you from any electronic surveillance.'

Carter and Erina nodded, following his logic.

'Once you reach the top, you launch your assault on the compound. Djoran has downloaded a set of up-to-date security codes, which I'll give you. He reckons once you're within a hundred metres of the compound, you can wirelessly hack into their system and shut down security.'

Erina cocked her head to the side and looked at Jacko directly.

'I know what you're thinking, Erina,' Jacko said, 'but trusting Djoran is the only option we have at this point. It's one of those times where we have to show some faith in our fellow man.'

'How do we find him?' Carter asked before Erina had a chance to respond.

'He assures me he'll find you. Take the satphone in case there's a dire emergency and you need me to bail you out. But he said to avoid making any calls on the island unless absolutely necessary. Their scanning devices pick up phone signals. He's figured out a way of making the occasional call to me safely, but you'd need to hook up with him first and follow his procedures to the letter.'

'What about the chopper?' Erina asked.

'The only one I could get comes with a pilot.'

'What's he like?'

'A real Pommy wanker. Wouldn't trust him as far as I could kick him, even with only one good leg. But he knows the area and has plenty of experience. He'll get you there and back.'

'How do you know?' Erina asked.

A big grin spread across Jacko's face. 'Because I only paid him a deposit.'

CHAPTER 7

The waitress placed a serving of chicken satay sticks on the table. The aromatic blend of hot oil, chilli and roasted peanuts reminded Carter of just how much he enjoyed Indonesian food and how hungry he was.

He took a stick, bit off a mouthful of hot, spicy chicken and savoured it for a moment before glancing at Erina. She took a napkin to hold one end of the stick and used a fork to pull the meat off one piece at a time.

She was still pissed off with him, he could tell, though he didn't know why. But clearing the air with Erina would have to wait a little longer. There were still questions to be answered. First up, he wanted to know if Jacko had any idea about what might've happened to the head of Trident's daughter. It still bothered him that the organisation had potentially been compromised.

He turned to Jacko. 'What've you found out about Callaghan's daughter?'

Jacko swallowed a mouthful of chicken.

'Apparently she's pretty wild, and this isn't the first time she's gone missing in action. Initially, I figured she'd just run off with some guy she'd met, but with the shit that's gone down in the last couple of days I wouldn't be surprised if the clan has nabbed her.'

He took a meditative pull on his beer. 'And if they have her, then Callaghan is their puppet. That's a serious worry, considering what the clan might be planning for Sydney.'

'He could've clued them in on where the city is most vulnerable and how to avoid security,' Erina said.

'Exactly what I was thinking,' Jacko replied. 'I'll make some enquiries, and give you a full run-down when you get back from the island.'

Carter nodded, knowing he could rely on Jacko to get all the necessary information and make any arrangements.

The waitress returned carrying a large plate of fried prawns and another of golden brown lumpia – spring rolls filled with minced pork and vegetables – with a bowl of sweet chilli sauce.

Carter picked up one of the rolls, took a bite and said, 'Are there any other operatives on hand we can call on?'

'As a matter of fact,' Jacko said, 'there are four guys from Detachment 88 staying at Candi Dasa. I've got a solid relationship with their immediate superior. I reckon I could line something up at a pinch. They're pretty fair operators, but they don't have anything like your skills or experience.'

Detachment 88 was the Indonesian counterterrorist organisation, so named to honour the eighty-eight Australians killed in the 2002 Bali bombing. They were funded and trained by American and Australian government agencies. Since 2003, they'd successfully hunted down, arrested and killed many members of Jemaah Islamiah and other suspected terrorist organisations.

The group attacked with sledgehammer-like efficiency, but lacked the subtlety and patience required for an operation like this. More importantly, there was every chance Samudra, with his wealth and influence, had corrupted sections of the organisation.

Carter liked to mull over all possibilities with an open mind. Often useful ideas emerged in the process. Bringing in some outside help had its merits. It meant they'd have backup and there'd be someone to help Jacko find out what Alex and the clan were up to in Sydney.

Erina rolled her eyes. 'Detachment 88 – you really want to get those cowboys involved?' There was an edge to her voice. 'You're saying six of us should go to the island and hook up with Djoran?'

Carter shrugged, deliberately casual, knowing it would infuriate her. He wanted to provoke her into an outburst, get her to admit what was bugging her.

'I could take a couple of guys and you could stay behind and work with Jacko,' he said. 'Start checking out what's going down in Sydney. And if there's trouble on the island, you'd be ready to bail us out.'

'Please tell me you're joking.'

'Just brainstorming.'

'There's no way I'm staying behind and you know it.'

'Look—'

'What makes you think you can come in like this and start running the show?'

'We need to work as a team and consider our options,' he said.

'It's a bit late to call yourself a team player. Let alone think you can call the shots. It's not your father whose life is at stake.'

He pushed his plate to one side and wiped the stickiness off his fingers with a paper napkin. 'You need to take the personal emotion out of this and get your head together.'

'Don't try to psychoanalyse me. Look after your own game.'

'We're in this together, Erina, but I can't work with you when you're like this.'

'Like what?'

'You've been pissed off ever since we left Woodforde's property. Now tell me what's got you so angry or god help me I'll team up with Detachment 88 and leave you here with Jacko.'

'I'd leave you behind if I didn't need you,' she said.

'Well, you do. So get used to it.'

'Once this is over you can fuck off and go surfing for all I care.'

'Suits me.'

She stood up. 'You're unbelievable.'

Carter turned to Jacko, who shook a clove cigarette out of its soft packet. 'Hey, don't look at me,' he said. 'I'm just organising the logistics.'

Erina looked directly at Carter. 'I'm not discussing this with you anymore.'

'Erina, sit down, please.'

She turned to Jacko. 'Sorry, big guy, just need to clear my head.'

She picked up her daypack from the floor and headed out through the front of the restaurant and down to the beach.

CHAPTER 8

Jacko inhaled on his cigarette, causing the tobacco and cloves to flare and crackle. He looked at Carter through the cloud of sweet-smelling smoke. 'You handled that well, champ.'

Carter moved his chair away from the table. 'No one ever accused me of being smart around women.'

'You're not wrong there,' Jacko said. 'But she's no ordinary woman.'

'Tell me about it.'

Carter took a long drink of water and looked through the open shopfront towards the beach. The backpackers had taken a break from their drinking game. Further down, Erina was walking across the hard sand towards the ocean with her hands in her pockets.

'She's still mad at me for leaving the order,' Carter said.

Jacko dipped the last spring roll in sweet chilli sauce, took a bite and washed it down with beer. 'Can't say I blame her. But I understand why you did what you did.'

'Thanks, mate, I appreciate that.'

There was a pause before Jacko replied. 'I'm not the one who's in love with you, though,' he said.

'Jacko, she hates me.'

Jacko shrugged. 'It's the flip side of the same coin.'

'If this is her idea of love, she has no idea what it is,' Carter said.

'And you do?'

Carter couldn't help but smile. 'Good point.'

'I'm none too flash with this relationship stuff myself,' Jacko said. He took a last puff on his cigarette and ground the butt out in the ashtray. 'There's a part of me that would've loved to have had a wife and a few kids.'

'Yeah?'

'Thought seriously about it ten years ago. A normal life, you know?'

Carter nodded.

'But it's not who I am. I made my choice and the order is family enough for me. It's a good life.'

'It has its moments.'

Jacko took a slow sip of beer, put the bottle down and said, 'I reckon you need to tell Erina how you feel and sort this shit out, right now, or it's going to cause trouble.'

'I know.'

'Getting involved when you're both in this line of work was always going to be tough. But you love her and she loves you. You both need to recognise the fact.'

'She's the only woman I've ever wanted.'

'Then man up and sort this shit out. The point is she's hurting and she's scared. Any dill can see that. You just have to talk to her.'

Carter felt himself nodding again. Jacko had got it right.

Jacko reached into his computer bag. 'In the meantime, this might cheer you up.'

He handed Carter a piece of A4 paper headed *Equipment Inventory*.

Carter read the list. Two Glock 18s with adjustable stocks and suppressors, two clips of nineteen hollow-point rounds for each weapon, a twenty-metre length of nylon cord, a pair of night-vision binoculars, three Emerson throwing knives, a blowpipe and a pack of drug-tipped darts. Everything he'd hoped for and then some.

Carter felt his shoulders relax.

Jacko reached into his pocket, pulled out a set of keys and handed them to him. 'You'll find everything in the usual place. You and Erina can crash there tonight.'

Carter took the keys and slipped them into the secure thigh pocket of his cargo pants.

Jacko then held up a red memory stick attached to a black lanyard and waved it in front of him. 'And this little beauty has every bit of information you'll need, including what I've just shown you.'

Carter hung the memory stick around his neck and slipped it under his T-shirt. 'I don't know how you pulled this together at such short notice.'

'Mate,' Jacko said, 'it's what I do. Now go out there, sort out your shit with Erina, bring Thomas and Wayan home alive and take this crazy motherfucker and his mujaheddin zombies down.'

Carter picked up his daypack and stood. 'I'll see what I can do.'

Jacko raised his bottle of VB in a salute. 'Good luck, champ. I've always got your back.'

'I know,' Carter said. 'Thanks, mate.'

He headed for the front of the restaurant without another word, but before stepping out onto the beach, he turned and gave Jacko a two-finger salute. Jacko dipped his head and returned the gesture.

—

Carter walked down across the soft sand towards Erina. She stood a few metres from the water's edge, her backpack by her feet.

Pink Floyd's 'Wish You Were Here' played from the speakers on the sand outside the cafe – another of his mother's favourite songs.

The air was calm and the sinking sun still had a gentle bite. A rolling wave broke out on the reef and a guy on a longboard paddled for it.

Carter dropped his pack on the sand next to hers.

'You've come to apologise?' she asked, looking out to sea.

'I came to talk.'

She turned to face him. 'Haven't you said enough?' She shook her head, incredulous.

'Thomas has always been like a father to me,' he said. 'You know that.'

'And that's supposed to make me accept what you did? If you really believe that, you should've shown him more respect. You just took off without giving any explanation or warning.'

'I'm sorry.'

'Sometimes sorry doesn't cut it,' she said. 'We both know this shit storm with the Sungkar clan could've been contained if you hadn't walked out on us.'

Carter clenched and unclenched his right hand. Finally they were getting to it. 'Erina, there's no point playing "what if". If Thomas hadn't made me sink that boat, Arung would be alive and none of this would've happened. No one could've predicted any of this. As I'm sure you understand. We all do the best we can with what's in front of us.'

'What you did was wrong. Leaving us was wrong. You betrayed the order.'

'I did what I had to do at the time.'

She stared at him without blinking. 'We needed you, Carter. You left us vulnerable. Thomas had come to rely on you more than you can imagine and was devastated when you disappeared. You're responsible for whatever happens to him – and to Wayan. Their kidnapping and the attack at Ubud are both on you.'

Carter opened his mouth to speak, about to argue, but then thought better of it. He heard Jacko's voice in his head: *She's hurting and she's scared. Any dill can see that. You just have to talk to her.*

He took a slow breath. 'When you cut me out of your life, I didn't handle it too well. I see that now. But do you understand how much I care about you? Have you ever thought about the effect you have on me?'

She'd always had trouble admitting fault or blame, and he didn't expect an apology from her now. But he needed to say it, to tell her how she'd hurt him – for his own benefit as much as hers. 'It was because of you that I left,' he said. 'At least that was a big part of it. I couldn't bear to be near you anymore, couldn't bear the way you treated me.'

In an instant her right hand flashed through the air, aiming for his head. He caught her wrist and held it tight. Then, with his left hand, he grabbed her behind the head and pulled her mouth to his.

She struggled to free herself from his grasp and then, suddenly, her whole body relaxed.

An electric charge ran up his spine.

Their lips met, and it was as if they'd never been apart, as if they'd always belonged together. The familiar chemical reaction came on with a rush, making him feel lightheaded and dizzy. The euphoria was almost like a drug, sending him into an altered state.

Then, just as suddenly, an exploding pain in his groin snapped him back into reality.

He released his grip on her and buckled over. 'Shit, Erina, what was that for?'

'Because I can and you deserved it.'

He looked up at her and grimaced, then walked in a circle until the pain started to subside.

'I get the point,' he said.

She stepped towards him and placed her hands around his face. He felt the gentle touch of her lips on his.

Behind him the waves lapped on the shore, and as their kiss grew deeper, her body trembled. He wrapped his arms around her and held her tight.

'I fucking hate you,' she whispered.

'Now the truth comes out.'

'I thought you'd always be there for me. I've missed you every day since you left.'

'I'm here now.'

'It seems I'm not as tough as I thought.'

'Perhaps you're human after all?'

She smiled. 'Let's not get too carried away.'

He leant in to kiss her again.

BOOM.

A loud explosion ripped through the late-afternoon air. Carter felt the force of it against his back. He shoved Erina down onto the hard sand and covered her with his body.

CHAPTER 9

Carter lay on top of Erina, his ears ringing from the explosion and the sound of people screaming on the beach.

She moved underneath him. He rolled off her, pushed himself onto his feet and stared through the billowing smoke in the direction of the Green Monkey Cafe. All that was left was a smouldering shell. The clan had once again got the jump on them with devastating results.

He reached down and pulled Erina to her feet.

'Fuck,' she said.

Unless Jacko had left the cafe before the bomb exploded, there was no way he could've survived the blast.

A film of charcoal slowly covered the sand. On all sides, people were shouting and screaming, running away from the point of the blast, including some who were bleeding from their injuries.

Carter felt like he needed to throw up, but he breathed deeply, trying to clear his thoughts. What had happened had happened – he needed to deal with the present.

'You stay here,' he said. 'Cover my back and see if you can identify anyone suspicious.'

'Okay.'

He ran across the sand towards the smoking ruins of the cafe, breathing in the smell of burning wood and seared flesh, the odour of violent death.

The table where the backpackers had been sitting was no more. He examined their charred and bloody remains, seeking any sign of life. He found none and moved to the entrance of the cafe and peered inside. All that was left standing was the iron stove and a coffee machine. The rest was flaming rubble and charred body parts.

Just inside the front door, he saw an arm, but no torso. He recognised Jacko's diver's watch, the face smashed.

He quelled the urge to cry out. Instead, he turned and walked towards the beach, struggling to put one foot in front of the other. Ten metres from the cafe he leant forwards with his hands on his knees and stared at the now black sand, feeling sick and numb.

From the direction of the airport he heard the wail of approaching sirens. He took a slow, deep breath, stood up, and looked at where the backpackers had been laughing and joking only a few minutes ago. The young kids had been caught in the wrong place at the wrong time, their lives cut short by a war that meant nothing to them. Their deaths were even more senseless than Jacko's. It was one thing to kill your enemy, another to take the life of innocents.

The sirens grew louder and more intense, indicating that ambulances and police vehicles were converging on the beach.

He turned and forced himself to stride swiftly over the sand towards Erina. Her pack lay open beside her, giving her easy access to a weapon should she need it.

'Jacko?' Erina called as he drew near, but he could tell by the tremor in her voice she already knew the answer.

He shook his head.

Her head dropped and she pounded her fist into her right thigh. 'Fucking bastards.'

'We have to go,' he said.

There was nothing either of them could do or say to bring Jacko back. They needed to keep moving.

'It's fucking madness,' she said, looking at him, her eyes welling with tears.

'I know.'

'Were there any survivors?'

'We can't help them.'

He didn't need to tell her the injured needed proper medical attention. The ambulances and police would be there in a couple of minutes.

The sirens grew louder. They couldn't afford to get caught up in a police investigation and have their departure for Batak Island jeopardised. He took her hand and squeezed it.

They gathered up their daypacks and began walking away from the cafe at a brisk but steady pace, not wanting to draw attention to themselves.

His body felt slow and heavy, but there was no looking back.

BOOK FOUR

CHAPTER 1

Legian Street, Kuta Beach, Bali, 7.20 p.m., 26 December

Charles Peacock stretched his lanky near-naked six-foot frame along the stained sofa, pumped his fist and yelled, 'Go, you Hammers!'

He was watching his soccer team, West Ham United, play Fulham on a small television set in his Kuta studio at the Peaceful Garden Apartments, which were anything but.

A couple of kids were crying in the apartment next door and heavy traffic roared along Legian Street, just a stone's throw away. A fan stuck on full blast whirred overhead, clicking to a rhythmic beat.

He adjusted the crotch of his navy boxer shorts and wiped the sweat off his face with a threadbare handtowel lying next to him.

Yet another siren wailed outside the open window, drowning out the football commentary. The blast he'd heard a couple of hours ago had stirred the local police into a frenzy of activity. Having served in the first Gulf War, he'd bet a sizeable sum on it being a bomb.

He turned up the television to drown out the distracting noise and looked at the half-empty bottle of Johnnie Walker Red Label sitting on the coffee table beside him. It was lined up next to a jug of water, a cracked glass, a foil of hash, a pipe, a razor blade and a disposable yellow Bic cigarette lighter.

Through an act of great will, he'd held off having his first drink of the day. He had a flying job the next morning at 6.30 a.m. and needed to be in control. He figured if he stayed straight and sober until 7.30 this evening, he'd be fine.

A West Ham striker scored another goal, making it 2–1 in their favour. He double-pumped his fist in the air and sung out, 'Yeeesss! We are the champions!'

Football was his religion and reminded him of how much he wanted out of this shithole of a country and to return home to the United Kingdom.

After fifteen years Bali had long lost its charm and he'd been trying to sell his helicopter for the last five months without a nibble, let alone a bite.

He sneaked a look at his watch: 7.25 p.m.

Close enough. After all, West Ham were now in the lead, a good enough reason to celebrate. He poured three fingers of whisky and a splash of water into the glass.

He lifted his drink, toasted the television and swallowed. The Johnnie Walker slid down his throat and warmed his stomach.

He let out a deep satisfied sigh, then bent over the table, cut a small chunk of black hash from the block with the razor blade, crumbled it into fragments between his thumb and forefinger and packed it into the black pipe.

As he lifted the pipe to his lips, a sharp double knock on the hollow plywood door made him look up.

His first instinct was to ignore it, but his dealer often called uninvited and he'd hate to miss him. His stash was getting low.

Another loud knock sounded.

He pushed himself up from the couch, pulled on a cotton shirt and a pair of baggy rugby shorts, then trudged to the door, mumbling, 'Hold your damn horses. I'm coming.'

The sweet smell of a clove cigarette wafted from under the door. He opened it.

Two well-dressed and clean-cut Indonesians stood in front of him. Both around thirty years old, they wore sandals, black trousers and batik shirts. The taller one stared at him through cold brown eyes.

'Are you Charles Peacock?' he asked in fluent English.

'Who wants to know?'

The man levelled his hard gaze at him. 'You don't need to know.'

Peacock ran his eyes over the two men. 'What's this about?'

'We have a business proposition for you. I understand you have a helicopter for sale?'

The taller Indonesian moved towards the doorway without being asked. His mate followed.

Peacock stepped aside to let them in. He stood just inside the door and watched them cast an eye over his apartment. Then he looked down the hallway to make sure no one else was there, closed the door and said, 'I'm listening.'

CHAPTER 2

Carter sat strapped into the front passenger seat of a red and black Bell 407 helicopter next to the pilot, cruising across the Indian Ocean at two hundred and thirty kilometres an hour towards Lengkuas Atoll, nearly eight hundred kilometres from Bali. After refuelling at an island en route, they expected to arrive in forty minutes.

He checked his watch and ran through the time line in his head. It was now 2.40 p.m., twenty-two hours since Jacko's death and just under two and a half days from when he was attacked in the surf at Lennox. If everything went according to plan, which he knew was unlikely, they'd rescue Thomas and Wayan that night from Batak Island and be back in Bali tomorrow, 28 December. They'd then set about determining the best way to deal with Samudra's planned terrorist attack on Sydney.

Erina was in the passenger seat behind, working on her computer. They'd met the pilot, Charles Peacock, at Denpasar Airport shortly before dawn. He'd been half an hour late, his breath smelt of whisky and their scheduled 6.30 a.m. departure was delayed until nearly 8.30. Peacock claimed the short notice he was given had resulted in a tangle of unavoidable problems that had caused the hold-up.

Erina had suggested to Carter that they knock Peacock out and fly the helicopter themselves, but he'd managed to convince her that they might need him and it was best to wait and see how the operation panned out.

They were both struggling to keep it together after Jacko's murder. There was no time for grief, no time to stop and try to make sense of his death. The violent attack had made their concern for Thomas and Wayan even more intense and the tragedy had brought them closer together. They'd slept in the same bed that night, just holding each other, silent. Though they'd barely even spoken, what they'd shared was more tender and intimate than if they'd made love.

Before going to sleep, Carter had made a promise to himself. Not only would he rescue Thomas and Wayan, but he'd take down Alex, Samudra and his mujaheddin or die trying. He hadn't chosen to start this fight, but after Jacko's murder he intended to finish it.

They'd woken at 5 a.m. and listened to the early-morning news on Asian CNN. It reported that the blast had killed an unnamed Australian, two Balinese cafe workers, three Swedish and two German backpackers and a man believed to have been the suicide bomber. Six others had been seriously injured and no one had yet claimed responsibility. Good luck or fate rather than good management had allowed Carter and Erina to escape unharmed.

He looked over his shoulder at her now, headphones in place. She was poring over the information from Jacko's memory stick. Throwing herself into a task was her way of dealing with uncomfortable emotion. She lifted her head and they exchanged the weakest of smiles. Carter turned to the front and sneaked a quick glance at Peacock. The long, lanky Englishman sat in the driver's seat staring stony-faced towards the cloudy grey horizon.

The muffled roar of the engine hummed through Carter's headphones, somehow comforting him. If all went according to plan, he and Erina would take the jet ski stowed in the rear cargo section to Batak Island and be there in just over an hour. Peacock would remain on the atoll with the helicopter until they returned with Thomas and Wayan.

Carter ran his fingers over the waterproof daypack that lay nestled between his feet, then slipped his hand into the thigh pocket of his pants. He felt the smooth steel of three drug-tipped darts and their hard plastic covers.

Using them on Peacock would be a last resort. But, like Erina, something about the man bothered him. They would need to be sure both pilot and helicopter remained on Lengkuas Atoll until they returned from Batak Island or called him in to pick them up.

—

Twenty minutes later, what looked like the haze of an island appeared on the horizon in front of them. Carter lifted the high-powered binoculars hanging round his neck.

A crescent-shaped beach came into focus, a curve of white sand about four hundred metres long. The water was blue and clear. Half-a-dozen children played at the western end in between two run-down fishing boats pulled up onto the sand.

He switched on the headset. 'I presume that's Lengkuas Atoll ahead?'

'That's where I was paid to take you.'

Carter refocused on the island in front of him. A couple of malibu surfboards lay in the shade of a palm tree. He made a mental note and scanned further down the beach.

A group of a dozen or so Indonesians were gathered at the eastern end. He zoomed in closer.

They were fanning out in military formation, carrying what looked like automatic weapons slung over their shoulders.

He swore under his breath.

Two things were clear. The villagers were expecting them and this was definitely not the atoll he'd seen last night on Jacko's memory stick.

He refocused the binoculars and a shot of adrenalin pulsed through his veins.

Two villagers were mounting a surface-to-air rocket-launcher onto a wooden platform.

CHAPTER 3

Carter turned to look at the pilot. Peacock was staring into the distance, apparently oblivious to the looming danger.

There was no way the guy was a born-again fundamentalist willing to sacrifice his life for Allah. From what Carter could tell, his only religion was alcohol, maybe drugs and probably the dollar. He might well have sold them out, but he didn't appear to be expecting any welcoming committee that might threaten his personal safety.

Carter spoke into the headset. 'Peacock, you need to cut the speed.'

He wanted to slow down rather than change course, so as not to alert the reception committee that they were onto them.

Peacock turned towards him. 'What are you talking about?'

Carter put a hard edge into his voice. 'Don't fuck with me. I'm not asking. Slow down now.'

Peacock spoke without looking at him. 'Back off, you Aussie dickhead. I'm flying this—'

Carter placed his hand on Peacock's shoulder and jammed his thumb into the pressure point at the top of the neck.

Peacock winced, let go of the control stick and yelled out, 'For Christ's sake.'

The helicopter slowed dramatically and wobbled. The nose dipped.

Carter braced himself with his feet, maintaining his grip on Peacock's shoulder. He knew exactly what was about to happen.

The helicopter lurched downwards, freefalling twenty metres before levelling off.

Erina's voice cut through the headset. 'What the fuck?'

The helicopter tilted hard to starboard, the nose pointing down at an acute and dangerous angle.

They'd start to dive at any moment.

He released the pressure on Peacock's shoulder.

Peacock snatched the controls. 'You crazy bastard! You trying to kill us?'

'Just getting your attention. You lied to us.'

The helicopter levelled out and hovered above the ocean without moving forwards.

'I did nothing of the sort.'

'If this is Lengkuas Atoll,' Carter said, 'Erina is the Virgin Mary and the reception committee assembling on the beach are the three wise men.'

'You're just being paranoid,' Peacock said, obviously trying to maintain the charade. 'It'll just be a couple of villagers out and about, wondering who we are.'

'Bullshit,' Carter said.

He thrust the binoculars in front of Peacock's face. 'Focus on the beach. West of the village. At eleven o'clock.'

Peacock grabbed them in his left hand and did as he was told.

Carter watched carefully to gauge his reaction and make sure the rocket-launcher came as a complete surprise.

Peacock swung the binoculars along the coastline.

Then he stopped and leant forwards.

'Sweet mother of God.'

The bravado had evaporated. He appeared to be genuinely shocked by what he saw.

'What the fuck is going on?' Erina asked.

Carter took the binoculars from Peacock, passed them to her and pointed to the beach.

She took hold of them and focused. 'Holy shit. Is that Batak Island?'

'You better ask Peacock,' Carter said.

Peacock said nothing.

Carter heard Erina unbuckle her seatbelt. She leant over Peacock and held a knife to his throat. 'Well?' she said.

'Yes,' Peacock said. 'That's Batak. But don't do anything rash. You need me.'

Carter looked through the binoculars again.

'Shit.'

The villagers were aiming the rocket-launcher directly at them and looked like they were getting ready to fire.

CHAPTER 4

Batak Island loomed a little over two thousand metres away.

Peacock sat rigid at the controls. Erina continued to lean over his shoulder, still holding the blade a few centimetres from his neck.

'Watch the knife,' Peacock said.

'Give me a good reason why I shouldn't slit your throat,' Erina said.

'You need me.'

'Keep talking.'

'That missile has a range of over three and a half kilometres,' Peacock said, shooting the words out. 'If they open fire, we can't outrun it. I'm your best hope.'

'You got us into this shit storm.'

'And I can get you out.'

'Convince me.'

'I'm ex–Royal Air Force. I've trained for this. I was one of the best. But to do this, I'm going to need a drink.'

'What do you think, Carter?' Erina asked.

Carter could fly a helicopter but was far from an expert and hadn't done so for five years. Plus, he'd never flown a chopper like this and he knew the Bell 407 was a sensitive beast.

It required deft handling, with three sets of controls. The collective control stick, positioned to the pilot's left, changed the pitch of the rotors and forced the nose to rise or fall. The cyclical control stick, situated just in front of the pilot, between his legs, adjusted the angle of the rotor blades, turning the bird to the left or right. Finally, there were the pedals on the floor, which controlled the tail rotor, counteracting the torque of the main rotors and stabilising the flight. They also helped turn the helicopter to the right or left.

The idea was to work all three controls together to create a smooth flight. Normally a skilled pilot used subtle pressure rather than any sudden or dramatic movement. In a situation like this the pilot needed to know his machine as if it was an extension of himself.

Peacock was their best option.

'Give the man a drink,' Carter said.

Peacock's whole body relaxed. 'There's a bottle in the rear port-side locker.'

Carter studied him. Blotchy, pale and gaunt, the guy was a burnt-out shell of a man. But he suspected a skilled pilot lay underneath the wreckage.

Erina placed an opened bottle of Johnnie Walker Red Label into Peacock's left hand. He lifted the bottle to his mouth and took a long pull. He then took a deep, satisfied breath and positioned the bottle between his thighs.

There was an immediate shift in his demeanour. The colour returned to his face and the set of his jaw hardened.

Carter raised the binoculars. A ball of fire was flying through the air, heading straight towards them.

Peacock had seen it too. He turned the throttle up full and adjusted the controls decisively and aggressively. The generous shot of alcohol had transformed him. Carter knew the hit was temporary. But it only needed to last long enough to get them to the island.

The helicopter's engine roared. The vibrating body started to shake and shudder like it was about to break apart. For a long half-second the bird's position remained unchanged.

Then the adjustments kicked in. The quivering helicopter swayed sharply to the left and the nose plunged towards the ocean.

Carter gripped the side of the smooth leather seat and concentrated on the slow inhalation and exhalation of his breath, aiming to become totally alert and yet detached, as if watching a movie.

Thomas said a man afraid to die was of no use to anyone. Panic guaranteed defeat, and in this case certain death. But if a man remained calm, regardless of circumstances, there was a chance of victory.

Carter entered an emotionally neutral zone – a place between life and death, where time slowed and everything around him became clear and still.

Peacock adjusted the controls and the helicopter hurtled to the right.

Carter thought the radical move might have averted a hit. But then Erina's urgent voice came over the headset.

'Hard right, Peacock. It's coming straight for the tail.'

Carter looked out the back window and saw the ball of flame heading straight for them. 'Must be programmed to track heat.'

'Yeah,' Erina said, 'us.'

Peacock adjusted the controls, but the warning had come too late. The missile slammed into their tail with a sickening shudder and the helicopter's rear end swung wildly to the left.

It kept going, spinning three hundred and sixty degrees.

Once around.

Then another full circle.

Again and again.

The sky flashed by the window.

Peacock worked the controls frantically.

In less than three seconds, but what felt to Carter like a timeless eternity, the helicopter came out of the spin.

It pitched forwards and swayed from side to side as if drunk.

'Rotor's down,' Erina said, her tone urgent but calm.

Carter looked over his shoulder out the window. The back rotor had been knocked out and a trail of black smoke ballooned behind them. But though the engine whined and screamed, they were still in the air.

The helicopter only had to hold together for another minute for them to reach the island.

Then everything changed again.

The engine shut down and the helicopter stopped swaying. Carter glanced at Peacock.

He took another slug of whisky. The combination of the alcohol and this latest threat galvanised him into action. He switched the controls back and forth at a great rate in a desperate effort to restart the stalled engine.

Peacock was making all the right moves, but so far without success. They seemed suspended in time and space, hanging in midair.

Then, like someone had pressed play in a video game, the nose pointed down and the helicopter started to plummet at an alarming rate.

The ocean rushed towards them.

Carter knew if they hit the water at this speed, the impact would kill them. Peacock had just 1.2 seconds to make the appropriate response.

He adjusted the collective control stick to his left. This flattened the blades, allowing them to be driven by the wind, and slowed their rate of descent to around two thousand feet per second. A step in the right direction.

Simultaneously, he manoeuvred the cyclical stick in front of him, positioning the rotors so they sustained forward momentum, and the helicopter headed in the general direction of the island.

Through the headset, Erina said, 'It seems you can drink and fly.'

A hint of a smile formed on Peacock's face.

If they continued at this speed and trajectory, they'd hit the water at a workable speed and have a good chance of surviving the crash – but Carter knew better than to make any assumptions.

The back of the helicopter began fishtailing back and forth. The nose jerked up and down in a bucking motion. Telltale signs of a giant bird in the throes of death.

Carter glanced over at Peacock again. The pilot's concentration and breathing were steady. Good signs.

The nose dipped to the near vertical.

They began freefalling again towards the on-rushing ocean.

Peacock needed to come up with the perfect counter move.

Carter said nothing, wanting to give him the space to allow whatever skill and ingenuity he possessed to come through.

The pilot worked all three controls at once, making all the right adjustments in his effort to wrest back his dominance of the plunging beast and flatten out the near-vertical dive.

Carter glanced at Erina. She gave him one of her short nods.

He nodded back at her and braced his feet against the front of the helicopter to protect himself from the crushing force of impact.

For once in his life the prospect of entering the ocean did nothing for him.

CHAPTER 5

The helicopter shook and vibrated, plunging towards the choppy water three hundred metres below and closing fast.

Peacock yanked back on the cyclical stick and the chopper jerked upwards like a parachute had shot out its backside, slowing their fall.

He worked the controls with fierce determination and concentration.

Back and forth. Left and right.

Carter noted that the helicopter decelerated further, but to give them a decent chance of survival, Peacock needed to level out their dive. The helicopter's belly rather than its nose needed to hit the water first.

Peacock pulled the stick back hard, flaring the helicopter's rotors and creating upward pressure on its body. Their downward velocity slowed and the wounded bird's nose lifted to a healthier forty-five-degree angle.

Ninety metres from the water, Peacock slammed the stick forwards, releasing the flare of the rotors. The stored energy in the blades pushed against the force of gravity, restoring the angle of the hull and bringing it practically parallel to the ocean.

Peacock had one move left. He raised the collective stick, slowing their fall even further.

Carter had to hand it to Peacock. It'd been a brilliant piece of flying.

Peacock took a final slug of scotch. In a few short seconds they'd smack into the brick wall of water.

'Brace for impact,' Peacock said over the headphones.

'Thanks for the tip,' Erina replied.

Carter clenched his neck muscles to stop his head from whipping forwards on impact.

An instant later the underbelly crashed into the hard surface of the water. The excruciating sound of shrieking, twisting metal filled their ears.

Carter was hurled forwards against his four-point safety harness, then thrust back into his seat.

The helicopter bounced once.

Twice.

It shuddered, then came to a stop.

A quick glance out the window told Carter the hull was intact and the buoyancy floats had activated. They'd crash-landed on the far side of the rocky headland, out of sight of the group of armed Indonesians.

Water started to flow into the cockpit. He unbuckled his seatbelt.

'Erina, you okay?' he asked.

'All good here,' she said, unbuckling her belt. 'But what are we going to do with Peacock?'

Carter turned towards the pilot. It wasn't a pretty sight. The force of impact had dislodged the Johnnie Walker from his lap, breaking the bottle and thrusting it upwards into his neck. Blood poured out of the jagged cut and down his front.

Carter checked his carotid pulse and said, 'Nothing can be done for him. He's dead.'

Erina bent over Carter and looked at Peacock.

'Shit, what a mess,' she said. 'Ironic that the bottle got him in the end.'

'At least he got us down and we don't have to figure out what to do with him.'

'That doublecrossing drunk just delivered us safely into the hands of the enemy. So much for flying under the radar.'

Water continued to pour into the cockpit.

'Come on,' Carter said. 'We need to get out of here before the bird flips.'

CHAPTER 6

Djoran lay flat on his belly at the edge of the rocky cliff, squinting in the harsh sunlight, praying to God for guidance.

The wounded helicopter bobbed up and down in the choppy water below, about a hundred and fifty metres from shore. He assumed it was Erina, Thomas's daughter, and his man Carter – despite the fact that he'd been told they would be arriving by jet ski.

The sun reflected off the transparent bubble, making it impossible for him to tell whether the people inside were alive or dead.

Though he'd prayed for their arrival, he dared do nothing to help. If he exposed himself and the clan's men captured him, there'd be no one to help Kemala, Thomas and Wayan.

It was almost like God was punishing him for praying for a specific outcome.

Djoran had devoted his life to Sufism. His religion had taught him to transcend the physical world, detach from all desires and live on a spiritual plane. Yet here he was on Batak Island caught up in a life-and-death struggle for a cause he believed in.

It didn't make sense, but Djoran had learnt many years ago that nothing in the world made sense and all one could do was follow one's heart and pray for divine guidance. God and his heart had led him to this point.

The helicopter door swung open.

Djoran saw a woman look around and then dive into the water, followed by a man. Both carried a small pack on their back.

They started swimming towards shore, stroking fast and smooth as if they were in an Olympic hundred-metre final.

The helicopter's nose dipped under the water, lifting the rear end to near vertical.

In a blur of movement the great bird flipped over and crashed onto its back, submerging the rotors and exposing its landing gear.

Slowly the helicopter started sliding under the water.

Ten seconds later all that was left were a few bubbles.

From the other side of the headland two outboard engines started up.

Djoran turned towards the sound.

Eight men sat close together in two overladen boats, chugging slowly towards the crashed helicopter.

It would take them less than two minutes to reach the headland.

He glanced in the direction of the two swimmers, halfway to the beach by now, and willed them to go even faster.

CHAPTER 7

At exactly the same time on the other side of the island, Thomas's eyes snapped open. He was in a cement cell, flat on his back on a hard wooden bench, his wrists and calves locked in iron manacles.

He looked up through the grille of the high solitary window above. The sun broke through a cloud and shone in his eyes. The angle of the light told him it was midafternoon.

Something caused his heart rate to quicken. Carter was nearby – he was sure of it.

A psychic thread had connected them ever since Carter first slouched into his Bangkok dojo, an undisciplined, troubled teenager with a prodigious gift for the martial arts.

Their bond had been instant – yet they differed in so many ways.

Thomas's mother had been a Chinese aristocrat; his father an American philanthropist. They had given him a life of privilege, and his upbringing had been rooted in Eastern religion and philosophy.

Carter's father had abandoned him, and his mother was a drug addict. The chaos of his childhood could have destroyed the sensitive young boy, if not for his innate strength of character.

Thomas had worked hard over many years to help Carter find his centre, quiet his demons and harness his talents. Though he'd been disappointed when Carter had left the order, he'd always known he would come back to the fold. The order was Carter's spiritual home, and Thomas had been both father and mother to him.

A groan came from the adjoining bench, where Wayan, also restrained by iron manacles, drifted in and out of consciousness.

Earlier that morning four of Samudra's men had beaten them with wooden batons and then chained them up like dogs.

Wayan had abused their attackers, causing them to give him an even harsher beating. They'd delivered vicious blows to his head and body.

Thomas, who had watched it, powerless to intervene, suspected they'd fractured the boy's collarbone and jaw, as well as creating severe internal injuries.

Since the beating, they'd been left in the cell without food or water, suggesting Samudra considered them already dead.

The naive courage of the young man's gesture had made Thomas want to weep. He saw Wayan, like Carter, as a surrogate son.

His fears for Wayan, the probable collapse of the order and the seemingly inevitable failure of his life's work had taken their toll on his spirit. Despair had engulfed him – a feeling he had hardly known, till now.

If Carter was nearby, most likely Erina, his courageous and headstrong daughter, was near too, but even that thought failed to lift his mood. Stopping Samudra and his jihad should have been their number-one priority, not rescuing him and Wayan. They should've recognised that his and Wayan's fate was ultimately unimportant, and that they were needed elsewhere. By listening to their hearts and not their heads, letting their feelings master them, they had failed him.

He adjusted his position slightly on the unforgiving wooden bench. His left ankle, which he suspected was fractured, screamed at the movement. Two broken ribs made breathing painful.

He let out a deep sigh.

The situation appeared hopeless. Even if Carter and Erina succeeded in freeing them from the cell, their actions, like Wayan's, would most likely prove nothing more than a brave but futile gesture.

CHAPTER 8

Carter and Erina ran down a dirt track through the jungle, Carter in front, their feet creating a rhythmical beat as they matched strides. A dense canopy of vines and leaves whipped them as they charged through.

Five minutes earlier they had reached the shore, sprinted across the narrow beach and burst through an opening in the dense vegetation, seconds before the approaching motorboats rounded the nearby headland.

The heat and humidity were intense, but their wet clothes clung to their bodies, providing some respite. Carter felt a heady mix of adrenalin and endorphins, a result of having survived the helicopter crash.

His plan to rescue Thomas and Wayan that night and get back to Bali by the next day, 28 December, now seemed impossible. Without the helicopter, they were going to have to come up with another way to get off the island.

Erina was behind him, not only keeping pace but pushing him to go faster. They'd covered a little over three hundred metres when they came to a clearing. He raised his right hand.

They slowed to a stop and stood next to each other, panting hard. He wiped the sweat dripping down his face from his eyes and listened.

The outboard engines had slowed to an idling putter, suggesting the boats following them had arrived at the site where the helicopter went down.

The fact that the bird had sunk without a trace would confuse their pursuers, making them suspect Carter and Erina might have been killed in the crash. But there'd been too little time for them to cover their tracks on the beach. It wouldn't take long for Samudra's men to figure out what had happened.

A distant sound caught Carter's attention above the noise of the engines: the manic excitement of barking dogs.

He and Erina listened for a little longer. The noise intensified. The dogs appeared to be heading straight for them.

Erina pointed west along the track. 'There's a stream about a kilometre that way. I saw it on the map just before we got shot down.'

'You sure?'

'Carter, I may be a woman, but I can read a map.'

———

After roughly six hundred metres the track widened, allowing Carter and Erina to run faster through the dense jungle, away from the village and the sounds of the dogs on the hunt.

To their left, towards the ocean, came the now much louder rumble of two outboard engines. The villagers' boats had started moving again, most likely patrolling the coast.

To their right the mountain range created a natural barrier that would make it impossible for them to turn inland and outrun the dogs. Finding the stream was their only option.

Carter grabbed Erina's arm.

'Hold on a sec.'

He'd heard something – sensed it, almost – over the sound of the dogs and the motorboats and the rustling of the trees.

'What is it?'

He put his hand to his ear and pointed into the jungle.

Erina nodded and followed him into the thick undergrowth. They crouched down together, screened from the track by a shield of dense foliage, and listened to the steady beat of approaching footsteps.

He slipped his pack off. 'Wait here and be ready to back me up.'

———

Twenty seconds later an Indonesian man with the whippet-thin build of a marathon runner charged around a bend in the path.

He ran past them barefoot, carrying a green cloth pack on his back.

Carter leapt out of the bushes, accelerated down the track after the man and caught up to him in half-a-dozen strides.

The man turned towards him, just as Carter launched himself through the air. He hit the guy with a flying tackle around the ankles and dropped him to the ground with a thud.

Carter wrestled him onto his back, pinned his shoulders with his knees, gripped his throat and clenched his right hand into a tight-coiled fist.

The guy grinned and said in English, 'Mr Carter – I am so very happy to have found you.'

'Djoran?'

'Yes, it is me. So sorry to startle you.'

Carter studied Djoran's clear brown eyes and the expression on his handsome face. He was struck by the man's openness and lack of guile.

He released his grip, stood up, put out his hand and pulled the guy to his feet.

Djoran gave him a broad smile. 'Thomas says you are a very good man.'

'I have my moments.'

Erina stepped out of the bushes, holding a Glock out in front of her with both hands, pointing it at Djoran's chest.

'And this is Erina,' Carter said.

He waved for her to lower the gun.

She hesitated, then did so.

Djoran held out his hand.

'I am so very pleased to meet you, Miss Erina,' he said. 'I have heard very much about you.'

She shook his hand, but said nothing.

'We're lucky you found us,' Carter said.

'Not luck,' Djoran said. 'God's will. And I have been watching very carefully. The wise camel driver trusts Allah, but hitches up his camel.'

'Too true,' Carter said. 'Now tell me about Thomas and Wayan. Are they okay?'

'They are alive. Being held prisoner in a cell within the compound. And my very dear friend Kemala is under twenty-four-hour guard.'

'Can you take us to them?' Carter asked.

'Hey,' Erina said. 'Shouldn't we first be worrying about the dogs?'

The barking was getting louder and more frenetic.

Djoran reached into his pack and extracted a plastic bag full of bloody raw meat.

'Are you going to feed them?' she asked.

'Not exactly. The meat is full of poison.'

He flung pieces into the bush on either side of the track.

'I hate to hurt animals,' he said. 'Even vicious beasts like these Rottweilers. But it must be done.'

He bowed towards the bush, where he'd thrown the meat. 'May God bless their spirits.'

Djoran turned to face them. 'Follow me, my friends. We must hurry.'

CHAPTER 9

The three of them ran in single file at close to full pace along another dirt track that cut through the thick jungle. Djoran led the way, followed by Carter, with Erina bringing up the rear. The barking of the dogs had ceased.

Djoran guided them through dense rainforest and two fast-running streams, which provided some relief from the energy-sapping heat and humidity. They'd been too short of breath to talk at any great length. Still, Erina was unusually withdrawn, Carter thought. She probably still harboured suspicions about Djoran. She wasn't one to trust people until they proved themselves. Then she was fiercely loyal.

From Carter's point of view, Djoran's timely appearance seemed a miracle, a gift from the gods.

After they'd been running for close to twenty minutes without stopping, they crested a small hill and Djoran raised his hand, indicating they should pause.

All three came to a halt. The sweat poured off Carter. He wiped it out of his eyes with the bottom of his T-shirt and looked down at the valley below, where a small village lay – half-a-dozen wooden huts with rough holes cut in them for windows. The sun lit up their rusted corrugated-iron roofs. Lazy wisps of smoke rose from the chimneys, the only sign that the village was inhabited.

'Please wait here,' Djoran said. 'I must make arrangements.'

Carter nodded, feeling grateful for the opportunity to bring his heart rate and breathing under control. He inhaled deeply and watched Djoran run down the hill, a bundle of boundless energy in a state of perpetual motion.

Erina dropped her daypack on the ground and stood with her hands on her hips, her face glistening with perspiration. She bent forwards, breathing deep and hard.

Down in the valley Djoran knocked at the door of one of the huts and went inside.

Erina's breathing returned to normal faster than Carter's. She stood up straight and said, 'I'm still not convinced we can trust this guy. This could be a trap.'

'Djoran's okay,' Carter said, still bent over and breathing hard.

He harboured no doubts about Djoran whatsoever. He'd only needed to look into Djoran's eyes to see the goodness shining in him. It was something that couldn't be faked.

'He's a Muslim training to be a mujaheddin,' Erina said.

'We can trust him.'

'How do you know?'

'Same way I know the difference between a shark and a dolphin.'

'Nice metaphor, Carter, but when you see a fin in the water coming towards you in shark-infested waters, it's prudent to entertain the possibility it might be a shark.'

Carter looked at her without saying a word.

'And,' she said, 'how do you know he didn't doublecross Jacko just like Peacock did?'

'I never trusted Peacock.'

'Let me remind you, we're on a tropical island in the middle of nowhere. It's governed by sharia law and hosts a terrorist training camp, which Djoran is part of. God knows who's hiding in those huts. I mean, where the hell is everyone?'

'Hopefully we'll find out very soon.'

After a silent minute they both watched Djoran walk out of the hut below, followed by two women wearing the white headscarfs known in

Indonesia as *jilbab* and dark, loose-fitting dresses, covering them from neck to toe.

Djoran waved, beckoning them to join him.

Carter watched Erina reach into her daypack, take out her Glock, lift her shirt and stick the weapon in the back of her trouser belt.

Her eyes locked onto Carter's as if daring him to challenge her. He shrugged and started walking down the hill towards the women, who looked like they were mother and daughter.

He stopped a metre from them and bowed. 'As-salamu alaikum.' *May peace be upon you.*

The older woman, carrying three large plastic bottles of water, returned the greeting and bowed her head. The younger one, who held a large cardboard box, gave him a shy smile.

Djoran held a cane basket in his left hand. 'We have food, fresh water and clean clothes.'

Carter smiled at the two women and said, 'Terima kasih.' *Thank you.*

They bowed and he watched them move away.

When they'd disappeared into one of the huts, he turned to Djoran and said, 'We don't want to put you or these people in any danger.'

Djoran grinned. 'Thank you, Mr Carter, that is very thoughtful of you. But we believe to live well we must live dangerously and trust God. Otherwise what is the point of this strange life he has given us? We all have the same enemy. That makes us friends. Friends help each other.'

'I thought Sufis didn't have enemies,' Carter said.

'In theory that is very correct,' Djoran said, 'but sometimes God moves our hearts in most mysterious ways.'

Erina stepped between them. 'That's all very interesting,' she said, 'but I suggest we get out of here and save the talk for later.'

'Too true, Miss Erina,' Djoran said. 'Come, I have a very good hiding place.'

CHAPTER 10

They had to crawl by torchlight through numerous dark tunnels to reach Djoran's hiding place, a dank, musty bunker the size of a double garage. The ceiling was just high enough to allow Carter to stand at the entrance without stooping.

Shadows from two hissing hurricane lamps danced like hypnotic snakes over the stone walls. Straw mats covered the earth floor. A low wooden table sat against one wall, surrounded by large dark cushions. A grey blanket hung over the opening to what was presumably another tunnel.

Carter felt himself relax. It was a good place to regroup before setting out for their assault on the compound.

Erina still seemed wary, he thought. She stood to one side near the wall. Her hand rested on her hip, near the Glock stuck in the back of her shorts. Maybe like him she was wondering who had lit the lamps and who was behind the blanket. He could sense another presence in the bunker.

'Is this what I think it is?' Erina asked. 'A Japanese bunker from the Second World War?'

Carter was pleased to see that she was willing to engage with Djoran, though he knew she was most likely masking her true thoughts.

'I see you know your history,' Djoran said.

'My father told me about these bunkers, but I've never seen one myself.'

Djoran smiled. 'During the Second World War, the Japanese built many bunkers throughout Indonesia and the Pacific Islands. The Allies never really engaged the Japanese in Indonesia, but elsewhere they had to dig them out one by one after much bloodshed. The Japanese soldiers preferred to die fighting rather than surrender.'

Carter wasn't listening.

He was staring at the grim-faced Indonesian dressed in black who'd just stepped out from behind the blanket, carrying a short-barrelled assault rifle in his right hand.

Carter recognised the weapon – an AK-90, developed by a Russian internal-affairs organisation and designed to take out assailants wearing bulletproof vests in urban environments. At such short range it'd blow a huge hole in anyone who got in the way. Fortunately it was pointing at the floor.

Erina had also seen it.

Before Carter had a chance to say anything, she whipped out her Glock from behind her back and aimed it at the Indonesian's head.

The stranger in turn raised his AK-90 to his shoulder and pointed it at her chest.

Djoran spun around on his heels. 'Muklas, what in God's name are you doing? These people are our friends.'

Muklas kept his weapon trained on Erina but directed his reply to Djoran, speaking in English. 'You think everyone is your friend. How do you know you can trust these two?'

Djoran waved his arms and shook his head. 'No. You are wrong about them. They are here to help Kemala. Their friends are in grave danger.'

'So what? By coming here, they put us and our operation in more danger.'

Muklas held his weapon steady at the optimum angle and positioned himself so that he covered both Carter and Erina. He'd clearly undergone some solid training. But Carter doubted he'd shoot unless directly threatened.

'God brought them here for a purpose,' Djoran continued. 'We must do his will.'

Muklas shook his head. 'Bullshit. Samudra needs to be taken out before he leaves the island. I'm calling in Detachment 88.'

Carter glanced at Djoran. His sunny disposition had clouded over and his fists were clenched.

'If Samudra learns they are coming,' Djoran said, 'he'll execute the prisoners on the spot. We cannot knowingly throw away the lives of the two innocent people being held captive.'

Muklas shrugged. 'They'll be killed anyway. We both know that.'

Erina never took her aim or eyes off Muklas. She asked, 'What does he mean by that, Djoran?'

Muklas jabbed his rifle in her direction. 'Shut up, woman.'

Carter felt Erina tense up. He switched his attention to Djoran, who bowed.

'Forgive me for not telling you earlier,' Djoran said. 'But I found out this morning that Samudra plans to execute Thomas and Wayan tomorrow evening at dusk.'

'Why would he wait till then?' Carter asked.

'He is leading a group of mujaheddin, of which I am a part, to Sydney on 29 December and he wants to use the execution tomorrow as a means to inspire confidence and courage in us. He says dusk is the magic hour when God is present. He will send the video out to thousands of followers around the world.'

Erina kept her Glock trained on Muklas. 'You mean he plans to film their execution?'

Djoran's head dropped. 'He's planning a demonstration of God's vengeance to be shared via a secure members-only website.'

The irony wasn't lost on Carter. Even a fundamentalist group intent on recreating the social order of the Middle Ages could harness the awesome power of modern technology, using it to spread their message of hatred and violence.

Carter took a deep breath and ran his hands through his hair. He turned towards Djoran. 'How long will it take us to get to the compound?'

'If you leave at midnight, you can be there in two hours.'

'Why can't we leave sooner?'

'It is too dangerous in daylight. Between midnight and dawn is when they have the fewest patrols. Besides, you need time to eat and rest. You will be very busy tomorrow.'

'Fair enough,' Carter said, deciding it was time to end the impasse between Muklas and Erina.

He stepped in front of Erina and looked down the cold black barrel of Muklas's assault rifle, letting his arms hang loosely by his side. He wanted to show Muklas that he did not fear him and at the same time give him every reason to back off.

Muklas held his rifle steady.

'You need to give us until six in the morning to rescue our friends,' Carter said. 'That's all I need.'

The dark eye of the barrel stared back at him.

Muklas raised the rifle a little. 'My only concern is for my Indonesian brothers and sisters. They live on this island in poverty and shame under crazy sharia laws. Samudra is a fanatical leader who poisons everything here with hatred. I don't care about your two friends. They are nothing to me. My people are everything.'

'Muklas, please,' Djoran said. 'If not for them, do it for Kemala.'

Carter raised his hand and looked Muklas directly in the eye. 'I understand what you're saying. It's tragic what Samudra has done to your island. But, like you, I can't walk away from my people. All I ask is that you give me until 6 a.m. If I fail to rescue them in that time, you can call in whoever you like.'

A strange combination of passion and fear emanated from Muklas's eyes.

'And if I get half a chance,' Carter continued, 'I'll kill that mother-fucker Samudra myself. I don't intend to let him leave this island alive.'

Muklas's mouth twitched with the hint of a smile. He took two steps back towards the rear wall of the bunker, so that he was out of Carter's reach, and lowered the rifle.

Carter turned to Erina. She dropped her Glock and returned it to the back of her belt.

Djoran stepped forwards, patted Muklas on the shoulder and turned to Carter. 'Very good. I am glad we are all friends. I will now show you the best way to get inside the compound.'

CHAPTER 11

Carter, Erina and Muklas followed Djoran to the rear of the dark bunker. They stopped in front of the grey blanket, which Carter assumed covered an exit tunnel leading towards the ocean.

Djoran pulled it back, revealing two red and white malibu surfboards propped against the left wall.

'You a surfer?' Carter asked.

'Oh no, not me,' Djoran said. 'But I understand you are very experienced.'

Carter entered the damp, musty tunnel. 'You could say that. Erina's also pretty handy.'

He knelt beside the ten-foot boards and ran his hands over the waxed decks.

Erina turned to Djoran. 'Are you suggesting we paddle these boards around the island to the compound?'

'Not all the way around,' he said. 'You would be picked up by their surveillance cameras two hundred metres before you approached it. Come with me and I shall show you what I have prepared.'

They followed him back to the wooden table and sat around it. Muklas, who positioned himself to Carter's right, still appeared to be wary of Erina.

Djoran reached inside a cloth bag and took out two rolled-up maps, two underwater breathing devices the size of large Cuban cigars and a set of three silver keys. He spread one of the maps on the table, placing the other on the floor beside him.

'Jacko suggested we go overland to the compound,' Erina said. 'You have a better option?'

'As much as I respect Mr Jacko's opinion, this island was my home for over twenty years. And, if I may say, in all modesty, I know every inch of it – and the clan's surveillance – better than anyone.'

Erina looked at Carter, seeking his opinion.

'As they say in the surf,' he said, 'you can't beat local knowledge.'

'I can assure you,' Djoran said, 'it is most inadvisable to travel overland to the compound at night. And now that you are expected, security will be much too tight to move during daylight hours. I have a better way.'

'Show us what you've got,' Erina said.

'We are here,' Djoran told them, placing his forefinger on the map. 'First you will paddle the surfboards east along the coast, past this village and then around the far headland, two and a half kilometres away. You will then cross this reef before reaching the cove.'

Djoran indicated a point on the other side of the headland at the far end of the island. 'Here you will find an underwater cave that leads directly inside the clan's compound.'

'What about the boats patrolling the coastline?' Carter asked, wondering just how much Djoran had thought his plan through. God and the devil were in the detail.

'They rotate, on average, at twenty-five-minute intervals, giving you enough time to reach the headland.'

Carter nodded. It was good, solid information.

'You see, I try to think of everything, Mr Carter. But as you would no doubt appreciate, we can never predict what is in store for us around the next corner. That is up to God and sometimes he chooses to test us in ways that do not appear to suit our immediate plans.'

Muklas stood up, shook his head at Djoran and said, 'You make it sound too easy.'

Carter and Erina turned to face him. 'What do you mean exactly?' Carter asked.

'I know these waters too. My father fished that reef for many years. If you try and cross it tonight, huge waves like mountains coming from the north-east will smash you onto the coral reef.'

'Mr Carter and Miss Erina are very experienced in the surf,' Djoran said. 'They will find a way through if God is with them.'

'Okay,' Erina said, 'let's say we're able to make it past the patrol boats, through the surf, then break into the compound and free Thomas and Wayan. How do we get them off the island, particularly if they're injured and in bad shape?'

'A very good question,' Djoran said, pointing at the map, his finger close to the eastern perimeter of the clan's compound. 'There is another secret bunker here, very similar to this one, but not as big. It has an entrance above the ocean at the bottom of a steep cliff. I prepared it many months ago as an escape hatch should I, or anyone else, need to leave the island quickly. In the cave you will find an inflatable rubber dinghy with a small outboard, a GPS navigation device and some food, water and medical supplies.'

Carter nodded to himself as much as anyone else. Djoran's plan just might work.

'You do think things through,' he said.

Djoran smiled. 'The best way to do God's will is to plan thoroughly.' He picked up the second map from the floor, unrolled it and indicated a point at the back of the Sungkar clan's compound. 'And God, through the Japanese, has provided us with more good fortune.'

He pointed at a different spot on the map. 'There is a hidden tunnel here leading to the bunker from inside the back perimeter, not so far from the cell where Thomas and Wayan are being held.'

'Just to be clear,' Carter said, 'you reckon negotiating the surf at the reef and entering the compound through the underwater cave is the best option?'

'It is, in my opinion,' Djoran said, 'the only chance you have.'

Carter looked at Erina, who nodded, then back at Djoran.

'Okay then,' he said. 'We leave at midnight.'

CHAPTER 12

After Djoran had run through his plan in detail, the four of them shared a meal of steamed rice, chicken and vegetables without saying very much, each lost in their own thoughts.

Djoran's plan was, in Carter's opinion, an inspired one. He'd done his homework and come up with something simple and yet totally unexpected that might allow them to get into the compound without being detected.

The plan came with more than its fair share of risks and challenges, but their way forward was clear. They'd make the necessary adjustments when things started to bend out of shape, as they inevitably would.

Erina ate slowly and was the last to finish. He could tell in this quiet space that thoughts of Jacko's death and the question of Thomas and Wayan's fate were weighing down on her. Carter resisted the urge to say something, realising it was best to give her the space to process what was going on in her own way. She'd pull herself together when she needed to.

He pushed back his chair, wanting to help clear the plates, but Djoran insisted he remain seated while he attended to them himself. Djoran put the kettle on the gas burner and offered them each a cup of instant coffee. All three said yes without any great enthusiasm.

He placed an open pot of brown sugar, two metal teaspoons and a can of condensed milk on the table, then returned to the gas burner and poured the coffee. After handing them each a steaming cup, he sat down again.

Carter took a sip of the bitter coffee. This was as good a time as any to let Djoran know about Jacko. Everything would then be on the table.

'I'm afraid I have some bad news we haven't shared with you yet.'

Djoran looked at him with evident sympathy. 'This does not come as a surprise, Mr Carter. I feel a deep sadness in both of your spirits. What has happened?'

'Yesterday afternoon Jacko was killed by a suicide bomber at a cafe in Kuta. I suspect Erina and I were also targets.'

Djoran remained silent for a moment and then said, 'This is a most terrible thing to hear. I liked Mr Jacko very much. He brought laughter into the world and was a very good man. A very caring man.'

'Can you think how Samudra could've known we'd be meeting there?' Carter asked.

Djoran took a sip of his coffee. 'I have no idea. He has been gone from the island for a few days and is due to return to the compound later tonight.'

He stood up. 'With your permission, I would like to say a Sufi prayer for Mr Jacko's spirit.'

'I'm sure Jacko would like that,' Carter said.

'Please, join me in a circle.'

Carter stood up and reached out his hand to Erina, having no idea how she'd respond to a Muslim prayer.

She gave him an ironic half-smile, clasped her palm in his and stood up slowly. The four of them formed a circle and bowed their heads.

'O Thou,' Djoran said, 'the cause and effect of the whole universe, the source from whence we have come and the goal towards which all are bound, receive the soul of Mr Jacko who has come to Thee.'

Djoran then spoke briefly about Jacko, highlighting his virtues. Carter and Erina also said a few words, each recounting a favourite memory of their fallen comrade and saying how much they would miss him. Muklas surprised Carter by saying he was very sorry to hear of their loss.

When they'd all spoken, Djoran continued his prayer. 'Please help us see Mr Jacko's death as a transition, a stepping stone across a threshold to a place where we have a chance to reawaken. We pray Thee offer him Thy blessing. May his life upon earth become as a dream to his waking soul, and let his thirsting eyes behold the glorious vision of Thy sunshine. Allah akbar.'

The four of them stood in silence. Carter felt some of his sadness lift. The ceremony reminded him that life and physical death were not necessarily the end of the journey.

All four sat back down around the table. Erina stared into her cup, as if searching for answers there.

Djoran noted this and asked her gently, 'Miss Erina, are you okay?'

'It's nothing. I'll be fine.'

She tried to speak lightly, but there was no mistaking the deep sadness in her voice.

Djoran gave her a warm smile that lit up his whole face. 'Please, share with us. It is most beneficial to release all dark thoughts and feelings into the universe. That way, God can cleanse your spirit.'

Erina sipped her coffee without looking at him and remained silent, obviously trying to push down whatever had been stirred up.

There was a pause, and then Djoran continued. 'We Sufis believe that in the afterlife we discover our time on earth was but a dream we have seen and a tale we have heard. Are you familiar with this concept, Miss Erina? I know your father is.'

'I believe in my father's spiritual principles and I try to live by them ...'

'And?' Djoran asked, filling in the silence.

Erina looked at him but couldn't seem to get any words out.

'Djoran,' Carter said. 'Why don't you tell us more about what the Sufis believe?'

He wanted to hear for himself as much as for Erina. He understood how grief lurked in one's soul like a shadow and needed to be brought into the light.

Djoran drank from his tin coffee cup like it was a sacred chalice and said, 'I do not wish to push my beliefs on anyone.'

'It's okay,' Erina said. 'Please go ahead.'

'Thank you,' Djoran said. 'We Sufis believe one should not allow the death of others to cloud our spirit. Death is part of life and should be celebrated. I am sure you are familiar with this idea, Miss Erina.'

'I understand the words,' she said, touching her heart. 'But I no longer feel them in here.'

Djoran nodded. 'The question we Sufis ask ourselves is: what do we take into the city of death except the sum of what our life has been? Death reveals what is important and what is not. By embracing death and its lessons during life, we can live with greater purpose. That is why we Sufis say, *Die before you die.*'

He smiled. 'For me these spiritual concepts are the source of great solace and guide me through the dark times towards the light. How do you see death, Miss Erina?'

She took a moment to collect her thoughts. 'Death is of course a part of life,' she said, hesitant at first. 'But those people who kill in the name of God have no idea how much pain and suffering they inflict on those left behind. I begin to wonder what the point of it all is.'

'And you have every reason to feel that way. What those misguided fanatics do is evil. They are the enemies of humanity and must be stopped. But it is the Sufis' belief we must strive to recognise we are all God's creatures and must never forget this great fact, or we become like those we despise. We must, I believe, seek justice and protect those who can't protect themselves. But seeking and justifying revenge can only corrupt our spirit.'

Carter saw Erina give a tiny nod. Djoran's humility had somehow got past her defences and touched her.

'I used to have faith,' she said. 'But what I've lost is my trust that God is on our side and will guide us where we need to go. After what happened to Jacko, and with Thomas and Wayan in such grave danger, I ask myself how I can surrender to a god who allows such terrible things to happen to good people. In moments like these I feel this life we strive to lead is all in vain and trying to serve God is a bad joke.'

Djoran let her words hang in the air and then said, 'One cannot understand divine logic. No human being can know God's will. That is beyond who we are. But we do need to follow the dictates of our hearts, align our intentions to our values and do what we believe is right.'

'In theory I agree,' Erina said. 'But at the moment I find it impossible to trust anything beyond my own strength, skill and willpower. I question whether the universe is guided by a friendly hand or one of hate and vengeance.'

Carter knew there was nothing he could say. Erina had echoed many of the thoughts and feelings he'd had when he'd left the order, the numbing soul sickness that came from being exposed to so much darkness and death.

Djoran put his hands in the prayer position. 'We cannot know what God has in store for any one of us, either in this life or beyond. When our faith deserts us, we must continue to ask for his guidance and act as if we believe in him. That is how we trust.'

Erina was nodding again.

'If we do this,' Djoran said, 'I believe great things will come to pass. While Thomas and Wayan are still alive, there is hope, and we must do what we can. If any of us die in our efforts, we must accept this as God's will. *What is, is.* Acceptance is true faith and will give us the strength and wisdom we need. There is more to life than what we can see and hear.'

'I want to believe that,' Erina said.

Djoran laid his hands on the table in front of him. 'Let me tell you something. My wife, Anisha, was killed in the Sari Club on the night of the first Bali bombing. She was celebrating the end of a marketing conference with two Australian business associates.'

A moment of profound silence followed, as if everyone was holding their breath.

'She was four months pregnant with our first child.'

A barely audible 'Oh my God' escaped from Erina's lips.

Djoran gently took her hand and placed it over his heart.

To Carter's surprise, she let him do so.

'Nothing takes away the pain of their loss,' Djoran said. 'But they live with me. I can feel my wife and unborn son in here, reminding me of God's omnipresence and compassion for all creatures. Their spirits tell me to keep going and that God loves us all.'

Carter was surprised to see Erina's eyes fill with tears. She never cried. They started to flow and she let them come.

CHAPTER 13

A few minutes after midnight Carter and Erina entered the warm thigh-high water from a small beach at the bottom of a rock cliff not far from Djoran's bunker.

Carter hitched up his black board shorts, while Erina had stripped down to her black bra and bikini briefs. After their talk with Djoran and a few hours' sleep, it was like a shadow had lifted from both of them and they were now acting as a unified team. The passionate moment they'd shared on the beach at Kuta had not been spoken of. This was neither the time nor the place to dwell on anything but the job at hand.

They stood next to each other in the dark, ten metres from shore, each steadying one of Djoran's surfboards against the incoming swell, rolling past them before breaking gently onto the sand behind them. It'd be a totally different story once they paddled around the distant headland, where they'd be forced to navigate their way through huge breaking surf.

First, though, they needed to paddle more than three kilometres without being spotted, something they couldn't take for granted.

Carter checked his watch. The patrol boat had passed by three minutes earlier, a hundred and twenty metres from shore. They'd start paddling in one minute.

Despite the challenges that lay ahead, it felt good to get started. A full moon and a glowing blanket of stars lit up the vast expanse of ocean, ruffled by a light onshore breeze. He noticed a build-up of thick clouds on the horizon, suggesting a change in weather conditions wasn't too far away. They would deal with that when the time came.

After finalising their plans, Djoran had headed back to the compound to resume his undercover role as one of Samudra's mujaheddin. He needed to remain close to Samudra to discover the precise nature of his plans for jihad in Sydney. It was their best shot at finding out what he was up to and stopping it.

Muklas, who had warmed to them after hearing of Jacko's death and understanding they were all fighting a common enemy, had set off an hour earlier to 'borrow' a fishing boat. He had promised not to act until 8 a.m. If they returned by then, he'd leave the island with them. Should they fail to show up, he had Carter's blessing to head for Java and personally inform one of Detachment 88's senior commanders of Samudra's activities and organise an attack on the compound.

What Muklas had said about the size of the waves around the headland had Carter slightly concerned. They might be facing conditions that even professional big-wave surfers wouldn't attempt without a jet ski tow-in during broad daylight, let alone at night on a ten-foot malibu. There was no point worrying now, though. He'd know more when they assessed the conditions firsthand.

Carter let go of his board and pulled his waterproof daypack tight against his body. He'd insisted Erina leave hers behind. She was a good surfer, but no match for Carter. He'd packed a T-shirt for each of them, Erina's light cotton trousers and their shoes into his own pack, along with the satphone and her computer, containing Djoran's security codes. The phone and computer were sealed in waterproof sleeves. Apart from that, he'd brought along only the essentials – one Glock, an underwater flashlight, throwing knives and the two breathing devices.

They lay on their boards and started paddling out to open sea across the moonlit ocean.

—

Eight minutes later they were halfway towards the eastern headland, two hundred metres from shore, when Carter detected a slight vibration in the water.

He glided to a stop. Erina did the same and pushed herself upright on her board. They both turned towards the faint growl of an outboard motor.

Roughly fifteen hundred metres behind them an arc of bright light moved back and forth across the water, heading straight for them. Obviously one of the patrol boats had deviated from their regular pattern. The plan had bent out of shape even quicker than Carter had anticipated.

He glanced at Erina, sitting on her longboard wearing nothing but her underwear, her eyes dancing between him and the oncoming spotlight.

They sat in silence. There was no way they could outrun the boat. The growl of the engine grew louder.

'You want me to be the decoy?' Erina asked.

'Yeah,' he said, though he was reluctant to put her at risk. There was no other choice.

'Great. Just make sure you hit the target with the first shot.'

CHAPTER 14

Erina sat upright on her board, waiting for the advancing spotlight to fall on her.

Both knew exactly what they had to do. She needed to distract the advancing clansmen so he had a clear shot to take them out. The plan's success depended on making the enemy look one way before striking hard from the other direction.

He paddled away from her, further out to sea, concentrating on each stroke, trying to still his mind for the critical moments that lay ahead.

His board came to rest roughly twenty metres from where she sat. The gurgling engine of the patrol boat was about four hundred metres from Erina now, closing on her at a steady pace.

Moving further away wasn't an option for Carter. It'd make a difficult shot impossible. If he fired from more than twenty metres, he might as well throw the weapon at their pursuers, for all the good it would do.

He sat upright on his board and kicked his legs to spin the nose around to face her.

After removing the Glock from his daypack, he switched it to a single round. He needed to make one shot at a time and didn't want any stray bullets spraying in Erina's direction. He sealed his daypack, slung it over his shoulder and knelt on the deck of his board.

The gusting wind roughed up the water. That, coupled with the roll of the incoming swell, caused his board to rise and fall at an irregular rate.

He spread his knees to steady the roll as best he could. He'd be shooting from an unstable platform at a person or persons facing side-on and bobbing up and down.

The fishing boat chugged forwards, now two hundred metres from Erina. In less than ten seconds the spotlight's ten-metre circle of light would fall on her.

He raised his arms in front of him and looked down the barrel, focusing on Erina's silhouette.

After rehearsing in his mind what he needed to do, he closed his eyes and breathed in. His shoulder, stomach and chest muscles were tight. He needed to get his emotions under complete control, switch from thinking to being and fully inhabit the moment.

When his eyes snapped open again, moments later, the boat's bright spotlight was dancing over Erina.

The moon had disappeared behind the gathering clouds and spots of rain spat on his back. Diesel fumes wafted through the night air.

He adjusted the board once more so the nose pointed directly at her.

She raised a hand to her eyes, defiant and vulnerable, playing the role to perfection.

He knew who'd got the toughest assignment on this job and it wasn't him. Being the bait in a high-stakes game like this required great emotional control and presence of mind.

Thirty metres from her, the patrol boat's helmsman cut back the throttle of the outboard engine to a rough idle.

The clan members had seen Erina.

The open aluminium vessel slowed, drifting to a halt about four metres from her, giving Carter a clear view of the two men on board.

An Indonesian Laurel and Hardy.

A tall skinny guy wearing a floppy white hat steered, working the dazzling spotlight from the stern. The other, short and fat, sat in the middle. An enormous cigar stuck out from the side of his mouth.

But there was nothing comical about the lethal weapon lying across his lap. An AK-47, a compact and reliable automatic rifle.

If the shooter used soft-nosed bullets, each shot would fragment on impact, causing serious tissue damage and resulting in certain death.

Erina gave away nothing and showed no signs of fear. She just smiled and waved at the Indonesian duo like they were two heroes coming to her rescue on a dark and lonely night.

He weighed up the odds and angles.

The AK-47 presented a problem.

The fat guy only had to squeeze the trigger once and over two dozen lethal rounds would fly through the night air.

Carter needed to take him out of the equation with his first shot and then bring down the skinny guy before he could reach his friend's weapon.

The boat drifted to within two metres of Erina.

The moment had come.

He adjusted his knees on his surfboard so they were fifteen centimetres apart and his weight spread evenly. He stretched both arms out in front of him again, locking his elbows this time and keeping the gun barrel parallel to the ocean.

Raindrops glistened in the beam of the spotlight.

A centimetre either way meant the fine line between success and disaster. Life and death.

The fat clansman raised the AK-47 and pointed it between Erina's breasts.

Carter lined up his head.

He held his arms relaxed and steady, imagining a force field of energy between him and his target.

Exhaling slowly, he squeezed the trigger.

Ever so gently.

The Glock roared to life.

CHAPTER 15

The moment he squeezed the trigger, Carter knew his shot had found its mark.

The fat Indonesian grabbed his throat, dropped his rifle and collapsed forwards with a thud.

Carter aimed the Glock at the spotlight.

Too late.

The intense bright light swung towards him, locking on his face, blinding him.

He heard movement on the boat. The second Indonesian was most likely scrambling for the fallen automatic weapon.

The harsh spotlight stayed focused on him, making the moving target invisible. There was no time for his eyes to adjust or for him to analyse what needed to be done. To have any chance of taking out the other guy, he had to surrender to unseen forces and shoot blind, almost immediately.

He inhaled to the count of three, closed his eyes and raised the weapon, trying to sense the Indonesian's position.

The master marksman has a target but never takes aim.

Carter exhaled slowly and experienced a moment of complete stillness between breaths. He squeezed off three shots in quick succession, shooting in a metre-wide triangular pattern.

An eerie silence filled the night.

Carter kept his eyes closed.

The sound of a body hitting the metal deck broke the spell.

The spotlight crashed forwards into the boat.

Carter opened his eyes, stuck the gun in the side pocket of his daypack and started paddling towards Erina.

She lay prone on her board, backlit by the soft glow of the fallen spotlight.

'You all right?' he called as he drew near.

She sat up, grabbed the bow of the boat and said, 'I'm fine.'

His board glided to a halt a metre from her. 'You did good.'

'I make a terrific decoy. But you didn't do so badly yourself. You hit the last guy shooting blind.'

'That was the easy part.'

Without waiting for a response, he stood on his board, put his weight on his back foot and stepped onto the aluminium boat.

The deck was slippery with fresh blood and guts.

'Just hang tight while I do some housekeeping,' he said.

'You think I can't handle a bit of blood?'

'It'll only take me a sec.'

He pulled his surfboard up after him and jammed the nose under the front seat. Its tail jutted forwards over the bow with the fin pointing upwards.

'Looks like a figurehead on an ancient warship heading into battle,' Erina said.

'A surfboard has many uses.'

He grabbed the fat guy under the armpits, dragged him to the stern, dumped him over the side and watched him float away from the boat, facedown.

'I reckon these two were just local fishermen,' he said.

'Yeah, armed with automatic rifles and happy to kill us.'

'I think they would've been pressed into service, not hardcore mujaheddin.'

'They made the wrong choice.'

He lifted the skinny guy off the deck and tossed him into the water after his mate, then moved to where she held onto the gunnels.

She took his outstretched hand and scrambled on board. He used a stray towel lying on the forward deck to wipe the blood and tissue off the middle seat.

'You did make a mess,' she said.

'Better them than us.'

The rain started to get heavier and patter on the deck. He settled her onto the now clean seat, picked up a tarpaulin lying in the bow and wrapped it around her shoulders.

'Don't go all chivalrous on me,' she said. 'I can look after myself.'

'I know.'

He understood what she was saying and why she'd said it. This was no time for softness or sentiment.

The sooner they got moving, the better. He climbed past her, turned the spotlight off and stowed it at the bow.

'What about my board?' she asked.

'We're leaving it. If we need to surf our way across the reef onto the island, we'll ride tandem.'

He then positioned himself next to the idling outboard engine and was about to put it into gear when a distant sound registered above the motor. They both turned in the direction they'd come from. He switched the outboard off.

Along with the freshening wind came the unmistakable *whump, whump, whump* of a helicopter and the shimmer of a spotlight dancing a hundred metres over the ocean, heading straight for them.

Without saying a word, he restarted the outboard motor, revved the engine and accelerated towards the dark headland looming in the distance.

CHAPTER 16

They rounded the headland in the open boat and faced the full brunt of the onshore gale and the angry nor'-east swell Muklas had predicted.

In just over five minutes the weather conditions had deteriorated, the rain having gone from a steady patter to a downpour. Sheets of water pelted down, creating an incessant drumbeat against the metal deck, and the wind whistled over them. Carter sensed, then saw, the huge shadow of an unbroken wave rolling towards them.

He steered straight for it, aiming to hit the oncoming wall of water at a ninety-degree angle. If the bow didn't hit square on, the boat would broach the wave sideways, fill with water and sink.

The bow thumped against the angry face, propelling them high in the air. He yanked the outboard engine towards him, turning the boat into the wave. The boat crashed through the lip and down the other side, before plunging them into the trough between the waves.

He turned the throttle and they accelerated parallel to the waves. They needed to generate speed before turning and ploughing into the next one head on. If they lost forward momentum, they'd be thrown back and risk being swamped by the following wave.

A quick glance behind told him the helicopter hadn't yet reached the headland, but it wouldn't be long.

Up ahead and to their left an invisible wave boomed onto the unseen coral reef like a clap of heavy thunder, punctuating the background roar of smaller but still sizeable waves crashing into the shallow water.

Erina turned towards him, shouting to be heard above the wind and rain. 'Muklas was right. The surf's definitely up.'

A minute later they drew level with a point where the incoming swell smacked onto the coral reef fifty metres to their left. They were still in deep, open water, and even though the waves were large and dangerous, they had nothing like the power and venom of those breaking in the shallow water over the reef, creating the mother of all no man's lands.

According to the map, which Carter could picture in his mind, they were two hundred and fifty metres from the underwater cave that led to Samudra's compound. To get to it, they needed to cross the reef.

Now that he'd had the opportunity to assess the conditions firsthand, he knew they'd never make it all the way through to the cave in the boat. The powerful waves would smash them to pieces on the sharp coral and drive what was left of them onto the rocky shore.

They crashed through another wave and accelerated along the trough between peaks. By the time they'd turned into the next wave, a plan had begun to crystallise in his mind.

As if to punctuate this moment of clarity, another unseen wave smashed against the reef and a cascade of sound exploded through the night like a bomb.

The only chance they had of getting across the reef was by catching a wave on the ten-foot board and surfing it tandem. This meant first taking the boat through no man's land, the only way to get to the take-off zone. Then they'd ditch the boat and surf across the reef to the calm deepwater channel on the other side. From there it'd be an easy paddle to the underwater cave. It sounded good in theory, but the execution would be another matter entirely.

He leant towards Erina and yelled, 'Steer the boat while I get the spotlight up.'

She turned her head. 'What's the plan?'

When he told her, it sounded even more outrageous than it had in his head.

'I've always wanted to ride tandem,' she said.

'This'll be your chance.'

'Anything else I should know?'

'When we abandon the boat, we'll leave the light on so they'll think we've capsized and drowned. What do you reckon?'

She didn't answer straightaway, appearing to be mulling over his words.

'That might just work,' she said.

———

In the lull between sets Carter and Erina swapped places. If anything, she handled a boat better than he did. But the surf was his sacred home and he'd be calling the shots.

He grabbed the spotlight and planted his feet wide on the vibrating deck, bending his knees and swaying in time with the violent motion of the boat, performing an unconscious dance with the elements raging around them.

He listened to the waves, trying to hear their pattern, so he could pick the best one in the set to catch and hold off turning on the spotlight for as long as possible.

They seemed to come in sets of four. The sound of the waves breaking on the reef told him that the first two in each set were shutting down viciously on the coral and should be avoided at all costs.

The third hit the reef at a good angle and broke evenly. The gusting wind blew offshore, which meant it'd hold the face up and give them a decent shot at riding the wave all the way across the reef.

Still, surfing this break on a ten-foot malibu tandem in the dark was a huge ask. Once the helicopter pilot spotted the light, they'd have only a few minutes to negotiate the boat through no man's land, get to the take-off zone on the other side and catch the right wave. They'd only get one shot.

But despite the grim odds, turning back was out of the question.

Carter flicked the plastic switch on the spotlight.

An arc of bright light lit up the take-off zone, leaving them exposed and vulnerable and illuminating an angry line of swell advancing towards the reef. He would watch this set rolling in, testing his theory.

The first wave, the height of a one-storey building, struck the reef about forty metres ahead of them at a sixty-degree angle.

The instant it hit the shallow water, the gnarly face jacked up, doubled its size and smashed onto the reef, creating an unrideable mass of boiling foam.

Carter glanced over his shoulder. The approaching helicopter still hadn't rounded the headland.

The second huge wave closed out on the reef, unrideable.

The third charged towards the reef, a two-storey boomer.

As he'd suspected, it struck the reef at a more acute angle than the others, had more water under it, and broke forming a perfect A frame. Bubbling white water peeled across the steep face in both directions.

One side broke to the left, towards their boat. The other passed over the reef towards the safety of the channel.

The fourth wave was smaller and closed out on the reef, leaving no face to ride.

The third wave in the set was the one to go for.

He turned the spotlight off and looked over his shoulder again.

The lights of the helicopter glowed near the headland.

'Erina,' he yelled. 'I need you to man the spotlight. When I give the signal, shine it in the same spot I just did.'

'Then what?'

'We find the take-off zone and catch us a wave.'

CHAPTER 17

Carter grabbed the vibrating throttle. He needed to navigate the boat through no man's land and the first two breaking waves of the set to reach the take-off point without being swamped and catch the third. It'd all come down to timing and a fair bit of luck.

He counted in his head as another set rolled in, listening as it broke onto the reef, and yelled, 'We take the boat into no man's land after the next wave.'

Erina shouted to be heard above the wind and rain. 'Just give the signal and I'll shed some light.'

The fourth and last wave of the set smashed against the reef.

Carter dropped his arm. Erina hit the switch and the spotlight came to life, throwing dazzling light across the angry ocean.

He twisted the throttle and followed the light, accelerating into the wild turbulence of no man's land. As the water became shallower, the breaking waves would pack ten times the punch of those forming in the deeper water where they were now.

Erina stood firm in the centre of the boat, her weight spread evenly and her knees bent at a slight angle, shining the spotlight on a wall of water towering towards them.

He lined up the bow at an acute angle to the steep face and accelerated. They'd need every bit of momentum they could muster to climb up and crash through the curling lip.

Erina grabbed a rope attached to the deck with her free hand to give her purchase and held tight, preparing herself for the rough ride to come.

The bow smacked into the arching face, which lifted them at a sharp angle. The outboard screamed and shook. The hull shuddered.

Erina maintained her position, shining the spotlight up the face of the wave and into the sky.

The craft lurched sideways.

Carter rotated the throttle to maximum, whipping the throbbing outboard motor back and forth to correct the boat's angle and generate more speed.

They smacked into the lip at close to perpendicular.

For a moment they hung in midair before crashing down the other side and ploughing into the trough below.

The deck vibrated. Sheets of white water poured over the sides. The sudden impact threw Erina forwards into the gunnels, jolting the spotlight from her grip. It fell facedown on the boat's deck.

She regathered her balance, dived to her left and grabbed the fallen light. Rolling onto her back, she shone it on the fast-approaching second wave of the set. It was gathering height as it rolled towards the reef.

The excess water washed over the deck, making it harder to generate the forward thrust they needed to crash through the next wave.

Carter grabbed a plastic ice-cream container attached to a rope with his left hand and started bailing. With his right he angled the boat away from the break.

Above the crashing of breaking waves, the dull roar of the helicopter's engine attracted his attention. He turned and saw its swaying spotlight heading in their direction. It'd only be a matter of seconds before they locked the beam onto them.

He turned back to face the wave and glared at the monster heading straight for them.

'Erina,' he shouted, 'kill the spotlight.'

'What?'

'Shut it down, now!'

She hesitated, then turned it off, plunging them into a dark void.

He couldn't see the oncoming wave, but now that he had an intuitive read on the break, he didn't need to.

Using both hands, he whipped down hard on the accelerator and pulled the engine towards him.

The motor screamed like a banshee. The bow lurched to the right. Water sloshed around the deck.

He sensed the second wave hovering above, rearing its head back, preparing to strike.

He twisted the throttle round full and aimed straight for it.

The bow blasted into the solid wall of water.

They started climbing at a steep angle.

The snarling lip crashed over them.

Water flooded over the gunnels and washed over the stern, slowing their momentum to a crawl.

He swung the engine back and forth in an effort to generate more speed.

They were barely inching ahead. Any second, the weight of water in the stern would drag them back down the face and into oblivion.

Unless he took drastic action, they were history.

In a desperate bid to shift momentum, he let go of the engine and threw himself forwards to the bow, hoping the movement of weight would propel them through the wave, like walking to the nose of a longboard.

The boat teetered at the critical point. He screamed to Erina, '*Get to the bow, now!*'

She threw herself forwards and grabbed hold of the bow, creating the momentum needed to push them through the lip.

The boat crashed down the other side of the wave into the deep trough. It was now two-thirds full of water. One more hit would sink them.

Carter scrambled to the stern and seized the throttle. He pointed the bow back towards the headland, where they had come from and where the helicopter now hovered, then twisted the throttle to idle and tied off the engine.

Erina was already on her feet, lashing the spotlight to the seat so that it pointed skywards.

They didn't need to speak.

He reached forwards, untied the surfboard and held it under his right arm.

She switched on the light.

He put the engine into gear and twisted the accelerator to one-third throttle.

The waterlogged boat started to gather speed.

They positioned themselves on the port side of the boat with one foot on the gunnel.

'Ready for a dip?' he asked.

'After you.'

He jumped into the choppy water. Erina followed a second later. He held the tail of the board while she climbed onto it. He turned his head and watched the boat chug away from them.

The spotlight from the approaching helicopter danced over the water, seeking them out.

CHAPTER 18

Carter pulled himself onto the board after Erina with his daypack strapped tight to his back. They both lay facedown, his chest arched over her smooth back and his legs pressed against hers.

In a few fleeting seconds the third wave in the set would hit shallow water, jack up and launch forwards, transforming the wind-blown rolling face into a steep and unforgiving precipice the size of a two-storey building.

The helicopter was moving away from them, making a beeline for the sinking boat heading back towards the headland, drawn by its spotlight bobbing up and down.

The decoy would give them enough time to get into position and make the take-off, but there'd be no second chances.

Erina remained perfectly still so as not to throw off the balance of the board, making his job a lot easier.

He needed to find the sweet spot, the one point on the face of the wave where they could take off safely at the right angle. To have any chance of surfing across the reef, he needed to position the board so they'd cut across the smooth face ahead of the crashing wall of white foam generated by the breaking lip.

If they positioned themselves too wide of the sweet spot, they'd miss the wave when it came and almost certainly get cleaned up by the next one. If they sat too far inside of it, the board would nosedive down the face and they'd get caught by the breaking lip. It'd pick them up and smash them onto the coral reef.

He lined up the board at forty-five degrees to where he figured the giant wave would break.

Erina's back muscles flexed under his chest.

He slid back a few centimetres so the nose tilted upwards a little more, reducing the risk of a nosedive, the biggest hazard when riding tandem. The board was now at the optimum angle and their weight distribution felt just right. The undertow started sucking them towards the approaching wave.

Once its arching face swept them up, he'd only be able to make fine adjustments, shifting his weight incrementally and leaning left or right to trim the board.

He moved forwards a centimetre and shouted, '*Hang tight!*'

He stroked hard and deep, his inner arms brushing past Erina's thighs.

The ten-foot board sprung to life, and as the full force of the wave took hold, they charged across the steep face, the bottom of the board whooshing against the water. They accelerated high above the earthly plane, perfectly in tune with the forces of nature. It felt like they'd been catapulted into another dimension, where the laws of gravity ceased to apply.

He leant into the wave, lifting them further up the face, the height of two stacked semitrailers above the water. The surf gods rode with them, guided them, as they hurtled through time and space.

The deck started vibrating.

He eased his weight off Erina's back and leant further into the curl, lining up the board so that they maintained height, speed and position and stayed ahead of the breaking lip, roaring a metre behind them. Any further back and the breaking section would eat them. Any further forwards and they'd be thrown off the wave.

This sense of dancing on the edge of oblivion made surfing big waves a profound and soulful experience. It was addictive, driving surfers to travel the world seeking the next adrenalin-fuelled high. And just when he thought it couldn't get any more intense, it did.

The lip curled over them, encasing them in a cylindrical tube of water – what surfers called a stand-up barrel – big enough to stand upright and stretch your arms out wide.

Their world became eerily quiet and pitch-black. They'd entered the zone known as the 'green room'. The mystical place every surfer longed to be. Like being suspended inside Mother Nature's womb. A moment of holy stillness surrounded by the surging power of nature, a fragile snapshot of perfection.

He slid his weight a fraction forwards to generate more speed, his chest pressing on Erina's back. He felt her muscles tense as the board flew across the face through the eerie darkness.

Nothing seemed real, except Erina's taut body beneath him.

One second they were deep inside the tube, the next they flew out onto the open face.

A rush of exhilaration raced through him. It was like they'd travelled to the other side of existence and returned to tell the tale.

For a serious surfer, nothing could ever match this experience, every micro-second tinged with the prospect of a watery death.

Yet such perfection couldn't last.

Sounds from outside their cocoon crashed in. They'd re-entered the real world, where the laws of time, space and gravity ruled.

Somewhere behind them, the helicopter roared. To their left, waves smashed onto the shallow reef.

More disturbingly, the angle of the board had changed, shattering the perfect symmetry they'd experienced inside the green room.

He shifted his weight further back and leant harder into the wave.

The board wobbled from side to side.

He yelled, '*Hold on!*'

Just as he spoke, the board nosedived, plunging forwards into the abyss.

The nose twisted and turned. The board rolled and bucked.

He tried to hang on, but the power of the wave wrenched the board out of his hands.

He grabbed Erina by the waist.

The full force of the wave crashed into his back, driving them down into the unholy depths of no man's land, spinning them around and around through the ink-black swirling water. There was no up or down or anywhere in between.

He had no idea how far down they'd been pushed.

His arms gripped Erina's stomach and squeezed tight, trying to maintain a secure hold.

Her skin was slippery. His legs entangled with hers.

He needed to get a better grip, somehow wrap his arms under her shoulders and his legs around her torso in a vice. Or he'd lose her.

He adjusted his arms to get a firmer grip.

At that precise moment the tumbling wave gave a violent jerk, picking them up and hurling them towards the ocean floor.

The surging wall of water twisted him to the left.

Her to the right.

He clutched at her waist. His grip started to slip.

One second he had hold of her.

The next …

She was gone.

CHAPTER 19

In the chaos of no man's land Carter was gripped by a feeling he almost never succumbed to.

Fear.

Erina was a good surfer and swimmer, but she wasn't anywhere near as familiar with this violent, out-of-control world as he was. In such extreme conditions she'd be vulnerable. And there was the distinct possibility that the board had struck her on the head, rendering her unconscious.

The thought of losing her terrified him.

The rampaging wave drove him down, down, down and spun him around and around. His arms flayed about in the darkness, seeking Erina among the chundering mass of raging water moving in every direction. The more he thrashed about, the more the ocean pummelled him, and he achieved nothing.

After a few minutes his lungs began screaming for oxygen. Just when he felt sure they'd burst, a moment of clarity descended upon him.

To survive in heavy surf such as this, you needed to understand, accept and ride out the wild whims and violent moods of the ocean with detachment, humility and patience. If you failed to do so, it would exact cruel vengeance. Thrashing about had only wasted precious air.

He ceased fighting and surrendered totally to the force of the ocean.

An immediate shift occurred. His body relaxed and his movement became effortless, like a cork bobbing in the water.

—

In its own time the ocean spat him out into still, calm water.

Carter's head breached the surface and he drew in deep lungfuls of air. The daypack remained secure on his back.

He trod water, circling on the spot.

The wave had transported him across the reef to the deepwater channel, but there was no sign of Erina.

He closed his eyes and tried to feel her.

His racing heart slowed and he tuned his senses to the world around him.

The rain had backed off to a gentle pitter-patter and the rolling swell lifted him up and down without breaking.

He sensed Erina nearby.

His eyes flashed open and he swam to his right.

After five strokes he saw her ahead of him, facedown in the water.

He took another four powerful strokes, took her in his arms and rested her head on his shoulder.

His elation at seeing her was short-lived.

She was unconscious. Barely breathing.

He felt the back of her head. His hand caressed a large swelling. The board had collected her skull, knocking her out cold.

He continued to tread water, kicking hard to keep her head clear.

He squeezed her chest and shook her in an effort to expel the water from her lungs and kickstart her breathing.

Her arms hung limp by his side.

His oxygen-starved legs started to cramp. The struggle through no man's land had taken its toll. He started dropping back into the water.

He forced his toes upwards to ease the cramp, then kicked even harder, still pumping her chest.

'Erina, come on.'

He reached around and forced two fingers into her mouth and stuck them down her throat.

A slight spasm rippled through her body.

He pulled his fingers out.

She shook violently. A warm river flowed down his back. He felt her heart beat and the rise and fall of her chest.

He eased her onto her back into the warm ocean, making sure her mouth and nose were clear, and then looked up.

A full moon shone through a break in the cloud cover.

Even though they were in the middle of the ocean off a remote and hostile island, he felt more connected to the universe than he could remember.

CHAPTER 20

Again, Thomas picked up Carter's presence.

He still lay on the bench in his cell. His body throbbed with pain, and he knew Wayan's condition had, if anything, deteriorated.

His perception had changed, though, and that made all the difference.

Like everything else in life, a person's response to suffering served a higher purpose. The challenges he faced in that cell were forcing him to look into his own soul and confront the truth.

He needed to walk his idealistic talk and reconnect with his fundamental beliefs. Nothing else truly mattered.

His personal ambition was simple: treat every test in life as a battle for personal power and face every challenge with humility and courage.

For Carter and Erina this philosophy was an interesting theory that they adhered to as best they could. For Thomas, though, it was the cornerstone of his life.

In the last few years, Carter had drifted away from his spiritual foundations, eventually walking out on the order. Thomas had only needed to spend twenty minutes with him to see that his rejection of the order and its principles hadn't worked for him. It was obvious, whether Carter realised it or not, that he needed to rediscover and commit to the path of the spirit. And so, Thomas now realised, did he. It was always easier to see what another man needed to do.

The true measure of a man revealed itself in the face of disaster. Thomas needed to get past the pain and focus on what needed to be done. The first step was to find the positives in his position.

Carter was nearby and wouldn't give up.

Furthermore, Samudra and his men's behaviour had reaffirmed Thomas's belief in his life's work.

Someone needed to make a stand against prejudice and hate, and protect those who couldn't protect themselves.

That was the order's primary purpose.

If he died that day, at least he'd die having fought for what he believed in.

That was something to be grateful for.

He felt himself recommitting to the principles of the order. Reminding him to: *Accept that what is, is. Expect the unexpected. And never give up.*

Whatever was meant to happen would happen. He just needed to do what he could in that moment.

For now, that meant waiting patiently for Carter and Erina.

CHAPTER 21

Carter wrapped his right arm lightly around Erina's chest and then, using a one-handed breaststroke, swam with her in tow across the relatively calm channel, away from the turbulence of the surf pounding on the reef and towards the rocky shoreline.

The cove was just under a hundred metres away; their silent swim took less than five minutes. They passed through a three-metre-wide opening and entered an oval pool of water, surrounded by rock walls on three sides. With the moonlight reflecting off the water, it was a place of uncommon beauty.

Holding Erina's arm, Carter jumped out of the water, grabbed her under the shoulders and pulled her onto a wide rock platform that ran along one side of the cove.

The full moon provided just enough light to see. He laid her on her back with her arms by her side. Her eyes remained closed. She was in shock, exhausted, and needed time to regain her composure and strength. For now, they were relatively safe, but the helicopter still hovered somewhere over the reef.

He removed his daypack, sat next to her on the smooth rock and took a few moments to get his bearings, watching her breathe in and out.

She was a rare woman, one of those special people who responded to extreme pressure with grace, poise and a dry humour. These qualities more than matched her outer beauty and were the true source of his attraction to her.

Part of him longed to tell her how relieved he was that she was okay, how much he cared for her and wanted to be close to her. But this was not the time to talk about his feelings, nor try to understand them. They'd sort out their relationship, whatever it might be, when the job was done.

He held her hand and squeezed gently.

She returned the pressure and slowly opened her eyes. He helped her to sit up, reached into his daypack, pulled out a bottle of water and placed it in her hand.

She took a long drink and then drew in three deep breaths. He put his hand on her shoulder and felt her body relax.

'How're you doing?' he asked.

She stretched her neck and touched the back of her head. 'Considering I've been hit over the head with a surfboard, swallowed gallons of water, almost drowned and vomited over your back, I'm pretty good.'

She began to cough and took another long drink. They sat in a comfortable silence for a while, neither wanting to break the spell of the moment.

They both knew instinctively when it was time to move. He held out his hand and helped her to her feet.

'That was some wave we caught,' she said, pushing her hair out of her eyes. 'I've never been tubed like that.' She paused. 'It was as good as you said it'd be.'

'The green room is a holy place.'

'I want to go there again.'

'We will.'

He led her along the rock ledge, counting off the paces from the entrance to the cove in his head.

Fifty-eight, fifty-nine …

He stopped, laid down the daypack and took out the flashlight. She drew level with him and they stood shoulder to shoulder on the coarse rock, looking down at the smooth surface of the water.

'According to the map in my head,' he said, 'the cave should be near here. I'll dive down, find the entrance and be right back.'

She nodded.

'If the helicopter heads this way, grab both breathing devices and my daypack. Then join me underwater.'

'Okay.'

———

He dived into the warm water, his eyes wide open, and started stroking for the bottom, holding the glowing flashlight in his right hand.

The bright arc of light lit up a school of small tropical fish whose colours covered the spectrum of the rainbow. In unison they turned to face the light, then darted off to go about their business. A metre-long blue grouper swam past at a lazy pace, ignoring him.

He dived another ten metres but saw no sign of the bottom.

The cave entrance was, he figured, further along. He switched the flashlight off and started floating upwards, the slow movement in the dark through the tranquil water relaxing his muscles.

His head breached the surface and he took a long breath.

Erina crouched on the ledge. 'We all set to go?'

'Hang on a bit longer. It's very deep here. I reckon the cave is about thirty metres that way.' He pointed further down the cove.

Erina picked up his daypack. He started to breaststroke parallel to the rock wall. She walked along the ledge, keeping pace with him. The helicopter continued to buzz over no man's land.

He stopped swimming after thirty metres and turned to face her. 'This should be about the spot.'

'Go,' she said.

He sucked in a lungful of air and again plunged headfirst into the watery depths.

The first thing he noticed was that the bottom was shallower, suggesting the entrance to the cave was nearby.

The second thing that struck him was that the beam of light lit up nothing but crystal-clear water.

There were no fish at all.

He stroked deeper. The flashlight illuminated the deserted sandy ocean floor.

Something wasn't right.

He shone the flashlight towards the cove wall and what he saw jolted his heart rate.

Come on, he thought to himself. *Give me a break.*

CHAPTER 22

The bright beam lit up a shark cruising slowly through the water towards him.

It was close to four metres long and probably weighed around five hundred kilos. He noted the dark stripes along its body.

A tiger shark.

They were apex predators, at the top of the food chain, and had a reputation for eating anything. Often found near reef breaks, they were one of the most dangerous sharks to be found in the Indian Ocean.

Its razor-toothed jaw hung slightly ajar, suggesting an enigmatic yet malevolent grin.

Carter switched off the flashlight. Adrenalin raced through his bloodstream, jacking up his heart rate.

For Carter, like most people, facing a shark wearing only a pair of board shorts was a worst nightmare. Death by drowning, burning, gunshot, knife, poison or snakebite seemed pleasant in comparison.

Sharks possessed a sixth sense, enabling them to detect the electromagnetic field emitted by any living creature in their immediate vicinity, able to sense as little as half a billionth of a volt.

The one good thing about spotting a shark was that it meant you were still alive. Usually they struck before you registered their presence.

He fought back the compulsion to shoot straight for the surface and jump onto dry land. Any sudden movement could attract the shark's attention and precipitate an attack.

He reminded himself that sharks weren't as a rule dangerous to humans. Ninety-nine times out of a hundred, a shark would swim away and leave you alone. He knew all this.

Still, understanding the cold facts was one thing. Refraining from freaking out when you saw a prehistoric monster up close and personal in its natural habitat was another matter entirely.

He forced himself to bring his heart rate under control. The shark might get him, but his fear would not.

He allowed himself to drift slowly upwards, his naked limbs feeling exposed and vulnerable in the darkness. His arm extended in front of him, seeking the comfort of solid earth.

His hand touched rock and he breached the surface. He rested his arms on the rock ledge and gulped the night air.

Erina stood by the water's edge. One breathing device hung around her neck; the other was in her left hand. The sealed daypack lay at her feet.

She looked at him in a way that made him feel transparent.

'What's wrong?' she asked. 'Couldn't you find the cave?'

'I did. But you need to wait here.'

'For what?'

'I need to check something.' He reached out. 'Give me a breathing device.'

She handed it to him.

Before she had a chance to say another word, he looped the attached lanyard around his neck and said, 'Be back in a sec.'

He stuck the rubber mouthpiece of the breathing device in his mouth, breathed in a lungful of air, slipped below the surface and propelled himself downwards, careful not to make any jerky movements.

Twenty metres under, he switched on the flashlight and swung it in a hundred-and-eighty-degree arc.

The shark he'd seen earlier was gone. Only one fish swam by, another blue grouper. Due to the groupers' size, shape and slow, gentle presence, sharks didn't instinctively see them as dinner. But all other life forms kept well away.

His flashlight lit up the cave entrance.

It appeared perfect for their purposes, big enough to drive a small car through.

Then it didn't seem quite so perfect.

Another shark, also close to four metres long, glided out of its mouth.

Carter was twenty metres from the shark and the same distance from the surface. He consciously relaxed his muscles. He needed to act like a fish in its natural habitat and avoid making any movements that'd signal he was afraid.

It took him a long fifteen seconds to drift to the surface, all the while picturing giant teeth tearing into his naked flesh.

Again, his hand touched the solid rock wall and, in one smooth movement, he pulled himself out of the water onto the safety of the ledge.

'So what's the big problem?' Erina asked. 'You look like you've seen your grandmother's ghost. What aren't you telling me?'

He could hide nothing from her.

'I just saw two tiger sharks swim out of the cave. I reckon it's a sharks' nest.'

'Sharks don't have nests. They mostly swim alone.'

'You try telling them that.'

'I don't know why you've got this thing about sharks. All you want to do is spend your time in the ocean surfing and yet you're scared of sharks. There's something screwy in that logic.'

'When this is over, I'll get some therapy.'

'Most shark attacks are mistakes. Dogs kill more people in one year in the US than sharks have in the last hundred.'

'That's all very well, but very few people swim with them in caves.'

'And it's the only way we can get into Samudra's compound?'

'Correct.'

She stood for a moment, expressionless, taking it in.

Then she looked into his eyes. 'Have you come up with a plan?'

'Swim through the cave without being eaten.'

CHAPTER 23

Carter and Erina eased themselves feet first into the warm water and swam down the side of the rock wall, following the beam of the flashlight strapped to the side of his head. He held a six-inch blade in his right hand.

When they were about twenty metres underwater, he put his hand out and signalled for Erina to stay where she was. He swam over to the metre-long blue grouper he'd seen earlier, cruising about four metres above the sandy bottom. Its saucer-like eyes stared at him and its large lips curled as if puckering for a kiss. He hated having to do what he was about to do, but he didn't have a choice.

He pulled the knife back and thrust the blade deep into the grouper's belly, twisting it up and around, creating a large jagged wound.

The innocent and normally slow-moving fish started to thrash violently in the water. Blood and intestines oozed out, spreading a pink cloud. For the sharks, the grouper's wild movements would be a dinner bell.

Carter did the same to a second grouper and slid the knife into its sheath, now strapped to his waist. He then motioned for Erina to join him.

They started swimming towards the cave at a steady pace. He breathed slowly through the rubber mouthpiece of the device and out through his nose, keeping his focus locked on the cave mouth, very aware of their relative position in the ocean's food chain.

He turned his head and saw a blur of movement flash through the water towards the wounded groupers. Most likely the shark he'd seen earlier. It tore into the wounded fish, creating a swirling cloud of red. Dinner had been served.

He squeezed Erina's hand. She returned the pressure and they continued to stroke towards the cave mouth.

The flashlight lit up the inside of the cave, a beautiful and dangerous world of bright coral.

They weren't dressed for the occasion.

Erina wore small briefs and a bra, while Carter was only in his board shorts. If they brushed against the coral, the sharp points would rip their skin and the scent of blood in the water could bring the sharks hurrying back.

Fortunately, the width of the cave gave them plenty of room to manoeuvre.

Carter glided through the opening, three-quarters of a body length ahead of Erina, careful not to make any sudden movements or get too far ahead of her.

They followed the light into the mouth of the brightly coloured tunnel.

When they'd swum about thirty metres, his insides turned ice-cold. He reminded himself that dogs killed more people than sharks and it was almost unheard of to see more than two sharks in an area like this.

He raised his free hand and stopped swimming.

The flashlight lit up another shark thirty metres away, cruising very slowly along the floor of the cave towards them. Clearly it didn't subscribe to the theory that sharks swam alone.

Erina moved up next to him.

He pointed down.

She involuntarily jerked backwards.

He grabbed her hand and switched the light off.

Feeling his way in the ink-black darkness, he positioned himself above her. He covered her back and wrapped his arms and legs around her, protecting her from the coral as they floated upwards towards the ceiling of the tunnel. She offered no resistance, clearly understanding what he had in mind.

He hunched his head and shoulders forwards, ensuring only his daypack, which covered half his back, made direct contact with the roof's coral lining.

Their bodies' natural buoyancy pressed upwards, holding them in place. Carter clung to Erina blindly, like a limpet, his heart pounding against her back.

He could feel Erina's heartbeat too. It was relatively steady.

Her hands squeezed his forearm, reassuring him.

He returned the gesture and clamped down on his breathing device.

Bloody sharks, he thought to himself and focused all his attention on the flow of his breath.

CHAPTER 24

After what seemed an extraordinarily long time, but in reality was less than a dozen heartbeats, there was a surge of water up ahead of them, indicating that the shark, whose massive body displaced a large volume of water, was moving towards them.

The shark had a simple choice to make. Either it'd strike them hard and fast or swim straight for what was left of the dying fish outside the cave, oblivious to all else.

The moving wall of current pushed against them with greater intensity. The shark was accelerating.

Carter tensed his stomach and shoulder muscles. Erina gave his arm a reassuring double squeeze.

He hugged her even harder. The worst-case scenario, he told himself, was that he'd get to die in the arms of the person he cared most about in the world.

Then the current jammed them hard against the roof.

He held his breath in the darkness, bracing for a ferocious strike when …

The current receded.

Followed by a profound and beautiful stillness.

He expelled the air he'd been holding in and started counting.

One thousand and one, one thousand and two, one thousand and three …

He released his grip on Erina and pushed her away from him. They separated slowly, like two isolated probes in deep outer space connected by an invisible bond.

He switched on the flashlight and the bright beam cut through the clear water.

The cave was empty – they seemed to be alone.

His gut and shoulder muscles relaxed. For now, the watery nightmare was over.

He shone the flashlight on Erina, who was already stroking towards the bottom of the cave.

She turned and gave him a thumbs-up sign, as if to say, 'I told you so.'

He reciprocated the gesture.

—

They swam through the dark tunnel. The only sign of life they encountered was a handful of crabs scurrying across the bottom.

After nearly ten minutes, the cave widened and the floor fell away another five metres. The temperature dropped and Carter's buoyancy decreased, suggesting less salt in the water.

He stopped swimming and pointed the flashlight upwards. The light refracted into the open air above them, indicating a large pocket. He swam towards it.

His head burst through the surface. He trod water and shone the flashlight about him. They'd reached the end of the tunnel and had entered the large rock-walled cavern Djoran had told them about.

To his right he heard running water and the hum of an electric motor, both impossibly loud after the underwater silence.

He switched off the flashlight, spat out his breathing device and turned towards the sound.

A weak light lit up six men dressed in army fatigues standing along a rock ledge, each pointing an Uzi at his head. His concern about the sharks suddenly seemed like a distant memory.

Erina's head breached the surface just in front of him.

She gave him one of her half-smiles. 'We need to discuss this issue you have with sharks,' she said.

'It's not our only problem.'

Erina looked up towards the armed men and said, 'You're right.'

A spotlight snapped on, filling the cavern with bright light.

He squinted.

'Out of the water,' a loud voice barked from above. 'Keep your hands where we can see them.'

Carter saw only one option.

He pulled himself out of the pool and raised his hands.

Erina followed his lead.

'Turn around,' the voice said. 'Put your hands on your heads.'

Carter and Erina did as they were told.

He sensed someone approaching from behind and braced himself.

BOOK FIVE

CHAPTER 1

Samudra's compound, Batak Island, 2.40 p.m., 28 December

Kemala Sungkar pulled her long black cotton skirt from under her knees and adjusted the multicoloured embroidered prayer mat beneath her.

She knelt upright and stared at the shadows thrown against the wall by the bars that secured the only window in her room.

By order of Samudra, her younger brother by seven years, she was being held in a small wooden bungalow at the back of his island compound, furnished with only a thin mattress and a single wooden chair.

How she detested him and everything he stood for. She had tried hard to focus on her prayers, but her constant anger made it impossible. One question consumed her: *how had it come to this?*

She was forty-six years old, and throughout her entire personal and professional life, the cornerstone of her daily existence had been her duty to family and her beloved religion, Islam. Now she was imprisoned by her own brother in the name of the God she loved.

She closed her eyes and focused on calming her racing mind. The problem was, when she became quiet – when she tried to pray – she had to face the undeniable and disturbing truth that she herself was in part to blame for this diabolical situation. Her own behaviour, her lack of action, had made it possible.

It was easy to see with the clarity of hindsight that growing up in a family with power and influence had made her ignorant and complacent. She'd been blind to the corruption and graft that were such an integral part of life in Indonesia, and to the suffering of the large mass of those less fortunate. But the clan's true rot had started with Arung, her older brother, after her father's death.

Like many women in her position, she'd never questioned the source of the family wealth that made her privileged lifestyle possible. For the last six years she'd been too busy flying between Jakarta and Palo Alto, completing an MBA at Stanford University, to think about who was paying for it, and how.

A sweet, pungent aroma drifted towards her from under the thick wooden front door. On the other side, one of Samudra's mujaheddin sat smoking a clove cigarette, no doubt cradling a standard-issue automatic rifle in his lap.

Earlier that morning her dear friend Djoran had taken a huge risk when delivering breakfast to her bungalow. Under the bamboo cover of her tray, next to her orange juice and fresh fruit, lay a large metal key, a small handgun, a silencer, a roll of black packing tape and a folded note.

The note lay open on the wooden floor beside her. She picked it up and re-read it for the third time.

My dearest Kemala,
It pains me to inform you that Thomas has been captured and badly beaten, along with Wayan. Carter and Erina were captured this morning also. They are all being held in the cell on the compound's western perimeter.
I am most saddened to say Samudra is planning to execute them early this evening and film the event.
The key I have provided will open the door to their cell.

You must free our friends, take them to the hidden bunker that I informed you about and flee from the island.

This is, I believe, your sacred duty.

My role is to stay close to Samudra and discover exactly what he is planning for Sydney. He has not as yet informed us of his intentions. Except that seven of us depart for Australia tomorrow.

Finally, I have provided you with a handgun and silencer. I know how much you deplore violence. But these are desperate times and we are called upon to perform desperate duties that go against our true nature and the highest calling of our faith.

Pray to God, but please do whatever it takes to free these people and get them and yourself to safety.

Have strength, my sister, and may God be with us all.

Your most loving friend,

Djoran

The key now hung around her neck, hidden under her loose-fitting garments, and she clutched it as her thoughts turned to the four people held prisoner by her brother.

Wayan was an ambitious boy, with the potential to bloom into a fine man and leader of his people.

She'd never met Carter. Though Carter had left the order, Thomas often spoke of him with warm affection, saying that if he reconnected with his spirit and true path in life, he was capable of greatness.

Erina remained an enigma to her. She felt the younger woman had never trusted her, always questioning her motives for befriending Thomas. Kemala often felt Erina was judging her and became very guarded, almost secretive, in her presence. She admired the younger woman's spirit and skill nevertheless, and hoped one day to be her friend. She saw much of Thomas in her.

Thomas was without doubt the finest man she'd ever encountered, the one she'd been waiting for all her life. She still remembered the moment when she recognised the stillness and compassion in his soft brown eyes.

She had loved him ever since that first fateful meeting in Jakarta, sharing tea after they met at a talk about Sufism in the modern world. For the first time in her life, and from that day on, she felt connected in mind and spirit with another human being without any reservation.

Her family hated the order, so a true relationship between them was impossible. Thomas, recognising the threat he posed to her safety, had never initiated any inappropriate contact. Still, she'd often thought longingly of how she might be with him.

Thomas lived a principled life – it was what had attracted her to him. He inspired her to look again at her own life, her own beliefs, and remove the blinkers from her sheltered eyes. Because of him, it became increasingly impossible for her to ignore the reality of her family's activities.

When Samudra became clan leader and his agenda became evident, she could no longer remain loyal to her family. Nine months ago, after much angst, she had taken Thomas into her confidence and told him everything she knew about her brother and the clan.

To her great relief, he recognised the enormity of the threat and together with Djoran constructed a plan to discover Samudra's true intentions and stop him.

Five days ago Samudra's chief lieutenant, the vile westerner Alex Botha, who they called by the Muslim name Abdul-Aleem, had kidnapped her from the family's compound in Jakarta and brought her here. She had been kept locked up in the bungalow ever since.

In that time, she had not laid eyes on Samudra and remained ignorant of what he intended doing with her.

For all she knew, he might wrap her in a sheet, lay her in a shallow grave and have her stoned to death, an archaic form of execution favoured by some Islamic fanatics. According to their strict interpretation of Islamic law, by stoning a sinner to death, the executioner cleansed the sinner's soul, thus allowing their spirit to enter heaven despite their moral transgressions.

The irony of murdering another person to cleanse them of their sins was not lost on her and brought the weakest of smiles to her lips. Her brother, in his self-righteous arrogance, would believe he was doing her an immense personal favour by killing her in this manner. To him, she was a delusional whore who deserved no mercy.

She was grateful for one thing: her mother and father were no longer alive to witness the shameful turn the family's business had taken, and its tragic fallout. Yet while they would have been appalled at where Arung and Samudra had taken the clan, they would never have forgiven her for moving against her younger brother.

Regardless of what her parents might have thought, she knew now what she needed to do, even if it threatened to destroy the Sungkar clan.

She stood and walked towards the thin dirty mattress on the floor, knelt down and lifted the top corner, exposing the handgun and silencer.

Samudra's fanaticism was like an incurable disease, festering and spreading. Ultimately, it would prove fatal for him and many others. She needed to put an end to the madness. Faith without action meant nothing. Her time had come.

She picked up the gun.

The metal felt cold in her hands. She observed the details of the small wooden handle, then checked the magazine and counted six bullets ready for duty.

Her heart started to race and her chest flushed with adrenal heat.

She placed the weapon back on the bed with the awe and care accorded a sacred icon. It both scared and excited her.

From this moment forward she knew nothing would ever be the same for her again.

CHAPTER 2

On the other side of Batak Island Samudra sat upright on his hammock at the rear of his five-bedroom property in the lush hills looking over the ocean. He threw his legs over the side and attempted to push the dark thoughts of his sister out of his mind.

His son, Osama, was playing with Ali, his pet monkey, a six-month-old long-tailed macaque, at the far end of the garden.

Praise be to God for the next generation.

The comfortable home was a short helicopter ride from the compound and had been built by his late brother Arung. It provided a constant reminder of Arung's untimely death at the hands of the order.

The sound of a fast-approaching helicopter shifted his attention to a far more pressing matter.

At the compound the night before, two of his men had demonstrated worrying signs of doubt about carrying out the planned jihad in Sydney, putting their families and existence on earth above eternal salvation.

Doubt was a spiritual malaise that would not be tolerated or allowed to spread through his men under any circumstances. His years of training with veteran mujaheddin in Pakistan and Afghanistan had taught him the necessity of eradicating such contagion.

His thoughts were interrupted by the aroma of warm chilli spices and fried chicken drifting across the humid air.

'Samudra! Osama!' his wife called from the kitchen. 'Lunch is ready!'

He stepped off the hammock and glanced over his shoulder towards the house.

The sound of the approaching helicopter would displease his wife greatly. For Premita, family lunch on Sunday was a sacred event. Particularly as he'd only returned last night from business and this would be his last meal with them before his departure for Sydney the next day.

If the helicopter brought the news he expected, he'd need to return to the compound without delay. It pained him to disappoint his very good wife. As befitting her role, she never questioned his duties as clan leader, even when he operated well outside the bounds of man's laws. But inside the family confines she saw herself as the undisputed ruler – making her the one person on earth whose wrath he feared.

A cry came from the far end of the garden.

'Gotcha!'

He turned towards his son, who was clutching his monkey by the tail.

The monkey shrieked and Osama squealed with excitement. 'I have you now!'

'Samudra! Osama!' Premita called again in a much sharper tone.

Samudra pointed his finger at Osama. 'You heard your mother. Leave Ali alone and wash your hands for lunch.'

'No!'

'You dare question your father?'

The monkey jumped up and down on the spot and started clapping.

Osama burst out laughing.

Samudra couldn't help but grin. He controlled the destiny of his clan and was the sole architect of the most audacious and holy plan for God and Islam since the attack on the Twin Towers. Like his hero, the great Osama bin Laden, he saw his life's purpose as striving to unleash death and destruction upon the enemies of Allah. When it came to his family, though – his son, his daughter and his wife – he was powerless.

Still, weakness was the wrong message to pass on to his son.

He glared at him. 'You want to experience the joys of God's heaven and live in paradise forever or burn in the fires of eternal hell?'

'Paradise, please.'

'Then do as you're told.'

Another call came from the back of the house, full of anger and impatience, causing them both to look around.

'Hurry up! Lunch is getting cold!'

Osama turned and ran towards the house.

Samudra looked up at the approaching helicopter and wondered how far the situation on the compound had deteriorated.

He reached under his white robe and ran his finger over the smooth handle of his sheathed kris, which he carried with him at all times. Then he patted the Beretta Bobcat, a small semiautomatic pistol, tucked inside a leather holster strapped under his armpit.

He thought of his beloved grandfather, Fajar, who had fought on the battlefields of Afghanistan, witnessing the defeat of the Russians. The great victory had galvanised Fajar and his Indonesian comrades, who saw themselves as fighters in a global struggle for Islam. By defeating the might of the imperialist Soviet superpower, they had proved themselves capable of achieving anything in the service of God.

On returning to Indonesia as highly disciplined and highly trained devotees of jihad, they continued the great work by carrying the flag of Islam and vowing to create a unified Muslim state worldwide.

Samudra had sworn on Fajar's deathbed that he'd pursue his grandfather's holy fight, striking fear into the heart of his enemies, no matter how long and difficult the struggle might be.

As much as he loved his wife and family, he needed to remember who he was and where his true duty lay.

CHAPTER 3

Samudra strapped himself into the passenger seat of his Robinson R22 Beta helicopter, placed the audio headset over his ears and scrutinised his second-in-command, Abdul-Aleem, who was absorbed in checking the controls.

At thirty-seven years of age, Abdul-Aleem was at the height of his physical powers, possessing the strength of a mighty elephant and the agility of a wild monkey. His extensive military and martial-arts background and inside knowledge of the order were most impressive.

He'd organised the placing of a GPS homing device inside Erina's computer at the film shoot near Boggabilla, enabling them to track her and Carter's movements every step of the way. They, along with Thomas and the young boy, would be executed at dusk.

Samudra recognised Abdul-Aleem's ingenuity and usefulness.

For now.

Abdul-Aleem flicked a few switches and the helicopter roared to life. He moved the control stick back and they lifted off in the direction of the compound.

Though the man had shown marked improvement in his character since converting to Islam, Samudra still believed that Abdul-Aleem was, at his core, a decadent westerner, and never quite trusted him.

Samudra was not naive. He recognised that the man's conversion in prison was most likely born out of his desperation to get out of jail rather than a true love of God and a desire to do his will on earth.

To insure against any weakness of faith or lack of loyalty on Abdul-Aleem's part, Samudra had promised him $250,000 once the jihad was successfully executed. Of course he never intended to honour the debt. In fact, by accepting the bribe, Abdul-Aleem had greatly hastened his own end.

Samudra switched his headset on and asked, 'What happened with Usif and Mohammed?'

Abdul-Aleem stared straight ahead. 'The stupid fools want to withdraw from the mission and be allowed to return home.'

'Not acceptable.'

'Agreed.'

Samudra closed his eyes, rotated his head from side to side to relieve the stiffness in his neck and thought through his options.

'What of the others?' he asked.

'No one else has uttered a word. But we must assume there is potential dissent in the ranks.'

'I presume the two men's families are on the island?'

'Yes. Both have wives and small children.'

'Excellent. And what are the men doing now?'

'They're playing football on the beach.'

'Radio ahead and have them all assemble on the top training field in formation. And make sure the families of the misguided are present as well.'

Abdul-Aleem turned to him. 'What do you need them for?'

'Just do as I command.'

Samudra switched the headset off and looked out the window away from Abdul-Aleem.

He answered to no one but God.

—

The helicopter climbed over the peak of the volcanic mountain that separated the two sides of the island and began its descent towards the U-shaped mujaheddin compound below.

Samudra peered through the tinted window at his creation in the name of Allah. The compound was surrounded by sea at the front, a steep mountain escarpment at the rear and sheer rocky cliffs on either side. The self-contained camp provided his men with everything they needed to prepare them for the great tasks ahead. He'd built a shooting range, two training fields, a gym, a communications centre and a weapons and explosives storage unit.

His eye was drawn, as always, to the sparkling white-tiled dome of the mosque, the compound's centrepiece, of which he was most proud. It offered a constant reminder to him and his men of their duty to God and their need to obey, honour and serve him.

He closed his eyes and recited one of his favourite passages of scripture to himself in his head.

Let those believers who sell the life of this world for the hereafter fight in the cause of Allah, and whosoever fights in the cause of Allah, and is killed or is victorious, we shall bestow on him a great reward.

One unerring truth governed his every breath. He was a mujaheddin, a holy warrior for God. Nothing else in existence mattered more than his sacred duty to Allah.

And every one of his men would soon be reminded of this fact.

CHAPTER 4

Twenty-four mujaheddin dressed in black caps and olive fatigues stood at attention in three rows of eight on the flat ridge of the compound's training field, forty metres above sea level.

Samudra positioned himself in front of them next to Abdul-Aleem and surveyed his assembled men. Seeing them in perfect parade-ground formation filled him with immense pride. Their demeanour and discipline were testimony to the hard work and training they'd endured and the respect they afforded him as their leader and obedient servant of Allah.

Usif and Mohammed, the two men whose fate hung in the balance, were in the front row and to the left. Their wives and children huddled together at the back of the ridge under the shade of a red calliandra tree.

Only Abdul-Aleem and himself carried arms. As instructed, Abdul-Aleem had an Uzi submachine gun slung over his right shoulder.

Samudra had rehearsed in his mind exactly what was required to ensure the group remained committed to their great objective, jihad. Not only must the men love God – most importantly they needed to fear God.

Samudra pulled himself up to his full one hundred and sixty-six centimetres. He maintained the smile on his face. It demonstrated to the men that his faith in the rightness of what God ordained was strong.

'Rejoice with me,' he said, speaking slowly and clearly. 'I am proud to announce that the order, a most despicable enemy of our clan, of Allah and of Islam, has been all but destroyed. We have captured four of its people, and this evening you shall all witness their death – a testament to the power of the one true God we all serve and the vengeance he wreaks on his enemies.'

He paused, allowing the men to drink in his carefully chosen words. He ran his sharp gaze over them, seeking out any visible signs of weakness or dissent.

'Even though we are few in number, we shall very soon strike a mighty blow for Allah. So long as every single one of you maintains your faith and is prepared to sacrifice all for God in performing his will on earth, we shall perform great deeds in his name.'

He raised his right hand high above his head in a salute to Allah. 'Jihad is the greatest thing you can do with your life. It represents the supreme service you can offer almighty God.'

Again, he gave the words time to sink in, then punched his right fist into the air. 'Rejoice! We are mujaheddin, holy warriors of Allah. Never, ever forget this great fact.'

A surge of passion rushed through him, lifting his heart rate.

'For your life to have meaning,' he said, 'you must live nobly and obey God's law, one hundred per cent. For God's warriors, sharia is more important than life itself. A human life without strict adherence to God's law means nothing.'

He clenched his fist in front of his face and raised the pitch of his voice. 'You must be prepared to forfeit your life for God and not cease your struggle until his law rules first this country and then the entire world. This is our sacred duty.'

As he spoke these words, many of his men nodded and their eyes shone. Their devotion warmed his heart.

He spread his arms out wide, the soft ocean breeze billowing his robe like a sail. He loved sharing his profound message, firing up the men's spirits with the power of God.

'Those who commit to jihad shall enter paradise, where mighty rivers flow beneath verdant bowers. Myriad physical delights in all forms, the sweetest of earthly fruits, shall be perpetually and abundantly available to you. This shall be your great gift for serving God in the supreme manner.

Do you understand this great fact? Do you understand the opportunity you have been given?'

The men, including Abdul-Aleem, replied in unison: 'Yes, sir.'

He wiped the smile from his face in an instant and frowned.

'But the reward for the unbelievers who defy God … is the searing fire of hell, where there is nothing but pain, suffering and degradation for all eternity. Do you understand this?'

'Yes, sir!' they shouted.

He marched along the line towards Usif and Mohammed. Eight months ago he'd recruited them from a poor fishing village on one of the Mentawai Islands off Sumatra.

When he reached them, he stopped and stared deep into their eyes, attempting to read their hearts and minds. What he saw displeased him greatly. Neither could hold his gaze.

'Do you love God?' he asked softly.

'Yes, sir,' they answered.

'Tell me then, why are you no longer of a mind to serve almighty Allah? Why is it you are unwilling to commit one hundred per cent to jihad and perform your sacred duty?'

Neither said a word.

'Are you not prepared to sacrifice all for God and experience the unimaginable pleasures of paradise?' he asked. 'Or do you prefer to live like animals and die like dogs before burning in hell for eternity?'

All that greeted him was grim silence.

'Answer me!' he yelled.

Usif, the skinnier of the two, dropped to his knees, put his hands in the prayer position and looked up at Samudra with pleading eyes.

'Forgive me. I am not yet ready. I do not wish to die.'

A wave of disgust rose in Samudra's stomach. The selfish coward began crying and whimpering like a baby. The man's weakness threatened the whole operation.

'Please, I beg you. Allow me to leave this island with my family, return home and live a normal life as a fisherman, a good husband and father. I am a good Muslim.'

CHAPTER 5

Samudra frowned at the pathetic man crying at his feet.

He hated to lose any of his mujaheddin, even a weak fool like Usif. At heart he was a compassionate man. He'd give him one last opportunity for redemption.

After all, Allah was truly merciful.

Samudra slapped him hard across the face with the back of his hand.

'Do you understand what you are saying?'

Usif began sobbing.

To think he had once treated this man like a son.

'Truly I say unto you, once you take an oath before your brothers and God, there is no turning back. This is your last chance for earthly salvation. Do you want to go to heaven or hell?'

'Please, for the love of God. I don't want to die.'

Samudra stretched his arms towards the earth, easing the tension in his shoulders, and looked away. He'd done all he could.

The time had come to do what God had called him to do.

He reached inside his robes and extracted the shiny semiautomatic handgun from its holster.

It glistened in the bright sunshine.

Usif started shaking, his eyes wide with terror and disbelief, only now appearing to grasp the dreadful wrath God visited on those who dared displease him.

Samudra switched the safety off and pointed the barrel at Usif's forehead.

Behind him a woman shrieked and a child let out a piercing wail.

Usif looked up at him through beseeching eyes, perhaps thinking his pitiful look might save him.

Samudra straightened his back and gently squeezed the trigger.

The gun jumped in his hand.

A flash of light spat out of the barrel, followed by a loud explosion.

Usif collapsed forwards onto the ground. A clean hole at the back of his skull began to ooze thick dark blood.

Samudra turned his attention to Mohammed.

The man stood rigid with fear. A wet patch formed at the crotch of his trousers and spread down his right leg.

The man was a disgrace and no mujaheddin.

A useless human being.

Samudra raised the gun and pointed it at his forehead.

Mohammed's eyes clamped shut.

Without uttering a word, Samudra squeezed the trigger.

The shot rang out and Mohammed dropped to the ground.

The women and children were now wailing and screaming with fear. A most disgusting sound, signifying a total lack of faith in God.

Samudra's attention shifted to the assembled men. They'd maintained their posture and kept their formation perfectly intact.

He'd trained them well.

CHAPTER 6

Samudra returned the weapon to its holster, ignoring the shrieking and wailing of the dead men's wives and children behind him.

He looked down at the fallen bodies, pleased to see that both were dead and already in hell. Their only purpose in life, as it turned out, had been to serve as an example to their brothers of the swift and dreadful price paid by those who forsook God's will.

He marched back to Abdul-Aleem and put out his hand. 'Give me your weapon.'

Abdul-Aleem hesitated and took half a step back.

Samudra glared at him. He would not tolerate disobedience from anyone.

Abdul-Aleem slowly unshouldered his Uzi and handed it to him.

He grabbed it with both hands.

The time had come to send a final, powerful message to the rest of his men.

This younger generation were too soft. It was time to toughen them up.

Samudra had taken inspiration from the Indonesian leader of Darul Islam, S.M. Kartosuwirjo, whom his grandfather had admired and fought alongside. He had divided the world into the 'Abode of Islam' and the 'Abode of War' and believed that Muslims must live by Islamic law alone. Laws made by man were an affront to God.

Kartosuwirjo had written: 'Eliminate all infidels and atheists until they are annihilated … or die as martyrs in a holy war. We are obliged to fight a third world war and bring about world revolution because God's justice in the form of God's kingdom does not exist on earth.'

These words gave Samudra's life its purpose. He would continue the great fight of his grandfather, as would his children and his children's children, until they achieved ultimate victory.

God's law would rule the earth, even if it took a thousand years.

—

Samudra studied the men standing at attention before him. They needed to be reminded that their lives and those of their families paled in significance compared to the will of God and the holy war of jihad.

Six of his men, plus himself and Abdul-Aleem, were heading to Sydney the next day for the first of his lethal attacks.

Doubt and insubordination could not be tolerated. There was no turning back for any of them.

He flicked the Uzi's safety switch to off and marched towards the families of the two dead men, twenty metres from where his men stood.

Samudra stopped in front of the two women and their children. A boy and a girl of around three and four years of age wrapped their arms around their crying mother and buried their faces against her stomach.

The other two young girls, who were between six and eight, hid behind the other woman, clutching her waist.

They all came from weak stock.

The girls' mother turned and looked at him through tear-filled eyes. 'Please,' she said, 'in the name of God, I beseech you. Have mercy on us.'

Samudra smiled. 'Your sins are forgiven.'

He saw hope flicker across her eyes.

He raised the Uzi and squeezed the trigger.

A stream of bullets sprayed out of the barrel.

He never let the smile of almighty God leave his face until the job was done.

CHAPTER 7

The distant, primal scream of two terrified women caused Carter's eyes to snap open. Despite the extreme heat and humidity, a cold shiver ran through him.

Along with Thomas, Erina and Wayan, he lay shackled inside an airless concrete cell. Old-fashioned iron manacles around his neck, waist, wrists and ankles pinned him to a coarse wooden bench, his arms stretched above his head. His joints were stiff and his leg and shoulder muscles ached.

He looked at the solitary window, high up and covered by a grille. The angle of the light filtering through the rusty bars told him it was early afternoon.

Thomas and Wayan were both out to it. They'd been drifting in and out of consciousness all day, and even when they were awake, their injuries made it painful for them to speak.

They had been given nothing to eat or drink since being dragged in the night before. Carter was dehydrated and weak. After dumping them there, the clan had left them for dead.

To his right Erina spoke in a hoarse voice. 'What the hell was that?'

His mouth was bone-dry. He twisted his head towards her, swallowed a couple of times, then worked his tongue to get some saliva flowing.

Before he could speak, two five-second bursts of intense gunfire from an automatic weapon cut through the air, drowning out the gut-churning cries of the wailing women.

'They're killing their own people,' Erina said. 'Why?'

'God knows,' he said. 'But we need to get Thomas and Wayan out of here and get back to Sydney before the new year.'

She worked her lips together and swallowed. 'The plan was to meet Muklas by 8 a.m. or he'd go to enlist Detachment 88's help.'

'I wouldn't count on them getting here anytime soon.'

'Any ideas?'

'Nothing is jumping out at me.'

Carter looked towards Thomas and Wayan. It worried him that even the gunfire had failed to stir them. If they didn't get food and water soon, they'd struggle to survive the night. Wayan in particular looked in a bad way. But there was no point saying anything. He and Erina both knew the score and were powerless to help.

Light footsteps approached and he glanced at her. She hiked her shoulders.

He turned his attention towards the cell door. A key clicked into the lock and it opened slowly.

A woman in full traditional Muslim attire stood in the doorway, a white jilbab wrapped around her head and face, revealing only her eyes.

Her gaze settled on Thomas. The love and concern he saw in her eyes convinced Carter it could only be one person.

'Kemala?' Erina asked. 'What are you doing here?'

Carter heard both surprise and distrust in her voice.

'I'm here to get you out,' Kemala said. Judging by her tone, she was far from confident.

Erina rattled her wrist. 'Do you have keys for the locks?'

Kemala shook her head as if she was disappointed with herself.

Outside, they heard two sets of heavy footsteps approaching the cell at a rapid pace.

'Get out of here quick,' Carter said.

Kemala remained at the doorway. 'I cannot leave.'

Her words were emphatic.

'Okay then,' he said in a calm, even voice. 'Come inside and close the door.'

She stepped into the cell and pushed the door shut.

'Now stand on the right-hand side of the entrance.'

She moved at once and stood with her back flush against the wall, so the door would open in front of her, creating a shield.

Her right hand slipped into the folds of her dark dress and, to Carter's surprise, extracted a compact Beretta 92 handgun with a silencer attached.

It only used .25 calibre cartridges, but at close range it'd get the job done.

CHAPTER 8

The gun shook in Kemala's hand, making Carter question whether she had what it took to pull the trigger and shoot a man in cold blood.

They'd find out soon enough.

Her dark eyes sought his.

He lifted his head a fraction and gave her a small, confident nod.

Outside, the footsteps stopped.

He turned to Erina.

Neither uttered a word. They were ready to seize any opportunity that presented itself, no matter how heavily the odds were stacked against them.

A key slid into the lock and turned, one way and then back again.

Carter mentally kicked himself for failing to tell Kemala to lock it.

The door flew forwards.

Two clansmen wearing fatigues and black caps marched in, dragging a body between them.

They dropped it on the floor like a sack of flour. One of them used the toe of his boot to roll the body on its back.

Carter turned his head as far as he could.

Muklas's dead eyes stared at him. There was a bullet wound in the middle of his forehead.

Carter swore to himself and clenched his hands into tight fists. He wondered how they'd caught him. Perhaps when Carter and Erina had failed to return to the bunker at the agreed time that morning, Muklas had chosen to come after them rather than calling in Detachment 88.

There was nothing to be done about that now. Kemala needed their help. She was hidden behind the open door.

He glared at the two clansmen in an effort to draw their attention to him. They returned his gaze full of cold hatred.

The taller of the two unslung an Uzi from his shoulder, pointed it at Carter's head and switched the safety off.

The shorter guy drew a handgun, a SIG, from his shoulder holster and moved to stand over Carter.

'Who unlocked the door?' he asked in perfect English.

'Dunno what you're talking about,' Carter said, keeping his tone conversational.

The guy pressed the cool barrel of the SIG against Carter's temple. 'Tell me who unlocked the door, you fucking arsehole.'

Carter said nothing.

The guy swung the SIG towards Erina's feet. 'Answer me. Or I blow this worthless whore's foot off and let her bleed to death.'

'Take it easy,' Carter said, wanting to keep the focus on himself.

The guy whipped the gun back and pointed it at Carter's right eye.

'It obviously wasn't one of us,' Carter said. 'We've been pretty much tied up.'

The man gave him a filthy look, no doubt itching to pull the SIG's trigger and personally send a westerner and a member of the order to hell. The only thing stopping him would be orders to keep them alive, for now.

'We'll see how smart you are in a couple of hours,' he said.

'Why's that?' Carter asked.

'That's when the first stone will smash your miserable skull to pulp. Samudra wants every one of the faithful to witness your execution. Unless I decide to shoot you first, like that worthless motherfucker.'

He pointed his gun towards Muklas's body, like he was proud of what he'd done.

'Go ahead,' Carter said. 'Put us out of our misery.'

To his right Erina cut in. 'Just be quick about it. Kill us in cold blood and go to hell.'

The guy with the Uzi jabbed the weapon towards her. 'Shut up, whore!'

Carter lifted his head. 'Come on and shoot, you gutless wonders.'

They were doing all they could to keep the two armed men's attention on them and away from the door that hid Kemala, hoping she would find the strength to shoot sooner rather than later.

The shorter man pointed his SIG at Carter and grinned. 'You think we're stupid. A quick death is too good for you western pigs.'

He reversed his grip on the weapon, held it by the barrel, and then, in a whipping motion, smashed the butt into the side of Carter's head, just above the temple.

A shooting pain exploded in Carter's brain.

He closed his eyes and gritted his teeth.

His mind felt like it was immersed in a heavy liquid, fuzzy and out of sync with reality.

A voice inside his head told him to relax, go to sleep and it'd all be over.

But he dug deep, fought off his body's overriding urge to shut down and forced his eyes open.

Warm blood flowed down the right side of his head and into his eye.

His vision blurred.

The guy with the Uzi aimed it at a point between his eyes, holding the barrel rock-steady.

Carter shook his head, as much as the manacle around his throat would allow, in an effort to clear his muddy thinking.

He heard the door to the cell creak and glimpsed a shadow moving out from behind it.

Kemala.

The guy lowered his Uzi and began to turn towards the door.

Carter tried to speak, to distract the guy, but no words came out, just a meaningless croak.

'You fucking cowards,' Erina screeched in a hoarse shout. 'Murdering unarmed women who can't defend themselves. Look at me and tell me you didn't just shoot defenceless Muslim women!'

Through his blurred vision Carter saw the clansmen turn towards her. She'd hit a raw nerve.

'What did they do?' she taunted. 'Show their faces in public?'

The guy with the SIG said, 'Shut your dirty mouth, bitch.'

Carter heard a fist strike Erina's face and her manacles rattle. She let out a muffled gasp.

Then four silenced shots spurted through the air, one after the other.

Carter felt himself slipping out of consciousness and drifting into a black void.

CHAPTER 9

As Carter came to, he heard loud moaning coming from the floor to his left. He had no idea how long he'd been out. His head felt like it was ready to split in two. He forced his eyes open and turned towards the sound, ignoring the pulsating pain.

The clan member who had struck him with the butt of his SIG lay on his stomach squirming. He'd been hit in the right shoulder and left thigh by low-calibre bullets. His weapon had skidded three metres in front of him.

His mate lay facedown to Carter's right, the Uzi near his head. He'd been hit in the right buttock and just below the shoulder.

They were down for the count, but not yet out.

Kemala needed to finish the job.

The final, deliberate shot – the one you took to kill a defenceless and wounded opponent – was by far the toughest, even for a trained assassin.

But in a situation like this, it had to be done.

Kemala stood paralysed in front of the open door, holding the Beretta by her side, staring at the wounded men.

'Shoot them,' Carter said, struggling to get the words out clearly.

She didn't seem to hear him. It felt like he was speaking underwater. The guy to his right started pushing himself onto his hands and knees.

Kemala didn't react.

The clansman to his left began sliding in slow motion towards the SIG, leaving a trail of blood.

'For God's sake, Kemala, *shoot*!' Erina said. 'Then find the keys to these locks.'

The woman just stood frozen to the spot, in shock, unable to take anything in.

Carter worked some saliva into his mouth and was about to speak when a gravelly whisper came from where Thomas lay.

'Kemala. You must finish this.'

She turned towards Thomas slowly.

The clansman was within a metre of the SIG, reaching out towards it.

'Trust God and be strong,' Thomas said. 'For all of us.'

Still she hesitated.

'Look what they did to Muklas. Do it for him.'

She glanced at Muklas's body. Her focus hardened and she turned back towards the man reaching for the SIG.

He had just gripped the weapon's stock.

She raised the shaking Beretta with two hands in front of her and pulled the trigger.

His body stopped moving.

She swung the weapon in a ninety-degree arc towards the other man, who was on his hands and knees, about to grab the Uzi. She pointed the Beretta at the back of his head and squeezed the trigger.

Another round spat out.

The man's body jerked as the bullet struck him between the shoulders. He collapsed and lay still.

Thomas spoke in a barely audible whisper. 'Good. Now the keys. Free Carter and Erina first.'

The Beretta dropped to the floor with a thud. Kemala stared at the bodies as if she couldn't believe what she'd done.

'It's all right,' Thomas whispered. 'You did what you needed to do. Ask God for forgiveness later. Now you need his courage.'

She bowed her head and mumbled what looked like a prayer. Then she took a few shaky steps forwards and started fumbling through the pockets of the guy who'd been wielding the SIG.

Carter heard the jangle of metal. Kemala stood and then came to his side. Her hands were still trembling as she unlocked the manacles around his throat, arms, waist and legs. He sat up slowly.

She ripped a section of cloth from the bottom of her dress and wrapped it around the wounds on his head before moving off towards Erina.

His whole body was numb, and his head continued to throb.

To his right Kemala hunched over Erina, who said, 'Thank you. I know that wasn't easy.'

He placed his feet on the ground and tried to stand. Pins and needles shot through his legs, forcing him to sit back down.

He worked his feet and ankles back and forth, flexing and relaxing the muscles to get the blood flowing. He glanced back towards Erina.

She tried to stand too, but couldn't.

'Let me help you,' Kemala said.

She put an arm around Erina's shoulders and supported her as they both shuffled towards Thomas.

Kemala unlocked his manacles, squeezed his hand and then moved towards the unconscious Wayan.

Carter managed to stay on his feet on the second attempt and walked over to join Kemala. He leant over Wayan and stroked his forehead.

There was nothing else he could do.

When Kemala had freed him, Carter lifted the boy up and gently placed him over his left shoulder, careful to exert minimum pressure on his chest and stomach, suspecting he had suffered internal injuries.

After balancing Wayan's weight evenly, he moved to the centre of the room, knelt down and picked up the Uzi lying next to the fallen clan member. The stock was slippery with blood.

'Come on,' he said. 'We need to move.'

Thomas was now on his feet. Kemala and Erina stood on either side of him, supporting him under his armpits, taking most of his weight. Erina held the SIG in her left hand.

Erina leant in to her father and said, 'We're so sorry.'

Her father's voice was still faint. 'There's nothing for either of you to be sorry about.'

With Erina and Kemala beside him, he started moving towards the door.

Carter followed, glancing at Muklas. He hated leaving his body behind, but they had no choice.

CHAPTER 10

The gathering gloom of dusk approached. The entrance to the tunnel that led to the bunker was set three-quarters of the way down a steep and rocky cliff, a hundred metres to the east of the compound.

The Japanese had chosen the entrance to the tunnel strategically. A rock ledge hid it from anyone looking down from above, and from the ocean below it would be invisible.

Carter sat just inside the entrance, where he could still see and hear what was going on outside. The air was calm, and gentle waves lapped against the rocks fifteen metres below.

Behind him Kemala and Erina tended to Thomas and Wayan. Djoran had stocked the bunker with food, water, basic medical supplies and a small gas burner, along with an inflatable dinghy, two oars and a small outboard motor.

For over an hour Carter had watched out for any clan activity.

Foot patrols had passed above him, but none had ventured down the cliff. Twice, the helicopter had buzzed overhead, causing him to move deeper inside the tunnel. And roughly every twenty minutes a fishing boat powered by an outboard motor cruised past. The next one was due in approximately ten minutes.

From above, in the creeping darkness, two Indonesian voices drifted down through the still dusk air.

Another patrol.

His right hand reached for the Uzi. He switched the safety off and cradled it in his lap.

Thirty seconds later the voices trailed off and he laid the weapon at his side.

This was the third patrol he'd heard, yet none had come exploring in the direction of the tunnel, which meant the mujaheddin must have remained ignorant of the bunker's existence.

As full darkness approached, the chances of anyone venturing down such rugged, steep terrain grew more remote, but it was still a possibility. In the morning they'd be far more exposed and vulnerable, and the clan's search would become more desperate and detailed.

Carter was loath to move Thomas and Wayan until their condition stabilised, but staying where they were any longer than necessary was out of the question. They needed to get off the island that night. He had the rubber dinghy prepped and ready to go. They needed to get moving shortly after complete darkness fell.

He sensed someone coming towards him from behind and Erina's voice echoed in the tunnel. 'Dinner is served.'

'I didn't know you cooked.'

She sat down next to him and handed him a plastic mug of steaming tea and two energy bars. 'I'm glad I can still surprise you.'

He placed the tea beside him, unwrapped a fruit and nut bar and took a large bite. He'd forgotten how hungry he was.

'How are they doing?' he asked.

'Thomas is in great pain,' she said, 'but he's eating and drinking. You know how strong and stubborn he can be – he'll recover.'

'And Wayan?'

'Still unconscious. His breathing is shallow and his heart rate is very weak. Moving him again will be extremely dangerous.'

Carter sat motionless, weighing up their options. They didn't have any. They needed to get off the island as soon as possible. It'd only be a matter of time before the clansmen found them. It was one of those decisions he loathed having to make, but it had to be done.

'We need to get Thomas and Wayan comfortably settled in the

dinghy as soon as it gets fully dark and we'll head off when there's a break in the patrols.'

Erina hesitated before answering and stood up. 'I'll tell the others.'

Carter took a sip of hot tea and stared out over the darkening ocean.

CHAPTER 11

At 9.20 p.m., Carter stopped rowing the heavily laden rubber dinghy and pulled in the fibreglass oars. They'd been travelling at roughly six knots for over an hour and a half – luckily, the outgoing tide was with them and had made the job easier.

Kemala sat at the bow, facing the stern. Erina was in the aft seat near the outboard engine and Carter was in the middle. Thomas and Wayan lay on their backs on the deck inside the gunnels on either side of the boat. Thomas's head faced the bow and Kemala. They had positioned the still unconscious Wayan with his head towards the aft section.

Carter glanced over his shoulder. The island and Samudra's compound were nothing more than a dull glow about ten kilometres behind them. The time had come to assess their position and consider starting the outboard engine.

The boat was laden with weapons and supplies, and they had pushed off from the rocky shore at 7.45 p.m. The plan was to reach the surf camp known as Legends, situated on a small island a hundred and fifty kilometres west of Sumatra, early next morning. Carter had set a course on the GPS device Djoran had provided and expected to be there in six to eight hours.

The camp had a full-time doctor and a light plane that made regular trips to Bali. Carter knew the owner, a former pro-surfer, well. He'd arrange for Carter and Erina to fly to Bali the same day they arrived

266

or the following day. They'd then head to Sydney from Denpasar Airport on either 29 or 30 December, depending on what obstacles they encountered in the meantime.

Hopefully by the time they touched down in Australia, Djoran would've discovered Samudra's plans for the terrorist attack. Putting himself into Samudra's head and taking into account the fact that the mujaheddin were heading for Sydney the next day, 29 December, it seemed highly probable that New Year's Eve was the likely date of the clan's planned attack.

But there was no point speculating about that now. First they had to get Thomas and Wayan to the surf camp.

Though Thomas had spoken only a few words, he remained conscious and seemed to be aware of everything going on around him. In contrast Wayan hadn't moved or uttered a word. They all knew deep down that it was only a matter of time for him. He needed urgent medical attention. There was little chance he'd survive the journey.

Carter kept reminding himself that they hadn't had a choice. Staying on the island wasn't an option. But that fact didn't make him feel any better about the decision he'd made.

He reached down and touched Wayan's forehead.

It was cold. There was no need to check his pulse.

Carter's head dropped. A numbness rose through his stomach and chest before settling in his heart.

He felt Erina's warm hand touch the back of his shoulder.

He ran his fingers down Wayan's cold cheek, triggering a deep-seated regret that he'd acted so selfishly over the last year by leaving and putting his own wellbeing above that of the order.

Maybe Erina had been right. If he hadn't left when he did, maybe all of this could've been prevented.

Erina climbed forwards and sat to his left. 'This is not on you,' she said.

'Sure feels like it.'

'No matter what I've said in the past, the truth is you've always done what you thought was right at the time. That's all anyone can do and I respect you for that.'

She put her arm around his shoulder, pulled him close and hugged him in silence for a few moments.

'Thank you,' he said, kissing her on the forehead before releasing himself from her embrace.

'You take a break,' Erina said. 'I'll sort out the engine and get us on our way.'

Carter moved forwards and knelt beside Thomas. He looked at Kemala, who was holding Thomas's hand in her own and wiping away a tear with the other.

After a few moments Thomas turned his head towards Carter and whispered, 'I know what has happened. It was inevitable. You did the right thing. We couldn't stay on the island.'

The boat rose and fell with the swell.

A gentle breeze brushed over them.

Carter stared across the ocean towards the dark horizon. The clouds blocked out the moon and stars as if the gods themselves mourned Wayan's passing.

'Whatever happens,' Thomas said, 'know that I am proud of you.'

Thomas started to cough. Kemala knelt beside him, lifted his head and held a canteen of water to his lips. He took a small sip.

'There's nothing further I can do in this fight,' Thomas said. 'It is up to you and Erina to stop Samudra and his clan. Leave Kemala and I at the surf camp. You need to get to Sydney as soon as possible. You will know what to do as soon as you hear from Djoran. He is very capable.'

He took a few shallow breaths. 'Don't make the same mistake I did and underestimate Samudra … he and Alex are a dangerous combination.'

'Understood.'

The effort of speaking caused Thomas to struggle for breath. 'I've never stopped loving you, Carter,' he whispered.

Carter wanted to tell Thomas how much he loved him too, but he couldn't get the words out.

Thomas touched his hand. 'Wayan, Muklas, Jacko – make sure their deaths count for something. I know you and Erina can do this. My heart and thoughts will always be with you.'

Carter bowed his head, surrendered to his emotion, and for the first time since his mother's death, allowed the warm tears to flow down his cheeks.

Behind him he heard the outboard engine start up.

BOOK SIX

CHAPTER 1

Sydney, Australia, early morning, 31 December

Three days later and six thousand kilometres from Batak Island, the sharp *beep beep* of his phone jolted Carter awake, signalling the arrival of a text message.

He turned towards the sideboard. The large numbers on the digital clock radio read 5.40 a.m. It took him a few moments to register where he was – the living room of the serviced apartment they had rented in Sydney's historic Rocks district. The Rosemount Apartments complex was on the edge of the CBD and a short walk from Sydney's picturesque harbour, which made it the ideal platform from which to mount a response to Samudra's expected attack.

According to a previous text from Djoran, who was somewhere in the city with Samudra's team of mujaheddin, either the Sydney Harbour Bridge or the Sydney Opera House was the likely target.

Carter sat up in the fold-out sofa bed and stretched his arms above him. He and Erina had flown into Sydney from Jakarta on false passports at 10 p.m. the night before.

She was asleep in the main bedroom.

His phone beeped a second time and he grabbed it off the glass coffee table beside the sofa.

The caller ID was blocked; there was no number. The message read: *Confirming 2nite. SH Bridge primary target. Details later. D*

Carter wasn't surprised. He and Erina had done their research and gone through various possible attack scenarios, and the Sydney Harbour Bridge seemed the most likely target.

The bridge was the focal point for the New Year's Eve fireworks. Half a million people would gather on the harbour and its foreshore that evening to watch five million dollars' worth of fireworks go up in smoke. It was high summer in Sydney, and the city's New Year's Eve celebrations were bigger than those held in Paris, London, Berlin and New York. The images would be broadcast around the world.

It was hard to think how Samudra could pick a better target.

Carter reached for the file Erina had put together on the bridge. He was hoping Djoran would give him the exact location of the attack later that day, but they'd already started preparing themselves. The more information they had, the better.

The Sydney Harbour Bridge was the tallest steel arch bridge in the world. Its highest point was more than a hundred and thirty metres above sea level and the arch spanned just over five hundred metres. The total weight of the steelwork was over fifty thousand tonnes. The almost fifty-metre-wide deck carried rail, car, bicycle and foot traffic between the CBD and the north shore.

Carter tried to put himself into the mind of Samudra. He figured the most likely place to mount an attack would be from one of the bridge's four pylons. The clan members could remain hidden in one of them and, from there, plant and detonate their explosives.

Two pylons stood at the northern and southern ends of the bridge and all were identical in design inside and out. The south-east pylon at the city end contained a museum and tourist centre, with a three-hundred-and-sixty-degree observation deck at the top. The south-west pylon, also at the city end, was run by the New South Wales Roads and Maritime Services and its CCTV cameras overlooked the bridge and surrounding roads. The pylons at the northern end incorporated venting chimneys used to extract traffic fumes from the Sydney Harbour Tunnel.

If he were Samudra, he'd choose the south-west pylon because of its access to surveillance cameras and proximity to the city – and because it was closed for business on New Year's Eve, unlike the south-east pylon, which was open to the public until 5 p.m.

He lay back down on the sofa and stared at a Sidney Nolan print, a Ned Kelly, hanging on the wall above him, which he'd failed to notice the night before. The lonesome outlaw sat on a red horse with a shotgun slung over his shoulder, staring back at him.

It wasn't enough simply to snuff out Samudra's planned attack for that night. Samudra and his organisation needed to be destroyed or they'd simply regroup and strike another day.

Having a specific target was a good start.

That evening provided the best opportunity they'd ever have to stop Samudra and the Sungkar clan in their tracks. The chance might not come again for a long time, if at all, and Carter meant to take it. It wouldn't bring Wayan, Muklas and Jacko back, but it'd give their death meaning.

Maybe it'd do the same for his own life.

CHAPTER 2

Carter pushed himself off the sofa bed and pulled on a pair of navy blue boxer shorts. His thoughts turned to Erina, still asleep in the bedroom. So close, yet so far away.

The night before, she'd made her position very clear, quoting the order's unwritten principle: *No emotional attachments on the job.* He'd retreated to the sofa, knowing better than to push her.

He'd wait another hour or so before waking her, he decided. She could do with the rest. In the meantime he switched on the television, hit mute and scrolled through to the weather channel. A synoptic chart filled the screen. Digital data streamed across the bottom.

SYDNEY. Hot and humid conditions throughout the day. Top temp 30 degrees Celsius. Humidity 87 per cent.

Southerly change forecast at 7 p.m. Strong wind warning for coastal regions. Up to 30 knots from the south-east.

Heavy rain expected tonight. Rough seas. Swell 3 metres and building.

The New Year's Eve fireworks on the Sydney Harbour Bridge will go ahead, regardless of weather conditions.

The first round at 9 p.m.

The final extravaganza on the stroke of midnight.

He turned the television off, then walked across the thick beige carpet towards the heavy curtains over the windows and drew them back. The floor-to-ceiling glazing revealed a spectacular view. The rising sun threw a pale pink and yellow dawn over the battleship-grey bridge and the glistening wavelike white sails of the Sydney Opera House.

As far as cities went, Sydney was close to his favourite. The beauty of the sparkling blue harbour and its emerald foreshores provided a soothing counterbalance to the close, crowded city with its cement, brick, concrete and sandstone.

As he looked out over the awakening harbour towards the open sea, footsteps padded behind him.

He turned.

Erina walked towards him from the bedroom wearing a long grey T-shirt and, from what he could see, little else. Her silky dark hair fell over her shoulders.

A rush of energy feathered up and down his spine.

'Any news from Djoran?' she asked.

He held the phone in front of her.

They stood in silence while Erina digested the information.

He forced his gaze from the swell of her breasts to the window and noticed three outside-broadcast vans parked under the bridge.

Sydney, eleven hours ahead of London and sixteen hours ahead of New York, was the first major city in the world to celebrate New Year's Eve, and the party was televised live, globally. By midmorning a whole fleet of media vehicles would descend on the glittering harbour and set up their cameras to capture the explosive magic of the evening's fireworks.

'So what's first on the agenda?' Erina asked.

'You're lining up the gear we need and I've got my meeting with Watto at 8.15 a.m.'

Last night he'd organised a meeting with John 'Watto' Watson, an old friend from the Australian Federal Police. They needed backup, and Watto was one of the few government agents he trusted.

'You really want to involve the AFP?'

'I have to at least talk to him.'

'You know it'll be their way or the highway.'

'We need a fallback position.'

'We're not going to fail, Carter.'

275

'I agree. But to quote Djoran, I have faith in us and God, but it never hurts to hitch up the camel. You never know how things will play out.'

She looked at him but said nothing.

He turned to the window and watched a green and yellow ferry chug past the Opera House and gently dock at Circular Quay, the city's bustling ferry terminal.

Erina moved to stand next to him, and their shoulders brushed.

After a few moments of silence she said, 'Perhaps you're right.'

He turned to face her. 'About what? The camel?'

'You can never be sure how things will play out,' she said.

'True.'

After everything they'd been through in the last few days and the uncertainty of what lay ahead that evening, he'd never felt so drawn to another human being in his life. He sensed the same electric charge running through her. It was like an invisible force field drawing them together, the current becoming stronger with each passing moment.

But it wasn't his place to make the first move.

She reached out her hand and caressed his bare shoulders. Her lips were moist and slightly parted.

'Remember what I said last night?' she asked.

'About what?'

'No emotional attachments on the job.'

She ran her hand over his chest, caressing the three-inch scar from an old knife wound above his right nipple.

'Well,' she said, 'I've been thinking.'

He held his breath. 'Uh huh.'

Her fingers slid down towards his stomach. 'I'm beginning to see it as more of a guideline than a rule.'

CHAPTER 3

Shortly after dawn Alex Botha, aka Abdul-Aleem, stood alone on the narrow open-air observation deck on top of the Sydney Harbour Bridge's south-west pylon, eighty-nine metres above sea level. He was waiting for his phone to ring.

Inside the pylon he'd set up an electronic blocking device that jammed any telecommunications transmissions, ensuring there'd be no breaches of security. If Carter or anyone who came with him entered the pylon, they'd be unable to call for help. He'd turn the device off when he needed to contact Samudra.

The incoming call would confirm two things: whether Samudra was laying out the trap for Carter and Erina they'd agreed on, and whether Alex would have the bank cheque for the $250,000 owed to him when they met later that night on board Samudra's boat.

He looked out across the harbour, feeling the excitement rise in his chest. The start of a hunt always stirred up his fighting juices. And this was personal, promising the sweetness of revenge.

Part of the reason he'd hung around Samudra for so long was his deep longing to see the order, and Carter and Thomas in particular, pay for their sins. He'd reached out to them for help in his darkest hour and they'd left him rotting in that stinking Indonesian prison, facing execution.

The order was full of self-righteous arseholes who'd used him and then discarded him, just because he'd needed to earn a little extra money to pay for his drugs. They'd cut him no slack whatsoever.

He patted down the dark grey T-shirt and black trousers he wore for the occasion. A jihadist cell with affiliations to the bikie gang Soldiers for Allah had supplied him and his men with the uniforms worn by the Australian Tactical Response Unit.

The uniform's jacket and body armour were hanging in the storeroom behind him, where Putu and Zaheed, his two best men, were resting.

Three members of the bikie gang and a clan member living in Sydney had smuggled them in at midnight the previous evening. Their contacts within harbour security had proved invaluable.

He extracted a cigarette from his coat pocket, clicked his silver zippo lighter and inhaled, drawing the warm vapour deep into his lungs.

His idea of prayer and meditation.

A martyr's death wouldn't be his fate that day or any other. That dubious reward belonged to the Putus and Zaheeds of the world. Later that night they'd be wired with explosives, guarding the pylon with their lives until their scheduled date with oblivion at midnight. Theirs was a crucial role. When the explosives they wore were detonated, it would set off a chain reaction, triggering the charges they had laid on the bridge.

To Alex it seemed a complete waste of resources to expend such highly trained and experienced mujaheddin on a suicide bombing. They'd been blooded in the battlefields of Pakistan and Afghanistan, but now they were on a mission from which there'd be no return.

As far as Samudra was concerned, of course, there were a million more where they came from. And for the two fanatical mujaheddin, jihad would be the defining act of their lives.

Naive fools.

That anyone would want to kill themselves or anyone else in the name of God made no sense to him whatsoever.

Never had, never would.

Fortunately for him, as a westerner with elite training in the order, Samudra considered him too valuable to sacrifice or doublecross. Though his commitment to jihad had been nothing more than a means to escape execution and exact revenge on Carter and Thomas, there was only one Alex Botha, only one Abdul-Aleem, and even though Samudra despised him, he also recognised his great value to his cause.

The two of them would witness the results of their carefully prepared plan together, sharing the rewards of all the work they'd put in. At 11.30 p.m. he'd use the hang-glider already in position on the gun deck above him to join Samudra on his launch moored in the harbour, ten minutes away. They'd detonate the bombs from there on the stroke of midnight before making their escape. It'd be a sweet moment.

His phone vibrated in his trouser pocket.

Samudra's familiar voice sounded over the line. 'Is everything ready?'

'Of course,' Alex said. 'We placed twenty-seven charges at the crucial structural points on the bridge late last night. That's forty kilos of high explosive altogether. I don't know if it'll bring the bridge down, but it'll create an almighty mess.'

'Excellent. God is indeed great.'

'Has the truck for the tunnel been prepared for the secondary attack?'

'I said it will be done and so it shall.'

'What about the trap for Carter and Erina? Is that being laid as arranged?' Alex asked.

Alex knew Samudra hated being questioned, but he believed in checking and rechecking every detail. It was what would bring them success that night. He didn't want to give Samudra any reason not to pay him.

'It shall come to pass,' Samudra said. 'But remember, we kill our enemies to exact God's vengeance, not our own. There is a difference between divine justice and man's.'

'Of course,' Alex said, happy to let Samudra occupy the moral high ground.

'We'll talk again in two hours,' Samudra told him.

There was a pause over the line.

'There's one more thing,' Alex said. 'You have my cheque as promised?'

'I said you shall receive what you are owed when the job is done. I am a man of my word. Allah akbar.'

Alex smiled. 'Allah akbar.'

The phone went dead.

He flicked the remnants of his cigarette over the side of the pylon.

It was all proving too easy.

CHAPTER 4

Carter strode down George Street in the early-morning sunshine, feeling rejuvenated and ready for what lay ahead.

After spending an hour in bed with Erina, it was like a missing piece of his soul had slotted back in place.

The lovemaking they shared was both tender and passionate, reconnecting their minds, bodies and spirits at the deepest level and bringing him to a place of inner stillness. Their union had left him with a sense of infinite possibility and rightness with the world, despite the craziness going on around him.

He weaved his way through a stream of human traffic, heading towards the cafe-lined foreshores of Sydney Harbour.

Most Australians were oblivious to the threat of a terrorist attack, thinking it could never happen on their own soil. It was in many ways a good thing, he supposed. Regular citizens didn't need to know the danger hanging over them.

A quick glance at his watch told him it was 8.05 a.m. He was due to meet Watto at the Oyster Bar, an open-air cafe near the Opera House, in ten minutes.

He'd known Watto for twenty years and always found him to be a straight shooter, but getting him to provide backup without any hard evidence was going to be a hard sell.

He crossed George Street at the lights and approached Circular Quay. A green and yellow ferry tooted as it left the dock, causing a flock of seagulls to lift off the dappled water like a white wave.

Watto was a career man, married with two teenage daughters, and his default position was to play everything by the book. The AFP procedures were the Ten Commandments of the personal bible he lived by.

If Carter was up-front and honest with Watto, he'd most likely bring something positive to the table. Definitely worth a shot. But Carter would need to tread carefully. If he told Watto the specifics of Samudra's proposed jihad, he'd feel compelled by his sense of duty to report the threat to his immediate superiors, triggering a series of events that would take the matter out of Carter's hands.

He wasn't prepared to let that happen, except as a last resort. He and Erina, operating off the grid, were the ones best equipped to stop the attack. Now they'd come together, part of him hated the thought of putting her in harm's way and facing the risk of losing her. But he couldn't afford to go there, even for a second.

Turning into the walkway that ran along the eastern side of the quay towards the Opera House, he checked his phone to see if there were any messages from Erina or Djoran.

Nothing.

He entered the cafe and stood a moment to look at the bridge towering over the harbour to his left. He sat at a corner table under an umbrella with his back to the water's edge, giving him a clear view of the stream of pedestrian traffic.

A gentle breeze blew off the water that lapped against the wall of the concourse behind him.

He ordered a long black and studied the crowd moving along the grey cobblestone promenade that ran between the harbour and the cafes and boutiques.

Two young children escaped from their parents and skipped towards the steel and concrete fence that ran along the edge of the harbour. They pointed in awe at a giant passenger liner docking on the western foreshore of the quay.

Carter's gaze fell on a group of young women dressed stylishly in western clothes and traditional Muslim headscarfs, posing in front of the water as they took photographs of each other.

At the same time, two surfie-looking blokes in rubber thongs, matching board shorts and T-shirts walked past, carrying an esky between them. In their free hands they each held a longneck bottle of beer, most likely preparing for a big night in front of the fireworks.

Carter smiled to himself at their enthusiasm for the occasion. Nothing like getting an early start to a good time.

Behind them he spotted the tall, erect figure of Watto, power-walking through the crowd. He wore a buttoned-up charcoal suit, a crisp white shirt and dark tie.

Watto caught Carter's eye, nodded and veered towards the cafe.

CHAPTER 5

Watto walked towards Carter's table and undid his middle coat button before dropping into the seat opposite.

'You've really stirred up a shit storm this time.'

'It's good to see you too, Watto.'

Watto ran his fingers through his dark, close-cropped hair. 'I checked the records. You're not even supposed to be in the country, for Christ's sake.'

Carter held up his hands, feigning surrender. 'Where's the trust? I had to take the odd short cut.'

A young waiter placed Carter's coffee in front of him. Watto ordered a double-shot skim flat white.

When they were alone, he leant across the table and said in a hushed tone, 'Seriously, mate, there's a warrant out for your arrest.'

'Yeah?'

'A double murder and assault with intent to cause grievous bodily harm. Was that one of your short cuts?'

Carter glanced down at his coffee to gather his thoughts. Obviously, Samudra had told Woodforde to contact the police and accuse Carter and Erina of assaulting him and killing his two gate guards on his Boggabilla property.

This new information changed the equation, pushing him and Erina further outside the law, making it extremely difficult for him to enlist the help of someone like Watto.

'There was a good reason,' he said.

'You've been in Indonesia too long. You're not on some remote island where you can do whatever you like and get away with all sorts of dubious shit. I should be dragging your sorry arse into custody.'

'There's something big that needs to be stopped.'

'Have you got any hard evidence?' Watto asked.

'Not exactly.'

'Just some information from a confidential source, I'll bet.'

'Something along those lines, but it's rock-solid.'

'What exactly do you want?'

Carter saw no point prevaricating. He looked Watto in the eye. 'I need a squad of half-a-dozen men at the ready, should I need to call them. No questions asked.'

Watto shook his head and opened his mouth to reply, but Carter didn't give him a chance.

'I also need total freedom to move wherever I like in the city and authority to access all public venues around the harbour.'

Watto arched an eyebrow. 'And when might you want all this?'

Carter took a slow sip of his bitter long black, let out a sigh and put it back on the saucer.

'Tonight.'

Watto shifted in his seat, clearly fighting to keep a lid on his growing irritation.

Though they respected each other, Watto came from a world with a different set of rules and values. He hated being asked to step outside the strict protocols he had followed all his working life.

He shook his head. 'There's no way on God's earth I can help you unless you're prepared to come downtown into the office, make an official statement and go through the proper channels.'

Carter understood where Watto was coming from, but it didn't mean he liked it or accepted it.

'You've gotta think outside of that tight little box you live in,' Carter said, deliberately baiting him. 'You can't always cover your arse to protect your pension plan.'

'Hey, I'm doing you a favour. I should be arresting you. And the last time I rang you wanting help, you told me the surf was up.'

Watto had asked Carter to travel to Sumatra to interrogate a suspected member of a terrorist cell being held as an unofficial prisoner by Detachment 88. Watto desperately needed information about a rumoured attack on the Australian embassy in Jakarta and saw this as a valid reason to circumvent official channels.

'Mate, I'd retired,' Carter said. 'I was living in Lennox. That was an unreasonable request.'

'And this isn't? You call me out of the blue on New Year's Eve wanting me to stick my neck out on nothing more than your word. All the while playing your cards close to your chest for fear the department I work for might interfere with your precious plans and do our job. Not going to happen.'

Carter drained his cup and pushed it to one side. 'I wouldn't be asking if this wasn't serious.'

Watto shifted in his seat. 'Not everyone can run around like an outlaw, following their own rules or making them up as they go. I work within the law. That's what separates me from the scumbags I bring in. That's the basis of a just society, in case you were wondering.'

'Gee, Watto, you sound like you're giving an orientation speech to new recruits at the police academy.'

'Don't get smart with me.'

'And don't patronise me. What I'm talking about is serious. We both know you're prepared to circumvent the law when it suits you. And you know that I'll do whatever it takes to get the job done. But it has to be my way.'

'Haven't you heard a single word I'm saying? You've killed people, left the country and re-entered illegally. Now you're asking me to break the law after you've taken it into your own—'

The waiter put Watto's flat white down in front of him, cutting him off mid-sentence.

Carter leant back in the chair and folded his arms. He'd known it'd be tough to get Watto to stick his neck out, even when everything had been straightforward and above board. With a warrant out for his arrest – a warrant for murder – the odds approached zero.

Watto was basically telling him he'd have to hand over the operation to the AFP or work outside the law on his own.

He thought of Ned Kelly on his red horse, shotgun slung over his shoulder. Maybe the maverick bushranger had been trying to tell him something.

'You heard about the bombing in Kuta?' he asked.

Watto shook a packet of artificial sweetener into his coffee. 'Of course. But a terrorist attack on a foreign tourist destination doesn't mean Sydney is under threat, which I presume is what you're insinuating.'

'Jacko was killed in the blast. It was meant for me and Erina as well.'

Watto looked straight at Carter.

'We were trying to rescue Thomas – he'd been abducted by an Indonesian clan, along with another of our operatives. Thomas is badly injured and the other guy was murdered.'

Watto placed his spoon into the saucer. 'So some serious shit, huh?'

Carter nodded.

'Why haven't you contacted Trident?' Watto asked. 'They have far greater discretionary powers than we do and they're who you're supposed to report to.'

'We believe Callaghan's been compromised. His daughter's missing and we suspect she's being held hostage.'

'Shit.'

Carter leant towards him. 'Look, all I need is until 11.15 p.m. and then I'll give you everything I've got. Promise. For now, all I need is some backup.'

Watto folded his arms. 'Mate, I'm telling you this as a friend. The smart thing for you to do here is to come down to headquarters, make a full statement and go through the proper channels. There are people trained and equipped to deal with situations like this, and if you do things by the book, we can call them in and use their full resources. I'll back you every step of the way.'

'You know as well as I do that the first thing they'll do is throw me in a cell and ask questions later. When the truth comes out about this, there'll be winners and losers in the official ranks. You need to decide what's right and who you're going to back.'

'You're confident you can get the job done?'

'Absolutely. I'm just asking for free rein until 11.15 p.m. and then it's all yours.'

Watto took a long sip of coffee and looked across the harbour towards the overseas passenger terminal, thinking over what he'd heard. When the federal officer turned back to face him, Carter knew what he was going to say.

'You're a clever bastard. You've painted me into a corner.'

Carter remained silent.

'All right,' Watto said, finishing his coffee and standing up. 'Here's what I can do.'

He reached into his coat pocket, pulled out a white card, wrote a number on it and pushed it across the table towards Carter.

'This is my new direct line. I'll put myself on duty until midnight. The moment you produce some rock-solid evidence I can act on, call me. I'll be ready with a squad of men. And I'll get you Callaghan's address and phone number. You should pay him a visit. That's the best I can do.'

Carter picked up the card and put it in his pocket. 'Thanks, mate.'

Watto walked towards the cashier.

'Watto.'

He turned and faced him.

'Coffee's on me.'

CHAPTER 6

Carter sat on the leather couch in the living room of their apartment and watched Erina make tea in the kitchenette with the same reverence Thomas reserved for the task. He'd just told her about his meeting with Watto and was waiting for her response.

She walked into the room carrying two steaming cups of fresh green tea.

'Having backup is good,' she said, 'but you're right, handing this over to the Federal Police isn't an option. Even if they manage to stop Samudra blowing up the bridge, we both know that's not enough. If he survives New Year's, he'll strike another day.'

'Exactly. We need to cut the threat off at the head. That means taking down Samudra tonight.'

She handed him a cup and sat down. 'Tracking down ruthless arseholes like him is what we do better than anyone else.'

Carter took a sip of hot tea and nodded, waiting. He knew she wasn't finished.

'But there is one thing that concerns me,' she said. 'It only takes one person with a vest packed with explosives to walk into a crowd of people and do untold damage. He might have more than one target.'

'True.'

'And what if he's counting on us thinking the bridge is the target while he's actually plotting something else?'

Carter, who had thought through the same possibilities himself, put his cup down on the table. 'You can never be sure of anything,' he said. 'But we need to be prepared and ready for the most likely scenario.'

She leant back in her chair, cradling her cup of tea. 'I'm listening.'

'There're a lot of ifs and maybes,' he said. 'And we're relying heavily on Djoran's intel. But I trust the guy – he's putting his life on the line. We have to make sure we're prepared when he delivers and also be ready for when Samudra makes a mistake.'

'Guys like him always do. And I have to admit I was wrong about Djoran.'

'There's a first time for everything.'

She smiled but didn't respond. 'Have you figured out the best way of getting onto the bridge undetected?'

Carter looked out the window. The bridge seemed to be looking over his shoulder, beckoning him, wherever he went in the city.

He leant back into the soft lounge. 'I've got a few ideas.'

'And they are?'

'I reckon we need to mount our assault via the water. It'll give us the best shot at reaching the pylon without being spotted and we won't have to deal with any of the security or crowds around the foreshore—'

The phone started vibrating in his thigh pocket. He took it out and checked the screen. The number was blocked. He put the phone on speaker and held it out.

'Carter here.'

'It's Watto. Got a pen?'

Erina got up from the lounge and grabbed a pen and notepad from the writing desk.

'Fire away,' Carter said.

Watto read out Callaghan's address and mobile-phone number and Erina wrote them down.

'Thanks, mate,' Carter said.

'One more thing.'

'Yeah?'

'We didn't have this conversation.'

The line went dead.

'What now?' Erina asked.

'I need to pay Callaghan a visit.'

'You want me to come?'

He shook his head. 'You need to go shopping. We'll discuss the details of the plan later.'

CHAPTER 7

Carter drove a rented white Toyota Hiace van away from the centre of the city along New South Head Road towards the up-market harbour-side suburb of Vaucluse, where Callaghan lived. He needed to extract any information he could from him about Samudra's plans.

He parked outside a large house under the shade of a leafy plane tree, just opposite Callaghan's place, and scoped the deserted street.

The only parked cars were a silver Mercedes convertible and a black BMW four-wheel drive. Considering the upper-middle-class surrounds, neither looked suspicious.

He stepped out of the van and locked the door. In this peaceful neighbourhood it barely felt necessary. The sleepy suburb was one of the wealthiest in Sydney and had one of the lowest crime rates. There was a complete absence of litter. All the gardens were neat and the lawns freshly mowed.

He crossed the street and followed a sandstone path through Callaghan's manicured front garden towards his spacious home. The sweet fragrance of frangipanis drifted through the air, adding to the feeling that nothing bad could ever happen in a suburb like this.

To his surprise a large stone buddha sat beside the door, greeting him with a warm smile. He pressed a buzzer and heard rhythmic chimes.

No answer.

Carter took a step back and looked up and down the front of the house, searching for an open window.

He pulled out his phone and dialled the number Watto had given him.

A musical ringtone sounded inside.

It stopped.

He knocked hard three times on the door and waited.

Shuffling footsteps approached.

There was a long moment of heavy silence, as if whoever stood on the other side of the door was making up their mind.

A gruff voice said, 'Who is it?'

'Russell Carter. We need to talk.'

A dog barked in the distance.

The door opened slowly, revealing a large man in his mid-sixties. He had a full head of silver hair and was only a couple of inches shorter than Carter. He would have been an imposing physical presence, except that his spirit appeared crushed.

Earl Callaghan wore a grey T-shirt and loose-fitting black Reebok tracksuit pants. His feet were bare. He had a solid three-day growth, his eyes were bloodshot and his skin an unhealthy grey.

The look of a man who'd come to hate himself.

He nodded at Carter. 'You better come in.'

It almost seemed like he was expecting him.

CHAPTER 8

Callaghan led Carter down a gloomy tiled hallway and into a large modern kitchen. The blinds were drawn, shutting out the view and the outside world. The mustiness of the air suggested the windows hadn't been opened for at least a week.

Dirty dishes stacked high filled the sink and an open box of crackers lay scattered across the marble bench next to a block of yellow cheese. Callaghan stared at the chrome fridge like he was being confronted with a major dilemma.

'Coffee?' he asked.

'No thanks,' Carter said.

'I need one.'

'Go ahead.'

———

Carter sat opposite Callaghan at a grubby white dining table. Toast crumbs littered the surface and tiny flies swarmed over a rotting bowl of fruit. A faint smell of cat urine hung over the house.

Callaghan lifted a steaming cup of instant black coffee to his lips with both hands and took a tentative sip. He was in a bad way, yet appeared relieved to have Carter there, probably ready and willing to unburden himself to someone.

Anyone.

A man could only hold dark secrets in for so long.

'You look like shit,' Carter said.

'I feel like it.'

Callaghan swallowed a large mouthful of coffee and stared at the table, looking like he wanted to throw up.

'What happened?' Carter asked.

They sat for a few moments in silence, interrupted only by the whine of a leaf blower a few doors down the street.

'Look at me,' Carter said.

Callaghan raised his head with great effort. Any arrogance he might once have possessed had been overtaken by a deep sense of shame and embarrassment.

'Start at the beginning.'

'Okay … the beginning.'

He rubbed his eyes like he was trying to focus his addled mind.

Carter remained silent, giving him space to ready himself. When interviewing someone, he liked to let the subject talk, keeping his questions to a minimum until they'd had their say.

'I got a series of margin calls during the financial crisis,' Callaghan said without looking at Carter directly. 'I was going to lose my house and have to pull my daughter, Vivienne, out of boarding school. It started out as a few harmless favours for a lot of money. Samudra just wanted my advice on a number of matters and asked me to give an IT consultant cousin of his some work. I thought I could control the situation. If he got out of line, I thought I could just shut him down.'

The pattern of corruption never worked any differently. The favours usually started out small and insignificant but gradually snowballed. It was the first compromise that did the damage.

'Then?' Carter asked.

Callaghan pointed at a framed picture on the kitchen wall. A young girl of about sixteen with long black hair wore a sombre expression and a grey school uniform. She stared at the camera with an air of defiant rebellion.

'Vivienne's seventeen now. Her stepmother walked out on us a few years ago, before that photo was taken. I wasn't a great husband – or father. I see that now.'

Callaghan paused and took another long swallow of coffee, looking like he was digesting what he'd just said for the first time.

Carter remained silent.

'Anyway,' Callaghan continued, 'Vivienne is a handful. Blames me for everything that's happened to the family. But I'd do anything for her.'

'Where is she now?'

'I never should've let her go to Bali after she finished her Higher School Certificate a few weeks ago. I can't say no to her. She's all I've got.'

Carter knew where this was heading. An intelligent and capable man had been sucked into a vortex from which there was no easy way out.

'Samudra grabbed her?' he asked.

Callaghan nodded.

'I'm presuming she's still alive?'

'Samudra's smart. Insisted I speak to her every day. Said if I didn't do exactly as he asked, he'd have her gang-raped and then killed. It tore me apart. Still does.' Tears welled in his eyes. 'I can't take it anymore.'

Carter read the pain and torment in his face, but as much as he empathised, Callaghan needed to see the pain his actions had inflicted on members of Carter's tribe. He'd given information to Samudra's clan that had directly resulted in Thomas's abduction and the deaths of Jacko, Muklas and Wayan.

'You think you and your daughter are the only ones suffering? Thomas and Wayan were kidnapped.'

'I heard,' Callaghan said, wiping his eyes with the back of his fingers. 'Are they all right?'

'Wayan's dead. So's Jacko MacDonald.'

Callaghan's head dropped.

'Six members of the order are in a hospital in Ubud.'

'And Thomas?'

'Badly hurt.'

Callaghan threw his head back, ran his hands over his face and muttered, 'Good God, what have I done?'

Carter let him sit quietly for a moment. He was surprised to find he felt nothing but empathy for this broken shell of a man, despite the choices he had made.

'Listen to me,' Carter said. 'What's done is done. All that matters is what you do now.'

'I'll do whatever I humanly can to make this right.'

'Tell me what you did for Samudra.'

Callaghan let out a slow breath. 'He said if I gave his consultant access to all our network passwords and email accounts, he'd release Viv on 2 January, unharmed.'

'So that's how they found us.'

'The consultant has been in there for two months,' Callaghan said. 'He has all our codes and has had full access to the Trident servers. God only knows what information they've siphoned off by now.'

'Do you know what Samudra is planning?'

'No. He never told me a thing. But my gut says it's big.'

'Your gut's right. Something Sydney's never seen before, and if our intel is correct, and we believe it is, it's happening tonight.'

'Fucking hell.'

Callaghan looked into Carter's eyes for the first time. 'What do you need from me?'

'Let me handle this without any interference from Trident.'

Callaghan nodded. 'You won't get any meddling from my end unless you ask for it.'

'And I need two official photo IDs from the water police, giving me free movement around the harbour.'

'You got it. Email me the photos and tell me where you want them delivered.'

Carter paused a beat. There was another thing he required and he knew it wouldn't be easy for Callaghan to deliver.

'There's one more thing I need you to do,' he said.

'Anything in my power.'

'The bridge is closed to traffic from 11 p.m.'

'Correct.'

'I need it shut by 9 p.m.'

'What?'

'No traffic on the deck of the bridge after nine o'clock.'

'Jesus Christ,' Callaghan said. 'I don't know if I can do that.'

'You have to. Even if you have to put a gun to someone's head.'

'I'll do my best.'

'No, get it done. I don't care how. It's not just Vivienne's life at stake. The lives of hundreds or possibly even thousands are at risk and their death will be on you.'

Carter waited long enough to make sure his message had struck home.

'I'll get it done,' Callaghan said. 'I swear to God I will.'

Carter looked into his eyes and knew Callaghan meant what he said. He took a small notepad and pen out of his pocket and wrote down his mobile number.

He slid it across the table to Callaghan and said, 'Ring me as soon as you can confirm.'

Callaghan took the paper and nodded.

Carter got to his feet. There was nothing more to be accomplished here.

He followed Callaghan to the front door. They stood outside on the porch. Some colour had returned to Callaghan's face. His eyes shone brighter.

'Thank you, Carter.'

'I haven't done anything yet.'

'You have.'

They shook hands.

'I'll bring your daughter back,' Carter said. 'That's a promise.'

'I believe you will.'

Carter turned and walked down the garden path and across the road to his van without looking back. To his left he noticed a black mini-van fifty metres behind where he was parked.

He climbed into the Toyota, fired up the ignition and then slowly pulled out and drove west towards the city skyline. He glanced in the rear-view mirror.

The mini-van pulled out from the kerb.

Carter accelerated down the wide street.

So did the dark van.

CHAPTER 9

Djoran had spent the last twenty-four hours on board a run-down ten-metre motor-launch, provided to the clan by a large cell from the outer Sydney suburb of Lakemba, which he'd discovered had a large Muslim community.

It lay at anchor two hundred metres from a wealthy-looking harbourside suburb. He could see the magnificent bridge and Opera House in the distance. Apart from that, he remained ignorant of where he was. He'd never been to Sydney before.

Samudra had called their third meeting of the day for 3.30 p.m., on the deck, and had just revealed the exact location of the planned attack on the Sydney Harbour Bridge. He'd sent Djoran below to make some tea, leaving himself, Jamal and Akeem, the two recruits from Aceh, sitting in the stern.

Djoran walked down the narrow stairs into the cramped galley, which reeked of diesel, spicy food and body odour. He put the blackened kettle on the stove and stared at a set of silver keys sitting on top of a rusty fridge.

One would open the rear cabin, where he knew Samudra had locked their mobile phones. He only needed one minute to send a message to Carter with the precise details of tonight's attack. About the time it'd take the kettle to boil.

Outside a loud toot caught his attention.

He glanced through the cabin window. A two-masted yacht packed with passengers cruised down the harbour, which was already filling with pleasure craft taking up their vantage points for the evening's spectacle.

His heart went out to the innocent souls on board, many of whom might die that night should he fail to contact Carter.

The launch listed and rolled in the yacht's wake. He put his hand against the cabin wall to steady himself.

He looked back at the keys sliding back and forth across the fridge, under no illusion as to what would happen to him should Samudra discover his betrayal.

Deep in his heart he knew that, in the grand scheme of God's universe, his physical existence meant very little.

Of supreme importance, though, was his ability to follow the dictates of his conscience. That meant doing everything in his power to stop Samudra from killing innocent people in the name of Allah.

He placed his hand on his thumping heart.

The time to cling to safety had passed. There was a time to let things happen and a time to make them happen. He might not get a better opportunity to contact Carter.

A man had the power to act, but only God knew the outcome of a man's actions.

He picked up the keys.

The third key he tried slid into the lock easily.

A tremor of fear ran down his spine.

He ignored it.

Fear represented a man's distance from God.

He turned the handle, opened the door and went inside.

CHAPTER 10

The afternoon sun had begun its descent towards the top of the bridge and Sydney's western skyline.

Carter and Erina walked up George Street towards the Rosemount Apartments at a brisk pace, blending in with the constant stream of pedestrian traffic.

'Did you manage to get everything on the list?' Carter asked.

'Of course. How did you go?'

He recapped his encounter with Callaghan and then outlined what'd happened after leaving Vaucluse.

The black van had tailed him into the city. He'd turned off Liverpool Street into Chinatown, jumped a red light, gone the wrong way up a one-way street, turned left into a dark lane beside the Happy Chef Restaurant and hidden there for ten minutes.

When confident he'd evaded the pursuing vehicle, he drove to a nearby car park and left the Hiace there, then headed towards Kent Street on foot to Paddy Pallin Adventure Equipment. When he'd returned to the parking lot, there was no sign of the dark van.

'How would they have known you'd be at Callaghan's?' she asked.

'Alex probably had someone keeping an eye on him.'

'So the clan know we're in Sydney and onto them.'

It was a statement rather than a question and something he'd already taken into account.

Before he had a chance to say anything more, his phone beeped in his thigh pocket – another text.

They moved to the side of the busy pavement and stood in front of the display window of a jewellery store. He read the text and then held the phone out for her.

2 men, maybe more + AA. SW pylon. Strike at midnight. Will detonate if threatened. B careful. D

Erina frowned. 'There's a good chance Djoran's been found out and they're using his phone to lure us into a trap.'

'It doesn't change a thing,' he said. 'Everything's a calculated gamble at this point.'

—

Carter stood next to Erina in the lift leading up to their serviced apartment. It came to a stop on the sixth floor. Carter's mobile started vibrating in his pocket.

They both stepped out into a deserted hallway. Erina entered the apartment, leaving the door ajar. Carter stayed where he was and answered on the fourth ring.

'Carter, it's Callaghan.'

'I'm listening.'

'It cost me, but I got it done.'

'Good job.'

'God bless you, Carter.'

Carter didn't know how to respond to that. He just said goodbye, hung up and stepped into the apartment, satisfied the last piece of the puzzle had fallen into place.

He closed the front door and stood just inside it.

'Was that Callaghan?' Erina asked.

'Yep, he came through.'

'Thank God for that. At least the bridge will be clear if things go pear-shaped.'

Carter turned and studied the living room. It resembled an army surplus store. Erina had arranged everything in neat rows on the carpeted floor.

She stretched out her hand as if presenting Carter with a feast and said, 'The banquet is laid.'

There were two Glock 18s, a SIG SG550, four throwing knives, three black cylinders containing C4 plastic explosives, a black pouch with acid in a small bottle, a roll of duct tape, detonators, two lightweight wetsuits, two pairs of Vibram five-finger shoes, climbing hooks attached to ten metres of nylon rope, one waterproof flashlight and a pair of wire-cutters.

Carter admired the four *hira shuriken* or five-point star knives, a favourite weapon of the Japanese ninja, lined up on a hotel pillow. *Shuriken* literally meant 'sword hidden in the hand'.

He picked one up and ran his fingers over the smooth surface. Thanks to hundreds of hours of training, he could fling three star knives in under a second and strike a target the size of a tennis ball at twenty paces.

His attention shifted to two items leaning against the side wall: two body harnesses and an Armaguard Magnogun-TX 7, an apparatus that looked like a high-powered spear gun with a flat head connected to a compact vacuum cleaner.

The Magnogun was designed to propel a magnetised metal head up to one hundred metres through the air. Once it struck metal, a powerful electromagnet was triggered, locking it fast. The section that looked like the dust-collection unit of a vacuum cleaner housed a hundred metres of cord and an electric motor.

'So fill me in on the plan,' she said. 'I need details.'

He had already told her how, after leaving the city car park, he'd driven to Dawes Point Park on the edge of the harbour near the Rocks to study the bridge and the two southern pylons. Now that they had a precise target, he was able to form a clear picture in his mind of the route they needed to take.

'The Hiace is parked downstairs with a double-seated kayak strapped to its roof,' he said. 'At 8.30 p.m. we'll set off from Rushcutters Bay and paddle for Fort Denison.'

Fort Denison had been built in the nineteenth century to protect the harbour from invaders. It was approximately one kilometre from the bridge and would shelter them from the full brunt of the building southerly.

'I've got hold of a couple of water police IDs courtesy of Callaghan, which will allow us to move freely around the harbour. Once the 9 p.m. fireworks finish, we paddle under the bridge and make for what looks like a maintenance walkway that runs from east to west below the bridge's deck. It's a separate structure that hangs a few metres underneath.'

'So the walkway crosses the width of the bridge – it doesn't run along the length?'

'That's right.'

'Where exactly is it in relation to the pylon?'

'About forty metres north of it, I'd say, out over the water.'

'So that's where the Magnogun comes into play?'

'Yeah, it'll get us to the bottom of the walkway.'

'And I'm presuming the walkway is enclosed in some sort of security fence?'

'Yeah, it looks about a metre and a half high, but it's quite open – lots of foot- and handholds from what I could see. We just have to climb up over it and jump down onto the walkway. From there, it should be easy enough to climb onto the bridge.'

'Yeah, if you're a monkey.'

'We'll do our best imitation.'

'I'd forgotten how much you like to do things the hard way.'

'Whatever it takes.'

CHAPTER 11

Djoran lay on his back strapped to the galley table, stripped naked, staring wide-eyed at the wooden ceiling, awaiting his inevitable fate.

Almost as soon as he'd sent the text message to Carter, Samudra had caught him in the rear cabin, still holding the mobile phone.

The keys and tea had been a trap.

Sweat trickled down his armpits. His breath came in short, sharp bursts and he was on the verge of hyperventilating.

He looked out the window at a bank of grey clouds floating high in the pale blue sky. Like them, his life would soon blow away and dissolve when his fleeting time on earth was over.

His training as a Sufi had taught him to recognise that a man was not his body. The body was merely a vessel for the soul. Whatever happened on the physical plane, his spirit would live on for eternity.

Above all else, he needed to remain true to the values and principles of his god. This was the core of his religion and the fundamental belief underpinning his life.

His spiritual practice and principles were about to face the ultimate test.

Death, he knew, was not far away.

He recognised three sets of footsteps treading down the stairs.

Samudra, Jamal and Akeem assembled around him, exuding the clinical calm of zealots who believed in the righteousness of their cause.

He swallowed hard and repeated his mantra over and over in his mind.

I am not my body.

Samudra leant over him, so close he could smell his bitter breath.

'For the final time, will you admit the error of your ways, confess everything you have done and beg forgiveness for your sins?'

Djoran said nothing.

Samudra lifted himself up to his full height. 'I am very disappointed in you. I'd hoped with all my heart that you were one of us, a true believer. But your spirit has been corrupted.'

Djoran turned his head to the right and looked through the window at a lush emerald headland. A soothing calmness descended upon him.

Samudra sighed. 'So you are going to be stubborn.'

He heard the *click, click, click* of a cheap cigarette lighter and breathed in the acrid smell of tobacco smoke.

Rough hands held his forehead.

Samudra placed electrical tape over his mouth, forcing him to breathe through his nostrils.

Jamal and Akeem stood back.

Djoran thought he detected excitement in their eyes, which saddened him. When he'd first met them, they were simple villagers with good hearts.

He closed his eyes. He knew what was coming and prayed to Allah for strength and compassion.

CHAPTER 12

Dusk was fast approaching when Carter settled behind Erina in the black double sea kayak moored in a protected cove at Rushcutters Bay, forty metres from the Cruising Yacht Club of Australia.

He ran his fingers over the aluminium paddle lying across his lap. A gentle swell rocked them up and down. It was 8.37 p.m. They planned to begin their one-kilometre sprint to Fort Denison at 8.40 p.m. before the first round of fireworks blasted off at 9 p.m.

Both wore lightweight black wetsuits, neoprene skullcaps and snug Vibram shoes. Water police IDs hung on lanyards around their necks. The IDs enabled them to move freely along the foreshore and through a barricade blocking an entrance to the harbour.

The water around them was calm, protected by the imposing Darling Point headland, where crowds were gathering to watch the fireworks. Out in the middle of the harbour, however, foaming whitecaps suggested that the predicted strong southerly change was well on its way.

The intermittent tinkle of loose rigging sounded through the still air, underscoring the distant murmur of the crowd. The lights from the tall masts of the hundred or so moored yachts shone across the smooth surface of the water, creating a pale yellow glow.

Erina brushed her right hand through the water alongside the kayak, then twisted her neck from side to side and stretched her arms out wide. Since they'd left the apartment an hour ago, she'd barely uttered a word.

Like Carter, she preferred a period of introspection to focus her mind before starting out.

He scanned the waters and shoreline of the enclosed cove. Nothing appeared to be out of the ordinary.

He squeezed his knees together against the SIG and the Magnogun resting between his legs, covered by a dark blue beach towel. Then he reached behind and patted his daypack, sitting in the scooped-out locker. It contained the Glocks, night-vision binoculars, gaffer tape, a bottle of acid, a lighter, the star knives, wire-cutters, throwing knives, C4 explosives and detonator caps. The ten-metre nylon climbing cord with attached hook was wrapped over his left shoulder.

His gaze shifted towards the expanse of the harbour, where the bridge and Opera House sat remote and aloof, dominating the darkening skyline.

It was 8.39 p.m.

The countdown before setting off created a small adrenalin rush. He felt like a foot soldier in the trenches, preparing to fix his bayonet and charge across the foreboding terrain between enemy lines.

He leant in close to Erina's ear. 'Ready?'

She nodded.

He dug his aluminium paddle into the murky water and pulled back hard. She did the same and they glided towards the winking lights of the fleet gathered on the harbour in front of the bridge.

As always, it felt good to get started.

CHAPTER 13

Just under nine minutes later the kayak drew level with the tip of Fort Denison. Carter steered into the lee of the island, giving them some protection from the wind whistling overhead.

The kayak bobbed up and down, smack bang in the centre of thousands of pleasure craft of all shapes and sizes, ranging from luxury yachts to stand-up paddleboards. They'd arrived in the middle of a floating carnival.

Carter laid the paddle in his lap. Neither of them uttered a word, using the last few minutes before the final countdown to tune into their surroundings, bringing themselves fully into the moment, ready for whatever came their way.

Ragtime jazz, occasional bursts of laughter and a constant stream of chatter drifted across the water from a party being hosted on Fort Denison.

The expectant buzz of the surrounding crowd reminded Carter of how little New Year's Eve usually meant to him. He'd never been one for public celebrations. New Year's had always been just another day.

He promised himself that next year, if there was a next year for him, he'd dive into the New Year's festivities and find out what all the fuss was about. He might, with a bit of luck, share it with Erina.

He pushed all thoughts of the future and what might or might not happen to the back of his mind. It was 8.56 p.m. and the clock was counting down.

Several spitting drops of rain landed on his face, followed by a sudden downpour. Concentric circles rippled across the surface of the water, radiating outwards.

Then, just as suddenly as it'd begun, the rain stopped. He sensed this was the prelude to a full-blown southerly buster.

At 8.59 p.m. the music and party noises began to peter out and an expectant hush fell over the harbour.

Erina turned and they exchanged a nod. They were both set.

He closed his eyes.

The crowd took up the ritualistic chant.

Ten, nine, eight, seven, six, five, four …

Carter's blood pumped faster.

Three, two, one …

A series of ear-piercing bangs ripped through the night as the first fireworks whooshed and then exploded overhead.

The crowd responded to the massive choreographed dance of colour and light with a symphony of oohs, aahs, cheers and squeals as millions of dollars went up in smoke.

Carter rocked back and forth in his seat, stretching his legs, arms and shoulders, enjoying the energy building up in his muscles.

The aerial explosions continued one after the other, as they would for the next eight minutes. The smell of gunpowder filled the air. He ran his left palm over the kayak's smooth deck as if calming a horse, his eyes still closed tight.

He felt neither cocky nor afraid.

Just ready.

CHAPTER 14

A series of loud explosions jolted Djoran back into full consciousness on the galley table, back into a world of physical pain.

What sounded like a rocket whistled through the air and exploded in the distance. Bright coloured light streamed through the windows.

For a moment he thought Samudra had succeeded in blowing up the bridge, but he soon realised it was just fireworks and gave thanks.

Warm blood flowed down his face into his right eye and his mouth.

Samudra had twisted and broken two of his fingers and smashed a fist into his nose. It felt like it'd been both splattered across his face and driven into his tortured skull, stabbing into his brain. Samudra had also crushed burning cigarettes into his chest, cheek and genitals.

Thanks to a power greater than himself, he'd remained silent throughout this violent torture and revealed no knowledge of the exact whereabouts or intentions of Carter and Erina. Nor had he renounced his steadfast faith in a loving God.

A feeling of humility and gratitude flowed through him. An unseen presence had protected his spirit and helped him tap reservoirs of courage he never knew he possessed.

Thanks to the divine strength bestowed upon him, he could return to his maker, join his beautiful wife and the spirit of his unborn child and rest in peace for eternity.

Stopping Samudra was now beyond his control. It rested with Carter, Erina and ultimately almighty God to determine the outcome.

He'd only met Carter and Erina briefly but had been struck by their presence and strong characters. If anyone could stop Samudra, they could, God willing.

He blinked the blood out of his eye, turned his head, stared out the window and recalled two of his most cherished lines from the work of his favourite poet, Rumi.

What strikes the oyster shell does not damage the pearl ...
What have I ever lost by dying? Why should I fear the next death?

Again, the familiar footsteps trod down the stairs towards him.

Flanked by Jamal and Akeem, Samudra stood over him holding a silver knife in his right hand.

Djoran knew his death was only moments away.

Strangely he felt nothing but love and pity for the three men who were soon to be his executioners. As the great prophet Jesus had said on the cross, 'Father, forgive them, for they know not what they do.'

He closed his eyes, not wishing to look upon their faces again before he passed through the veil of death to the hereafter.

The sharp knife struck his throat. A moment of intense pain was followed by a feeling of drowning in his own blood.

He gagged and his body started to shake.

He took one final breath, and on the exhalation, a peace that surpassed all human understanding flowed through every fibre of his being.

Like the mystics of old had written, a man could transcend the suffering of the physical world and enter the world of spiritual ecstasy and eternal peace.

Allah akbar.

CHAPTER 15

Eight minutes after the first rocket exploded, the noise from the fire-works ceased.

The sweet sounds of silence descended over the harbour.

After a few seconds a collective sigh was breathed and the harbour erupted into a symphony of raucous clapping and cheering. The crowds thronging the foreshore whooped and shouted, and the boats packing the water tooted their horns.

Carter's eyes snapped open.

Two lightning bolts ripped through the night air, illuminating the bridge's arch like a scene from a horror movie, followed by a violent double clap of thunder that silenced the crowd.

It struck Carter that nothing human beings conjured up could match the power, majesty and violence of the natural world.

Then, the sky opened.

Sheets of rain bucketed down, providing the perfect cloak for their run to the bridge – like the heavens had their backs covered.

Another bolt of lightning ripped across the sky, followed by a dark clap of thunder.

Erina turned to face him. Her eyes shone like twin flames, lit from within.

She was ready.

In perfect unison they dug their paddles deep into the choppy waters and pulled back hard.

Small orange lights lit up both ends of the walkway they were heading for, providing a beacon through the driving wind and rain that lashed them from behind.

—

'*Stop paddling!*' Carter yelled to be heard above the raging elements.

The kayak glided into the deep shadow of the massive bridge, directly underneath the maintenance walkway. The bridge's dark underbelly protected them from the torrential rain, but the driving wind, which had been at their back coming down the harbour, now buffeted them from the south-east, pushing them in a westerly direction beneath the bridge.

Carter dug his paddle into the water and executed a perfect J stroke. The bow swung a hundred and eighty degrees to face the Opera House and the teeth of the howling gale.

He needed to stall the kayak long enough to fire the Magnogun accurately, so that the magnetic pad would attach itself to the bottom of the metre-wide walkway.

Erina swivelled around in her seat at the bow and faced him. They both dropped their legs over the side to stabilise the craft.

It reminded him of being in the surf at Lennox when the wind blew strongly onshore and only the most desperate surfers ventured out.

'You think Alex might've planted snipers underneath the bridge?' Erina asked, almost shouting to be heard over the wind.

'We'll find out soon enough,' he yelled.

He reached into his bag, grabbed a harness and handed it to her. She slipped it over her shoulders and buckled it up. He lay back and stretched his torso along the sleek deck of the kayak.

Once settled, he placed the stock of the Magnogun to his shoulder, lined up a metal panel on the bottom of the walkway roughly fifty metres above them, and pulled the trigger.

The recoil jammed the butt into his shoulder, pushing his end of the craft into the water. The metal pad flew through the darkness towards its target, the nylon cord uncoiling behind it.

The Magnogun-TX 7 was designed to propel the pad with tremendous force, allowing it to cut through the most turbulent weather.

After counting to ten, Carter sat up and pulled down on the cord, hard, hoping the first shot had stuck. The sooner they got onto the bridge, the better.

The Magnogun held firm.

He laid the gun on the kayak deck and took the climbing cord and hook off his shoulder and handed it to Erina. She put it over her head so that it hung diagonally across her body and secured it off with a rubber tie so it wouldn't unravel.

While she got herself organised, he clipped on his harness, slung his daypack on his back and fastened it tight.

The stern faced west, the most likely direction for a sniper. That meant his back created a human shield protecting Erina.

He handed her a phone in its waterproof case. 'If anything happens to me, call Watto. The number is preset. Just press 1.'

She strapped the phone onto her arm. 'Will do.'

Without needing to say anything, they shuffled towards each other, still sitting, until their knees touched in the midsection of the kayak.

They clipped their harnesses onto either side of the Magnogun.

He double-checked everything was secure and gave the cord a final pull. 'All set?'

She nodded. 'Beam us up, Scotty.'

He shouldered the SIG and pushed the green button on the side of the Magnogun, activating its internal drive.

The cord tightened and pulled them closer together. They each held it in one hand to steady themselves.

Slowly, the device lifted them into a standing position before pulling them off the kayak and upwards into the night.

CHAPTER 16

Samudra looked through the water-streaked cabin window towards the bridge and smiled. He was sitting in the galley of the launch he commanded, moored off Watsons Bay, not far from Sydney Heads, rocking back and forth in the wind.

Rain lashed the deck above, reminding him of the many tears the heathens of Sydney would shed in the morning and the days, weeks, months and years ahead.

God was indeed great.

Everything was in place.

The two men who had been with him on the boat, Jamal and Akeem, were on their way to the second target, the Sydney Opera House foreshore, with C4 explosives packed into the vests hidden under their shirts. No one would give them a second thought among the packed crowds in the foul weather.

A truck packed with explosives – a chariot of destruction – was heading for the Sydney Harbour Tunnel.

Ubal, a member of the Lakemba cell, would join Samudra on the motor-launch shortly.

Abdul-Aleem would not be coming on board as he presumed, or collecting his $250,000. This would be his last job for the clan. His usefulness had come to an end.

The men under his command, Zaheed and Putu, had been instructed by Samudra to shoot Abdul-Aleem when he attempted to leave the pylon on his hang-glider shortly before midnight.

In future only true believers would be allowed into the clan's inner circle.

His mind turned to the midnight explosions. The sound of God's vengeance would reverberate around Sydney and then the world.

By 12.10 a.m. all of the brave mujaheddin who'd come with him to Sydney would be dead, only to be resurrected as heroes enjoying the magnificent fruits of paradise they so richly deserved for their noble acts of courage and devotion.

That was not his fate. God had even greater plans for him.

Following the climactic moment where his jihad became reality, he'd use the launch's dinghy to land at Watsons Bay. He'd then travel to a safe house in Lakemba with Ubal, who'd made all the arrangements. In the morning he'd leave this accursed country and return home to the loving arms of his wife and family.

His thoughts turned to the traitor Djoran, for whom he'd once held such high hopes, and now felt such bitter disappointment.

To his credit, the man had demonstrated great courage at the end of his life. Samudra had to admire him for that, even if he was deeply misguided and would spend eternity in hell.

The mobile phone vibrated in his breast pocket. He took it out and looked at the number. It was Abdul-Aleem.

He held it to his ear. 'Yes?'

'Carter and Erina have been spotted coming onto the bridge from the water as I predicted.'

'That is indeed good news. Proceed as planned.'

'Yes, sir.'

Samudra clicked off.

He gently stroked the keypad of the phone with his forefinger. To unleash the wrath of God on Sydney, all he needed to do was dial a number and hit send.

The phones would vibrate simultaneously around the harbour, detonating the explosives his men wore on the bridge, near the Opera House and inside the truck. If anyone tried to tamper with the bombs, they'd explode instantly.

The men would die as heroes and enter paradise, as was their wish.

A bolt of energy shot through him. He'd never felt so close to God.

CHAPTER 17

Carter and Erina dangled from the nylon cord with the gusting southerly buster blowing them back and forth in an arc.

The harness dug into Carter's chest. He held onto the ascending cord with his left hand and the trigger guard of the SIG with his right, aware of how exposed and vulnerable they were.

Time, always elastic, slowed. All of his senses were heightened, enabling him to take in every detail of the world around him.

He looked up. The bridge's underbelly loomed cold and malevolent, casting an ominous shadow of energy that sent a tingle down Carter's spine. It was as if the bridge knew it was under threat.

Its crisscrossing steel girders and metal beams formed an intricate pattern of interlocking angles, all providing myriad potential hiding spots. If a sniper was concealed on one of the metal struts, there was nothing he and Erina could do to defend themselves.

He shook off these counterproductive thoughts and looked to the south, towards the city, seeking inspiration. Thousands of bright lights shone through the slanting rain, homes and offices to hundreds of thousands of people ignorant of the threat facing their city.

His gaze swept a hundred and eighty degrees over the twinkling nightscape of Sydney's harbour suburbs, stopping at Luna Park. The huge lit-up clown face grinned at him as if amused by the folly of their endeavour and wishing to share the cosmic joke of human existence.

The Magnogun pulled them steadily towards the base of the walkway, now less than fifteen metres away.

A strong gust of wind blasted them. He gripped the cord tighter. Erina's cold wet cheek brushed against his. He looked into her eyes and saw no sign of fear, only alert anticipation.

Without thinking, he stroked the small of her back with his left hand. She gave his right shoulder a gentle squeeze. The shared touch was one of the most intimate connections he'd ever felt.

—

The Magnogun clicked to a jolting stop. They hung in the centre of the metre-wide walkway, buffeted by the wind.

Carter pushed the SIG back into its holster and said, 'Time for some monkey business.'

'Okay, you big ape,' Erina said, 'show us what you've got.'

A steel bar ran along both sides of the base of the walkway, suspended about fifteen centimetres below it.

He reached out with one hand, grasped the cold wet metal bar closest to him and hung from it by one arm. Then he unclipped his harness and swung his body around, reaching out to grab hold of the bar with his free hand. He hung there at full stretch, facing Erina, who was still attached to the Magnogun.

'Nice move,' she said.

The bar was slippery from the rain, making it hard for him to gain a firm hold.

'I'm going to need a leg up,' he told her.

'No kidding.'

He tightened his grip on the bar and raised his right leg towards her until his foot found her cupped hands.

She held his foot firmly. He pulled himself up as if doing a chin-up and pushed off her hand as she gave him a final shove. The combined force thrust his body up into the air and he grabbed onto the metal bars of the security fence above with his left hand and then his right. Clinging tightly, he scrambled one foot, then the other, onto the bar he'd just been hanging from, and pulled himself up into a standing position.

He yelled down to Erina, 'Your turn.'

Erina repeated his manoeuvre and hung from the metal bar to the right of where he was now standing. This was the riskiest part. He needed to get a firm hold of Erina to pull her up.

He gripped onto the security fence hard with his left hand and then leant out and down towards her, bending his knees until he could reach her with his right hand.

Their hands locked on each other's wrists and he pulled her up next to him.

They took a moment, standing beside each other, holding onto the rungs of the side of the metal walkway, giving their arms and hands a chance to recover.

The southerly buster whistled through the struts and rigging, and the walkway shook and shuddered. Looking over their shoulders, they peered down at the dark waters of the harbour fifty metres below.

'No point hanging about here admiring the view,' Erina said.

'I guess not,' Carter replied.

He stretched his right hand upwards and started climbing the fence, using the crisscrossing metal bars as footholds. On reaching the top, he jumped over and dropped onto the metre-wide metal floor below. Erina followed closely behind, leapt down and squatted next to him.

He studied the creaking dark shadows of the metal structures above them.

'See anything?' Erina asked.

'Nothing – but I have a creepy sense of being watched.'

'Me too.'

'Let's go.'

—

Carter led Erina across the walkway towards the western side of the bridge, holding the SIG in his right hand. The thin soles of his Vibram shoes made him feel light on his feet, connected to and part of the cold metal structure underneath.

They moved at a steady, even pace, the wind pushing them as if urging them forwards.

His gaze flicked from left to right, but he saw nothing suspicious.

A semi-enclosed metal cage made of galvanised steel grating was attached to the end of the walkway, connecting it to the deck of the bridge above. They passed through its rectangular entrance, stopped in the centre and looked up. A metal lid sealed what looked like an access point leading up the inside of the cage onto the deck.

'An internal ladder would've been nice,' Erina said.

'So would a hot coffee.'

Carter stretched upwards and pushed hard against the metal cover. It didn't budge. There was no way round or through it. As he'd always suspected, they'd need to climb up the outside of the cage.

There was a rectangular opening at the end of the cage, almost like a window, giving a view out over the water, and they moved towards it. Carter leant out over the top of the chest-high security railing, turned his head and looked up.

He liked what he saw. The front of the cage, a metre and a half wide, ran approximately ten metres up the outside of the bridge, stretching all the way to the top of the security fence on the main deck.

A flat metal grid formed its roof. Once they'd climbed up the outside of the cage and onto its roof, they'd be able to jump over the barbed-wire security fence that ran south to north along the side of the bridge, and land on the bridge's deck on the bicycle lane. There was no need to utter a word. Both understood that climbing the cage and getting onto the bridge was the easy part.

The hard part would come if a squad of Alex's men were in position above, armed with automatic rifles, waiting for them.

But they could only deal with one problem at a time. Carter had a motto in situations like this: *If in doubt, keep moving forward.* Waiting any longer would change nothing.

Erina pulled the climbing cord over her head, untied it and handed it to Carter. He slung it over his right shoulder and pulled himself up onto the open metal ledge of the cage. He stood facing Erina, holding a bar above him with his left hand for support.

His daypack hugged his back and the SIG hung over his left shoulder.

He shrugged the climbing cord off his shoulder into his free hand, then uncoiled two metres and dropped one end towards Erina.

She took hold of it with both hands.

If he discovered the way forward was clear when he reached the bridge's deck, he'd pull the rope twice to signal for her to come up and join him.

He leant away from the cage and balanced outside over the water. He let two metres of the top end of the rope drop below him and began twirling the hook in the air.

After half-a-dozen spins, it had gained enough momentum. He hurled it upwards towards the top of the cage, releasing the rest of the cord as the hook flew through the air.

The hook landed on the flat top of the cage. He pulled the cord hard to make sure the hook had caught and turned to Erina.

It felt like that instant before taking off on a giant wave, where everything hung in the balance. He had no idea what was waiting for him up there on the bridge's deck.

Alex and his men had probably been on the bridge for over twenty-four hours, and once he pulled his head above the line of sight, he'd be totally exposed.

'If I don't signal you within three minutes,' he said, 'call Watto.'

'Carter?'

Erina let the word hang in the air.

'What?' he asked.

She shook her head. 'Nothing.'

He started climbing.

CHAPTER 18

By 10.04 p.m. Erina and Carter had reached their target, the entrance to the south-west pylon on the main deck of the bridge. Footlights bathed the pylon in a golden glow, making them both easy targets, but there was nothing they could do. Shooting out the lights would only draw attention to their position.

Erina was working on the lock of the thick grey metal door with acid and picking keys while Carter covered her back, swinging his SIG in an arc, scanning the deck.

It looked like an urban wasteland from an end-of-the-world disaster movie. Wind and rain swirled over the concrete and steel structures. Street lamps lit up the bike path, two railway tracks and the eight empty traffic lanes. All four pylons were illuminated.

So far everything had gone to plan. They'd worked together like dancers in a ballet, each anticipating the other's moves. They'd jumped down onto the bike lane from the top of the cage without incident. Erina had picked a lock that opened a gate in the security fence that separated the bike lane from the train tracks and the pylon. They then climbed down a four-rung yellow ladder onto the tracks, ran to their right along the sleepers and finally pulled themselves up onto a wooden deck right by the entrance to the south-west pylon.

Carter kept a keen lookout as Erina worked. There was still no sign of human activity, but once they passed through the pylon door, they'd be in territory controlled by the clan. It all depended on when Alex chose to make his move against them.

Sun Tzu, the famous Chinese military strategist, would've approved of the clan's strategy.

The clan had chosen the location of the battle well. They'd arrived first, occupied the high ground and were numerically superior. They'd be watching and waiting for their enemy from a position of safety and had given themselves plenty of time to prepare and execute an ambush in an enclosed space. Once inside the pylon, Carter and Erina would have nowhere to run, making escape almost impossible. The odds were all in Alex and his men's favour.

Yet Carter knew that in any fight there was always something you couldn't plan for. And that something invariably made all the difference.

Their job was to find it.

'We're in,' Erina said.

He turned around. The door was slightly ajar and the lock was smoking.

'Cover me,' he said.

She stepped away from the door, gripping her Glock in both hands and holding it out in front of her. Carter pushed the door open, his SIG pointing forwards, cocked and ready.

He moved into a small, gloomy stairwell, barely illuminated by light coming from above. He counted twelve metal steps, a metre wide, leading to a small landing, from which a second set of steps led upwards to another landing, then another.

According to their research there were three levels above the main deck: the first floor, a second floor, and then a rooftop level, partially covered, but with an open-air balcony. They would have to climb sixteen staircases and nearly two hundred steps to reach the lookout that surrounded the roof of the pylon.

Erina closed the door and forced a throwing knife into the lock, twisting and breaking it so that it jammed. She then slid two more throwing knives under the door and pushed them forwards so they formed a tight wedge.

She gave the door a good shake. It appeared to hold firm. It wouldn't deter a determined force, but at least they'd hear anyone coming in.

Carter gripped the SIG lightly and started walking up the metal steps on the sides of his rubber shoes, not making a sound.

Erina followed one step behind.

CHAPTER 19

Forty metres above Erina and Carter, Alex once again stood on the narrow, open lookout on top of the pylon. He was looking west down the harbour towards the waterside suburb of East Balmain, waiting.

Zaheed and Putu stood on either side of him, wearing full Australian Tactical Response Unit uniforms concealing vests stuffed with C4 explosives. One carried a Heckler & Koch MP5 submachine gun, the other a Mossberg 500 pump-action shotgun.

Alex ran his fingers along the smooth scabbard of his beloved samurai sword, the Drying Pole. The beautiful two-handed sword, made famous by the master samurai Sasaki Kojiro, was roughly one and a half metres long and designed to hang from the waist. According to legend the blade embodied the soul of the warrior who possessed it.

With studied reverence he unsheathed the weapon with his right hand. Spots of rain glistened off the polished blade. He held it in front of his face and pointed it upright, the top of the handle level with his chin, searching for his image on the naked blade, but the angle of the light made it impossible.

Taking great care, he placed the sword on top of the low ledge that encircled the balcony. The ledge was chest-height, and was the only barrier against a fall of nearly ninety metres to the ground below. On the south-east pylon, whose rooftop lookout was open to the public, there was a clear plastic shield to protect visitors, but no such protection was offered here.

He'd use the ledge later that night to good effect, when he met Carter and Erina face to face.

Reaching into the thigh pocket of his trousers, he extracted a tablet computer. During the day he'd run a cable up to the lookout and connected it to a router, allowing him to link his tablet wirelessly to the pylon's security cameras.

He checked the screen and pressed Camera B.

Sure enough, the shadowy images of Carter and Erina filled the screen. They were climbing the stairs from the deck of the bridge to level one. Carter held an automatic weapon and Erina a handgun.

He picked up his phone and dialled the number of Hazeem, the leader of his second unit. The group of three were in position on the bridge, waiting behind the south-east pylon for his signal.

They'd trained on Batak Island with Samudra and himself for eight months and had been working with the Sydney cell based in Lakemba.

'The targets have made their entrance,' Alex said. 'Move the men into position in two minutes.'

'Yes, sir.'

Alex clicked off.

The endgame, when he had his target helpless and cornered, ready for the kill, was always his favourite part of the hunt.

His thoughts turned to the men from the Sydney cell. Unlike Zaheed and Putu they had no combat experience. Under normal circumstances they'd be no match for the likes of Carter and Erina.

But this wasn't going to be anything like a fair fight. More like shooting blind barracudas in a concrete pond.

So long as they delivered Carter and Erina, he didn't care what happened to them.

He picked up the Drying Pole and held the blade in front of him, pointing it south-east towards the city lights. The sword was thirsty.

A thin smile spread across his face.

326

CHAPTER 20

When they reached the first floor, dimly lit by overhead halogen lights, Carter motioned for Erina to check the two large rooms to their right while he covered the stairway. She reappeared a minute later and whispered, 'All clear. Just a lot of stored equipment.'

They started up the stairs to the second floor, Carter leading the way, but after just a few steps, he raised his hand and stopped.

Two bodies wearing fluorescent lime-green jackets lay facedown in pools of blood on the metal landing above them. They had been shot in the back of the head, execution style.

Carter continued up the stairs, knelt beside the bodies and gently turned them over. They were men, Caucasian, in their early thirties. Their jackets carried the New South Wales Roads and Maritime Services logo. Just a couple of government workers unlucky enough to be rostered on for New Year's Eve.

More than anything else Carter hated seeing innocent people murdered because they'd inadvertently got in some madman's way.

He was sure Alex had used their deaths to send a message. He was waiting for them above and he wanted them to know it.

Erina stood next to him and said under her breath, 'Fucking bastard.'

Carter stood up, raised the SIG to shoulder height and carried on up the stairs one deliberate step at a time, Erina's soft tread coming half a pace behind his.

Just before they reached the second floor, he signalled for her to stop again. He leant against the metal railing and listened, holding the SIG in front of him.

He heard nothing.

He crept up the last few stairs and then, holding his gun out in front and keeping his finger lightly on the trigger, he scanned the room.

In the centre were more stairs, leading up to the lookout on the roof.

Old CCTV camera equipment, extension cords, cardboard boxes of fireworks and a pile of lime-green security jackets were heaped against the south wall.

None of that held his attention.

What did, though, were the two large sliding doors on the eastern and western sides of the room. Both were painted black. He filed the information away and kept looking around the room.

In the right-hand corner on the eastern side two open laptops sat on a wooden desk. On the floor next to it two large cardboard boxes were stacked one on top of the other. One was labelled *INFUSION CRYSTAL FOUNTAINS*, the other *PEGASUS SKYROCKETS*.

In the corner opposite the desk, on the western side, was a hooded figure sitting on a chair.

Erina moved up behind Carter. He pointed forwards and signalled for her to cover his back. He wondered if the hooded figure could be a booby trap. But there was no way of knowing.

He walked to the back of the stairs and stopped a metre from the figure. It wore black pants, a loose-fitting black jacket and dark green thongs. An executioner's hood hung over its head. Both arms were secured behind its back around a steel pole that ran up the wall.

On closer inspection Carter noted that the feet were delicate and their toenails painted a shiny blue. He was almost certain he knew who it was.

'Vivienne?' he whispered.

The figure jerked and the hooded head nodded.

'My name's Carter. I'm here to help. Are you wired?'

The captive shook her head.

'She could be a plant,' Erina whispered behind him.

He moved towards the girl cautiously, then reached out and felt around the hood for any detonation devices. Finding none, he peeled the hood off slowly, revealing a slightly older and edgier version of the young woman he'd seen on the wall of Callaghan's kitchen.

She now had spiky short black hair and silver nose and eyebrow rings, but her intense dark eyes were unmistakably the same, blazing with an equal mixture of fear and defiance.

Grey electrical tape with a slit in the middle covered her mouth.

'I'm going to take the tape off,' Carter whispered. 'I'll try to be gentle, but it might sting. It's important you remain very quiet.'

He grabbed the corner of the tape. 'On the count of three.'

She nodded.

'One, two …'

He tore the tape off in one sharp movement.

'For fuck sake,' she whispered, her eyes welling from the pain. 'You nearly ripped my piercing out.'

He noted a small amount of blood around a ring in her lower lip. 'Sorry,' he said. 'You okay otherwise?'

'Yeah,' she said. 'Where's the rest of the rescue team?'

Carter glanced over his shoulder at Erina. 'We're it.'

'You're fucking kidding me.'

'Listen, I need you to answer some questions.'

'Aren't you going to untie me first?'

'Be quiet and listen.'

'No way am I telling you anything until you untie me first – I'm freaking out here.'

Carter didn't have time to waste and knew when he was beaten. He put his hands on her shoulders. 'Okay. Just stay calm.'

She nodded.

He reached into his daypack and used a throwing knife to slice through the ties binding her wrists and ankles.

As she shook her arms and legs, he asked, 'Do you know how many men Samudra has on the bridge?'

'Six. A South African – a real arsehole – and the two Indonesians who dragged me up here. They all had guns. Three more came an hour or so ago and left. I never saw their faces.'

'Are they on the top level?'

'I think so. People have been going up and down the stairs all night.'

'What else can you tell us?' Erina asked.

Vivienne motioned her head in the direction of the desk. 'The computer on the right is linked to the surveillance cameras. The arsehole was in here for over an hour this afternoon setting it all up. You might want to check it out.'

CHAPTER 21

Erina sat in the chair behind the computer screen. Carter stood at her shoulder with his SIG at the ready.

She hit some keys and the screen came to life. Five icons appeared – *Entrance, Level One, Level Two, Outside/Bridge Deck* and *Lookout*. Each was linked to a video-surveillance feed.

She clicked *Entrance*.

Clear.

Next she clicked the icon *Outside/Bridge Deck*.

Carter leant forwards. The screen showed murky images of three armed men dressed in uniforms moving across the train tracks towards the pylon.

One carried a pump-action shotgun, the other two automatic rifles. Each weapon was fitted with a high-tech night scope. They had enough firepower to wipe out two football teams in three seconds flat.

Carter studied the men. Though they wore body armour and heavy boots, none possessed Alex's imposing physique.

Erina clicked on the *Lookout* icon.

The screen was black, as if someone had placed tape over the camera lens.

'You thinking what I'm thinking?' she asked.

'Yeah,' he said, almost certain that Alex and his men had stationed themselves on the lookout one floor above. 'Time to call in the cavalry.'

'What the fuck's going on?' Vivienne asked.

'Hold tight and stay put,' Erina said and handed Carter the phone.

He pressed 1, hit dial and put it to his ear.

The phone rang twice.

An automated female voice came on the line. 'Your service is temporarily unavailable. Please try again later.'

The phone clicked off.

'What is it?' Erina asked.

He handed her the phone and said, 'No service. I'll bet they've got a blocking device covering the inside of the pylon.'

Before she had a chance to respond, the lights went out, plunging them into total darkness.

A loud thump echoed somewhere beneath them.

'Fuuuck,' Vivienne said. 'What was that?'

'Sounds like we have visitors,' Carter said. 'Keep quiet and come over here by us.'

He guided her into a crouch next to Erina, who'd dropped to the floor. Erina shone the light of the phone screen onto the cardboard boxes stacked near the computers.

From below, another loud crash reverberated through the pylon.

Carter counted three sets of footsteps. The men had broken through the door and were inside, tramping up the first set of metal stairs, not caring who heard them. They sounded as if they were pumped full of arrogance and bravado, suggesting they were relative amateurs.

He turned towards Erina, who was ripping open the carton marked *PEGASUS SKYROCKETS*.

'Are you planning on putting on a private fireworks display?' Vivienne asked her, sounding incredulous.

'Something like that,' Erina said. 'Here.' She handed Vivienne the phone. 'Make yourself useful and give us some light.'

Vivienne held it in her right hand. Carter could tell she was trying to control her nervous shaking.

Erina extracted four rockets from the open box and then took five *INFUSION CRYSTAL FOUNTAINS* from the other one.

'What exactly have you got in mind?' Carter asked.

'I'm going to take Vivienne up the stairs towards the roof and stay with her,' she said. 'I'll set up the fountains and rockets along the way. We want to give the late arrivals a bright welcome.'

Carter knew exactly what she meant and said, 'You're quite the hostess.'

'You never get a second chance to make a first impression.'

He opened his daypack and laid it on the floor. Vivienne shone the light over it while he extracted a plastic lighter and a roll of grey duct tape. He handed them to Erina.

She grabbed Vivienne's hand and hurried up the stairs. Carter stuffed the phone back in the daypack and took out his Glock. He then threw the pack under the wooden desk and slid in after it, facedown.

His shoulder, hip and left leg pressed flush against the wall. He held the SIG near his right shoulder with his finger on the trigger and placed his Glock by his left hip within easy reach. He had a feeling he'd need all the firepower he could gather.

He remained still, breathing softly and listening to the steady thump of footsteps moving towards him. The three men had already reached level one and were heading for the second floor. The beat of their boots had changed – they were cautious now, moving more slowly.

Carter imagined himself in their position. They'd be pumped full of adrenalin, holding their rifles to their shoulders, peering through their night scopes, seeing the world as a series of glowing green shadows.

The sounds of the marching boots changed again.

They'd stepped onto the second level. They were metres away, moving much more slowly now.

He heard Erina above him, lighting the fireworks.

He squeezed his eyes shut tight, placed his hands firmly over his ears and started counting.

One, two …

He never got to three.

BOOM. BOOM. BOOM. BOOM.

CHAPTER 22

Carter lay perfectly still under the table.

The four rockets detonated one by one, like a cluster of small bombs exploding. Then, with his ears ringing, he heard the whooshing sound of the crystal fountains.

Each whoosh heralded a shower of bright coloured lights that'd make the night scopes useless and disorient the three men hunting him.

An automatic rifle barked.

Rat tat tat tat ...

A split second later another joined in, followed by the double *BOOM BOOM* of the shotgun.

The three guys were spooked, shooting blind – but that didn't make their bullets any less deadly.

Lead smashed into steel and brick, echoing around the enclosed chamber. The acrid smell of gunpowder and smoke filled the air.

Then the firing ceased.

Above him the sound of the fountains swirled.

He heard a high-pitched voice nearby shout in Indonesian, 'You see him?'

They'd still be blinded by Erina's lightshow.

'Diam.' *Shut up.*

Carter opened his eyes.

From the floor under the table he saw three sets of black trouser legs and boots near the top of the stairs, forming a tight triangle.

Bad move. They should've spread out.

He picked up the Glock and threw it across the room.

There was a moment of silence followed by a loud clatter as it bounced against the opposite wall.

The boots turned towards the sound.

A burst of gunfire from the automatic rifles sprayed the far wall.

The shotgun boomed.

Carter slid in a smooth movement from under the table, holding the SIG. There was still enough light from the fireworks to see his targets.

He rose to his feet, raised the SIG to his shoulder, took aim and squeezed off three shots.

The first shot hit the closest man in the side of the neck. The second got the next man between the back of his helmet and the top of his body armour. Carter shot the last guy in the throat when he turned towards him.

The three men collapsed to the ground.

The last of the fireworks gave a final splutter and died.

Carter started moving towards the stairs in the silent darkness.

Then stopped.

Somewhere above him, a door opened and closed.

A set of heavy footsteps came racing down the metal stairs.

He looked up into the darkness.

Erina's loud scream echoed around the pylon. 'CAAAAAARTEEER!'

A chilling dread cut through him.

Something dropped on the floor.

It bounced once … twice …

CHAPTER 23

Carter ran back towards the desk and dived under it.

He threw it on its side, sending the computers flying, using the front surface as a shield. He then curled himself into the foetal position and covered his head with his arms.

Time froze.

Erina's scream still echoed in his mind.

He held his breath and braced himself for what he expected was a grenade.

There was nothing he could do but wait.

He had to hand it to Alex. He'd thought through every scenario in detail and had kept one step ahead.

BOOM.

An ear-splitting explosion ripped through the pylon.

A hail of shrapnel whistled through the air, bouncing off the cement walls and drumming against the tabletop.

For the briefest of moments he thought he'd defied the odds and avoided being hit. Then a wave of intense pain hit him in the back.

It started just below his right shoulder and shot up his neck to the base of his skull, like he'd been jabbed from the inside with a red-hot poker.

He flinched, tensing his back muscles, and lay still. If a ligament or muscle had been severed or a bone broken, he was in trouble.

There wasn't a moment to lose. Alex might send someone down to finish him off.

But this was no time to rush, either. He forced himself to sit upright, unzipped his wetsuit and peeled the top off his shoulders.

Another wave of searing pain made him clench his jaw.

He breathed into the pain and worked his forefinger into the wound, probing deep into his flesh.

The tip of his finger touched two pieces of rounded metal the size of cherry pips – shrapnel from a frag grenade.

The two bearings were lodged just below his right shoulder joint. They must have bounced off a wall or the stairs before slamming into him. He hadn't exactly won the lottery, but a direct hit would've shattered his shoulder, making a tough situation close to impossible.

He wiped the sweat from his forehead, relaxed his back muscles and dug in again, probing even deeper.

It took all his focus to counter the shooting pain.

Just when he thought he could take no more, the two smooth bearings popped out and rolled on the floor like a couple of loose marbles. He let out a jagged sigh.

Getting the shrapnel out of his body was a good start.

He pushed himself to his feet one-handed, walked over to one of the dead guys, knelt down and tore a long strip off his shirt. He stood up, wound it round his shoulder and tied it off.

The crude dressing would stem the bleeding and support his shoulder joint for a while at least.

He rotated his shoulder back, then forwards.

Good enough.

Slowly, he worked his arm back into the wetsuit and zipped it up with his left hand.

He felt for his daypack in the dark, then found the table and righted it. Squatting beneath it, he would be hidden from Alex's surveillance cameras – at least he hoped he would be.

Carter opened the daypack, shone the phone light inside and took out three drug-tipped darts and two star knives.

He stuck the darts under his tongue and slipped the ultra-slim star knives into two velcro pockets in each arm of his wetsuit, just above the inside of his wrist. It'd take an extremely thorough search to detect them.

The phone read 11.06 p.m. He turned it to full volume, set the alarm for 11.15 p.m., and stepped back out onto the second floor.

Without warning the overhead lights burst back on.

Alex's voice boomed through overhead speakers. 'If you want to see Erina and the girl again, you'll come up the stairs to the lookout, unarmed. Keep your hands where I can see them.'

CHAPTER 24

Carter started up the stairs towards the top level of the pylon. Perhaps Alex had planned to separate him and Erina all along, knowing it was always easier to pick off two individuals than a team.

He'd seen a map of the south-east pylon, which was open to the public. The top level was a single room known as the 'indoor lookout', which provided tourists with a view of the harbour when the weather was inclement. It had a door opening onto a three-hundred-and-sixty-degree open-air lookout deck that wrapped around the room's four walls. The layout of the south-west pylon was the same, but the indoor room was used as a storeroom. On top of the storeroom's roof was a gun deck, which could be reached by a pull-down metal ladder. During the Second World War the four pylons had been taken over by the military, and gun parapets were built and used as anti-aircraft posts, which were never removed.

He mounted the final set of steps, half expecting to be greeted by armed clansmen. But he saw no sign of anyone. Just a cluttered rectangular room filled with cardboard boxes of electrical equipment, more disused CCTV cameras, aluminium stepladders and cleaning equipment.

One feature stood out. The eight smallish windows that surrounded the room had been painted black, like the sliding doors on the floor below.

The door to the outdoor lookout was closed. He pushed the throbbing pain in his shoulder out of his mind and breathed in. His body might be wounded but his mind and spirit were strong and ready.

From the other side of the door he could feel the energy of Alex and his men. They'd be wielding automatic rifles, whereas he was armed with a phone, three darts and a couple of ninja star knives.

To an outsider his position would appear hopeless.

But he knew better.

In a life-and-death battle the rules were different. It took far more than mere numerical superiority and firepower. Such moments tested a man to the core, stripped him bare of everything that was false, revealing his true self and enabling him to perceive more than could be seen with the naked eye.

He glanced at the phone.

11.08 p.m.

So long as Alex resisted the urge to simply shoot him on sight the instant he stepped onto the rooftop balcony, he was in with a chance.

Knowing Alex as well as he did, he figured he'd take a perverse pleasure in tormenting him before the final execution.

Carter turned the handle and pulled the door open a crack.

'I'm coming out,' he said. 'Unarmed.'

He raised his arms high and used his elbow to shove the door open.

The balcony was narrow – it was just one and a half metres from where he stood to the chest-high ledge that surrounded the lookout – but it ran the full length of the western side of the pylon, about twenty-five metres, before disappearing around the corner at each end. He stepped through the door onto the rain-soaked floor, placing him in the dead centre of the western lookout deck.

There was no room to move or hide.

The door slammed shut behind him.

He turned his head to his left.

Five metres from him a clan member dressed in a Tactical Response uniform pointed an MP5 directly at his head. The butt of the weapon was pressed into the man's shoulder and, though clearly tense and nervous, he appeared to know what he was doing.

Carter slowly turned his head to the right, keeping his hands high.

Eight metres away, towards the northern end of the balcony, another clan member stood flush against the western wall. He was dressed identically to his mate and held the blade of a six-inch kris dagger against Erina's throat.

Her eyes flicked towards him. Silver gaffer tape covered her mouth. She appeared to be unharmed apart from bruising around her right eye and a small cut on her forehead from which blood trickled down.

Vivienne was about three metres behind Erina, tucked away in the north-west corner. She sat upright on a metal bench attached to the balcony wall with her mouth taped, hands and feet tied and her dark eyes wide open, staring at him.

Carter noticed something glint on the ledge a couple of metres in front of Erina – a samurai sword. He recognised the blade at once as the Drying Pole, which Alex had stolen from him. He intended to get it back.

Alex emerged from around the corner of the northern wall and stood just in front of where Vivienne sat, speaking softly into the mike of a bluetooth headset. He placed what looked like a GPS tracking device in his thigh pocket and stared at Carter with the cold-hearted intensity of a hungry predator.

The group stood frozen, as if Alex had pressed the pause button and they were waiting for him to hit play.

CHAPTER 25

'Drop the phone,' Alex said in a calm, almost sympathetic voice. 'You won't be making any calls.'

Carter let go of it and put his foot out to break its fall. It slid across the wet floor to the cement wall opposite him.

'Zaheed,' Alex said, speaking in Indonesian. 'You know what to do.'

The clansman to Carter's left strode towards him and pushed him hard against the closed door.

Carter kept his arms raised with his hands extended high above his head.

Zaheed glared at him and jammed the MP5 muzzle into Carter's stomach.

He then ran his hands over his torso, patting the outside of his arms and his legs, pressing his shoulder wound for good measure and sending a sharp stab of pain up his arm. But Carter didn't care. He'd missed the star knives.

'He's clean,' Zaheed said in Indonesian.

'Check his mouth.'

Zaheed dropped his rifle level with Carter's crotch.

'Open wide,' Alex said. 'Or he'll blow your balls off.'

Carter opened his mouth.

Zaheed's calloused index finger probed Carter's gums and forced its way under his tongue.

He extracted the three darts and held them up in the light, grinning.

'Kerja baik,' Alex said. *Good work.*

Zaheed threw the darts against the ledge wall, where they scattered.

A sloppy move. They might prove useful later if Carter got his hands on them.

Zaheed resumed his position five metres to Carter's left, pointing the MP5 at his head.

Carter stayed silent.

Alex swaggered past Erina like an alpha lion about to pounce on an old and weakened enemy.

Carter turned to face him, bracing himself for a physical assault.

Alex stopped half a metre in front of him and looked into Carter's eyes.

'You've always been a lying, doublecrossing arsehole. And for some reason unfathomable to me, you think your shit doesn't stink.'

He pulled his right fist back under his armpit.

Carter tensed his abdomen.

With a grunt Alex let fly, putting his whole body and spirit into the blow. His fist slammed into Carter's solar plexus like a sledgehammer, bruising the stomach muscles and knocking the wind out of him.

'That's for leaving me to rot in prison,' he said.

Carter bent forwards, drawing in lungfuls of air, straining to keep his hands high with his palms facing Alex. He needed to maintain his poise and let the clock tick down.

'Stand up straight,' Alex said. 'And keep your hands in the air.'

Carter did as he was told.

Alex again pulled his fist back and threw his whole body behind a second punch. His fist found its mark, striking Carter in the centre of his rib cage with terrific force.

Carter tried to roll with the savage blow and keep his hands up but he heard a distinct crack on impact and felt a fierce pain shooting through his side.

Alex had either broken a rib or torn the cartilage away from the bone.

Beads of sweat rolled down Carter's face. He breathed into the hurt, reminding himself that pain was just a state of mind.

Alex snarled and said, 'And that's just for being you, a fucking arsehole.'

His fist flew through the air again, aiming for the bridge of Carter's nose.

Carter rolled his head and turned it side-on. The vicious punch struck his cheekbone, causing waves of searing pain to pulsate through his skull.

His head rang from the blow to the jaw as tears welled in his eyes. He tasted blood in his mouth. A right molar had come loose.

Alex turned and picked up the Drying Pole from the ledge. He held the sword by his side with the blade pointing down.

Carter knew what was coming.

Alex intended to prove his superiority and savour his victory, which he saw as a foregone conclusion.

He'd want to delay the deathblow as long as possible, using Carter's old sword to complete the job.

Carter took a slow, deliberate breath. He couldn't afford to let Alex keep playing his sadistic game and incur any further injuries.

He needed to engage him.

He looked past Alex, caught Erina's eye and gave her a tight nod.

They weren't beaten yet.

CHAPTER 26

Carter clenched and unclenched his left fist and spread his weight evenly on the balls of his feet. The fight was approaching its climax and as yet he hadn't even looked like landing a blow. But he knew it was the final shot that counted.

Another long slow breath helped push the pain in his shoulder, ribs and jaw from the forefront of his mind and lock it away.

He needed to buy a few more precious moments. Any one-on-one battle must first be fought with the eyes, then from the heart and finally through the body.

'What happened to you, Alex?' he asked. 'To cause you to hate so much?'

'What do you think, man? The order was my family. Thomas was my father. You were my brother. But you used me as a pawn for all those years and when I was no longer of any use, you and Thomas deserted me when I needed you most. Now you're going to pay for it. Face it, Carter, it's over for you – and the order.'

'Don't you even care that these lunatics plan to kill and injure God knows how many innocent people? It's not too late to save them.'

Alex gave a tiny shake of the head. 'You've never understood me, Carter. My belief is that most people are mindless sheep, barely alive. Their death doesn't concern me one way or the other.'

Carter motioned his head towards the two clan members. 'At least these two believe in something bigger than themselves. All you care about is yourself.'

'Someone has to,' Alex said.

Carter's gaze flicked towards the clansman holding Erina. He didn't move a muscle.

Alex took a step towards Carter. He raised the sword with two hands, drew it up behind his head and then swept the blade down, creating a swishing sound through the air.

The tip of the sword stopped a centimetre from Carter's throat.

Carter didn't blink.

Alex motioned for Carter to move backwards, south along the look-out deck.

Again, he did what he was told and began walking, one cautious step at a time. Adrenalin surged through his body, giving him a feeling of mental clarity. Alex kept pace with him, holding the sword at the side of his throat, a self-satisfied smile etched across his face.

Carter kept moving backwards until the top of his calves hit a metal bench attached to the ledge. The end of the line. It wouldn't be long now.

He glanced to his right. Zaheed had moved and now stood four metres from him, halfway down the southern lookout deck, out of the others' line of sight. His MP5 remained trained on Carter's head.

Alex adjusted the Drying Pole so that the tip of the blade pointed at Carter's heart, now beating fast. Another surge of adrenalin pumped through his veins, causing him to tighten and then relax his muscles.

Some adrenalin was good. Too much drained your focus.

'Get onto the ledge,' Alex said.

Carter needed to play the game out as long as possible, so he continued to do as he was told.

Turning his back on Alex wasn't an option, though. Carter placed his left foot on the metal bench and then his right, keeping his movements slow and deliberate.

At the northern end of the lookout Vivienne was slumped forwards. Her body bent over her lap as though she couldn't bear to watch.

His gaze searched out Erina.

She stood rigid. The other clansman still held the dagger at her throat. For the first time he read fear and doubt in her eyes.

Alex frowned and said, 'I won't tell you again.' He still held the point of the sword at Carter's heart.

Carter used his hands to lift himself onto the thirty-centimetre-wide ledge and sat there for a moment, thinking.

The storeroom no longer protected him from the gusting southerly wind. He was now at the mercy of the elements. He looked over his left shoulder at the ninety-metre drop to the ground. There was no escape that way. He turned back to Alex.

The smile had returned to his face. 'Get on with it,' Alex said. 'There's no point trying to delay the inevitable.'

Carter took a slow breath, embracing the pain that ran through his body. He pulled his feet up onto the ledge and then slowly stood up, keeping his knees bent and his arms loose by his side.

'Lift them,' Alex said.

Carter raised his arms to shoulder height, making his position even more vulnerable.

He adjusted his right foot back, maintaining his balance, like he was riding a surfboard on a steep wave.

The sound of plastic flapping caused him to look up at the gun deck above the storeroom.

He couldn't see directly onto it, but he glimpsed the black wings of what could only be a hang-glider. It explained how Alex intended to get off the pylon, save himself and most likely meet Samudra before the midnight fireworks.

Carter pulled himself up to his full height.

Alex held the Drying Pole in two hands pointing up at him.

Carter stared across the top of the polished sword into Alex's dark brown eyes.

The clock in his head entered the final countdown.

Ten, nine, eight ...

He took a slow breath in.

Alex moved one foot slightly backwards, adjusted the angle of his sword and squared his shoulders. He swept the Drying Pole back with a dramatic flourish, gripping the handle tight.

His gaze dropped, signalling his intention.

He planned to cut Carter's legs off at the knees.

Three, two, one.

The chorus from the Rolling Stones song 'Street Fighting Man', an anthem from Carter's youth, blared at full volume from the phone lying on the deck.

His mum had played it when he was a kid. He'd always loved the lines about the sound of marching, charging feet and how the time was right for fighting in the street.

Alex's eyes swung to the phone.

Carter was already in motion.

CHAPTER 27

The 'Street Fighting Man' chorus created the split-second opening Carter sought.

His thought processes accelerated and the world around him slowed. He felt a pure and total clarity.

He grabbed the star knife from under his left wetsuit sleeve and flung it at Zaheed to his right.

The Indonesian's MP5 clattered on the ground. He clutched his right eye and collapsed backwards.

Carter had already moved on.

As he whipped the other star knife from his right sleeve, he looked to his left and saw Erina stabbing the second clansman's throat with his own dagger.

It had all happened in less than a second.

The chorus was still blaring as Alex swung back to face Carter, pulling his sword back behind his head in one swift, fluid motion, poised to strike at Carter's legs.

Carter threw his arms forwards, pushed off hard with his legs and leapt high over Alex's head, tucking his knees underneath his chest.

The Drying Pole's blade flashed close beneath his heels.

Carter hit the cement floor a metre behind Alex, landing sideways and breaking the impact with his good arm before rolling onto his feet, a molten sea of agony surging through his battered body.

Alex spun around and faced him with the sword raised high over his head.

He started his forward strike.

But Carter was quicker.

He'd already flung the second star knife towards Alex.

The knife struck its target. One of the five blades buried itself in Alex's exposed throat.

The Drying Pole and then Alex dropped to the ground.

Carter stood still, his breath coming hard and fast.

Alex lay on his back, holding his throat in an effort to stem the bleeding. He stared at Carter in a state of shock. His arrogance had given way to a look of bewildered disbelief.

The phone sounded another round of the 'Street Fighting Man' chorus.

Carter picked up the Drying Pole, keeping his attention on Alex, and held the sword by his side. It felt light in his hand.

Behind him the phone went silent.

He looked around and saw Erina freeing Vivienne.

The clansman who'd been holding the dagger at her throat lay motionless on his back, almost certainly dead.

Carter moved to the southern end of the walkway and looked down to where Zaheed lay on his back, not moving. The life had drained out of his body. Carter checked for a pulse but was careful not to disturb Zaheed's clothing. He and his mate were no doubt wired with explosives. This wasn't over yet. Carter needed to get off the bridge and find Samudra before he could trigger the detonators.

He returned to Alex and knelt down beside his head. A pool of blood had spread out around his shoulders onto the wet cement.

Carter removed the star knife from his throat, then placed his hand over the jagged wound and applied downward pressure. He needed to find out where Samudra was.

Two sets of soft footsteps approached. Erina and Vivienne stopped at Alex's feet.

Alex looked up at Carter and whispered, 'You know I've been thinking about killing you every day for the last two years.'

'That was a waste of time,' Carter said.

'It kept me going.'

'Tell me where Samudra is.'

Blood dribbled from Alex's mouth, which had twisted into a sneer. 'You think I'd betray him to you? At least I have the satisfaction of knowing you failed and will be forced to live with the consequences.'

'Don't worry,' Vivienne said to Carter. 'I know where Samudra is and how to find him. I heard them talking on the phone downstairs. Alex has a GPS device on him with the coordinates set.'

Erina looked down at Alex. 'You should be more careful when you talk on the phone. You never know who's listening.'

'Fuck you,' Alex said.

His head dropped to one side but his dead eyes remained open, staring into the night as if trying to figure out where it had all gone wrong.

CHAPTER 28

Erina, Vivienne and Carter stood over Alex's body. They all needed a moment to gather themselves before facing what lay ahead.

Thanks to the adrenalin pumping through his veins, Carter barely registered any pain.

He had retrieved the palm GPS navigation device from Alex's trouser pocket and held it in his left hand; the still thirsty Drying Pole, now returned to its scabbard, was in his right.

The sword would serve as a powerful reminder of what he'd been through and learnt. He remembered the words of Miyamoto Musashi, the great samurai who had defeated the sword's original owner, Sasaki Kojiro, in a famous bout between the two men on an island off Japan. Musashi had said the only difference between himself and Kojiro was that he used his sword not to conquer the world but rather to advance his spirit. Musashi had used his fighting skills only to perfect his craft and serve others.

Carter looked up into the dark sky. Alex's blade had passed a hair's breadth from his body. It could so easily have been him lying on the cold, wet cement, or broken and twisted at the foot of the pylon.

He didn't necessarily believe in fate or destiny, but he acknowledged the karmic logic of the universe, of cause and effect. Now the fight was over, Alex's death appeared inevitable.

Carter glanced at Erina, then at Vivienne, both lost in their own thoughts.

He looked down and saw the scowl on Alex's lifeless face. It revealed the bitter fruit of such an existence – a hollow life and a lonely death.

Alex had abandoned the principles of the order and become driven by ego and the fulfilment of desire, his decline hastened by his use of heavy drugs. Carter had seen the man unravel bit by bit, his soul corrupted by a life of hedonism and the pursuit of his own interest at the expense of others.

Carter recognised the parallels with his own life.

He had allowed his desire for Erina to consume him until he sought to control her, and had been frustrated when she denied him that control. He'd shown Thomas not the love and respect he deserved but pride and anger, rejecting his authority not because it was unjust, but because Thomas asked him to put the order's interests ahead of his own.

He'd walked away from the problems confronting him rather than facing them.

He'd abandoned the people who loved him and relied on him and instead pursued his own selfish ends.

He'd given up his spiritual beliefs and practices and sought oblivion in physical sensation.

He knew now that he had made the wrong decision. His world had become narrower since leaving the order, and he'd suffered a deep and unshakable unease, almost a sickness, that had only ever been momentarily appeased by the surf.

He was caught in the turbulence of the spiritual no man's land created by his ego, and eventually he would drown. If he wanted to avoid Alex's fate, the only way out was to return to the order. By submitting, by allowing himself to be guided by its principles, he could transcend the chaotic waves of the material world and reach calm water. He could know peace.

A surprising wave of compassion for Alex washed through him.

He leant forwards and closed Alex's eyes.

CHAPTER 29

Five minutes later Carter stood on the gun deck, strapped into the harness of Alex's hang-glider, facing the wind. The flexible black wings fluttered above his head, pulling at him as if an unseen force was impatient to pluck him from the earth.

Vivienne and Erina stood on either side of the glider. They held the struts in place against the wind, ensuring Carter remained earthbound long enough to make a final check of everything before lifting off.

He'd taped two high-powered bombs made up of C4 explosives from his pack to its nose, turning the simple hang-glider into a flying kamikaze missile.

The C4 consisted of explosive chemicals and a plastic binder substance; he'd moulded it into a couple of oval balls the size of a small bread roll and then embedded a detonator cap in their hearts. The jury-rigged bombs would detonate on impact.

Erina held Alex's GPS device in front of him at eye level.

A blinking red light flashed on the screen, marking a point off Watsons Bay near Sydney Heads, roughly six kilometres from the bridge.

That's where he expected to find Samudra.

'The light hasn't moved,' Erina said.

'Good.'

She stuck the palm computer into a side pocket of his daypack and zipped it up.

'You'll call Watto?' he said.

'You don't need to worry about things at this end,' she told him. 'Vivienne and I will take care of it. You take care of Samudra.'

He pressed the button on the side of Alex's bluetooth earpiece and heard a dial tone. The earpiece and Alex's phone were now synced, and tucked into the neck of his wetsuit. Samudra would, he suspected, call at any minute to check in with Alex.

As a final preparation Carter made sure the night-vision binoculars hanging around his neck were secure. Then he pulled the daypack tight against his body and clasped the roll of duct tape in the side pocket to make sure it was still there.

A fresh gust of wind surged in his face.

It was 11.40 p.m.

'All set,' Erina said. 'Now get this done.'

'Will do. See you next year. You know where I'll be.'

She reached out her free hand, still holding onto the strut with the other, and squeezed his shoulder. 'That's a date.'

He nodded at Vivienne, who smiled for the first time and said, 'Take the motherfucker down, Carter.'

Still holding onto the controls with his left hand, he gave them a thumbs up with his right.

Time to go.

Vivienne and Erina released the struts.

The strong southerly lifted the wings.

He gripped the steering bar as tightly as he could, held his breath and clenched his stomach muscles to counter the waves of pain stabbing through his ribs.

Then he took three steps forwards and leapt into the abyss.

The hang-glider surged high above the pylon. Two seagulls, lit up by the lights from the bridge, hovered alongside, appearing to take a sympathetic interest in him.

He leant forwards on the controls, pointing the hang-glider's nose towards the dark waters below. His injured arm hung by his side.

For half a second the man-made apparatus quivered in the air as if making up its mind what to do. Then it lurched forwards and plunged down, a black flying ghost.

He didn't look back.

CHAPTER 30

Roughly a hundred metres below Carter, twenty-three-year-old Youssef bin Hassan, dressed in green overalls and wearing a Lakers baseball cap, drove the diesel truck marked *Rapid Transfer* into the underground Sydney Harbour Tunnel, heading towards the city's northern suburbs.

His boyhood friend Faisel Aman sat in the passenger seat wearing matching overalls and cap. They travelled in silence.

They'd joined the Lakemba cell a year ago. This was their first and last important assignment. They'd been told to wait in the truck until midnight, when the bombs inside would detonate.

Death held no fear for Youssef.

He and Faisel would die as heroes for Allah, bringing honour to their families. They'd receive their reward in the afterlife and spend eternity enjoying the fruits of paradise.

On reaching the first breakdown bay, Youssef pulled over to the left as instructed and turned the hazard lights on. They stepped out of the truck and placed seven orange witch's hats around the vehicle at regular intervals.

They got back into the front seat. Youssef typed a text into his phone: *Have reached target.*

He pressed send.

The reply came back a minute later from Samudra. *Good work. Allah akbar.*

CHAPTER 31

Carter stalled the glider so that it hovered about a hundred metres from Watsons Bay, towards the far eastern end of Sydney Harbour, close to Sydney Heads and the open sea. The wind blew into his face from the south-east.

He looked down at the dark waters fifty metres below and then over his shoulder at the bright lights of Sydney. The only sound was the vibration of the wings.

For a moment he wondered how many people would be awake, sitting in front of their television sets waiting for the midnight fireworks, hoping it would signal the beginning of better things for the new year.

He shrugged the thought off, hooked his wounded arm under the steering bar and extracted Alex's palm computer from the daypack with his other hand.

The blinking light was in the same spot, marking a point halfway between the Watsons Bay shoreline and South Head, where he could see a fleet of around fifty pleasure craft gathered in the lee of a headland reserve.

He returned the computer to its pocket in his daypack, brought the binoculars to his eyes and scanned the fleet.

Samudra would choose a position on the edge of the other boats, most likely the closest to Sydney Heads, to facilitate an easy getaway.

The furthest boat to the north of the fleet was a shabby-looking cabin cruiser rolling with the gentle swell.

He focused the high-powered binoculars on two men standing in the bow.

Bingo.

They were Indonesian. One of them was Samudra, dialling a number on a mobile phone.

If Samudra stuck to his schedule, he wouldn't be detonating the bombs until midnight.

However, if Alex or his men had failed to meet a prearranged reporting deadline, it might spook him into striking prematurely – making whatever Carter did too late to stop him.

Samudra put the phone to his ear.

Alex's mobile started vibrating under the wetsuit against Carter's chest, just below his neck.

He checked the time.

Ten minutes to midnight.

He ignored it. He wanted to hold off making contact until he was in his final dive.

After four more rings it fell silent.

Carter lined up the midsection of Samudra's launch with the armed nose of the glider, pointing the man-made bird towards the ugly craft at a forty-five-degree angle. The hang-glider quivered for a moment in the darkness and then dropped into its final dive.

A bolt of energy surged from the centre of his *hara* and he let out a deep 'haah', his version of a battle cry.

He grabbed the roll of duct tape and lashed the controls into place with one arm, breaking the tape off with his teeth.

Satisfied the hang-glider was locked onto its target, he lifted the binoculars to his eyes for the final time.

An enlarged image of Samudra's normally smiling face stared straight at him. A nasty scowl twisted his features, but there was no look of recognition – not yet.

He'd probably seen the glider, expecting Alex. When the phone failed to answer, he'd most likely suspected something was amiss.

Carter saw Samudra take the phone out of his pocket and dial once more.

Alex's phone vibrated against his chest again.

Carter took out the phone and pressed answer on the third ring, keeping the binoculars trained on Samudra.

'Abdul-Aleem,' Samudra barked. 'What's going on?'

Carter said nothing.

'Are you there?' Samudra said, his voice urgent. 'Is that you on the hang-glider?'

Silence hung over the phone line. A drop of rain spat in Carter's face.

'Alex is dead,' he said.

'What? Who is this?'

'Carter.'

'It can't be.'

'Afraid so.' Carter paused to let the information sink in. 'Don't even think about hanging up and dialling the number,' he said. 'I'm on the hang-glider and you're lined up in the night scope of my sniper rifle.'

Samudra lifted his head and stared at the glider.

'I can see you clearly,' Carter said. 'You just lifted your head. Make one wrong move and you're dead. So is the man next to you.'

He saw Samudra peer into the night, holding the phone in his left hand. It was too dark for him to make out whether Carter carried a rifle.

'You start dialling, I start shooting,' Carter said. 'Drop the phone. I don't miss.'

'You're bluffing.'

'Try me.'

A gust of wind caused the glider to accelerate.

The nose of the makeshift missile was perfectly lined up with the midsection of the launch, less than twenty metres away.

Would Samudra choose self-preservation over jihad? Carter would have to wait to find out. He unclipped the harness and pushed himself away from the struts, letting himself drop towards the water. Whatever was meant to happen would happen. He'd done all he could.

CHAPTER 32

Carter plunged into the cool water and kicked and stroked to propel himself towards the bottom of the harbour.

After a few seconds the water shook and churned violently.

Carter had no idea how Samudra had responded to the dilemma he had posed. Had he dialled the number to detonate the explosives or dived over the side to save himself?

He'd bet on the latter.

A giant watery hand grabbed hold of him and thrust him even deeper underwater.

He relaxed and went with it.

There was no use fighting.

Less than four seconds later the water stopped moving.

Carter stroked and kicked upwards until his head burst through the surface.

Sucking in a lungful of air, he stared at where the launch had been.

The hang-glider had made a direct hit. All that remained on the surface were fragments of floating plastic and wood.

A couple of the other boats in the fleet had capsized and several more had rammed into each other.

People were yelling and waving their arms. Some were inexplicably cheering. Thankfully no one appeared to be seriously injured.

Fifteen metres away he spotted a lone figure swimming towards shore using a cross between a frantic freestyle and a dog paddle.

Samudra.

He'd opted to jump overboard rather than dial the number, choosing to save himself rather than die a martyr's death. His rhetoric had proved hollow when put to the ultimate test.

Carter started swimming towards him, his gaze never leaving the back of his head.

Samudra was no swimmer. He thrashed his arms and made slow progress. Even one-armed, Carter caught him in a dozen strokes.

Samudra turned and faced him, defiant. Treading water seemed an effort for him; his arms splashed about as he struggled to keep his head above water.

'You cannot harm me,' he said. 'You have no idea of my power. If you lift a finger against me, God will strike you dead.'

'Let's put that theory to the test, shall we?'

'If it's money you want, I'll give you whatever you ask. Name your price.'

'I don't have a price.'

Carter kicked hard and strong, propelling his torso out of the water, reaching out with his arm and putting his hand on the crown of Samudra's head.

A look of alarm and indignation crossed Samudra's face. He swung one arm in the air, trying to swat Carter's hand away, with no effect.

Carter gripped his hair and held him at arm's length.

'I'm warning you in the name of Allah,' Samudra said. 'No matter how hard you try, you cannot defy the will of God. Djoran tried to do that and for his efforts I slit his miserable throat.'

'You fucking arsehole.'

Carter allowed grief and anger to well up inside him, allowed himself to feel them.

'You cannot defy God's will,' Samudra said.

'No man can know what God's will is,' Carter said. 'But I know what it's not.'

He kicked his legs harder, pushing his torso further out of the water, and forced Samudra's head under, holding him down using every ounce of his weight.

Samudra kicked and thrashed, trying to grab Carter's arm and break his grip, but Carter was far too strong.

Forty seconds passed.

The thrashing subsided, growing weaker, and then finally stopped.

From down the harbour Carter heard the distant roar of the crowd counting down the new year.

Four, three, two ...

Horns and whistles sounded.

Carter held his breath. Samudra might've dialled the number before he jumped.

He still held the man's head underwater.

A distant explosion rocked the night.

He looked down the harbour towards the bridge.

A dazzling spiral of white light flashed above it.

Then, after a brief pause, another set of explosions erupted.

The skyline was flooded with every colour of the rainbow, throwing myriad multicoloured reflections on the water.

The Sydney Harbour Bridge stood firm.

Amid the mayhem people were clapping and cheering.

He heard the opening line of 'Auld Lang Syne': '*Should old acquaintance be forgot ...*'

He thought of his friend Jacko, of Muklas, Wayan and Djoran.

They'd all shown ultimate courage in playing their role. Any success he'd had that night was founded on their sacrifice.

The ugly truth was not everyone made it home.

Another explosion rocked the night.

The Harbour Bridge erupted with showers of dazzling pink, green, purple, red and orange.

Waves of sparkling silver stars shot into the night, exploding with bursts of colour.

A moment of quiet darkness followed. Then, as if out of nowhere, two bright pink hearts burst in front of the bridge, surrounded by an orb of golden light.

Blue lights spelt out one word.

LOVE.

He released Samudra's head, and his lifeless body floated to the surface and drifted away.

CHAPTER 33

Carter trod water, watching the spotlight from the police launch speed across the harbour towards him.

Erina stood in the bow, composed but smiling.

The launch swerved and slowed to a halt, sending a bow wave of broken water towards him, lifting him up and then dropping him down gently.

Erina, still dressed in her wetsuit, climbed onto the gunnels and dived into the harbour.

She disappeared under the water and surfaced a metre and a half from him, pushing the hair out of her eyes.

He swam towards her and, with one arm, gathered her around the waist.

They bobbed up and down with the gentle swell, locked in each other's embrace and cocooned in their own private world.

She kissed him gently on the lips. 'We got it done.'

'At a cost.'

'It's who we are.'

'I know.'

He held her tight.

'I love you,' he said.

'I love you too, Russell Carter.'

EPILOGUE

Darkness was fast approaching on a big Sunday out the back at the point of Lennox Head.

There was not a breath of wind. The water was smooth as glass and the dying sun was only minutes from slipping below the green hills running behind the town of Lennox.

Carter sat alone in the take-off zone, watching a swell roll in from the north-east, hoping to catch a final wave before the light disappeared altogether.

It'd be his last surf at Lennox for a few months at least. He was heading to Bali in the morning to train some new recruits for the order and, to his surprise, was looking forward to the challenge.

In the gathering gloom a familiar voice yelled out to him. 'Hey, Carter!'

Carter turned to see Knowlsie pulling up next to him.

'Haven't seen you around for yonks,' Knowlsie said. 'You been on holidays?'

Carter paused a beat. 'Something like that. What've you been up to?'

365

'Visiting the rellies in Perth. And I'm now in Year Ten. Man, it's full-on.'

'You'll be sweet.'

'Dunno about that.'

'Just do what you do in the surf. Charge every test. You're a smart kid.'

A broad grin spread across Knowlsie's face and his eyes dropped as if embarrassed.

'Hey,' he said, changing the subject, 'one of my mates reckons he eyeballed you arm in arm with a hot-looking woman. Is that your new girlfriend or something?'

'Wouldn't say that exactly.'

Erina had left the day before for Burma – there was trouble on the Thai border at the refugee camps – and he didn't know when he'd see her next. He'd miss her, but their relationship was what it was.

Both needed to do what they needed to do. Their duty to the order came first.

Thanks to Callaghan the order had more autonomy now. And Thomas had undergone his own personal jihad, becoming far less autocratic and more willing to listen before making decisions.

He'd begun to trust the group's intelligence, rather than dictating to it. That was, in part, due to Kemala's softening influence. She and Thomas were now 'officially' in a relationship.

Kemala was the first woman to be endorsed as head of the Sungkar clan and was in the process of reforming it, endeavouring to instil in all its members the profound spirituality at the heart of Islam – something many in the West could learn from, including Carter himself.

'Hey, Carter,' Knowlsie said, pointing out the back. 'Big set coming.'

A snarling double overhead wall of water reared up fifteen metres out to sea, promising to form a perfect arching barrel.

'It's all yours, big guy,' Carter said, expecting it to be the last rideable wave of the day.

Knowlsie gave Carter a grateful nod, turned and started stroking hard for it.

The wave reared up. Carter took great pleasure in watching the kid leap to his feet, gun his board down the line and charge like he'd always told him to.

Carter turned back out to sea.

From nowhere another perfect wave rolled in from the deep, the biggest of the session. It rose up and towered triple overhead, the size of a small building, forming a steep wall of water.

He spun his board around, powered into the wave and sprung to his feet in one fluid motion.

The lip curled. His board raced across the near-vertical wall of smooth water. He dropped down the face and lined up the barrel peeling in front of him.

The board accelerated. He crouched even lower and charged forwards.

A thick wall of water broke over his shoulder. He entered deep inside the holy vortex of the green room, covered by a cascading curtain of crystal liquid.

For some reason unknown to him, a reason that had nothing to do with Islam, Christianity or any other religion, he thought of Djoran and whispered, 'Allah akbar.'

ACKNOWLEDGEMENTS

The number one lesson I've learnt from running creative writing courses at the Writers' Studio over many years is the power of a group of people working together with a common purpose. This creates a magic synergy that takes everyone's stories to another level. *No Man's Land* has benefited from a lot of input and I'd like to thank and acknowledge everyone who has helped me on the journey, roughly in chronological order.

First and foremost I'd like to thank everyone who has ever participated in a creative writing class at the Writers' Studio. You guys have been my greatest teachers and source of inspiration. You've been instrumental in maintaining my love and passion for writing and my thirst for greater understanding of the art and craft.

I've also profited from participating in many writing programs. I'd particularly like to acknowledge the Maui Writers' Conference and writing teachers James Rollins, Garry Braver and James N. Frey. They helped me see the power of a story with well-motivated characters and dramatic conflict so that a reader wants to keep turning the pages.

Filmmaker George Miller has been a source of inspiration and creative wisdom over many years. His commitment to excellence and passion for storytelling is remarkable. He was instrumental in prompting me to write an action/adventure style thriller.

I am grateful to literary agent Selwa Anthony for her ongoing encouragement and guidance. When I first sent her the opening chapters of *No Man's Land*, she said she loved it, and her enthusiastic feedback and counsel kept me going.

To fellow fiction writer Alex Gilly, reader Drew Keys and scriptwriter Nick Lathouris, thank you for your intelligent and generous input into the story.

To my buddies Phil Pick, John Malone and Geoff Moss, thank you for your ongoing support and patience. And to Lynette Arkadie, thank you for your wisdom and encouragement to keep the faith and always move forward in pursuit of the dream.

A special thanks to Joanne Symonds for all your help at the Writers' Studio and for having our back when Kathleen and I had to really focus on getting the final edits done.

I also feel very fortunate to have had Elizabeth Cowell edit *No Man's Land* and manage its production. Her professionalism and skill were inspiring, and working with her has been an education. She really understood my characters and what I was trying to do with the story, and never settled for anything less than the best I was capable of, for which I am very thankful.

Kevin O'Brien did a masterly job as proofreader. Kevin and Elizabeth were painstaking in picking up inconsistencies and errors. Any mistakes that may remain are solely my responsibility.

I felt a real buzz of excitement when I saw the final version of the cover. Thanks to Eugene Tan and Debbie Baker at Aquabumps for providing the photograph and Luke Causby for his evocative cover design that captured the feel and mood of the story.

A special thank you to business consultant Jim Stackpool for his guidance, encouragement and support over many years helping me develop the Writers' Studio while encouraging me to prioritise my time to complete *No Man's Land*. His guidance has enabled me to navigate the way forward with confidence and clarity, enabling me to get the job done in the face of one challenge after another.

Finally, I wish to thank my partner in life and at the Writers' Studio, Kathleen Allen. She is responsible for giving the story heart and emotional depth. Most importantly, she dedicated herself to me and to making the novel as good as it could be. She worked with me on every line, challenging, supporting and questioning me every step of the way. Our creative conflict has often rivalled the relationship of Carter and Erina and played out in cafes across Sydney. I literally couldn't have written this book without her and am very blessed to have her in my life.

So thank you, Kathleen, and everyone who has helped and supported me along the way.

CPSIA information can be obtained at www.ICGtesting.com
Printed in the USA
BVOW01s1313020315

389935BV00002B/18/P